Half *the* World *in* Winter

Also by Maggie Joel

The Past and Other Lies
The Second-Last Woman in England

Half *the* World *in* Winter

MAGGIE JOEL

ALLEN&UNWIN

First published in Great Britain in 2015 by Allen & Unwin
First published in Australia in 2014 by Allen & Unwin

Allen & Unwin
c/o Atlantic Books
Ormond House
26–27 Boswell Street
London WC1N 3JZ
Phone: 020 7269 1610
Fax: 020 7430 0916
Email: UK@allenandunwin.com
Web: www.allenandunwin.co.uk

A CIP catalogue record for this book is available from the British Library.

Paperback ISBN 978 1 92526 652 8
E-Book ISBN 978 1 92526 794 5

Set in 12/17 pt Minion Pro by Bookhouse, Sydney
Printed in Great Britain

10 9 8 7 6 5 4 3 2 1

For Richard, Dominic and Rebecca
—sorry I didn't end up using the dinosaurs or the aliens

PROLOGUE

The West Midlands: December 1880

BY THE TIME IT ARRIVED at Dawley, the 1.55 p.m. local train from Shrewsbury to Birmingham was already twelve minutes late. It had left Shrewsbury two or three minutes behind schedule, was further delayed by signals and other trains ahead of it and now three additional third-class carriages were being attached to the rear of the train to accommodate a large Sunday school excursion party. This would add a further eight to ten minutes to the delay and the stationmaster peered at his fob watch and shook his head.

Seamus Proctor, the driver of the train, waited in the engine's cab, smoking patiently. His fireman, Evans, pulled off his cap and mopped his brow with a rag, streaking his face with oil as he did so. It was a bitterly cold afternoon but the heat from the boiler was fierce.

'This'll slow us down,' Seamus remarked, nodding his head towards the rear of the train where the additional carriages were being hurriedly attached.

He had buried his wife the previous day.

The railway company had allowed him the day off. The funeral had been held in the morning, the ground so frozen you wondered how the gravediggers had been able to dig her grave. It had been a brief ceremony: the rector had had a streaming cold and there had been another burial party already gathered at the church gate.

Seamus leant out of the cab window watching the stationmaster's frantic attempts to supervise the coupling of the new carriages and he thought about his dead wife. They had been married twenty-seven years.

'Company won't like this,' replied Evans, standing up and leaning on his shovel so that he could stretch his back. 'Three carriages behind the last brake-van.'

Seamus made no comment. He was aware of the railway company's regulations and he was aware there was nothing actually stating how many carriages could or could not be placed behind the final brake-van. It wasn't usual, it might be frowned on, but it wasn't against regulations. Besides, the railway company would be more concerned about the additional time lost if they stopped to move the brake-van to the end of the train.

Evans had said nothing to him about his wife's death. It was quite likely Evans did not know. Why would he? Seamus had said nothing. It was no one else's business. This morning he had got up at the usual time, made his cup of tea and his breakfast, carved a hunk of bread and cheese for his lunch and left the house before dawn. Just as he always did.

He smoked silently in the cab as outside the party of Sunday schoolchildren and church people surged along the platform and boarded the train.

He lived in a small railwayman's cottage in a purpose-built terrace behind the station. They had lived there, he and his wife, since the day of their wedding. Twenty-seven years. He had been a young man then.

A passenger, a young fella in a cap and his Sunday-best shirt, came hurrying up the platform holding the hand of a little girl, his daughter perhaps. The girl skipped and twisted this way and that to see everything, jumping when a burst of steam shot from beneath the engine and startled her. Seamus took the end of his pipe out of his mouth and smiled at her and she smiled back and waved. The young fella, her dad, spoke to her sharply, and the little girl pouted. Seamus winked at her and watched as they boarded the third-class carriage behind the engine.

When his shift ended, late in the evening, he would return home to an empty house.

A blast from the stationmaster's whistle and an urgent waving of his flag indicated they were—at last—ready. Seamus gave two short blasts from the train's whistle, startling a circling crow, released the engine brakes, opened the throttle and they eased out of the station.

'Twenty-one minutes late,' observed Evans.

The bell of the internal communication cord rang once. It was the test ring the head guard was required to make on leaving every station where carriages had been attached or removed. Regulations stated it was supposed to be rung prior to leaving the station, not once they were under way. Seamus gave a resigned pull of the cord in acknowledgement.

They now had fifteen carriages, including the three just added, plus the engine, the tender, a luggage van and two brake-vans, one behind the luggage van, one behind the twelfth carriage.

'It's the fair,' said Evans, shouting above the roar of the engine. 'In Wolverhampton. There's a big fair on.'

Seamus shook his head. A fair on the Sabbath. And in December! Whoever heard of such a thing?

There had been frosts the last seven nights and this morning there had been a sprinkling of snow in the fields around Shrewsbury. Ice hung from the trees and from the eaves of the cottages they passed. The third-class carriages would be bracing—though, no doubt if you were going to a fair, you would put up with it. The cab of the engine was the only place to be on such a day. That, or before the hearth in your home.

He thought of the hearth in his cottage, which would be cold when he returned home.

The distance to Wolverhampton was eighteen miles and it was, by and large, a straight run aside from the Sutton Hill incline and the tunnel a mile or so further on. Beside him, Evans shovelled coal into the firebox for all he was worth, pausing only to check the pressure gauge.

The train shot through a cutting that soon became an embankment with a slight and steadily increasing gradient as the line ahead passed over the canal at a place called Lea's Crossing. All the signals were in the 'clear' position so the train was able to pick up speed. It was travelling at around thirty miles per hour as it approached the bridge.

'Shall I make a brew?' shouted Evans, slamming the firebox shut and breathing heavily through his mouth.

Seamus nodded at his fireman. The signal at the approach to the bridge was also clear. At this rate they might pick up two or three minutes—unless someone decided to attach more carriages at Wolverhampton. The train was already straining under the additional weight and they lost a bit of speed on the incline before rattling over the bridge. Seamus glanced down and saw that the canal beneath them was frozen solid, a barge tethered unnecessarily to a mooring. It wouldn't be going anywhere today.

When he saw the stationary goods train on the line ahead of him his first thought was that it must be on a siding. In the second that he realised that there was no siding, that the train was on their line and that they were going to hit it, he shut off the steam, threw the engine into reverse and gave out a whistle to tell the guard to apply his brakes. Beside him, Evans had dropped the kettle and was frantically applying the tender brake. Instantly the cab was filled with steam and the horrifying screech of the wheels braking and sending up sparks, and the thump of the couplings behind them straining.

'We're going too fast,' shouted Evans. Seamus knew they were travelling too fast. He knew that their combined brake-power would not stop the train in time. He wondered why all the signals had been in the 'clear' position—could he have misread one of them? He thought about his dead wife.

The Birmingham-bound passenger train hit the stationary goods train at twelve minutes past three in the afternoon. The engine and tender ploughed into the rear of the goods train, throwing the last three wagons of that train off the line and down the embankment. The engine and tender of the oncoming passenger train were crushed and almost completely destroyed by the force of the collision.

The driver and the fireman were killed instantly.

The third-class carriage behind slammed into the tender and was thrown from the tracks on the other side to the goods wagons, coming to rest on its side some yards from the line. Carriages two and three were also taken off the line, their couplings braking, and rolled into the canal. Carriages four, five and six and the luggage van were all swung to the left, destroying the walls of the bridge but remaining upright. The first brake-van's front wheels came off the rails, its axles breaking and its wheels flying off and coming to rest some yards away. The second brake-van and the remaining nine carriages, including those carrying the Sunday school excursion, remained on the lines, sustaining only broken axles and damage to their interiors.

The time from the engine cresting the bridge to the last carriage coming to a standstill was twenty-three seconds. In the circumstances it was a miracle only three people died.

CHAPTER ONE

London

NINETEEN CADOGAN MEWS WAS A smart, double-fronted, white-painted terrace in a row of such dwellings erected in the early 1850s for gentlemen of business and their families. It was situated in a discreet and elegantly proportioned laneway off Cadogan Square in a part of Bloomsbury just then becoming fashionable. The house had been purchased originally by Mr Samuel Jarmyn, entrepreneur and wealthy industrialist, in the autumn of 1854, soon after its completion. Following Mr Jarmyn's sudden and unexpected demise not long after, it had become the home of his only son, the current Mr Jarmyn, and his family.

It was a five-storey house, including the below-stairs rooms and the servants' quarters in the attic, which allowed for a gentleman of not-insignificant means along with his wife and up to six children, plus a staff of four, to live quite comfortably. And during the current Mr Jarmyn's tenure, the house had contained all these people. But now Mr Jarmyn's eldest son had gone up to Oxford and first one and now a second housemaid had departed at short notice and, since June, the curtains had remained drawn and every mirror in the house was covered.

It was now early December and by late afternoon it was bitterly cold in the house but still no fires were lit in the grates.

Dinah Jarmyn, coming in from the garden, pulled her shawl closer about her shoulders, and wondered if her father would ever allow another fire to be lit in the house again. She had recently turned eighteen but as the family had been unable to observe the day Dinah had slipped from girlhood to womanhood silently and unseen. Her hair was now up and she had her own calling card but as she and her mother made no calls this meant very little. Dinah was her father's child, perhaps more than his other children, having his watchful grey-green eyes and the long Jarmyn face, the blunt jawline and slender nose. What she inherited from her mother was harder to define. 'You will be a great beauty like your mother, Dinah,' Mr Jarmyn had observed solemnly a few nights earlier, and the way he had said it had made it seem like a judgement.

Dinah shivered. Two of the housemaids had left already. Better, they had told the housekeeper, Mrs Logan, to seek employment elsewhere than to stay in a house that was forever cold. And who could blame them? thought Dinah. Would she, too, not depart given the choice? But she did not have a choice: she had no position to resign from and there was no employment she could seek elsewhere.

The grates were swept clean—a boy had come during the summer and flushed out the chimney, leaving soot on the carpet which Mrs Logan had tried in vain to hide but that her father had, inevitably, seen and railed against. The boy had not been back—though, as the chimney had not been used since, his presence was hardly required.

It was curious though, that despite no fire having been lit since June, still one could smell burning.

Dinah shivered a second time, turning to close the door to the garden behind her with numbed fingers. She had ventured out to cut some of the first winter jasmine from the steep bank at the end of the garden and intended, now, to take the bright yellow flowers upstairs to arrange them in a vase. She laid the flowers on the hallway table then paused. She had found, in amongst the tangle of jasmine roots and the damp and rotting last-summer foliage at the base of the ancient sycamore, a button: brass, round, a tunic button, green-tinged and dirt-encrusted where it had lain in the undergrowth. She rubbed at the dirt just enough to make out the circular inscription *Montis Insignia Calpe*, words which Dinah, not having a word of Latin, could not translate.

She looked up. The ground-floor rooms were all silent. Her father had gone out immediately after lunch stating neither his destination nor his purpose which, on a weekday, would have meant a meeting of the board of directors. But on a Sunday afternoon, what business could he have?

Dinah rubbed her hands briskly together, placed the button on the silver letter tray on the hall table and went upstairs in search of a suitable receptacle for her flowers.

—⁓—

As Dinah surmised, her father, Mr Lucas Jarmyn, had not attended a meeting of the board of directors. He had gone out, though his business had taken him only as far as a bench in nearby Russell Square where he had sat for a time talking to no one and, to the casual observer, doing nothing very much at all, and now he had returned and was upstairs in his study going through the monthly accounts.

The accounts were, strictly speaking, his wife's affair and in the early years of their marriage Mrs Aurora Jarmyn had run the household with the precision, zeal and authority of a ship's purser. But in recent times his wife's control of the accounts, indeed her interest in them, had waned. As often as not it fell to Mrs Logan to settle the monthly accounts and to reconcile the various household expenses. But, whilst relying on one's housekeeper to keep the household afloat might suit some men, Mr Jarmyn preferred to cast an expert eye over the figures himself. Not that he had ever had reason to fault the estimable Mrs Logan, who was in her accounting abilities as she was in all aspects of her housekeeping, which was to say, flawless.

He reached the end of a long column of figures and was pleased to observe that the figure Mrs Logan had recorded tallied with his own. He paused, knocking the ash from his cigar into the grate, where it lay in a small grey pile and where it would remain until someone thought to sweep it away as this fireplace, like every fireplace in the house, was empty and unlit.

But Mr Jarmyn no longer felt the cold.

—◊—

In a small room on the second floor, directly above Mr Jarmyn's study, Uncle Austin, formerly Major Austin Randle, late of the 8th King's Hussars, was also at home that Sunday afternoon, though as the major rarely left his room and never ventured beyond the front steps of number 19 Cadogan Mews, his presence went unremarked. The little finger of his left hand was missing, sliced off in battle on a frozen Crimean plain close on three decades earlier—a deformity that might play on other men's minds. Today the loss of his little finger was not Uncle Austin's most pressing concern: he was, at this moment, balancing on the window ledge of his second-storey room cackling delightedly at the pigeon that had just alighted on his arm.

Mrs Logan, the estimable housekeeper whose monthly figures Mr Jarmyn was even now perusing, came into the room just at the point at which Uncle Austin was preparing to launch himself off the window after the pigeon and into certain oblivion.

Mrs Logan held the elevated position of housekeeper at 19 Cadogan Mews despite being only in her thirty-third year, and after three years with the household was a veteran of Uncle Austin's unusual flights of fancy. She wasted no time now in fainting or hysteria, nor any of the customary responses that the sight of an old man making ready to jump out of a second-floor window might elicit. Instead she hurried into the room stating firmly, 'I don't think so, Major!' and made a grab for his coat-tails at the critical moment, thus preventing a very nasty accident.

Lord knows, they did not need another nasty accident in this house, thought Mrs Logan as she hauled the mildly protesting old man back into the room and made fast the window. And who, she tutted, had left the windows unsecured? Annie, the housemaid, was the most likely candidate, a girl whose grasp of even the most rudimentary concepts was limited. But as Annie had, last night, quit the household there was little chance of asking her.

It was annoying, Annie quitting like that (here Mrs Logan tugged on the window fastening to assure herself it was secure) and only a month after Agnes quitting. '*Too cold*'! Whoever heard of such a thing? In other households, a girl came to the house at age ten and stayed until she either got married, was pensioned off or died. She didn't stay five minutes then hand in her notice claiming the house was too cold.

Mrs Logan turned her attention on the old man. The major was seated quietly in an armchair. A pleasantly attentive smile suggested he was happily awaiting her ministrations and, not for the first time, Mrs Logan wondered if the old man had even the slightest idea who she was. His small black eyes watched her with a keen intelligence that belied the aborted leap of death of a moment earlier and, were it not for the missing finger and the scar, he could have been any elderly gentleman sitting down to his four o'clock cup of tea and toasted muffin.

The scar was hard to ignore. It snaked from mouth to temple, slicing the left side of his face in half. At its deepest point the groove was perhaps a quarter of an inch thick, and a vivid purple-red that changed colour occasionally when the major got upset. The shot that had caused this scar had been fired by a sharp-eyed Cossack at Balaklava in the autumn of '54. It had penetrated his skull and a small piece of it was still lodged there today. What was left of the major following this encounter with the Cossack was this black-eyed old man who sometimes sat patiently awaiting his tea and sometimes attempted to leap from his second-floor window.

It was to be hoped that the major was no more aware of his circumstances than a newborn baby was of its. And yet often he was quite lucid: a memory of childhood perfectly recalled, a fellow officer minutely described. But of the last twenty-six years he remained steadfastly unaware. He was Mrs Jarmyn's uncle, her father's younger brother, though he often greeted Mrs Jarmyn as though she were a complete stranger. Whom he imagined all the other people in this house were, the Lord alone knew. Still, he was always very polite when he ran into them.

'There now, Major, all safe and secure,' Mrs Logan observed, giving the window lock a final rattle. 'We'll leave the flying for another day, shall we?'

—⁂—

Annie the housemaid had quit. But she had not left quite yet.

On the floor above Major Randle's room, in an attic with a steeply sloping ceiling that, for two years, she and Agnes had shared, Annie sat and contemplated her future.

She had quit.

It was not something she had thought she would ever do. Yet here she was on her final morning with her small bag already packed, and here was the chipped enamel jug she had daily washed from but never would again, and there the narrow bed she had lain in, shivering.

Would she have taken this step had Agnes not already done so a month earlier? She wasn't sure. They had talked of it, the two of them, in the dark when the family were asleep downstairs, and it had been Agnes who had first said she was going to quit.

'But where would you go?' Annie had replied, pulling the flannelette sheet up to her chin because with Agnes's words a vast chasm, pitch black and bottomless, had opened up before her.

'Don't matter. Away from here. Away from *her*,' had been Agnes's reply. ·

But these were just words. Anyone could say 'I'm going to quit', couldn't they? It didn't mean you were actually going to do it.

But Agnes *had* done it. Annie had come into their room one Tuesday afternoon after lighting up to find Agnes jamming her few belongings into a battered old trunk, her face set hard and angry.

'I've quit. Told 'em I've had enough,' had been her explanation and Annie had stared at her, open-mouthed.

'But why?' Though she knew why, of course.

'*I 'eard her!*' was all Agnes would say. And truth be told Annie did not care to hear more.

She shivered. They had both smelt the burning, smelt it every single day. The drawing room always smelt of burning. You couldn't escape it. But what had Agnes heard? She had heard *her*. But *what*, exactly?

14

Whatever it was, Agnes had gone and exactly where she had gone (*'I got a sister in Bethnal Green, she'll help me. I'll get another place, if I want one. Maybe I don't want one'*) Annie did not know.

So Annie had gone on alone and though Mrs Logan had said another girl would be joining them shortly, the new girl wouldn't be Agnes, would she? And in the meantime Annie was alone, upstairs in her room, shivering, her feet blue with cold, the major stalking the downstairs rooms and planning who knew what mischief.

And the ghost. The ghost was in the drawing room.

A creak downstairs made her gasp. It was the floorboards settling, just the floorboards.

Last evening, when darkness had long fallen and the house was in shadows and the light from the lamp in the hallway had flickered in the draught, the master had ordered her to fetch something from the drawing room.

She had stared at him, panic-stricken. They never went into the drawing room, and certainly never after dark, not even the family! But the master had said, 'Annie, there is a book I require in the drawing room. Please fetch it for me.' And because she had gaped at him, he had added, impatiently, 'It is the Squires, girl. *Squires' Study of the Workings and Evolution of the Railway Steam Engine,*' as if knowing the title of the book might somehow make a difference. As if he thought she could read.

She had fled his gaze and tried to locate Mrs Logan but Mrs Logan could not be located so Annie had found herself standing outside the door to the drawing room, in the dark, with the shadows flickering all around her and her hand that was raised to the door handle shaking so violently she wondered if she would be able to open the door at all.

And that was when she had heard it: the whimper of a small child in terrible pain. Instantly the smell of burning was all around her, suffocating, smothering, choking her. She had shrieked and run for the stairs, had bolted for her room and when Mrs Logan had sought her out some time later, her bag was packed and she had uttered the words she had thought she would never utter: *I quit.*

Mrs Logan had been furious, as well she might be, losing both her girls one after another, but there was nothing to be done about it. Annie had said she was quitting and quit she would and no amount of coaxing and reasoning and demanding was going to change that. And this morning the daylight and the sliver of weak December sunshine that crept in through the narrow attic window changed nothing—somehow it was late afternoon already. She had intended to leave first thing.

Annie picked up her bag and left the room that she had, for two years, shared with Agnes, and scuttled down the back stairs. She had said her farewells to Mrs Logan and Cook already, and she had no wish to run into the family, especially the master.

At the back door she put down her bag and pulled on her mittens. It was cold outside, she could already feel it. She unlatched the heavy bolt, picked up her bag and let herself out, almost falling over Mr Gladstone. Steadying herself she bent down to fondle his furry orange chin but, having spent an unprofitable night prowling the streets, Mr Gladstone was in no mood to be friendly and he shot inside and was gone. His dismissal was somehow final so that she felt an odd pang. The area steps were icy and she picked her way cautiously and stood at street level. There was a frost on the ground that the weak sunlight had failed to melt. A few remaining leaves, blown by the strong winds last night, were banked up against the railings. The plane trees that lined Cadogan Mews were quite bare now.

She pulled her shawl tighter around her shoulders and left the house.

—⁂—

Cook, watching Annie's departure from the basement kitchen window, shook her head and rolled her eyes and made a *tch!* sound with her tongue.

That one was as daft as the other one who had left the previous month, thought Cook, and she used the occasion of Annie's departure to stop work and place her floury hands on her hips. And what the household was going to do now that both girls had upped and gone she did not know and she had an idea Mrs Logan did not know either, for all she said she'd have a new girl start in a day or two.

What new girl? Cook wanted to know. No one had come to the house, no position had been advertised so far as she was aware. And what was they all meant to do in the meantime, she wanted to know, with meals to be prepared and on the table morning, noon and night and no one to help her except the boy who came mornings to deliver the coal? Well, there was nothing for it: Mrs Logan would have to serve.

Outside Annie had paused at the top of the area steps and was now looking from left to right as though she had forgotten which way she was going.

It was a pity, Cook decided as she resumed her kneading of the dough, that folk didn't forget things more easily.

It was the girl. The dead girl. It was all they thought about. And why? What good did it do? Hadn't she lost four children herself in her time, and a husband too come to think of it, and never a word of it mentioned to anyone and hardly a thought either, all these years. Two dead in their cradles, buried before their first birthdays, poor little mites. One drowned in the river on New Year's Eve, the last dashed beneath the hooves of a horse crossing Whitehall. As for Mr Varley—for there had once been a Mr Varley—he had perished off the Irish coast, shipwrecked during a freak storm en route to New South Wales, along with two dozen other souls, and never missed nor grieved for. All dead. All so many years ago she could barely see their faces now. The two babies so young she had to remind herself what she had christened them.

She paused again, wiping a floury hand across her forehead. The kitchen was warm no matter there was a frost outside and ice already forming on the outside of the window.

And look at Mrs Logan who'd lost her husband not so many years back and her newly married, you didn't hear Mrs Logan making a fuss about a dead girl, did you?

Satisfied at last with the texture of the dough, Cook squeezed it into three waiting baking dishes and slid them with the aid of a long wooden spatula into the range. The smell of baking bread would soon fill the whole house and, like as not, Master Jack would be down demanding a piece soon enough.

He wouldn't get any.

Cook wiped her hands again and sat down with a sigh onto her rocking chair and reached for her pipe.

Annie had gone, disappeared from view, and Cook instantly forgot her.

—⁓—

As Cook predicted, the aroma of baking bread rapidly infused the house. It crept up the back stairs to the hallway, easily overpowering the fragrance from the winter jasmine Dinah had brought in from the garden and not yet arranged in a vase, and it seeped into the first-floor drawing room, neutralising, for a moment at least, any other odours that lingered there. Onwards it went, slipping beneath the closed door of Mr Jarmyn's study, causing him to pause in his perusal of the accounts and, just for a second, forget himself.

Gathering force, it surged upwards, reaching Uncle Austin's room on the second floor so that the old soldier lifted his grizzled head like a ponderous, elderly spaniel and, for a fleeting moment, remembered another loaf of bread baking in another range in his mother's kitchen fifty years earlier.

The last place it reached was the schoolroom at the top of the house where Mr Todd, one-time Classics master at Harrow and long since retired but who (due to a poor investment decision involving a mine and a small South American nation whose name Mr Todd could no longer recall) found himself forced to give private tuition to the sons of gentlemen. The sons in question were Master Gus Jarmyn, eleven, and Master Jack Jarmyn, ten, and at this moment they were in the midst of a Latin translation. Or rather Master Gus was in the midst of a Latin translation, his pen gripped tightly, the nib poised and shaking ever so slightly an inch above the exercise book that had once belonged to his elder brother, Bill, his tongue poking out of the side of his mouth as he pondered the phrase *iter itineris* and wondered whether to translate it as 'journey' or 'road'.

By contrast, seated beside him, his brother Jack was recalling with exquisite pleasure the pictures from the book he had been reading the night before, an illustrated work charting the development of the English soldier and his uniform from the Normans to the present day. His reading the previous evening had brought him to the Hundred Years War and he was recalling, in minute detail, the armour worn by King Henry's knights.

As the smell of baking bread reached them, Mr Todd sat back in his hard little wooden chair and let out a contented 'Ahh!' Gus momentarily forgot about *iter itineris* and Jack briefly left the battlefield of Agincourt.

—⁓—

The only part of the house the baking bread failed to penetrate was the bedroom of Dinah's mother, Mrs Aurora Jarmyn. This bedroom, a large room on the second floor and overlooking the mews, was sealed from such intrusions. The door was shut and a thick, padded draught-excluder was wedged firmly along the bottom of the door, beyond which no light, no sound, no smell could pass.

The curtains were not quite fully drawn so that a shaft of sudden and unexpected December sunlight struck the carpet and fell across Mrs Jarmyn, who sat in an upright chair before her writing table. A diary was open on her desk and she noted that it was the fifth of December.

Six months had passed.

She looked up, closed the diary. Laid her hands on the table. How could six months have passed?

She placed the diary in her desk drawer and turned the key but made no move to get up. Mrs Jarmyn was impervious to the smell of baking bread that now permeated the whole house. But unlike her husband, she was not impervious to the cold that had crept into the very foundations of the house and would not be dislodged.

She shivered.

CHAPTER TWO

BOTH HER PARENTS WERE LATE for dinner.

Dinah picked up her napkin, slid it from its silver ring and unfolded it on her lap, realising as she did so that she had left the winter jasmine on the hallway table and that the delicate flowers would, by now, have faded. She felt a small pang of remorse and her eyes flickered around the table wondering who might have noticed. Opposite her Gus was frowning in concentration at something, and she knew it could not possibly be winter jasmine that absorbed him so. Beside Gus, Jack was fiddling crossly with his collar, his face pink with his exertions.

'And I jolly well have it on good authority that Old Toddy was quite wrong with that marking,' Gus announced and Jack, to whom this statement appeared to be aimed, gave up on his collar and retorted with a huge shrug.

'I don't see that it matters either way. And on whose authority anyway?'

'Bill's. He said Toddy was a frightful old fraud with his Latin and that he only really knows Greek.'

Jack now looked confused. 'Weren't we doing Greek?' he asked, a doubtful look creeping over his face.

Gus seemed about to reply to this surprising question from his younger brother when their mother joined them, coming in and seating herself at one end of the table, and smiling brightly at them all. Gus instantly closed his mouth.

Her mother looked beautiful this evening, Dinah saw. It was a beauty that seemed to transcend every little horror and tragedy whilst retaining, somehow, a memory of each of those things. It made your heart ache at the same time as it made your spirits soar. She wore a shawl wrapped closely about her thin shoulders and long kid gloves in a soft ivory white which served, also, to hide the scar that disfigured her arm. Her mother slid slender arms around herself for a brief moment as though to hug herself and appeared to stifle a shiver. It seemed she must surely make some comment about the coldness in the dining room and Dinah felt the muscles of her stomach tense.

Instead her mother said, 'Well, my dears, and what have you all been up to today?'

Dinah felt her muscles release and she spoke first as she, with Bill absent, was now the eldest.

'I went into the garden this afternoon as I wanted to cut the first winter jasmine to make an arrangement.'

'Did you dear? How lovely. But where are they?'

Dinah thought of the flowers, probably wilted and faded by now, lying where she had left them on the little side table in the hallway. She would get Mrs Logan to remove them.

'There were only one or two. It was too few to make a proper arrangement . . .'

'Oh. What a shame. Perhaps you could press them?' Her mother smiled brightly again.

It was odd, Dinah realised, how her mother only smiled brightly now. She never just smiled. It was always this intense, almost fierce smile, a smile that dared one to contradict it. A smile that sent a chill through one. She made no reply to her mother's suggestion.

'Gus?'

'Oh. We did Latin prep,' said Gus, aiming a significant look at Jack. 'We had a test and I did rather well although there was a point of contention when Toddy—Mr Todd—disputed one of my translations.'

'Did he? Well, no doubt he knows best, dear, being a Latin master.'

Gus flushed indignantly at this suggestion.

'Jack?'

Jack, who had returned to the problem of his collar, was caught out by her question and appeared to cast about for some suitable reply.

'I've been reading about the British Army,' he replied at last and beside him Gus rolled his eyes but Jack instantly warmed to this subject. 'It's really very interesting, Mama. Did you know the average French soldier at Agincourt wore thirty pounds of armour? *Thirty pounds!* Whereas the English bowmen wore virtually *no armour at all* and consequently they were quite mobile and that is probably what contributed to them winning. That, and their exceptional skill at archery,' he concluded.

Beside him Gus groaned.

'Good Heavens!' replied Mrs Jarmyn as though she had only that morning been pondering the Battle of Agincourt and now all her questions had been answered. 'That is most interesting,' she added, at which point even Jack appeared to realise his mother's interest in the uniforms of the English soldier did not equal his. He seemed to deflate a little and fell silent.

'And I have been busy too!' announced Mrs Jarmyn unexpectedly and, almost imperceptibly, they all tensed. No one said, 'Have you, Mama?' but it did not seem to matter for Mrs Jarmyn continued unbidden.

'I have been planning a holiday! There! What do you think of that?' She did not wait to hear what they thought of that, instead plunging ahead with her plan. 'We shall travel to Paris and perhaps spend one or two nights there then take the train to Florence and from there to Venice. And—what do think?—the Brightsides will be in Venice in the spring! We shall stay at their villa or perhaps take one of our own. It will be an education! What do you think of that?'

The Brightsides were Mr Jarmyn's sister, Meredith, and her husband, Travers. Uncle Travers was an ecclesiastical publisher, a one-time cleric himself though now, for reasons never adequately explained, minus a parish. Aunt Meredith was the God-daughter of a former bishop of Coventry and Lichfield and seemed to have made a dreadful mistake with her choice of husband. Why her mother wished to holiday with the Brightsides was not immediately clear to Dinah. Nor, she could see, to her two brothers. But her cousin Rhoda would be there, she presumed, and she and Rhoda were almost of an age and, for the most part, friends. Roger, who was her only other cousin and Rhoda's elder brother, would not be there because he had recently gone off to become a soldier.

No one had yet remarked on Mrs Jarmyn's plan and Dinah felt it incumbent upon her as the eldest in Bill's absence, to offer some response. 'How marvellous,' she suggested, and looked to her brothers but Jack and Gus seemed to have nothing to add.

'Venice is always at its best in the springtime. The weather will be perfect,' said Mrs Jarmyn, needing no further affirmation of their wholehearted acquiescence.

And now Dinah understood, or thought she did. Florence, Venice—Italy. It would be warm. Warmer than here at any rate. And it would be away. Far, far away.

'Will we still have to have lessons? Will Mr Todd have to come?' asked Jack, and Mrs Jarmyn laughed her high tinkling laugh, seemingly unaware that Jack was in earnest.

'I expect we would have an Italian tutor,' suggested Gus. 'Mr Todd is all very well for your run-of-the-mill Greek but he's hardly up to scratch for Ancient Rome or modern Italian, one would have thought,' he added, his grievance with the ageing tutor clearly still fresh in his mind.

'Of course Mr Todd must come! We must all go! Just wait till I tell your father!'

And as though he had been summoned, they heard footsteps outside as their father approached. It seemed an eternity that he crossed the hallway and put his hand on the doorknob and Dinah sat quite still and silent, waiting. Across the table Jack was still fidgeting and she tried to catch his eye to make him stop.

At last the door softly opened and she caught a whiff of tobacco and tweed and the something that she thought of as 'the world of business', whatever that was, she was never quite certain, but it always preceded her father into a room. She studied her napkin, observing the way it had curled naturally back into a roll even though she had removed it from its ring. At the final moment, just as Mr Jarmyn reached the table, she looked up, the correct expression ready on her face. What that correct expression was she could no more describe than she could describe the smell of business but she saw that expression reflected back to her now on the three other faces around the table.

Mr Jarmyn pulled out his chair, lowered himself into it and repositioned the chair beneath the table. He reached for his napkin, removed it from its ring, placed it on his lap and only then did he look up, appearing to notice the various members of his family observing him in silent anticipation.

Dinah was aware of an uncomfortable sensation in her stomach that felt like hunger pangs yet she felt no desire for food. It hadn't always been like this. Now it had become their routine.

'Good evening,' said Mr Jarmyn, making this remark to his wife, and the absence of the words 'my dear' at the end of this greeting was as stark as the absence around the table of the two other family members (though Bill was merely at Oxford).

'Good evening, Lucas,' replied her mother, and Dinah averted her gaze to avoid seeing that bright smile or her father's answering frown.

'Good evening, Dinah. Gus. Jack.'

'Good evening, Father.'

'Good evening, Father.'

'Good evening, Father.'

It was a relief, of sorts, to get that part over and done with. Dinah settled her shoulder muscles into a softer posture.

'Well. Tell me about your day. Dinah?'

'I've been arranging flowers, Father, from the garden . . .'

'Have you? I don't see any.'

Dinah thought, not of the flowers, but of the old tunic button she had discovered in the garden and instead of offering some reply to her father she stared mutely at him. Perhaps he needed no reply as he turned instead to Gus.

'And Gus? What have you been up to?'

'Studying hard, Father.'

'Good. Good. And you, Jack?'

'And I too, Father.' No mention of Agincourt now.

'Good. Good,' said their father a second time. He pulled out his fob watch and studied it for such a long moment it seemed that what he was reading there must surely be more than just the time. They waited and eventually he put the watch away.

Dinah stared straight ahead, determined not to glance at her mother, who was seated at the far end of the table. Her mother poured herself a glass of water from the carafe then slowly rotated the glass on its coaster, seeming to study the colourless liquid within. Her hand shook ever so slightly. Their father had not addressed her, had not asked what she had done that day. It was as though their mother was not there at all.

Mrs Jarmyn cleared her throat and Dinah bit down on her lip. It seemed that her mother must speak, that she might even mention her wild plans of a moment earlier. But she said nothing and, on the other side of the table, one of the boys let out a tiny sigh.

'And where, do you suppose, is our dinner?' remarked Mr Jarmyn as though just that moment realising it was nearly ten past six and no dishes had yet arrived from the kitchen. 'Dinah, call for Annie.'

But before Dinah could reach for the bell the door opened and Mrs Logan herself entered, her normally smooth, calm features unusually flushed, and even more unusually, she was carrying the silver soup tureen.

'Mrs Logan. You appear to be carrying a soup tureen,' observed Mr Jarmyn. 'May one inquire as to the reason for this sudden demotion in your position in my household from housekeeper to maid?'

'Certainly, Mr Jarmyn,' Mrs Logan replied, manhandling the large tureen with surprising dexterity. 'We find ourselves temporarily deficient in staff to the tune of two housemaids. The soup is quail and leek.'

'I see,' Mr Jarmyn replied grimly, receiving the news of another housemaid's departure in the same vein as he did the advent of Cook's quail and leek consommé. 'I suppose we had better have some of it, then. Don't want Cook quitting on us too.'

He leant back in his chair to allow Mrs Logan to serve him, which she did with a measured concentration that seemed out of all proportion to the task at hand. Having satisfied herself that Mr Jarmyn's soup bowl was suitably filled, Mrs Logan moved on to their mother. Dinah had no wish to experience Cook's quail and leek soup but it seemed that her father had spoken for them all and they each submitted in turn as Mrs Logan wielded her ladle before discreetly withdrawing. Dinah picked up her spoon and submerged it slowly into the pool of liquid in her bowl. The soup, as was often the case with Cook's soup, defied any particular colour or texture but still managed to coat her spoon with a sticky residue.

They ate the soup in silence aside from the tiny and unavoidable slurps as they each took a sip. Dinah concentrated all her energy on making no sound at all and she achieved this until she realised she was taking none of the soup into her mouth and that the pool of liquid in her bowl was not going down. A drop of soup made its way onto her tongue where it scalded her, then slid down her throat and into her stomach where it congealed, a thick indigestible mass. She remembered as a girl being hungry all the time, feeling ravenous before meals, spooning great quantities into her mouth, receiving each new dish with relish. Now she could no longer eat. She wished Mrs Logan would remove the soup.

'Father, we are to go to Venice,' said Jack, and beside him Gus stirred uneasily.

Where *was* Mrs Logan? Surely she must realise they had finished the soup? Perhaps they ought to ring for her?

'Indeed?' said Mr Jarmyn, putting down his spoon and studying his youngest child with interest. 'And when are we to make this journey?'

At this, Jack appeared to lose confidence, looking to his mother for confirmation.

'Oh. It was a little scheme of mine,' said Mrs Jarmyn with a modest laugh. 'You know, Lucas, how delightful Venice is in the springtime—'

'No indeed, I have not had the pleasure of visiting it at that time.'

'—and how educational it is, especially for young children? The Brightsides, of course, will be there. They are taking a villa.'

But neither the time of year nor the anticipated educational value of the trip, nor even the allure of spending an extended amount of time with the Brightsides appeared to hold much sway for their father, who met her remarks with a stony silence.

'Shall we be going, Father?' asked Jack, the idea, once planted, not easily dislodged.

Beside him Gus scowled. 'Of course we are not going,' he hissed.

Jack was at once outraged. *'But—'*

'Be quiet.' Mr Jarmyn did not raise his voice but both fell instantly silent.

Where was Mrs Logan? Why did she not take away the soup bowls? Dinah smoothed out the creases of her napkin again and again, her fingers digging into the embroidered monogram.

'We will *not* be going to Venice,' said Mr Jarmyn slowly and deliberately. 'And I would prefer there to be no further mention of the subject. Is that clear?'

Jack and Gus nodded silently.

'Oh, but it seemed like such an agreeable idea!' said Mrs Jarmyn chattily and seemingly impervious to the chill that had settled over the dining room. 'Dinah thought it was a grand scheme—didn't you think it a grand scheme, Dinah?'

Dinah stared at her mother but was spared from answering by Mrs Logan who finally emerged with the next course.

But it was not the next course Mrs Logan had brought. It was the silver letter tray from the downstairs hallway into which, in another era, callers had left their cards. Nowadays it was generally used when telegrams arrived and it was such that Mrs Logan now offered to their father.

'A telegram, Mr Jarmyn,' she explained, offering him the tray. 'And there is baked sole in asparagus jelly with parsley sauce.'

'I will have the sole, Mrs Logan,' said Mrs Jarmyn, and it seemed inconceivable to Dinah that her mother had just attempted a witticism.

Her father, at any rate, chose to ignore it, taking the telegram and nodding to Mrs Logan, who wordlessly withdrew. He opened it at once, using his fish knife to slit the envelope. He unfolded the slip of paper, reviewed its contents expressionlessly, refolded it and replaced it in the envelope, placing the telegram beside his plate. There it remained as the sole in asparagus jelly with parsley sauce was served, consumed and removed, so too the roast loin of mutton and the baked pear pudding that followed it.

Once, Dinah realised, her mother would have said, 'Not bad news I trust, my dear?' But now Mrs Jarmyn remained silent for there could be no bad news left. They had had it all already.

—⁓—

There had been another railway accident and this time three people were dead—two employees of the railway and a young child travelling with its father.

This much Lucas Jarmyn had established from the telegram that had arrived during dinner and from a second one delivered to him by Mrs Logan an hour or so later. Both came from Kemp, a fellow director of the railway line and a man Mr Jarmyn usually took pains to avoid.

After dinner he retired to his study and sat contemplating the two telegrams over a glass of port. The dinner had not been a pleasant experience. It seldom was. And the arrival of the two telegrams had merely made things worse.

He frowned, avoiding that other presence in the room: it hung over the empty fireplace, a portrait of his father, the elder Mr Jarmyn, a solidly built man in late middle-age sporting enormous whiskers and a florid complexion and wearing a collar, hat and morning coat in a style that had been briefly fashionable in the late forties. As a child Lucas remembered his father sitting for this very portrait during one exceptionally warm June and the maid having to be on hand with a sponge and a jug of iced water to mop the old man's face when the perspiration got too much. Mr Jarmyn Senior had been enormous by then, barely squeezing his bulk into the chair in which he was seated, though the portrait, painted by a young Royal Academy artist with an eye to further commissions, merely suggested a man of generous rather than excessive proportions.

But Samuel Jarmyn had started life from humble beginnings and perhaps, no matter how wealthy one became in later life, one never really got used to having enough to eat. Born at the turn of the century, the son of an impoverished Spitalfields silk weaver, Samuel Jarmyn had by the early forties somehow scraped together enough capital to build a railway line to transport coal, iron ore and wool to and from the newly industrialised towns of Wolverhampton and Birmingham and had, overnight, become extraordinarily wealthy. His company, the Wolverhampton and Birmingham Freight and Passenger Railway Company, had been listed publicly in 1851 and, following an extension of the line as far as Shrewsbury, renamed the North West Midlands Railway. It was no longer a family-owned company but, as Mr Jarmyn's only son, Lucas was the majority shareholder and held a lifetime seat on the board of directors.

It was a role he sometimes disliked.

At a time when railway accidents rivalled cholera as the main cause of premature death amongst the working population, the NWMR held a safety record unmatched by its rivals: it had more accidents per stretch of line than any other railway in the Kingdom—more derailments and signal failures, more passenger fatalities and employee injuries, more coronial inquests and Board of Trade inquiries, and more column inches in *The Times* than the Midland, the Great Western and the North Eastern combined. Truly, it was said, the passenger on the North West Midlands Railway took his life in his hands when he purchased his ticket and stepped into the brown-and-salmon liveried carriage. A famous *Punch* cartoon showed a young man being offered a ticket to travel on the NWMR or a place in Wellington's army to face Napoleon on the battlefields of Waterloo. '*The young fellow's dilemma!*' was the caption. The cartoon was oft cited in business circles and a copy had been framed and placed on the wall of Mr Jarmyn's own club in St James.

Lucas reached for the first of the two telegrams and cast an eye over it for the fourth or fifth time, contemplating this further evidence—should any be needed—of the continuing carnage on his father's railway and the uneasy reputation the line had earned for itself. And yet it was difficult to see beyond the fact that the railway provided his—and his family's—livelihood. This house, the servants (those who still remained in his employ), the clothes his children wore and the expensive education provided to them, his membership of the club in St James, all paid for by the endless trainloads of coal and passengers trundling between these distant towns.

There would be a damning report in *The Times* tomorrow. Well, so be it. The company would offer to pay the railwaymen's funeral costs and there would be a small annuity for the widows. The usual letter of condolence would be forwarded to the dead child's father.

He finished the port in a single gulp and gazed at the tumbler in his hand. A lot of men had shaken his own hand at his own child's funeral last June though he could not remember a single one of their faces.

He reached for the decanter and was disconcerted to find it empty. Ringing vigorously for Annie, he was further disconcerted when Mrs Logan answered his summons.

Of course, Annie had quit. He looked away as Mrs Logan entered the room and the frown that had clouded his face since dinner deepened, though the arrival of his housekeeper could hardly account for this. She had a strong face, though he was not at this moment looking at it, a strong North Country face. No, that was not quite right—it was her character that was strong, he decided, and it was this strength that showed in her silent, thoughtful demeanour. *Could* one's character show in one's features? He did not know.

'Mrs Logan. We appear to have run out of port as well as housemaids. Are you in a position to rectify either of these deficiencies?'

'I trust I am in a position to rectify both, Mr Jarmyn. I have fetched a bottle of the Quinta Dos Santos '58 from the cellar and the agency are sending us a girl tomorrow afternoon.'

There was a silence, then, 'Are you running my entire establishment single-handedly, Mrs Logan?'

'It would appear so, Mr Jarmyn.'

He nodded and watched as Mrs Logan coolly decanted the '58, her hands moving smoothly and skilfully and with the minimum of fuss and, now as he glanced up at her face, he saw the same calm concentration there.

'You will have noted there was no wine served with the dinner?' she inquired in her soft North Country voice.

'I did,' he replied, turning back to his contemplation of the two telegrams, but when she had retired from the room, he found he had no stomach for the port. He had lately discovered a horror of drunkenness.

—⁓—

'There will have been another accident,' remarked Jack, and Aurora, standing outside the boys' room, paused to listen. She pictured her youngest son with his hands in his pockets imitating the way Bill stood, the voluminous *Boys' Compendium of the English Soldier: His Uniform and Weaponry as Used in the Greatest English Battles*, whose heroic and blood-curdling pages had consumed him for the past fortnight, open on the bed beside him. 'There'll be an article in *The Times* for certain,' Jack added, because this was not their first railway accident and they knew how things would be.

'Telegrams do not always mean there has been a railway accident,' Gus corrected, the meticulous one, the contrary one. 'In actual fact,' Gus continued, 'in most households the arrival of a telegram would not signify a railway accident at all. It would, more likely, announce a wedding or someone's arrival somewhere or, on occasion, the death of a distant relative.'

'But here it usually means a railway accident,' Jack observed.

They fell silent but Aurora hesitated outside their door. She did not venture up to the children's rooms in the attic often, and the room directly next door to the boys' room she had not set foot in for many months. She had been absent, she realised, and perhaps her children had needed her. But six months had passed and things would be different from now on. She would go into the boys' room to say goodnight to them. She would write to Bill before she retired for the night, and tomorrow she would take Dinah to her dressmaker and together they would pay some calls. She had wanted them all to go away together, to Italy perhaps with the Brightsides, it had seemed like such a practical idea, but Lucas had forbidden it. But he would come around. In the meantime she would say goodnight to her children.

—∿—

There had been a railway accident.

Mrs Logan had known it as soon as the boy had delivered the telegram in the middle of dinner.

'Got three more of these to deliver before I get off,' the boy
had announced importantly, pausing on the back step to adjust
his chinstrap and await a coin. 'Next one's over Hampstead
way. Take me best part of an hour to get there in this weather,
I s'pect.'

'To what address?'

The boy's eyes narrowed. 'Can't say, can I?'

A second coin was passed to him, which he slipped into his
tunic pocket. 'Coburg Square. Give you the name, if you like?'

But Mrs Logan did not need the name. She already knew
it: Mr Porter Sinclair, a director, like Mr Jarmyn, of the North
West Midlands Railway. The other two telegrams would be
going to Mr Hart of Aldgate and Mr Freebody of Mayfair.

When a second telegram had arrived at the house an hour
later and Mr Jarmyn had retired to his study, her suspicions
appeared to have been confirmed.

The port decanter in his study had been almost empty.
Annie ought to have noted this and informed her at once,
but Anne had quit and the decanter had gone unfilled. So
Mrs Logan had made her way down to the cellar and dug out
the correct bottle, but before she had had time to decant it
Mr Jarmyn had rung for it.

The study was on the first floor in a small room at the rear of
the house and, in answer to Mr Jarmyn's summons, Mrs Logan
had knocked briefly at the door before going in. The room
was lit by a single lamp attached to the wall and bookshelves
lined all four walls, reaching to ceiling height. Aside from the
two jardinières overflowing with ferns, the chiffonier by the
window, an occasional table near the fireplace and the work

table in the centre of the room, the only furniture were the two Louis XIV chairs, in one of which Mr Jarmyn had been seated.

The telegrams had lain opened and unfolded, on the work-table on which the crystal decanter and his empty glass stood, almost as though Mr Jarmyn had placed them there for her to read.

But why would he do such a thing? His business was of no concern to her.

She had opened the new bottle and stepped back at once. She disliked the smell of port. The deceased Mr Logan had developed a taste for it early on in their short marriage and, with him being in the wine trade, no doubt this was a useful taste for him to acquire but, three years after his death, the richly sweet odour and the glistening crimson hue of the stuff—so like freshly spilt blood—had, as she decanted it, induced an image of her dead husband that was so vivid and so unexpected she had had to stifle a gasp: Paul Logan standing frozen, now and forever, beside the shuttered window in their two-room tenement, holding aloft a tiny tumbler. It was night-time, of course—wasn't it always night-time in that place?—the room in shadows, lit only by a guttering candle, the meagre light catching the dark liquid in his tumbler and creating a myriad of crimson, flickering points. That was his final night on Earth. The following morning he had left and was killed. They had been married less than three years.

She blinked, shutting out the past.

The two telegrams delivered earlier in the evening had lain open on the table, confirming that there had been an accident and that three people were dead.

So be it. They would all know about it soon enough. It would be in the newspapers tomorrow for certain. It was carelessness then that had caused Mr Jarmyn to leave the telegrams lying open like that where anyone might see them.

'Are you running my entire establishment single-handedly, Mrs Logan?' he had asked, not raising his head to look at her face.

'It would appear so, Mr Jarmyn.'

And he had nodded as though this was only to be expected.

CHAPTER THREE

May 1880

THE HOUSE HAD NOT ALWAYS been so cold. It was not so very long ago that fires had been lit in the grates.

Sofia Jarmyn, a bright child of nine years of age, had once played in this house. A child at once unremarkable and precocious: adorable and irksome in equal quantities; eager to turn her hand to whatever games her brothers suggested and irritated by her role as forever the youngest in a large household; striving to mimic her elder sister and impatient to be her own person. She attended dance class, she practised her scales, and on warm summer afternoons she painted watercolours in Regent's Park and watched, fascinated, as the raindrops transformed her carefully constructed creations into abstracts. At night she turned the pages of picture books filled with malevolent fairies and naughty children whose transgressions never went unpunished and, like her sister and her brothers before her, she dismissed such nonsense and decided it need not apply to her. She was, in short, a little girl.

On an afternoon in the final week of May the last crocuses and daffodils had fallen away and the delphiniums and hydrangeas were beginning to take their place in the boxes that lined the windows of Cadogan Mews. The sun had risen early if sluggishly and had endured throughout the day, though veiled by a sickly yellowish cloud of London smoke. It was a day for running very fast down a steep grassy bank, for hitching up dresses and paddling barefoot in shallow streams as tiny transparent newts swam in circles at your toes. It was a day for climbing trees and hiding when your name was called.

'Stand still, Sofia, please!' said Mrs Logan crossly.

'Will I be allowed to stroke the horse's nose?' said Sofia, trying for all she was worth not to wriggle. For today she was to ride in a hansom cab with her mother and, whilst it was quite exciting to ride occasionally in an omnibus with Dinah, to ride with her mother in a hansom cab with a horse, that was beyond anything!

'If you do not let me tie you hair properly you won't be going anywhere.'

But Sofia ignored this because her mother had promised, which was worth more than any threat from Mrs Logan. Besides which, the promise had been made at Easter and Sofia had waited weeks—*weeks!*—for this day. She was not about to have it taken from her.

'Dinah!' she called, seeing her elder sister go past her door, and Dinah put her head in and smiled.

'Is it today you are to go with Mama?' she said.

'Yes! And we are to ride in a hansom. I expect I shall be allowed to stroke the horse's nose.'

'They do bite, you know,' Dinah observed, but with a smile to take the sting out of her words.

'Not if you do it right,' said Sofia as though she were an expert on such matters. Then she sighed. 'I wish you were coming with us.'

'But I can't—I have a caller coming. Besides, it is your outing, not mine. You should enjoy all Mama's attention for once without me getting in the way.'

'Yes, that's true,' agreed Sofia thoughtfully. She would like to have all Mama's attention. That seemed incredible, unprecedented. She felt a little giddy and sick at the enormity of it. And, as if her imagination had conjured her up, her mother appeared now in the doorway and Sofia turned crimson with delight for now the outing would begin. And not only that, but her mother had dressed in Sofia's favourite blue taffeta gown that shone with different hues of turquoise and emerald like a peacock's tail when it was caught in sunlight. She wore her pearls, just a single string as it was daytime, and her third-best kid gloves, which were midnight-blue to complement the gown. She looked, to Sofia's eyes, like a figure from a fairytale who danced at midnight at a ball in a magical palace and quite probably wore glass slippers. Her mother did not, of course, wear glass slippers, but that was the impression she gave.

'Are you ready, darling?' said Mrs Jarmyn from the doorway, and when she said this she smiled as though she was looking forward to their outing every bit as much as her daughter was.

Yes, Sofia was ready! She had been ready for hours! And she wanted to shout out, *Let us go! Let us hurry!* But something in her mother's poise and bearing as she led the way downstairs forestalled her and instead she followed in dignified silence, her chin held high. For today they were not visiting the monkeys at the zoological gardens or the ducks in the park or choosing toys from the toy shop, they were visiting Mama's dressmaker. Sofia was to have her own dress made for her by Mama's dressmaker in Bond Street. She was to be allowed to choose the fabric and the style herself, so long as it was appropriate, and in a week there was to be a party at which she would be allowed to wear the new dress.

'Have you thought about what type of dress you are going to choose?' her mother said as they paused in the hallway to put on hats and gloves.

Sofia *had* thought! Indeed she had thought about little else: 'A princess line with a cuirasse bodice in sapphire or perhaps crimson silk, but certainly not in green and not in taffeta though I do like taffeta but I think it will be a little stiff and bothersome to wear.'

Her mother tried very hard not to laugh, instead raising both eyebrows. 'I am not sure that sounds entirely suitable for a little girl,' she observed.

'But I wish to look as beautiful as you, Mama,' Sofia replied artlessly.

Mrs Logan had gone outside to whistle for a cab and, as one drew up, Sofia found she no longer wished to stroke the horse's nose because she had outgrown such things.

It was, then, a day for riding in hansom cabs, for marvelling at the carriages and omnibuses in Regent Street, for viewing the fine ladies in Bond Street in their elegant gowns and their brightly coloured parasols and the ostrich feathers in their hats. It was a day to have your first dress made for you.

Instead, it was a day when none of these things happened.

Instead, an hour or two later nine-year-old Sofia ran indoors from the garden blindly, furiously, her face hot with unshed tears, ran upstairs and pushed open the first door she came to. She came to the drawing room, where a fire was burning.

At 19 Cadogan Mews, as at each of the grand merchants' houses in Bloomsbury, fires were lit by the maid—in this case, Annie—in the kitchen, the morning room and the bedrooms early each morning before the family awoke. The dining room and drawing rooms fires were lit only in the late afternoon as the curtains were drawn and the lamps turned on. The grates had to be swept and the fenders and the fire-irons cleaned daily throughout the cold months when the fireplaces were in use. At the end of May, as she swept and polished and cleaned and blacked, as she manhandled the coal up from the scullery in a large metal bucket then struggled to ignite the fire, Annie may have been counting the days till the official start of summer. Or she may have been more concerned with keeping her hair and her skirts away from the fire, for many a poor girl had been horribly burnt by a stray ember catching her skirts alight, though in truth it was more likely to be the young ladies in their gowns of silk and satin and their increasingly lengthy frills of gauze and tulle who were at risk rather than the maid in her brown Holland dress. But still, Annie took no chances.

The fire was lit.

At a little after five o'clock, Mr Jarmyn arrived home from his office in the City. The overzealous eighteenth-century tambour clock in the drawing room chimed the quarter hour as he came up the front steps and let himself in, and the other clocks throughout the house would follow two minutes later. But in those two minutes the world turned upside down.

A scream was heard, a scream so terrifying and dreadful it pierced the heart and chilled the soul. Mr Jarmyn, still in his hat and coat and gloves, charged at once into the drawing room. The boys—Gus and Jack—arrived in a tumble at the top of the stairs and their father, seeing them, called out, '*Stay out, go back upstairs!*' and the boys had turned, their faces ashen, half at his words, half at the smell of burning. Mrs Logan arrived next, coming down the stairs, her face stricken, in time to see the maid, Annie, running from the room, screaming, her hands over her face, and almost knocking over Cook—puffing and panting, her face scarlet—who had just ascended from below stairs. Dinah too, coming in from the garden, her face a little flushed, saw the maid run from the room and instinctively her hands flew up to cover her own face, mirroring Annie though she had not seen what the girl had seen. Someone in the drawing room had slammed the door shut so Dinah could not identify who was in the room and who was not, but beyond the door she could make out voices and a dreadful screaming that would not cease and now shouts, a thump and someone crying out.

The door opened and Mrs Logan came out, seemingly quite calm though her eyes were terrible and her face was utterly drained of colour. She put a hand on the doorframe to steady herself, not speaking at first.

Their cousin Roger Brightside was there, Meredith and Travers' boy, and when Mrs Logan said in a slow, steady voice, 'Someone must get Dr Frobisher,' he said at once, 'Let me go!' and plunged down the stairs, glad it seemed to have something to do. The front door opened and slammed shut and footsteps clattered down the front steps and away.

Dinah could not move, her fear rendering her motionless.

'Go upstairs,' Mrs Logan ordered, pushing Dinah back, but not before Dinah had seen the door to the drawing room open and her father stagger out, a bundle wrapped up tightly in what appeared to be the drawing room hearthrug held in his arms. It was a heavy, awkward bundle and he carried it with shaking arms and so very carefully up the stairs towards the bedrooms, Mrs Logan hurrying after him.

Despite Mrs Logan's insistence she go upstairs, Dinah found herself in the drawing room doorway where she stopped, unable to set foot within. Grey and steaming coals lay in the hearth, and an overturned plant pot and splashes on the walls and mantel suggested someone had tossed water on the grate to put a fire out. Uncle Austin—when had he got here?—was crouched in the corner of the room, rocking silently back and forth. And her mother too was there, standing in the centre of the room, making no sound, her face frozen, her clothing burnt and black on one arm. The smell was everywhere, of burning. Burning clothing, burning rug, burning hair, burning flesh. The room was filled with smoke and Dinah ran to the window and fought with it then flung it open. She thrust her head out and gulped down the London air that they usually tried so hard to avoid. The sudden draught of cold air sucked much of the smoke out of the room but not the smell. The hearthrug had gone and the carpet was a different shade where the rug usually covered it. The carpet closest to the grate was blackened and singed. Nothing else in the room was burnt—except for Mrs Jarmyn, whose arm was seared red and already blistering.

'Who?' said Dinah. Her mouth was dry and no further words seemed to want to come.

No one answered her and her mother fainted.

At length Roger returned with Dr Frobisher, who ran immediately up the stairs and went into one of the bedrooms, pushing Mr Jarmyn and Mrs Logan out and closing the door so that Mr Jarmyn paced the corridor. Mrs Logan poured him a whisky and Dinah took some herself though she detested it and could hardly hold the shaking glass to her lips. No one spoke. It was as though they had all lost the power of speech.

A commotion erupted downstairs as the other maid, Agnes, returned from her day off and was met by the by-now-hysterical Annie. Mrs Logan had to run downstairs to hush them, only to find that Cook had administered her own hysteria-cure already and the girl was sitting on the floor rubbing the side of her face, the newly returned Agnes staring at her, pale and frightened.

When Dr Frobisher emerged his face too was pale and he took Mr Jarmyn into his study. Then he went to Mrs Jarmyn who had been carried up to her room, and administered a draught and left a balm for her burn.

No one mentioned a name. No one said, It is Sofia. No one dared to ask, How is she? Will she be all right?

Outside darkness had fallen and, as he finally took his leave, the doctor shook his head, saying: 'She will not last the night,' and the look he gave said: And that is for the best.

But she did last the night. And there followed a terrible time with the child alive, though barely; unable to speak, to eat, to drink even; in such silent and terrible pain it was more than anyone could bear. Mr Jarmyn remained constantly at her bedside, leaving her room only to pace and tear at his hair in the hallway. Mrs Logan, pale but calm, ministered to her night and day. The boys were kept away and crept about the house like beaten dogs. In another room, Mrs Jarmyn, her arm bandaged, and heavily sedated on the draughts Dr Frobisher had left for her, lay in her bed, unable to speak.

The house grew cold as Mr Jarmyn forbade any fires to be lit in the grates and, when the maid forgot or had not heard his edict, and he caught her laying out the coal in the morning room, he railed in furious anguish against her until she ran in terror and he railed against the fireplace as though it was a malevolent being that had acted wilfully.

May slipped into June but the house grew colder. Alone in her room Dinah prayed nightly that her sister would die. And eventually, after ten days, she did.

CHAPTER FOUR

December

A COLD WIND BLEW THROUGHOUT the night, whipping up the leaves from the plane trees in nearby Cadogan Square and sending them swirling down Cadogan Mews. When the wind abated, at a little after six o'clock, the mini-tornado of late autumnal leaves came to rest where they fell, strewn across road and pavement, and plastered to walls and lampposts and front steps in a decaying, sodden mass.

The occupants of number 19 had passed a restless night for which the incessant whistling of the wind down the narrow laneway, and the rattling of every window in the house, and the repeated banging of a door somewhere in the distance, were only partly to blame.

Mr Jarmyn had endured a particularly troubled night and had risen before the dawn intending to get to the office early.

His wife did not appear at breakfast and he ate his veal cutlets with only the boys and Dinah and the lead story from *The Times* for company. As the lead story was taken up with yesterday's fatal crash on the accident-prone North West Midlands Railway, he abandoned the newspaper and listened, instead, to a rambling account of the Battle of Crécy from Jack. A five-hundred-year-old battle had seemed preferable to a day-old catastrophe on one's own railway. Eventually, and perhaps sensing her father's growing irritation, Dinah cut short her brother's oration and they completed their breakfast in silence so that it had been a relief to push back his chair and announce his departure for the office. As Lucas went upstairs to his study, Dinah followed as though she would speak to him but something caused her to change her mind for she made instead for her own room.

The door of the drawing room was ajar, he saw with surprise. The room had lain vacant and unused since May yet someone was in there, or had recently been in there. It could not be one of the housemaids as both girls, apparently, had now departed. It was Mrs Logan then, returning something or fetching something from the room. It could not be one of the family who spent their time in the morning room.

As he stood there, disconcerted and perhaps even a little unnerved, the door to the drawing room opened wider and Aurora came out. For a moment husband and wife regarded one another. Lucas opened his mouth to make some remark but the remark remained unspoken as he looked over his wife's head and realised that the curtains in the drawing room were opened, that a narrow shaft of winter sunlight had found its way in through the window and was striking the dusty crimson carpet.

'Lucas,' said his wife, drawing his attention back to her, and he realised she was in a gown of deep lavender, instead of the black crape she had worn at breakfast every day since she had risen from her sickbed in late June.

Six months. It was the sixth day of December and their half-year of mourning had, it seemed, ended. In the room behind her the mirror that hung above the mantelpiece had had its black covering removed. The room would need to be redecorated, he realised; there would be callers now and whilst they could utilise the morning room still it was awkward having a room out of commission. There would be dinner parties too, presumably, though he could not for the moment picture either himself or his wife presiding over such an event ever again. Yet he knew it would be so. Well, so be it. It would be best to get Mrs Logan to organise it. It was not something he could ask Aurora to do.

And meanwhile his wife was standing before him in a gown of the deepest lavender. He found he had nothing to say to her.

'Had you forgotten what day it is?' she inquired. She had been waiting here to tell him, he realised. She believed the arrival of this day somehow changed things.

'Your grasp of such matters, as always, exceeds mine,' he replied with a brief bow.

She looked down, a tiny frown creasing her brow, and seemed to wish to say more but instead gave him the quickest ghost of a smile and turned and went upstairs.

Lucas watched wordlessly as she ascended the staircase, her feet seeming to glide up the stairs without touching them, and his mind went back to that very first meeting, the dinner twenty-two years ago at the Chelsea home of Mrs Cassandra Randle, Aurora's mother. A dinner in honour of whom or in the presence of whom, he could not now recall. His own presence that evening had been entirely on account of her father, the Honourable Griffin Randle, MP, one-time member of Mr Peel's government and already by that evening many years deceased. The Hon. Griffin had, sometime in the 1840s and in his capacity as undersecretary, assisted in the smooth passage of the Bill of Parliament permitting the building of Samuel Jarmyn's new railway along with the necessary compulsory land purchases that accompanied it. A notorious scandal a year or two later had meant Randle's political career had ended abruptly and in disgrace and, aside from the annual payments of dividends to his estate (he had, at the time of his early death, been in possession of a substantial number of shares in the said railway) there had been no contact between the two families since. But an invitation to dinner had been made and Lucas, out of curiosity more than politeness, had accepted.

It was a decision, made with little thought at a time in his life (aged just twenty-two and having inherited the directorship of a railway) when he had first begun to question the world and his own place in it, that had changed his life forever.

The evening had been taken up almost exclusively with Mr Darwin, whose book had just been published. There had been much silly chatter about apes and fish in which he had taken little part, being entirely concerned with the young lady seated opposite him whom he had already surmised was Aurora, his hostess's eighteen-year-old daughter and only child of the late Hon. Griffin. He had had a vivid impression of deep, grey eyes observing him, just for a moment, over the rim of a wine glass, of rich chestnut-brown hair in ringlets as was the fashion of the day. She had worn—he could recall it in detail even twenty years later—a crinoline gown in a blazing scarlet silk with bell-shaped sleeves, the silk brocaded and finished with some delicate piece of lace at the cuffs. The cut of the gown left both shoulders exposed but unlike every other lady at the table she wore no shawl to cover them. He had not exchanged so much as a single word with her throughout the meal yet once the evening had broken up he had paced up and down outside her window for the best part of an hour, and the lamps were being extinguished in his own street before he had eventually reached his home.

He shook his head to rid it of this two-decade-old memory. How was it, he asked himself, that his wife's feet seemed to glide up the stairs without touching them? It was a trick of her gown, surely, the way it covered her feet. All ladies glided in this way yet it seemed to him now that she did not quite touch the Earth. He remembered that he had thought this very same thing the evening he had met her, only then it had seemed miraculous. *She* had seemed miraculous. Now it seemed . . . inhuman.

He turned away. He needed to go to the office and, making his way downstairs, he retrieved his coat, hat, gloves and umbrella and left the house.

—⁂—

Dinah realised she no longer wished to help people.

The realisation came as the mid-morning sun crept in through the dusty Georgian windows of the Town Hall and cast long shadows across the elegantly proportioned chamber where the five members of the committee for the Society for the Alleviation of Misery, Poverty and Misfortune Amongst the Poor and Destitute of London sat.

The realisation came not so much as a sudden revelation, more as a gradual dawning. At the commencement of the meeting she had been a willing and enthusiastic member of the committee; by the time Miss Parson had delivered her report on the Society's recent dispersal of funds and her proposals for the forthcoming year, Dinah had lost her desire to help.

An hour ago, after breakfast, she had reviewed herself in the mirror in her room and her fingers had slid uneasily over the unfamiliar mauve of the new gown she had put on. She had got used to wearing black: at first it had seemed grotesque, a heavy, suffocating reminder every minute of every hour of every day of the loss they had suffered. They had gone out—one or two necessary visits to dressmakers and the like—and people had looked at them descending from a cab, entering a shop, making some purchase, and had not seem them, the Jarmyns, had not seen *her*, Miss Dinah Jarmyn; they had seem a Family in Mourning. The Jarmyns had ceased to exist. But now they were to reclaim themselves. They were to cast off their black and don lavender and mauve and dove-grey. They were to make calls and they were to receive callers. Soon there would be a dinner party. Her mother had already begun preparations.

Outwardly, she presumed that to her fellow committee members, she looked just as she always had. She had resumed her seat on the north side of the committee table, in what had been—until six months ago—her usual spot a little to the left of centre, facing the window, with Mr Dunleavy on her right, Miss Joseph on her left. She wore her second-best bonnet (it was considered poor form to overdress for the Society), her weekday gloves and a light cashmere shawl over her dress that had barely kept the chill out that morning over breakfast, but that in this room, where a fire was crackling in the hearth not five feet away, was proving a trifle warm. Her face had displayed polite interest as Miss Parson had stood up to give her report and it still displayed polite interest as Miss Parson now placed her figures before her on the table and sat down again.

But somewhere behind that polite interest something had quietly died.

'Thank you, Miss Parson. A most thorough and interesting report,' said Mr Briers, who was chairing the meeting. 'And, may I add, most prettily presented.'

Miss Parson, who was an ardent emancipist, bristled visibly. 'I am not here to "present prettily", Mr Briers. I am here to save lives.'

The idea of Miss Parson, who, as well as being an ardent emancipist, was five feet tall in her boots and not a day under seventy, saving lives clearly tickled Mr Briers who indulged in a hearty chuckle then had to wipe his eyes with a large handkerchief.

Dinah smiled though she had not been paying attention. In the months since she had attended her last meeting very little appeared to have changed—excepting, of course, herself. But it seemed the other members of the Society could not see this change—and why should they? She did not wish them to see it for it was not a change for the better. They would, she felt, recoil if they saw her as she saw herself. She looked down at her hands resting demurely on her lap. She did not feel demure. She slid her hands further beneath the table, out of sight.

'Miss Jarmyn? I recall you were particularly impassioned during that meeting,' prompted Miss Joseph on her left, peering at her over a pair of pince-nez perched on the bridge of her nose.

Dinah stared at her. *Had* she been impassioned? It seemed impossible now to imagine. Yes, there had been a discussion, quite a heated one, if she remembered correctly. Miss Joseph had wanted to make placards and to picket Parliament. She had wanted to commandeer a series of rooms and houses all across the East End where the homeless and those in need of emergency shelter might stay free of charge. She had wanted to distribute food at schools to encourage the children to attend and their parents to let them attend. At the time these suggestions had seemed wild and exciting, revolutionary even, and Dinah had listened, amazed, and, when Miss Joseph had finished, she had applauded enthusiastically.

Now they seemed absurd.

'Miss Jarmyn?'

'It was so long ago . . .' Dinah replied. 'But, you are right, Miss Joseph, of course. I *do* remember and I *was* impassioned. It is just that now . . .'

She floundered again. What *did* she feel? And why did they peer at her so, leaning across the table and peering just as though her opinion mattered when she knew it did not. She wished they would stop.

'Now I find I am *not* impassioned. Now I find that . . . I do not seem to mind as much.'

'Oh.' Miss Joseph looked affronted. 'Do you mean you do not mind as much about my ideas or do you mean you do not mind which way the committee votes on the issue?'

What Dinah meant was that she did not care if they sheltered the homeless or fed children or saved fallen women or provided for the destitute. She no longer cared about the poor of London. Or anywhere.

But what she said was: 'I think I would like to be out in the sunshine walking in the park with the leaves rustling beneath my feet.'

'So would I!' said Miss Parson unexpectedly. 'Come, my dear!' And she jumped to her feet and held out her arm to Dinah and together they left the meeting and went out into the chilly December morning.

—∞—

In Half Mitre Street, at a point midway between St Paul's and the Bank of England, another meeting was under way. At the London office of the North West Midlands Railway Company a hurriedly convened meeting of the board of directors was in progress though, an hour into the meeting, little progress had been made.

'This is intolerable!' exclaimed Mr Freebody, who was the oldest director on the board and yet the one most prone to outburst and liberal thinking.

'Acting in haste is not the answer, Freebody,' countered Mr Sinclair, chairman of the board.

'*Haste?* I wonder does anyone around this table understand the meaning of the word?'

'Indeed we do, Freebody,' replied Mr Kemp, who was the youngest and newest member of the board and yet its most conservative. 'We all recall the haste with which a new type of rolling stock was introduced onto the line in time to fulfil certain standing orders and before the rolling stock had been properly and fully tested. We all recall the carnage that resulted.'

Sitting opposite Kemp, Freebody thumped the desk with his fist and his face suffused with colour. '*Damn* it, *I* was the one who pleaded for restraint, was I not? The minutes will bear me out on this, I think, Kemp.'

'Gentlemen, please!' called Sinclair, holding up both hands in a conciliatory manner. 'I think we are all agreed this is a dreadful mishap and that our immediate response is settled: to wit, myself and Jarmyn will journey to the crash site tomorrow and will stay to attend the inquest which I understand is to take place at Wolverhampton on the eighth. We can assume the public inquiry will commence some three to four weeks after that, for which various papers and statements will need to be furnished by us. Funeral costs for the fatalities will, of course, be covered by the company as a gesture of goodwill, and annuities arranged for the widows of the dead driver and fireman. This much is settled.'

'How proficient we have become at dealing with a major crash,' observed Lucas, not looking up as he held a match to his cigar.

'It is our future course of action for which we must find consensus,' continued Sinclair, choosing not to reply to this. 'Obviously we will await the outcome of the inquiry but as I see it, it boils down to one thing: money. It is a simple enough equation—the introduction of additional safety measures at a certain cost to the company resulting, in the short term at least, in a drop in profits. Alternatively, no introduction of additional safety measures, meaning profits remain steady though public confidence, and no doubt the share price, continues to fall.'

He held out both hands, palms upwards, offering his two solutions to the floor.

'*No!* Sinclair, this is *not* acceptable,' countered Freebody. 'Why must we await the outcome of the inquiry when we surely already know the reason for the crash and, more to the point, it does *not* boil down to money. It boils down to lives—Christian souls. The souls that are in our care for that briefest of moments and whose safety we are, at present, in no position to guarantee, whose safety we toss aside with scant regard.'

'These are working people, Freebody,' remarked Kemp, mildly. 'People who travel third-class. The luxury and safety these people now take for granted would have been unimaginable thirty, forty years ago—when your father was running this line, Jarmyn. Now we pander to these people as though they were first-class passengers.'

And of course Kemp was perfectly right. In the forties the third-class carriages on the then Wolverhampton and Birmingham Railway had been simply goods wagons: low-sided, unroofed and with no seating whatsoever. The third-class passenger travelling across open country on a longish journey in the dead of winter risked death by exposure. Indeed, a number of fatalities citing this as the cause of death had actually been recorded in the early years of the railway. And that wasn't all: the unfortunate traveller having survived the elements, risked, if the train braked suddenly, being tipped out of the low-sided carriage resulting, almost certainly, in a broken neck. The 1880s passenger could consider himself mollycoddled by comparison.

The fifth member of the board, Mr Hart of Aldgate, had remained silent for much of this lively discussion. He now moved restlessly in his chair. 'One hundred and eighty-five deaths,' he announced into the silence. He spoke in a calm voice, expressionless and low and the other four members of the board turned towards him. 'Since the line opened. Since 1841. That's almost five deaths a year.'

'Less than five a year?' scoffed Kemp, throwing up his hands in disbelief. 'Good God, do any of you have any idea how many people are killed crossing the streets in London each year? How many infants perish before their first birthday? How many have died of scarlet fever, cholera, consumption, this year alone? *Five a year!* It is hardly what one would describe as an epidemic.'

'This absurd bickering about statistics is getting us nowhere,' Sinclair interrupted. 'As stated, Jarmyn and myself will make our way up to the crash site first thing tomorrow. We have already made contact with the Board of Trade inspectors. There is little else that can be achieved until the inquiry.'

'What do we know of the fatalities?' Freebody inquired. 'And the injured?'

'Very little of the injured,' said Lucas. 'The two deceased employees were . . .' he peered at the page on the table before him '. . . driver Proctor and fireman Evans. Both employees of the company for a number of years. One leaves a widow and two small children, the other was himself recently widowed and leaves no dependants.'

'Well, that's a saving,' observed Kemp.

'The other fatality was a nine-year-old girl travelling with her father. The man sustained only minor injuries, I understand.'

Sinclair nodded slowly. 'As chairman, I had better attend the two employee funerals, speak to the widow, that sort of thing. And the father—what sort of man is he? Likely to kick up a fuss?'

'I doubt any man would take such a loss without a fuss, Sinclair,' said Lucas, and he felt the other men in the room shift uncomfortably. 'But if you are asking whether the man has the resources and education to take out an action against us, I am afraid I am not in a position to judge.'

'And the cause of the accident?'

Kemp made an impatient sound. 'We have gone over this, Sinclair. What is the point in trying to pre-empt the inquiry?'

'Inquiry or no inquiry, there seems little room for doubt: it was frozen signals,' said Freebody.

'I say again, what is the point in pre-empting the inquiry?'

'It is early December, Kemp,' replied Freebody slowly and distinctly. 'We are at the start of winter. There have already been frosts. How likely is it, do you think, that the signals will freeze again before spring? Before the Board publishes its inquiry?'

But for once Kemp did not seem inclined to offer an opinion.

—⁓—

The sun was still discernible through the clouds, though intermittently. The park's formal municipal flowerbeds were bare but for a scattering of decaying leaves and splitting conkers, and the fallen chestnut leaves crunched underfoot, crisp with the final vestiges of this morning's frost.

'Such a relief to be out of that horrid room,' observed Miss Parson, giving a little skip and kicking playfully at a pile of leaves that lay in their path, which was disconcerting in a woman over seventy and Dinah was faintly scandalised.

They sat down on a park bench and watched as a cluster of small boys attempted, with much commotion but little success, to launch a kite.

It was a relief to be out, it was invigorating! And yet Dinah's thoughts returned, unbidden, to that morning: she had gone up to her room after breakfast but not before she had seen her mother emerge from the drawing room and announce to her father, almost as a challenge, *'Had you forgotten what day it is?'*

Had he forgotten? Dinah had paused on the stairway wishing she had not overheard, wishing she had not seen his response. For the occasion of throwing off mourning should herald a new start, should it not? At the very least it ought to mean a return to how things had been before. Yet the opposite had happened: her mother's words had evoked a look from her father that contained all the chill of a winter, deep and without end.

The kite had failed to launch, was being dragged faster and faster through the fallen leaves until it snagged on a branch and stuck fast. The boy who held the string yanked and yanked and his cohorts shouted and shouted until the paper tore and the balsa wood frame split and the game was ended.

Her father's coldness made no sense. He could hardly blame their mother for what happened. If there was anyone to blame—

Dinah reached down and snatched up a handful of leaves in her fist, crushing them and releasing a damp, earthy odour. She dropped the crushed leaves and wiped her hand on her cloak.

'You must think me very selfish,' she remarked, realising as she said this that she did not care if Miss Parson thought her selfish or not.

'Oh, my dear Miss Jarmyn.' Miss Parson patted her hand, a little sadly it seemed. 'I am an old woman—though I take pains to deny it—and I have seen and experienced a great many things in my lifetime. Why, would you believe, I can remember the bells ringing out over the city and dear Papa coming home to tell us Napoleon had been defeated at Waterloo?'

This did make her very old indeed though the relevance of it was not immediately clear to Dinah.

'Such a different time! So very, *very* long ago. So many, many people gone, so much changed. Such a safer world we live in now, a rational world, a world of Industry and Science and Good Works. Sometimes it feels as though we have come as far as we might, that man has reached his zenith.'

Dinah nodded though she did not believe man had reached his zenith; was not entirely sure what a zenith was.

'But we must guard against complacency, Miss Jarmyn. For, mark my words, there is still much to be done. So much, indeed, that at times it feels almost daunting.' She gave a little sigh. 'Sometimes our ways must seem tediously laboured to you, perhaps even ineffectual. I have often thought it myself. But there is good work being done. Little by little, step by step, we make a difference. And there are other committees to join. The work, I fear, will never dry up.'

The work will never dry up. Dinah gazed ahead of her and these words came to her as though from very far away. She watched a squirrel dart across the grass, pick up a fallen acorn, pause, listening, then scamper up the nearest tree and away.

Winter was here.

'What will you do?'

Dinah cast about for a reply. What *would* she do? She could scarcely begin to think.

'There is so much to do . . .' she began but found she could not complete her sentence.

'That's the spirit! I think we understand each other,' said Miss Parson, patting Dinah's hand with a kind smile, and Dinah returned the smile and realised they did not understand each other at all.

CHAPTER FIVE

London and the Midlands

MR JARMYN WAS GOING AWAY. He was catching the morning train from Euston, changing at Birmingham onto the NWMR and travelling on to Wolverhampton. Though he had not said so specifically to her, Mrs Logan understood that he was to visit the accident site and to attend the inquest. He would be away some days.

Mrs Logan considered the items she had packed for him and wondered if she had included enough freshly laundered shirts. He had not said how many days he would be away so it was difficult to decide. In the end she placed one additional shirt in his valise and closed it. It would be colder up there. She had noticed the difference in climate herself, coming down to London, though Mr Jarmyn did not feel the cold. She opened the valise and placed a thick wool scarf inside and closed it again.

He had been out for his early morning walk. Now she heard his footsteps below on the front steps and a moment later the front door opened so she picked up his luggage and proceeded downstairs. He was knocking mud from his boots and reaching for the silver tray in the hallway to see what the first post had brought as she came down the stairs. He looked up and as usual she could not read his expression.

'Mrs Logan,' he said. And he smiled. 'Ah, you have my overnight things?'

'Yes, Mr Jarmyn. Will you be leaving before lunch?'

'Yes. I'll eat at Birmingham. Please inform Mrs Jarmyn that I will send a telegram when I am in a position to know how long I shall be staying. Is she risen yet?'

'Not yet. She is to go out later this morning with Mrs Brightside, I understand.'

He nodded and for once she felt that she could read his expression and it was one of relief.

'Then I shall detain you no more. No, don't bother,' he said as she went to the door to hail him a cab. 'I've a cab waiting for me.'

He took the valise and she held the door open. There was something on his mind, she saw, for he passed her with a frown, his head slightly bowed, and she almost said something to him. What, she did not afterwards know, but a moment later Mr Jarmyn had boarded the waiting cab and was gone and she had said nothing.

She closed the front door and for a while did not move. He would be catching one of his own trains from Birmingham though he would not be travelling on the stretch of line where the accident had occurred. Did that concern him? But of course it would not: he was a director of the railway. And how likely was a second accident so soon after the first?

She had ridden on Mr Jarmyn's railway herself once, three years ago, in the weeks following that other great crash, a much worse crash, the one at Wombourne. At that time, in the immediate aftermath of that dreadful accident, she had not even considered the danger of travelling on a train, of passing the very place where so many souls had just perished. What, then, *had* she been thinking, a recently bereaved widow journeying south with only a trunk and a portmanteau containing all she owned, travelling alone to a grand house belonging to a grand gentleman in the grandest, the greatest, the most frightening city in the world? Surely she must have been anxious and filled with trepidation? But she could not recall. She had an idea she had not been anxious, or not at first.

She had arrived at the grand house in the narrow, silent mews off the elegant, tree-lined square late on a Thursday afternoon in the first week of January to find her telegram had arrived only an hour before her and Mr Jarmyn himself, still at the crash site, had not troubled to inform the rest of the household of her arrival. A flustered maid had taken her to a ground-floor reception room and left her there. A cab had drawn up in the street outside and eventually Mrs Jarmyn had swept into the room and declared, '*I am afraid there has been some kind of an error.*' Those had been her exact words, no greeting, no introduction, and in her hand Mrs Jarmyn had held the telegram which had arrived that morning and which she now handed to the new arrival as though it were a summons from the court.

She had been dismayed. In his interview with her Mr Jarmyn had explained his household, briefly, in the manner of one who had much on his mind at present, and the household had included a Mrs Jarmyn, naturally, and five children. Mrs Logan had imagined, therefore, a lady who was grave like her husband. She had imagined a lady who was serene and composed, perhaps austere, certainly stately. She had not expected this person barely five years her senior, a woman of startling beauty and a high colour with furious grey eyes and a telegram in her hand which she brandished like a weapon. A woman who walked into a room and said, *'I am afraid there has been some kind of an error.'*

Inside Mrs Logan had faltered. Outside she had stood firm.

'I am Mrs Logan. Am I to understand you were not expecting me, madam? This is very odd as Mr Jarmyn himself offered me the post of housekeeper—'

'I hardly think that likely. We have no need of a housekeeper, Mrs . . . ? We are not Clarence House or Balmoral. We are, as you see, a modest household in Bloomsbury. We have two maids and a cook. Why would we have need of a housekeeper? I am afraid you are in error, Mrs . . . ?'

'Logan. And yet Mr Jarmyn offered me a position and I accepted and here I am.'

And she had left her home and everything that she knew to come south and she would not flinch. What direction the discussion might have taken had not a second telegram arrived at that moment, Mrs Logan was saved from finding out. This second telegram, sent, somewhat tardily, by Mr Jarmyn himself appeared to settle the matter, for Mrs Jarmyn had read it and swept from the room without another word. A maid had been sent to escort the new arrival to a vacant upstairs room where she had unpacked and remained until, a day later, a cab had driven up to the front steps and Mr Jarmyn himself had arrived home.

Exactly what had transpired between husband and wife upon his return she never found out but immediately afterwards Mrs Jarmyn had boarded a cab and departed on a visit to a relative in Cheltenham where she had remained for a fortnight.

With Mrs Jarmyn gone Mrs Logan had been presented with the keys to the cellars and to the pantry and to the drawers where the various household accounts and ledgers were stored. She had been given custody of the accounts and ledgers with the understanding that once Mrs Jarmyn returned they would oversee these tasks together. Yet after a fortnight Mr Jarmyn, taking valuable time away from the accident inquiry to journey to Cheltenham himself, had returned with his wife and Mrs Jarmyn had shown not the slightest interest in sharing these tasks with the new housekeeper; indeed she appeared to wash her hands of the whole thing, maintaining an aloofness towards her housekeeper that had not thawed in the intervening years.

Mrs Logan had wasted little time. She had sorted and re-arranged. She had dismissed suppliers and sourced new ones. She had overseen tasks that had gone unsupervised for years and she had reorganised rosters and duties that were badly in need of reorganisation. She had, in short, discovered a talent for housekeeping. She had also found herself lonelier than she could have believed possible.

That had been three years ago and she had not travelled on a train since that day and could not, now, imagine herself travelling north again. Something very bad would have to happen first.

She went slowly back upstairs.

She had been instructed to oversee the redecoration of the drawing room and, though it had not been said out loud, she understood that this was to be done discreetly and tactfully, and preferably when none of the family were around to witness it. Consequently, an appointment with a man from Whiteleys had been arranged for this morning and would, it was hoped, be concluded before Mrs Jarmyn returned from her shopping expedition. The work itself would need to be done at carefully arranged times over the next two to three days; that is, before Mr Jarmyn's return.

At eleven o'clock she opened up the drawing room and showed the man in. He was the salesman type: showily rather than tastefully dressed and armed with a bag of samples. She had not explained the reason for the redecoration as it was not the man's business, but she stood on the threshold of the room and found she was hesitant, even now, to enter.

'Funny smell in here,' the man remarked and Mrs Logan went into the room rather than reply to this observation. And perhaps it did not require a reply as the man was already kneeling down to examine the carpet, peering at the wallpaper, holding up the material of the curtains to the daylight. 'Old fashioned,' was his conclusion. 'Crimson. You don't want crimson any more. It's all mauve and magenta and dove-grey. Softer shades. And *café au lait* if you want to be considered very daring.'

'I feel fairly certain the family do not wish to be considered "very daring",' replied Mrs Logan. 'I suggest we go with softer shades. Only the carpet and the curtains require replacing, not the wallpaper.'

'Sticking with the crimson flock?' said the man from Whiteleys, clearly unconvinced. 'Well, that limits your choice. What goes with crimson flock?' He pulled out his samples and explained the various merits of each, which appeared to come down to which important houses and families had which type of material.

Mrs Logan was unswayed by what type of curtain material the Duke of Westminster preferred and instead allowed her choice to be made solely on the basis of what might look right. The man from Whiteleys seemed to find this a novel way to make a decision but he duly recorded her orders.

'What else?' he went on, keen to conduct further transactions. 'Chairs need re-upholstering? A new mirror? Light-fittings?'

Mrs Logan hesitated. Should the fireplace be bricked up? The thought had crossed her mind earlier but it was a big step and not one she was prepared to make without authorisation. Was this what Mr Jarmyn would want? Or would it be merely a constant reminder? But wasn't everything a constant reminder?

'No, that will be all,' she decided.

'Right-oh. We'll be round first thing, then.'

'No, not first thing. After ten o'clock and only until noon. You may do as much as you can during that time. Then, if need be, you shall return at the same time the following day. That is imperative. And when you leave, if you have to return, there is to be no evidence that you were here. Do you understand?'

'Surprise, is it?' nodded the man from Whiteleys. 'Lovely,' he added unenthusiastically.

When he had gone Mrs Logan returned to the drawing room. There was a smell, it still lingered, but now it was muted, you had to seek it out. The man from Whiteleys had noticed it at once which perhaps meant he had a good nose. Or did it mean she had got used to it? Could you get used to the smell of burnt flesh?

—∾—

'Your notepaper needs to say: "We have suffered a loss but we are now out of first mourning. We are still very much distressed but we are looking forward cautiously, though with no loss of faith, to the future."'

Less than a mile away in Bond Street Aurora Jarmyn looked at her sister-in-law blankly. Meredith Brightside was her husband's only sister, younger than him by a year, and with the same long face, blunt jawline and narrow nose, the same grey-green eyes that peered at you unblinking if you said something stupid or surprising. Yet where Lucas had an unwavering belief in his place in the world Meredith wore a look of vague but persistent disappointment—as well she might, Aurora reflected, being married to Travers.

'Can my notepaper say so much?' she replied.

'It can and it shall! Come!' And Meredith took Aurora's arm and led the way through the door of the stationer's shop outside of which they had been standing for some minutes amidst the midday bustle of Bond Street shoppers. 'It is all in the depth of one's black-edged border,' Meredith added, speaking in lower tones now that they were inside the shop.

'My notepaper has black-edged borders and has done so since June,' retorted Aurora, surprised to find herself feeling quite indignant. 'And what's more,' she went on, 'my black-edged border is of a standard depth. I have it on good authority from my printer.'

Meredith stopped in her tracks, clearly scandalised. 'My dear sister-in-law, I am very much afraid you have been duped. What is this "standard depth" to which you—and your printer—allude?'

'Half an inch, I believe.' Really, Meredith was quite the stickler on occasion.

'Half an inch for the first three months of mourning, certainly. After that the border decreases to one-third of an inch. At six months it decreases to a quarter of an inch then in increments of a tenth of an inch over the succeeding six months depending on the nature of the loss and one's relationship to the deceased.'

Aurora gazed at her sister-in-law in silent fascination and for a moment was at a loss to know how to reply.

The shopkeeper, who had been hovering anxiously in the background since they had entered his shop, used this momentary pause in the conversation to jump in. 'Madam, please forgive me, but am I to understand you seek notepaper and that a bereavement has latterly taken place?'

Aurora slowly inclined her head.

'My services are at your disposal, madam, at this difficult

time. Might one inquire as to the length of time that has elapsed since the tragic loss occurred?'

Meredith nodded in a 'You see!' sort of way.

'Six months,' said Aurora.

'Ah, then madam will be requiring the purple-edged notepaper.'

Beside her, Meredith started. 'I beg your pardon?'

'The purple-edged border. It is quite the custom now, after the first mourning has been concluded. Then at nine months one graduates to navy or maroon, depending on—'

'A purple border!?' repeated Meredith.

'Graduating to navy or maroon.'

'My good man, I do not know from where you have gleaned your information, but I can assure you that all the books recommend gradations of black. There is no mention of purple whatsoever. Nor yet, of navy or maroon!'

'Madam is most certainly correct. However the custom of Her Majesty—'

'The Queen uses purple?'

'Quite so.'

Meredith appeared stunned and again Aurora took a moment to regard her. As far as she could recall, her sister-in-law had had no occasion, at least during the twenty or so years that she had known her, to use black-edged notepaper. And yet she evidently found the subject worthy of a not inconsiderable amount of her time and energy. By contrast, Aurora, who had every reason to make a detailed study of the subject, found that her energy and her patience had both run out.

And she was fast going to join them. She turned and walked out of the shop.

'Aurora! Your order!'

'I will have whatever Her Majesty has,' she said over her shoulder as she re-entered the chaotic stream of Bond Street shoppers.

It had been a mistake to allow Meredith to bring her here. She had done with mourning, there was no more mourning left in her. And yet her sister-in-law, no doubt with the best of intentions, seemed determined to prolong it, to revel in its intricacies.

Am I really going to grade my notepaper from purple to navy or maroon? Aurora asked herself, as she stood amidst the swirl of hurrying shoppers. It had all seemed possible yesterday. She had ordered the downstairs curtains and shutters to be opened, the covers over the mirrors removed (it was a shock to see oneself in each of the mirrors that hung above the fireplaces). She had made a number of calls and received a number of callers in return and the world, it appeared, had not changed so very much in six months. This morning Lucas had departed first thing without a word to her so that she had come down to breakfast and had had to pretend to Dinah, to Mrs Logan, to know of his plans. She understood that the railway accident must be uppermost in his mind yet it was disappointing he must be absent. And yet they had made it, she and Dinah and the boys, through that first day, and no doubt they would make it through this second day and each day after that would be a little easier.

A carriage drew up at the kerbside and a mother and daughter got out, the mother a fussy-looking lady in masses of ivory tulle and a train that got caught in the door of the cab, the little girl perhaps nine or ten years old, who waited impatiently for her mother then got too close to the horse and shrieked in terror when it pawed the ground and snorted. Perhaps they had an appointment with their dressmaker.

Aurora felt a coldness seep up from the paving stones and spread rapidly through her body. *'Have you thought about what type of dress you are going to choose?'* It was a moment before Aurora recognised these words as her own, spoken six months ago; that the words had sounded so clear and distinct yet no one could hear them but herself. That Wednesday afternoon in the final week of May, a strange, a foreboding day that had hung around longer than any day ought, when the sun had been cloaked the whole day by a queasy yellowish haze, not the usual London smoke but something altogether more menacing. It had been a day for staying in one's room and peering down at the world through smoke-encrusted windows, for writing impassioned letters to people one had long ago lost touch with and would never meet again, for remembering all those who had passed. It was her youngest child's ninth birthday.

'Are you ready, darling?' she had asked and she had glanced at the clock on the mantel for she and Sofia were to take a cab to her dressmaker in Bond Street and the traffic was bound to be tiresome, coupled with which she and Lucas had a dinner to attend that evening. They ought to have started the venture much earlier but there had been a series of callers that morning, making lunch late, and now here they were and it was mid-afternoon already. It was inconvenient and she had wanted to say, Do please hurry up, darling, but she had not done so for

77

it was Sofia's birthday and she had wanted the child to enjoy her day.

'I wish to look as beautiful as you, Mama,' Sofia had said and Mrs Logan had gone outside to whistle for a cab.

As one had drawn up, Jack had returned bloodied from a cricket match, Gus a step or two behind carrying cricket bats and pads and quick to apportion blame: 'Mama, I did tell him not to stand there. I did warn him.'

'That's where you're meant to stand!' Jack had replied, indistinctly, cradling his injury, which appeared to be a tooth knocked out that caused a surprising amount of blood to spill down the front of this shirt. In the confusion of the next few moments Aurora had run to her stricken son, Mrs Logan had called to Annie to get hot water and a towels ('He is not in labour, Mrs Logan!') and Agnes had been dispatched to fetch Dr Frobisher. The party had moved indoors and the blood flow had been stemmed and Jack had been made to hold his head back though it was not, he had protested, a nose bleed at all. He had merely lost a tooth—not a very good tooth either, not one he actually needed—and Gus, who was nothing if not thorough, had produced the tooth in question, which he had retrieved from the cricket green.

Unsurprisingly the outing to the dressmaker had been abandoned. Too much time had passed, the traffic would be tiresome, they had a dinner to attend and now this! Her son with a cricket injury and blood on the drawing room carpet and Gus sporting the dislodged tooth like a gruesome hunting trophy! It was hard on Sofia but it could not be helped. 'We will go to the dressmaker another day,' Aurora had said, one eye on the clock and the other on a tiny spot of blood that had got onto her gown, and when Sofia had pouted and stamped her foot and eventually burst into tears Aurora had sent her out into the garden.

'Madam? Is it you, madam?'

In Bond Street the mother and daughter had gone and instead the face of some opportunistic street urchin came into focus, the wretched creature thin and lank-haired, her face streaked and gaunt, on her head a bonnet minus its lace, and around her shoulders a shawl, patched and torn.

'I fought it was you, madam. I seen ya from 'cross the street.'

Aurora experienced a moment of disorientation. It was the maid. Agnes. Annie. One of the maids who had quit. At once Aurora stood up straighter and inclined her head to acknowledge the girl's presence. What did she want? Money, presumably.

'I know I shouldn't, madam,' the girl went on, curtseying awkwardly then taking a tentative step closer, 'but I'm desperate, see. I can't find work. I'm a hardworking girl, madam, you know it's the truth, but I can't find no work.'

Aurora lifted her chin and addressed a place just above the girl's left ear. 'I am sorry for your misfortune, Agnes, but you should not have been so hasty to leave our employ.'

'Annie. It's Annie. I tried to stay on after Agnes left, honest I did, but I couldn't . . . I couldn't, on account of . . .' The girl stopped, her mouth working but no sound coming out. There was something half-pleading, half-fearful in her eyes. 'On account of the *ghost*,' she whispered at last.

And Aurora thought, surely I have misheard her.

She had not misheard. The coldness spread over her body a second time, creeping out along her limbs and it seemed, for a moment, that she could no longer feel her feet, her legs, her arms. It seemed that she must surely have invented the girl's presence and put those words in her mouth. But she had not invented the girl. The girl was standing before her now, a look of dismayed terror on her face.

'*There is no ghost!*' Aurora whispered, grabbing the girl's shoulder and holding it tightly. 'How *dare* you say such a thing?'

The girl's dismay was palpable yet she clung doggedly to her story. 'Swear to God, madam, we 'eard it! Agnes and me, *we both 'eard it.*'

Aurora let go of the girl's shoulder and reeled away and she had almost reached Piccadilly by the time Meredith finally caught up with her.

—⚬—

'Really! *The Times* has surpassed itself!' exclaimed Sinclair, shaking that morning's edition of the newspaper with unsuppressed rage. '"*Amidst the mangled wreck of carriages the anguished cries of the sufferers could be heard long into the night, rendering the scene most terrible to behold.*" Is it a piece of journalism, one wonders, or a passage from some lurid Gothic fantasy?'

Lucas did not answer. Unlike his colleague he was not reading about the aftermath of the company's worst accident in three years in the pages of *The London Times*, he was viewing it right now first-hand.

They had arrived at Wolverhampton mid-afternoon and, with the line still closed, had hired a carriage to take them the rest of the way to the accident site. Sinclair had been silent most of the journey. The vivid accounts of the crash clearly infuriated him yet it was more palatable than witnessing it in person through the carriage window.

As they drew alongside the track Lucas saw a bridge strad-dling a canal—the remains of a bridge: its abutments on one side were utterly destroyed. The engine, tender and a third-class carriage of the ill-fated train lay on their sides some distance from the line, the mangled remains of a goods wagon now hardly distinguishable from the engine that had ploughed into it. Further down the embankment a gang was working with ropes and pulleys and a team of horses to remove two other carriages from the canal into which they appeared to have rolled. The remaining carriages, the luggage van and the brake-vans had been removed from the site but all around was a littering of broken glass and twisted metal and fragments of bricks. Over it all was a thin covering of frost and Lucas shivered.

Their carriage had stopped. The driver got down, pulled open the door and lowered the steps but for a moment neither of them got out. The foreman of the work gang and another man in a frock-coat buttoned up against the cold had seen them. The foreman stopped work and regarded them from a distance, not coming over, but the frock-coated man began to pick his way over the frozen ground towards them.

'Mr Jarmyn and Mr Sinclair, is it?' he inquired, offering them his hand as though they were meeting outside church after Morning Prayer. 'I'm Standish, district superintendent of locomotives. Pardew is my foreman.' He indicated the foreman, who gave a brief nod and returned to his work.

Lucas descended the steps and shook the man's hand, ashamed of his reluctance to leave the carriage.

'What is the situation? Our last communication indicated that salvage work had commenced and I can see that much has been achieved already.'

'Indeed. I arrived here myself just a few hours after the accident occurred and a most dreadful sight it was then, sir, as you can well imagine. Needless to report, the work of recovering and tending to the injured and the dead went on into Sunday night and through Monday but by lunchtime all had been removed, the more seriously injured being transported by a fleet of hired carriages and by special train to the Royal Infirmary at Wolverhampton. Others to the Red Lion Hotel and the Queens Arms Hotel, both at Dawley. Work continued through the night and into this morning to clear and repair the line so that it may be in use again at the earliest opportunity.'

'And the deceased?' said Sinclair, looking beyond Standish towards the horizon where the smoke and chimneys of a small village could just be seen.

'The bodies were secured in a van and held overnight at Dawley Station. They now reside, as I understand, at the infirmary, awaiting identification. We know who they are, it is a formality only. The driver and fireman being listed on that day's duty roster, it made identification a straightforward matter. The father was with the child when it died but he was rendered insensible by the shock and was unable to make formal identification straight away.'

'What news of the injured? We had heard upwards of thirty, some gravely?'

'Yes. The more serious cases are at the infirmary. The injuries are mostly compound fractures, concussions and internal bleedings. There has been at least one amputation. Some poor souls remain insensible and are not expected to recover. There was a Sunday school party in one of the carriages but, by God's grace, the party escaped, for the most part, unscathed. You are here to attend the inquest?'

'Yes,' confirmed Sinclair. 'It is scheduled for nine o'clock tomorrow morning though no doubt it will be adjourned. With any luck we shall be on the noon train and home again by evening. Tell me, why are the constables here?'

Lucas had noticed them too. A small contingent of uniformed constables patrolled the fringes of the crash site.

Standish nodded. 'There were pickpockets in the immediate aftermath of the crash. People came at once when they heard what had happened. By the time I myself arrived the place was swarming. Many were tending to the injured but others came simply to stare, as you can well imagine, and into this swarm a number of miscreants inevitably were drawn. The crowd caught one man red-handed and, by the time they had finished with him, I believe he would have been glad to have been handed over to the constables.'

'It is the worst sort of crime,' observed Sinclair.

'Indeed, sir.' Standish shifted from one foot to the other then back again. 'There was a second incident though of a different nature late on Sunday. A crowd had gathered at the station and they had got hold of a rumour that the engine of the ill-fated train was faulty or the track poorly maintained or both. All strenuously refuted by myself and others, naturally, but once they had got hold of the idea the crowd would not be dissuaded. There was some ill-feeling. The stationmaster was jostled and knocked down. A window was smashed.'

'There was nothing in *The Times* about it,' Lucas replied.

'They dispersed soon enough when the constables were called and things have remained quiet since. I trust it was merely a result of high emotions in the heat of the moment.' Standish gave a quick smile. 'Do you wish to see the site of the collision, gentlemen?' he offered, seeming anxious to change the subject.

They began to pick their way across the ground towards the bridge and when he looked down at the frozen, uneven ground Lucas saw a man's shoe, crushed and soiled, before him. A little further on was a chain from a man's watch, a scrap of a lady's handkerchief, a third-class ticket stub, the stem of a clay pipe, and an unidentifiable item of clothing, mangled and torn and darkly stained along one edge though whether from the damp or from blood he could not tell. So intent was he on the dark stain that he missed his footing and tripped, putting out a hand to steady himself, and looking down he saw a small cylindrical pinkish-grey object at his feet. At first he could not make out what it was, so incongruous did it look amongst the twisted chunks of metal and the splinters of wood and the rubble, and he crouched down and went to pick it up. Then he saw that it was a human finger, sliced clean off and frozen solid. A woman's finger, the nail neatly trimmed, the skin puckered but clean.

He stood up and lurched away from it, keeping his eyes on Standish who was ahead of him.

'Here,' Standish was saying, indicating with his arm the point of contact with the goods train. They walked wordlessly up the line in the Dawley direction until they had reached the final signal before the bridge. It was in the 'danger' position. They stood beneath it and observed it for some minutes.

'This signal has been changed since the accident?' inquired Lucas finally.

'That I cannot say, sir. I have not spoken to the signalman who was on duty at the time, being more concerned with the salvage operation, as you see. The government official, a Captain Greenaway, was here yesterday and spoke to the man, I believe, as well as to the head guard and the stationmaster at Dawley, but I cannot say what the outcome of these discussions was. No doubt we shall hear at the inquest.'

'If the signal was in the "danger" position and the driver failed to spot it and to stop in time then clearly it was driver error that caused this accident,' pronounced Sinclair, turning to head back down the line.

'And if the signal was frozen in the "clear" position and has since *un*frozen it is *not* driver error,' Lucas countered.

'Look around you,' said Sinclair, pausing to wave his arm at the icy scene of destruction before them. 'There has been a frost each day since the accident. Do you think this signal would have unfrozen when the air temperature has not got above freezing these last three days? It is driver error, mark my words.'

'Convenient for us if it is,' remarked Lucas, when they were out of the hearing of Standish.

Sinclair rounded on him angrily. 'Contrary to what you evidently believe, Jarmyn, I am just as concerned about finding out the truth of this matter as you are. It does not assist matters if we hide from the truth, however ugly it may prove.'

'Knowing the truth privately and acknowledging it publicly being two very different things, Sinclair. Do you share my views on both points, I wonder?'

'You pre-judge me just as you seem to think I have pre-judged this case.'

'Then I trust I shall be proved wrong.'

'And I trust I shall be proved right. The implications for this railway if I am not are . . . awkward.'

Standish had caught them up and had evidently heard Sinclair's earlier statement.

'The company can hardly be held responsible for a frost, surely?' he remarked and he gave the same quick smile.

CHAPTER SIX

London

LIEUTENANT FORBES HAD COME TO dinner. He was sitting opposite Uncle Austin at the table in his uniform, all gold epaulettes and shining gold buttons and gold braid at his cuffs and collar. Odd that his tunic was scarlet rather than the usual dark blue of the 8th Hussars, and he was not wearing his sword at his side, so far as Austin could make out. This was strange but not half as strange as the fact that the very last time Austin had seen him, Lieutenant Forbes had been cut in half by a Cossack sabre at Balaklava in '54.

And now he had come to dinner. And so far as Austin could tell, he was miraculously in one piece again. Was it a trick? No one around the table seemed in the least bit surprised by the lieutenant's sudden and unexplained return to health. Indeed, to life.

But then none of the people around the table (who they were, he was not quite sure) had witnessed the lieutenant's grisly death. Or had they? One couldn't be sure of that either.

No, they were children, mostly. And the grave young gentleman at the head of the table whom he ran into from time to time, and the enigmatic but very captivating lady whom he had an idea was married to the grave gentleman and was perhaps his own niece, for he felt certain he had known this lady when she was a child and it was unsettling now to see her thus grown up.

'How did you *do* it, eh? How did you do it, Forbes?' he asked, leaning over the table at the chap, needing to understand.

Lieutenant Forbes leant back in his chair warily as though alarmed at being addressed and instead of answering he looked at the other people around the table.

'I am sorry, Roger. You remember he gets a little confused?' said the enigmatic lady. She turned to Austin with a smile. 'Uncle, this is Roger Brightside. Travers and Meredith's son. You remember? He's a lieutenant and he's just been assigned to the 58th. He's about to join his new regiment. They are to sail to the Transvaal in a few days.'

Austin nodded enthusiastically and had no idea what the woman was talking about.

Lieutenant Forbes, meanwhile, was smiling grimly at him. 'Major Randle, sir, I hope you are keeping well?' he said and Austin was bewildered. Was the fellow a ghost? An apparition?

'That Cossack,' he reminded the lieutenant. 'Big Russian fellow with a shashka—big sabre-thing with a damned sharp edge. Fellow came out of nowhere. You didn't stand a chance. How'd you do it, eh? Saw you cut clean in two—left to right. Only your legs left standing.'

'Uncle, please.'

'You saw someone *cut in two*?' said one of the children, the boy sitting to his left, the child's eyes boggling with delighted horror.

'Jack, please do not encourage him. I'm sorry Brightside, my wife's uncle has a colourful and somewhat . . . selective memory. When does your ship sail?'

'In two days' time, sir, the thirteenth. We sail from Portsmouth to the Cape then round to Durban. Should take around three weeks, I understand. I should be joining my regiment around the New Year. And that fellow Kruger will be routed before the end of the month, I shouldn't wonder. I only hope they hold off till I get out there.'

The fellow was cocky. Lieutenant Forbes had never been cocky before, but then he had cheated death, he could afford to adopt a bit of a swagger. It was unnerving, though, no doubt about it. One moment the fellow was dead, the next he was sitting down to dinner.

But some very strange things had happened recently, Austin remembered, and for a moment his eyes filled with tears.

—◊—

Cousin Roger was wearing the uniform of the 58th: a scarlet tunic and blue trousers with red piping, a spotless white belt across his chest and highly polished knee-high black boots. His tunic buttons bore the Latin inscription *Montis Insignia Calpe* (which was something to do with Gibraltar) and on his cap badge insignia was a Sphinx to honour the regiment's 1801 Egypt campaign. His uniform was, therefore, as different to that of a cavalry officer at the Crimea as it was possible for a uniform to be.

Jack, carefully studying his cousin across the table, was not aware of this, not having reached the Crimean War yet in his *Boys' Compendium*. He did know that, in his uniform, his cousin cut a very dashing figure indeed and that people, especially the young ladies, tended to notice him. Not Dinah, of course, she had barely given him a second glance but that was just Dinah.

'And how are things in the Transvaal?' inquired his mother, as though she was inquiring after the health of Roger's parents.

'Well, in a nutshell, Aunt, this fellow, Kruger, has declared the Transvaal independent of British rule. So General Colley, who is governor of the region, has responded by assembling a column of troops. I understand the general now has around a thousand men at his disposal—including a naval detachment—and is poised to advance whereas Kruger has perhaps a few hundred Boers at most. Colley is in a pretty unassailable position, one would think.'

Jack nodded eagerly. He knew much of this already, of course—after all, one read *The Times*—not that it had ever been a topic for discussion at the dinner table before.

'My regiment—the 58th—is already there. It is simply a matter of my joining them before the thing kicks off.' He aimed this last remark at Dinah as though she had some special interest in the affair but Dinah was playing with her napkin ring.

'And this region, the Transvaal,' said Mr Jarmyn. 'It is strategically important? It is rich in natural resources? It is part of a trading route?'

Roger nodded. 'Presumably, sir.'

Mr Jarmyn nodded with a small sigh. He had returned from the crash site of the wrecked train the evening before after four days in the Midlands and it seemed to Jack his father was more taken up with trains than war.

'What will it be like when you get there? What will you have to *do*?' asked Gus doubtfully and Jack turned to his brother.

'Don't you know *anything*?' he retorted scornfully. 'Cousin Roger is an officer in the British Army! What do you *think* he will be doing?'

Instead of looking embarrassed Gus turned to him patiently. 'Which means *what*, exactly?'

'Soldiering, of course.'

'You don't know.'

'Of course I do. It means foraging and drilling and inspecting kit and keeping your uniform in order and looking after your men and keeping your rifle clean, and . . .' He looked towards his cousin.

'Quite right, Jack,' confirmed his cousin. 'You know a lot about it. Are you going to be in the army yourself?'

'Jack will be going to Oxford, like his brothers,' said his father.

This was met by a short silence during which Cousin Roger concentrated on his Windsor soup and Jack glared furiously at his own plate and felt something burning inside him. Their cousin had come to dinner and yet they were expected, he and Gus, to sit still and say nothing, to hold no opinion, to not actually exist.

And Jack remembered that his sister had lain mortally injured and in terrible pain in an upstairs room for ten days before she had died and that he and Gus had not been allowed to see her. He blamed his father for that too.

'Where the Devil is everyone?' said Mr Jarmyn, irritably. There was no sign of any of the servants and he reached over and pulled the bell rope but after a minute still no one had come.

'Dinah.'

'Of course, Father,' and Dinah got up so speedily one wondered if she hadn't been sitting there waiting for the excuse.

'I certainly hope to go up to Oxford,' announced Gus into the silence.

—⚬—

Dinah was glad to have left the dinner table. The room, despite the bone-jarring cold, was stifling. She did not at once go in search of Mrs Logan but stood, lost in her own thoughts, in the hallway.

They had played together as children, she and Roger. He was Bill's age and she a year younger but as small children they had always got on better than she and Rhoda or he and Bill, dressing up in old clothes and acting out little stories—Roger had enjoyed the silly fairytales of youth as much as she, when Bill had scoffed and Rhoda had felt left out and run off in tears to be consoled by her nurse. Silly, childish games that had ended abruptly when Roger's father had been given what would prove to be the last of many ministries and the family had leased out their Great Portland Street house and relocated to the North. When the ministry had inevitably failed and the family returned Rhoda had seemed barely changed—an unfortunate flat 'a' in her speech the only outward sign of her time in the North. But Roger was on the cusp of manhood in his final year of schooling and ready to embark—quite against his father's wishes—on a career in the military. Dinah had, she remembered, been unprepared for this change in him.

But she must find Mrs Logan. Dinah hurried downstairs.

Things were not going to plan in the kitchen. Dinah stood in the doorway as a great burst of steam blasted from the range, and emerging from the steam as would an apparition from the underworld Cook appeared, her face streaming moisture and glowing redly, her sleeves rolled up and her vast forearms wielding a massive cauldron. As the steam thinned Dinah saw Mrs Logan bending over the new maid (a girl with the unlikely name of Hermione) whom, it appeared, was in some distress.

'Is everything all right, Mrs Varley?' Dinah asked, though it clearly was not.

'Ha!' replied Cook, shaking her head.

Mrs Logan looked up and smiled wearily.

'We have experienced a small domestic accident, Miss Jarmyn. Nothing life-threatening.' She frowned then, as though she had said something she wished she hadn't and Dinah thought, Yes, Mrs Logan is good in a crisis. She excelled at accidents. Small or otherwise.

'Folk in the kitchen when they shouldn't be, gettin' in the way when they have no business to be in the way,' muttered Cook, slamming the huge cauldron down onto the stove top and reaching for her pipe to take a consoling puff, and Dinah wondered if Cook was referring to her or the new maid. The look that Cook now aimed at the new maid seemed to settle the point.

The maid, Hermione, sobbed quietly and Mrs Logan patiently dabbed something onto her forearm.

'Is the girl burnt?' said Dinah. The words had a queer sound to her ears.

'A scald. Just a scald from the steam. Not a burn,' said Mrs Logan firmly. 'We will be up directly, Miss Jarmyn. Please tell Mr Jarmyn all is well and we will be up directly.'

Mrs Logan wanted her gone and Dinah was glad to go. She wished she had not come down. She went back up the stairs and paused for a moment outside the dining room. She could hear Roger's voice on the other side of the door.

That last term of the boys' schooling, when Bill had been furiously working for his final exams and Roger had given up any pretence of taking exams and had already joined the militia as a cadet, he had been a regular visitor at Cadogan Mews, biding his time till he was free of school and could join the regiment full-time. One afternoon in late May something quite extraordinary had happened and, as with most extraordinary things, it had begun quite innocently.

He had lost a button from his tunic. It was a solid brass button from his uniform jacket and, though he was only a cadet, it was the genuine thing. It even had the words *Montis Insignia Calpe* inscribed on it, which Roger said was the motto of Gibraltar, awarded to the regiment for some very important action during some important campaign. He had been very put out at the button's loss.

They had only gone out into the garden in the first place because the delphiniums and hydrangeas had begun to bud and the sun had risen early if sluggishly and had endured throughout the day, though veiled by a sickly yellowish cloud of London smoke. It was a day for being out in the garden. They had sat in the lowest boughs of the ancient sycamore that had stood since childhood days, their heads in the past, their talk of the future. And Roger had lost a button from his tunic. Together they had scoured the undergrowth to locate it.

Roger had despaired: 'I cannot return minus a button!'

But Dinah was all practical advice: 'You must say you were set upon by a gang of desperate ruffians and in the ensuing melee it was lost.'

Roger had given up the hunt and now stood and regarded his cousin. 'That's your suggestion?'

Dinah had nodded. It was a good suggestion. She was quite proud of it. Yet she could not tell from Roger's expression if it were the silliest suggestion in the world or the most extraordinary.

As it turned out it was not the suggestion nor the loss of the button that was extraordinary. It was what had happened next: Roger, her cousin, her playmate, had taken her in his arms and kissed her.

If the birds had stopped their song and the breeze had turned to snow and all the buds on the delphiniums and hydrangeas had sprung at once into bloom she would have been less surprised. Indeed it was quite possible that all these things and more had happened, Dinah could not say for sure.

Her surprise, great as it was, was then utterly eclipsed: 'Dinah,' he had entreated, clasping both her hands in his. 'I want us to marry, I cannot imagine being with any other girl. There is no girl in England who is like you and I cannot bear for some other chap to win your hand. Dinah, say you feel the same way. Say you will marry me!'

There was no other girl in England like her! The very ground at her feet had trembled and the sun, which had been sluggish all day, dazzled her.

That was six months ago. Dinah stood now outside the dining room door, waiting to go in, and when she did go in she formed her mouth into a smile that was not really there.

'What sort of gun do you have?' Jack was asking and Dinah sat down and nodded to her father, who had raised an inquiring eyebrow at her.

'Well, nowadays your average British infantryman uses a single-shot breech loading rifle. It has a sword bayonet that fixes on the end for close combat,' said Roger.

He paused, his eyes sliding uneasily to Uncle Austin who had fallen into a thoughtful silence but whose vivid contribution to the conversation a few minutes earlier was still fresh in everyone's minds.

'Not that close combat is common any more in modern warfare,' Roger went on. 'Cavalry charges and hand-to-hand is all very well for old-fashioned campaigns but it is all artillery and marksmanship these days.'

'Cousin Roger came top of his class at marksmanship, didn't you, Cousin Roger?' said Jack, practically bursting with pride at this family achievement.

'Second, actually,' Roger corrected. 'But I came top at swordsmanship. And I was commended for my horsemanship.'

'How clever!' said Mrs Jarmyn, obligingly. 'Though if there

are to be no cavalry charges or hand-to-hand this may not prove very useful?'

'An officer of the British Army must be conversant with all aspects of warfare,' Roger explained. 'But these things are one thing in basic training. It is how a fellow acquits himself in the field of battle that counts.'

The door opened and the new maid edged tentatively into the dining room, her arm bandaged, and balancing a serving dish which she awkwardly moved to her other hand. She made her way over to Mrs Jarmyn, who caught the girl's eye and gave a brief shake of her head and the girl, mortified, scuttled to the other end of the table to serve the master first. The dish emitted a savoury, slightly fishy aroma, and Dinah realised she wasn't very hungry.

'I am sure you will be a credit to yourself and your parents, Roger,' said Mrs Jarmyn. 'I know that Travers, in particular, is very proud of your achievements.'

As Uncle Travers had always anticipated Roger following him into the clergy and, upon Roger's entry into the military, had expressed his bitter disappointment to them all at this very table not eight months earlier, her mother's statement fell a little flat.

Perhaps Roger felt it too, as his reply was almost a challenge.

'I shall be the best soldier I can be. Soldiering is the most honourable profession there is for a gentleman.'

And though he did not look at her as he said this, Dinah knew it was aimed at her. It was all aimed at her.

But Dinah was watching her uncle, formerly Major Randle of the 8th Hussars, as he rocked back and forth, silently weeping.

—∿—

'Will you hail a cab?' Mr Jarmyn inquired, shaking Roger's hand as he stood in the Jarmyns' front doorway at the end of the evening.

But Roger eschewed a hansom. Certainly it was a cold night but it would be worse in the Transvaal. He would not take a cab.

'It will be summer though, won't it, in the Transvaal?' Dinah said as he departed, perhaps the first thing she had said to him all night, and her father laughed and patted her shoulder, the idea of his daughter sitting poring over a globe and understanding the hemispheres and longitude and latitude clearly amusing him.

So Roger set off on foot, westwards towards Great Portland Street, and yes, technically Dinah was right. It would be summer in the Transvaal but it was very much winter here and he turned up the collar of his greatcoat. He turned into Cadogan Square, pausing on the corner to look back at the mews. He was to depart in two days' time so this may very well be the last time he would see any of his cousins before he sailed. Had they realised that? Jack had realised it. Uncle Austin didn't realise very much at all. Uncle Lucas had been unimpressed, he could tell that. And his Aunt Aurora had seemed preoccupied. What about Dinah? Had it meant anything at all to her?

If it had, she had been as cool as you like about it! That was Dinah, wasn't it? Cool as you like. Always had been. Not like Rhoda, fainting and screaming and carrying on like a girl. Dinah was all composure—and that was just what a chap wanted in a girl, wasn't it, composure?

For a moment he faltered. It was not what he wanted. This was the last time she would see him before he sailed for the war. Did one want composure at such times?

She had written to him in June, a day after her sister's death, telling him that it had been a terrible mistake. She could not marry him. That he should tell no one what had happened.

It was grief, he had known that and he had understood though it had wounded him almost beyond endurance to wait. But six months had passed and still she would not see him.

Instead she had said, *'It will be summer though, won't it, in the Transvaal?'* And she was right. Half the world was in winter yet there, south of the equator, it would be summer. The thought filled him with wonder.

Perhaps he had not made it clear to them, the nearness of his departure? That this must, surely, be the last time he would set foot in their house before he sailed, before he went off to fight in a war?

He turned and took a step back towards Cadogan Mews. He would tell them, make it quite clear. Make it clear to Dinah.

But as he looked, the lamps on the ground floor of number 19 were gradually extinguished and a moment later the upstairs lamps went out too.

So instead he turned away and continued on his journey, westwards towards Great Portland Street.

—⁂—

Cousin Roger had gone and the boys had stood at their bedroom window and waved him off.

'Do you remember, Lucas,' said Aurora, waiting in the drawing room doorway as he came back upstairs, 'Roger falling out of the monkey puzzle tree in the garden? I can see him now, sitting on the lawn rubbing his knee, crying, and Dinah, perched on some upper branch, pouring scorn on him from above. And now he is a lieutenant in the 58th and about to depart for war. How quickly they grew up.'

'Indeed,' said her husband, with a frown, passing her and going into the drawing room.

'Thank God Bill is at Oxford. What can Travers have been thinking, allowing his only son to become an officer in the infantry? I always assumed Roger was to have followed him into the clergy.'

'Apparently that was not Roger's plan,' Lucas remarked. 'Sons, it seems, no longer regard their fathers' wishes when choosing their careers.' He returned to his chair but instead of reseating himself he merely collected his spectacles and his newspaper and made to leave the room.

'My uncle was a little agitated by Roger's presence,' Aurora observed, forestalling his departure. Dinah had been agitated too, she added privately, but this was a conversation for another time.

'As well he might,' Lucas replied, pausing and studying the front page of the newspaper.

'My uncle came to visit us at my father's house when I was a very small child,' she remembered. 'I recall him being a rather frightening and blustery man with loud boots and a louder voice. He never called me by my name, just called me "little girl". And the next time I saw him it must have been the spring of '55, years after Father's death, and the war in its second year.'

The man who had been returned to them had been an imbecile, barely coherent, a shambling, shuffling, frequently distressed casualty of a war that was still raging and with no one to look after him. So Mrs Randle, somewhat against her will, had provided him with a home. And there he had remained until Mrs Randle's own death four years later, at which time Uncle Austin had been uprooted for the final time and brought here, to Cadogan Mews. The major was into his mid-seventies now, having outlived his brother by thirty years and his sister-in-law by twenty and, aside from the occasional attempt to hurl himself from a top-storey window, looked likely to outlive them all.

And now another war seemed set to rage in another distant corner of the world and more young men were set to die horribly and far from home, yet always there was this stream of boys ready—nay, *eager*—to sign up for it, oblivious, it seemed, to their likely fate. Jack, she had noticed, had been in thrall to his older cousin. If Jack were to become a soldier—

Something swelled up in her chest making it difficult for her to catch her breath.

If Jack became a soldier, this current war would be long over but there would be another, there was always another. Lucas wanted Jack to go to Oxford but he would not; the days when sons, especially younger sons, did what their fathers wanted were gone. Jack would go into the army and perhaps he would die. What then? Ten years might have passed. She might have ten years until that point, until the next death.

She stood in the doorway but Lucas would not look at her, and her anxiety about her nephew and her son was, for the time being, forgotten. Lucas would not look at her! Even when he spoke to her, his eyes were always elsewhere. It was not anger, it was something else, something worse. He had come to her bedside in the first few days following Sofia's accident; even in her delirious state she had been aware of his presence. But one morning he had not been there. He had ceased to sit with her, he no longer entered her room. Death had turned him cold. It had turned them all cold and yet Lucas had turned from her even before Sofia had died and all her attempts since then to reach him had failed.

'Unless there is anything further you wish to say, I shall retire,' Lucas said.

There was nothing further she wished to say. He departed, giving her a brief nod. A draught blew in through the gap in the curtains and Aurora hastily closed them. A second draught crept in beneath the door. The very air was icy.

—⁓—

'Say you will marry me!'

But I am not yet eighteen and you are to go off to join your regiment and we are first cousins, our parents cannot wish this—all the things, in short, that Dinah might have replied, she did not. They certainly occurred to her for Dinah was of a practical nature, but what she said was:

'Oh! Yes! I will marry you!'

For in that moment the world had shifted and instead of the faceless, nameless stranger of her imaginings she now saw a future where the person at her side was Roger, whom she adored more than anyone else. That one could feel such happiness was a revelation! The fears and dread of a girl on the edge of womanhood vanished, replaced by a bright and warming certainty. She would marry her cousin Roger.

Yes I will marry you. This is what she had said and when one says these words one expects them to endure. One does not anticipate that they will be revoked; or at least, if they are to be revoked, then not in almost the same breath in which they are uttered. But now that one extraordinary thing had happened, a second happened almost at once. For Sofia had spied them.

Whether nine-year-old Sofia had been standing at an upstairs window looking out when she spied the two cousins in the garden below, or whether she had wandered of her own volition into the garden in order to enjoy the late May sunshine was a moot point. She came at them out of the dappled sunlight, a malevolent sprite materialising from the underworld, or this is how it seemed to Dinah.

Sofia's reaction to her elder sister and her cousin caught in this most compromising of positions was decided and unequivocal. A look of dazed horror passed over her face, followed at once by one of almost unimagined triumph. For now she had the power to make or break! Hers alone was the decision to give or to destroy and when you are nine years old and forever the youngest in a large family and a girl to boot, your position was negligible at best.

Often you went completely unnoticed.

So Sofia darted away, giving a little skip of pure glee, and aware only vaguely of her sister's hot pursuit. The race was a one-sided affair, the nine-year-old Sofia too filled with her heady new power to think through her escape and running straight to the French doors of the morning room, which were locked, as they always were until at least the first day of June. Consequently Dinah caught her up and grabbed her by the arm.

Perhaps, if Dinah had done the thing more delicately, had she reasoned and negotiated, had she cajoled, had she offered an inducement, the outcome might have been different. But something extraordinary had just happened to Dinah and now it had been ruined before it was even properly formed, and so in her fury and dismay she grabbed her sister's arm roughly.

'I *won't* let you spoil it!' she cried.

But Sofia would not be bullied. '*I'm going to tell! You cannot stop me! I shall tell Father!*'

Dinah slapped her once, hard, across the face.

The garden, which had been alive with birdsong, fell silent. The children playing noisily in a neighbouring house ceased their game. The carriages in Cadogan Square became still. The city stopped.

The first to move was Sofia. Her nine-year-old frame rocked and her face seemed to freeze into a mask then tears sprang to her eyes. The elation of a few heady moments evaporated in an instant. She shook herself free and ran from her sister into the house and up the stairs and pushed open the first door she came to which was the door to the drawing room where, inside, a fire was burning.

CHAPTER SEVEN

London and the Midlands

THE FIRST OF THE THREE funerals was held in Dawley on the second Monday in December, a week and a day after the train crash. On that day the sky hung heavily over the Earth leaving only the narrowest of spaces for man and his structures and rituals. The tiny Norman church clung to a hillside a mile from the town, its churchyard crammed already to bursting with the dead of eons. The walls of the churchyard had crumbled and, in places, had fallen quite away.

At eleven o'clock a small procession climbed up the hill towards the church, bent into the wind and holding onto their hats. Some wore black armbands. Others had black streamers tied around the crowns of their hats. The man from the railway company, Sinclair, wore a black frock-coat and a top hat and carried a cane. The path through the churchyard was overgrown and choked with brambles so that a way could only be found by following the muddied footsteps of the man ahead. An enormous black crow cawed from the uppermost branch of the wizened and ancient oak tree that had stood sentry over the churchyard since the Middle Ages. A second crow, older and battle-scarred, watched from the apex of the moss-covered lychgate, and its single black eye was the only object that glistened on this blackest of black days.

For it was the funeral of the little girl.

Sinclair followed closely in the footsteps of the clergyman who led the procession of mourners up the hill. He had had a difficult journey—the line was still closed and would be for some days yet. He had been obliged, once again, to hire a carriage at Wolverhampton and make his way across country by means of the roads and laneways. The carriage had become stuck three times in the mud and it had seemed likely he would not make the funeral at all. However here he was and let it not be said that the North West Midlands Railway Company did not care about its employees or its fare-paying passengers, even the poorest of them.

The procession had reached its destination: a four-foot by three-foot hole cut out of the frozen ground by the gnarled hands of a watching gravedigger, the man's frame so bent and ravaged he seemed as old as the churchyard and could as well have been digging his own grave. The vicar—a man not long past his youth but with a marked stoop like a pit worker and a face disfigured by smallpox—began his business and beside him Sinclair pulled out his watch. He had a habit, newly formed, of polishing its surface with his handkerchief. He did this now, with slow, methodical movements, feeling the smooth polished surface of the object through the newly laundered linen of the handkerchief. It was a gentleman's pocket watch made for him by John Bennett of London. It had cost six pounds and seven shillings. The watch had an ivory open-face dial with roman numerals and the exterior was hand-engraved. The fob chain was gold and the key brass. Sinclair had ordered the manufacture of the timepiece himself. He polished the watch a final time and placed it carefully in his pocket. The clergyman, he noted with satisfaction, was making good time. At this rate he would spend the night at Wolverhampton and be back in London by the following afternoon.

'I am the resurrection and the life. Those who believe in me, even though they die, will live, and everyone who lives and believes in me will never die.'

There were many men at the little girl's funeral. One of these, naturally enough, was the girl's father, Thomas Brinklow, a man born and raised within the shadow of the great iron foundry that dominated the town. A man who had begun work young and married young and did not expect to die an old man. A man whose only child lay in the coffin in the four-foot by three-foot hole in ground. As for the others who stood in solemn and respectful silence at the grave's edge, some were neighbours of the grieving man, some brothers and cousins of his wife's, but who the other men were, Thomas did not know—curious townsfolk, perhaps, who had heard about the railway accident and wanted to see for themselves, and men from the inquiry. One, a gentleman in a tall black hat and long black frock-coat, had shaken his hand before the service. All of them had given their names but he hadn't taken any of them in.

'Blessed are those who mourn, for they will be comforted.'

After the train crash Thomas had been taken to an infirmary where a surgeon had bandaged a gash on his temple. He wore the bandage still as his head throbbed more or less constantly and made him sway dizzyingly if he moved too fast or tried to think. It brought bile to the back of his throat, though it may not have been the lump on his temple that caused this.

His child, whose name was Alice, had died in his arms. One moment they had been riding along in the third-class carriage, fighting for room in the confined space, feeling the jolt as the wheels went over some points, the next she had been a broken thing in his arms, her blood seeping out onto his clothing. He did not remember anything after that, had come to in a bed in the infirmary surrounded by the injured. He was not badly hurt, they had assured him, yet he had been unable to speak or move in his bed. He had lain in the infirmary not speaking, not moving, awaiting his wife's arrival. But she had not come and he was glad and dismayed.

For his wife had refused to accompany himself and Alice to the fair. Not on the Sabbath, she had said, and he had not realised before that moment how stubborn she could be, his wife. And how stubborn he could be. Sunday was his only day off—what other day could he take his little girl to the fair? Why would God deny them this one pleasure, he reasoned, when their lives were otherwise a never-ending grind, grind and more grind, morning till night, day after day, year after year? Was this what God intended for His children? It was not what he, Thomas Brinklow, intended for his child. They would go to the fair. Besides, he had promised Alice and she would be disappointed. His wife, tight-lipped, had chosen to remain at home.

And now Alice was dead and his wife blamed him for her death.

'We brought nothing into the world, and we take nothing out,' recited the vicar in a deadened and dreadful tone that denied hope or joy or justice, at least in this world. He scooped up a handful of loose earth and cast it over the coffin, stepping back to indicate the mourners do likewise, pulling a handkerchief from his pocket and absentmindedly wiping the dirt from his fingers.

Thomas cast his own handful looking away so as not to see where the dirt landed on his daughter's coffin. He had no handkerchief and the dirt remained on his hands.

The burial was completed and the procession made its way back down the hill. When he saw the gentleman in the tall hat and the frock-coat climbing into a waiting carriage, Thomas understood that this was the man from the railway company. The door slammed shut and the carriage moved off, becoming bogged in the mud and the ice and, if he had wanted to, Thomas could have easily caught it up and spoken to the man but his heart was black and he could not move. Which was as well, for the man from the funeral company now arrived to present Thomas with the bill for the cost of the burial, which was four pounds. Thomas had assumed the railway company would pay. Four pounds was more than he earned in a year.

The carriage had freed itself and driven off and the funeral party had moved off down the hill but the gravedigger had remained. He now dug up the little girl's grave and retrieved the cheap pieces of timber that had made up her coffin. He rolled the girl's body back into the grave and scattered a thin layer of soil over her but he left the hole open for the next burial, which was due at midday.

The churchyard was crammed to bursting but still the people kept on dying.

—⁓—

The following morning, a Tuesday, Dinah found her mother winding wool in the morning room. She wordlessly came and joined her on the sofa, taking the skein of wool off her hands and submitting to her mother's winding. They sat in silence for a while.

'I have resigned from my committee, Mama,' said Dinah.

This was not intended to shock, indeed she hardly expected her mother to mind much at all, yet when Aurora had reached the end of the ball they had been winding and attempted to tie it off but the strand would not be tied, in a sudden and inexplicable rage her mother hurled it across the room, springing to her feet and upsetting the workbox so that pin-cushions, knitting needles, threads and scissors and bits of embroidery scattered in all directions.

'*Oh!*' she exclaimed in fury or dismay and strode over to the window, thrusting her palms out behind her as though to push the chaotic scene, and her own outburst, from her.

A little shocked, Dinah quickly dropped to her knees to retrieve the fallen items, scooping up the escaped balls of wool and attempting to instil some order in the confused tangle. It could not, she reasoned, be the announcement of her resignation from the committee that had caused such a reaction. She placed the things in the workbox and tried to think what to say.

'But tell me, why have you resigned from your committee, Dinah?'

It was her mother who spoke from her position at the window and her voice was perfectly normal as she gazed out over the mews, her back to the room, but her right hand began to rub her left forearm, the place where she had been burnt in the fire.

'Because I no longer care about the poor,' Dinah replied, trying not to watch her mother rubbing that same spot over and over. 'And it seems hypocritical to sit on a committee whose aim is to help the poor when one no longer cares about the poor. So I resigned.'

'Yes, I can see how that would be hypocritical,' Aurora replied after a moment's thoughtful silence. 'And what will you do instead?'

What *would* she do? Dinah did not know.

'You shall marry, of course,' said her mother, not waiting for a reply and ceasing, at least for the moment, her incessant rubbing. 'Have you had a proposal, I wonder?' and here she gave her daughter a quick, sharp, shrewd glance.

'No, Mama.'

'Oh.' Another short silence ensued during which her mother appeared to feel that these words warranted some form of comfort for she added, coming over and seating herself near her daughter, 'Never mind, dear. Plenty of proposals will come your way. More—in my experience—than one really wants, so that one is required to rebuff, which is never a very pleasant event for either party. And if many are not forthcoming then certainly one or two shall be and really, one is all that is required, is it not? I mean to say, one can only accept one proposal. More than one proposal is simply . . . superfluous.'

Dinah picked restlessly at the balls of wool in her mother's workbox. The conversation had turned in a direction she did not like. And now she had lied. Each lie, she noticed, became marginally easier than the one before.

'I wonder if Cousin Roger has set sail yet for the Transvaal,' she said to quell her own thoughts; but why say *that*, of all things? 'Perhaps he is already at sea?'

'I couldn't say, dear,' replied her mother. 'No doubt your Uncle Travers and your Aunt Meredith will keep us abreast of events. Communication is so much swifter than it was in my youth. When your Uncle Austin was so gravely injured in the Crimea, it was upwards of three months before my poor mama heard a thing about it. Now, people can sail to the Cape in two or three weeks and the telegraph means we will hear of a death in a matter of days. Of *hours*,' and she gave a little sigh then selected one of the balls of wool and resumed her winding, not with any sense of purpose but rather to occupy her hands, which seemed inclined to move of their own volition aimlessly and without end.

Dinah thought about her mother's words and it seemed to her no great marvel that a person could find out in a matter of days, of hours, that someone far away had died. They were still dead. She shivered with sudden cold and realised she could no longer feel the fingers around which her mother was winding the wool.

The clock in the hallway began to chime the hour just as the front doorbell rang. A moment later Mrs Logan appeared with the silver tray on which two cards were laid.

'Ah,' said Mrs Jarmyn, putting down the skein of wool. She glanced at the cards. 'It is your cousin and your aunt,' she said, nodding to Mrs Logan to bring the callers in and for an extraordinary moment Dinah thought she must mean Roger but it was Rhoda, of course, who followed Aunt Meredith into the room.

'Aurora. How lovely you're looking,' her aunt announced, greeting her sister-in-law with a kiss. Both mother and daughter wore gowns of brocaded silk, Rhoda's in a brilliant shade of crimson and Aunt Meredith's in a more muted pale grey with Aunt Meredith carrying a reticule and a parasol made of the same fabric. They both sported cashmere shawls in deference to the chilly December wind. Dinah had once or twice made the mistake of believing her aunt a little foolish—she had, after all, married Uncle Travers—but a look here and a word uttered there had persuaded her otherwise so that she now wondered if Meredith, had she been born a boy, would not have turned out every bit as determined and forthright as her father who was a director of a railway. It was a question that could never be answered as Meredith's life was the same round of calls and shops and dinner parties and dress fittings and charitable committees as it was every other lady in her acquaintance.

'And how is Lucas?' said Meredith, arranging herself on one of the upright chairs and indicating to Rhoda that she should take the other.

'Lucas?' repeated Aurora looking up, and for a moment her restless hands were stilled and a bewildered expression crossed her face as though she could not be expected to answer such a question, though surely it was a natural enough inquiry from her sister-in-law. 'He is not here,' she replied and she reached over to ring for the maid. Her mother's reply had not answered her question but perhaps it did not matter for Meredith had leant forward with an urgency that suggested her inquiry was but a pleasantry and this visit was something more than merely social.

Dinah looked past her aunt and tried to catch Rhoda's eye. They were the same age, she and her cousin, separated by just two months, and as very small children she and Roger and Rhoda had climbed trees and fished for newts in the pond. In more recent times the two of them had attended dance and music classes together, which had suited Rhoda much better than the tree climbing and the newt fishing. Today, oddly, Rhoda sat in mute consternation.

There was something, she had not been mistaken. Her aunt passed a nervous hand over her eyes. 'Aurora, I must speak to you about a most urgent matter.' She spoke in a low voice and, seated beside her, Rhoda's cheeks coloured and she cast her eyes downwards. 'Something rather dreadful has occurred: Travers has forbidden Roger to sail with his regiment.'

This was, somehow, the last thing Dinah had expected and she heard herself gasp and her hands flew to her mouth. But no one noticed. No one even looked at her. Her mother, who not a quarter of an hour earlier had reacted with a fit of inexplicable temper when winding the wool, received this news of family calamity with an unruffled calm.

'This is unsettling news, Meredith. But surely it is a little late for Travers to forbid anything of the sort? At this stage Roger failing to sail would, I am reasonably confident, amount to a dereliction of duty.'

'So I explained to him yet he would not listen! He is adamant Roger shall not sail.' Meredith moved restlessly in her seat, seeming unable for a moment to speak then her voice dropped almost to a hush: 'He claims it is an affront to God.'

'How so?'

'The Ten Commandments! Thou shalt not kill.'

Aurora dismissed the Ten Commandments with a wave of her hand. 'But surely Travers cannot be so literal? These sorts of things are . . .' she cast about for the a suitable word '. . . a guide, merely. A suggestion. He cannot think them a foundation on which to build one's life?'

There was a startled silence.

'Naturally that is what he believes, Aurora. How can he not? He is a clergyman. How can any of us *not*?' Meredith turned to Dinah and gave a little laugh. 'Dinah, did you realise your dear mama had become a heathen?'

But Aurora rejected her sister-in-law's suggestion with another wave of her hand: 'I am no more a heathen than you are, Meredith. I merely express the opinion that I prefer to use the Bible as a guide rather than a literal truth.'

Dinah felt the presence of Mr Darwin and his book loom heavily over them. Her father possessed a copy of the book in his study, which he judiciously removed from view whenever

Uncle Travers or other members of the clergy visited lest he cause offence. Dinah was reasonably certain her mother had not read the book and took no interest in the study or the origin of species. She was also reasonably certain her mother was not a heathen, in which case why had she said this? She found it unsettling.

'But Aunt Meredith, what will my uncle do?' she asked, anxious to forestall further theological debate. 'About Cousin Roger, I mean? He cannot truly mean to forbid him, can he?'

'He can and he does!'

'But in practical terms, what does it mean?' said Aurora, taking the wool from Dinah's hands and placing it in her workbox.

'A rift. He will be disinherited. Travers has declared he may never enter the house again. That his name never more be spoken!'

'Oh!' Dinah felt tears prick her eyes and she was dismayed.

'How like Travers,' observed her mother as she reached over a second time to ring for the maid. 'Where is that girl? Dinah, go and see—'

But before she could get up, Hermione announced her arrival with an awkward curtsy.

'You rang—'

'I did. Twice. We are in need of refreshment, Annie. Ask Mrs Logan to bring the sherry.'

The girl curtsied and left.

'Who *is* that?' said Aunt Meredith in a low voice, once the door had closed. 'It is not your usual Annie, surely?'

'No. She left.'

'They both left,' added Dinah.

'Is this one also called Annie?'

'No, I don't suppose so,' replied Mrs Jarmyn.

'Her name is Hermione,' supplied Dinah.

'Hermione!' repeated Aunt Meredith. 'Whatever next?'

'But Cousin Roger?' Dinah prompted, anxious to learn what had transpired between her uncle and her cousin.

'Roger is to sail this very evening,' said Aunt Meredith. 'From Portsmouth. There is to be a great send-off and we were to have travelled down, Roger expected us to be there. But last night—the last night before he sails—Travers made his announcement and Roger said did his father care more for God than he did for the Empire? And of course Travers was very much shocked and said that, should Roger sail, he would never speak to him again and would consider him dead and no longer his only son. Roger, suffice to say, left the house in a rage. And Travers went to the church to pray and he did not return all last night.'

'How dreadful!' cried Dinah and she looked to her cousin for reassurance, though what reassurance Rhoda could provide she did not know and indeed her cousin returned her look, pale and a little frightened, and offered no comfort.

'Quite so,' agreed her aunt. 'I was to go to Portsmouth—indeed, I had purchased a new hat on the strength of it—and now I confess I do not know what to do. We are at sixes and sevens.'

She looked at her sister-in-law who had remained silent since Hermione had departed.

'And *does* Travers care more for God than for the Empire?' Mrs Jarmyn inquired now.

Aunt Meredith opened then closed her mouth, clearly nonplussed by the question. 'Yes,' she said at last. 'I believe so. At least, I have never heard him express it in quite those terms. We have never had to make such a distinction before.' She frowned. 'Can it really be, Aurora, that one must choose between the two? It has always seemed so simple before. God and Empire were always on the same side, were they not?'

'Is God British, then?' said Mrs Jarmyn. She had picked up the skein of wool again and now placed her pince-nez on the tip of her nose.

Aunt Meredith regarded her sister-in-law in some surprise. 'What a ridiculous thing to ask, Aurora!' she replied with a little laugh.

'How can you laugh?' burst out Rhoda. It was the first time she had spoken and her words silenced the room.

Dinah sat perfectly still staring straight ahead. There was nothing she could say to her cousin, no look she might exchange. The memory of the afternoon she and Roger had spent together in the garden swirled about her, enclosing her and separating her from her cousin and her mother and her aunt as surely as if they sat atop two different mountains and no bridge connected them.

CHAPTER EIGHT

BILL JARMYN STOOD ON THE platform at Paddington Station beside the quietly steaming train and lit a cigarette. He had travelled up from Oxford that morning, sending his luggage on ahead. He had a solitary portmanteau at his feet, which was just as well as there appeared to be no porters to be had in London. Once he had got the cigarette alight he picked up the portmanteau himself, tossed his ticket at the man on the ticket barrier and set about hailing a hansom.

London's climate seemed milder than Oxford's, he observed, a consequence no doubt of all the people. Even on a Saturday morning the place was teeming. He had not noticed when he lived here. Now, after the graceful domes and spires and the learned laneways and quads of Oxford, London seemed vulgar. Gauche.

Bill had been in Oxford for a single term but it felt like a lifetime.

The cab dropped him in Cadogan Mews. He paid the man and stood before the house, looking up, and aware of a range of emotions that were, for the most part, unsettling.

He had been away at school taking his final exams in May, returning home briefly, in the first week of June for his sister's funeral, then he had departed again, on a pre-arranged tour of Italian antiquities with the family of a school friend. There had been talk of the trip being cancelled but in the end it had seemed best if he go. On returning to the house in the autumn he had found his family subdued. Withdrawn. Father had taken him down to Oxford on the train, had seen him settled in his rooms, and departed. Hardly a word had been exchanged between them aside from the formalities of the trip. It had not been the commencement of his time at Oxford that he had envisaged.

Now it was December and the Jarmyns' front door sported a discreet wreath of holly and ivy in acknowledgement of the season but with deference to the second period of mourning in which they now found themselves. Bill pushed the door open and stood in the hallway for a moment, listening.

'Hullo there. Mrs Logan? Anyone?'

The house was silent.

A girl appeared at the top of the stairs, emerging from the drawing room with a tray in her hand. Her left arm was heavily bandaged. She paused and stared at Bill expressionlessly.

'Hullo. Who are you?' Bill asked.

The girl continued to stare.

'Where are Annie and Agnes?'

'I couldn't say, sir,' replied the girl. 'Should I get someone?'

'Only if you want to. Here, you can take my bag up to my room. It's on the second floor. Second door on the left,' he added, as he had an idea she wouldn't know and would not think to inquire. 'Where is everyone?'

'I couldn't say, sir,' said the girl a second time, viewing the portmanteau and the tray of tea things still in her hands and clearly having difficulty reconciling the two items.

'Don't bother, I'll take it up myself.' And he picked up his case and started up the stairs.

'Oh Bill. There you are.' His mother appeared at the top of the stairs, her eyes a little glassy as though she had just woken from a nap. 'Hermione, take Master Bill's case up to his room.'

'Hermione!' said Bill, in some surprise, turning to look at the girl who was once more wrestling with the problem of the tea tray and the case. 'Don't bother, Mama, I can manage it on my own. Did my luggage arrive?'

'I have no idea, dear. I expect so. Mrs Logan will know.' His mother came down the stairs, meeting him halfway and submitting herself for a kiss. She pulled away after the briefest second. 'Come, your father is away at present but Dinah and the boys are here. We'll have afternoon tea in the drawing room. Hermione, tell Mrs Logan we shall have afternoon tea in the drawing room,' and the maid stood in some confusion holding the tray of tea things which she had just that moment removed from the drawing room.

'Lord! It's like an icebox in here,' said Bill.

'My rooms are on the ground floor, facing the quad, which is good from the point of view of chaps dropping in and so on.

But very bad from the point of view of disturbances and chaps dropping in when you're working or whom one doesn't actually *want* to drop in. And then again I am facing the pond, which is a source of great entertainment most weekends as someone invariably ends up in there. Some of the fellows even make a wager out of it: you know, whose turn is it this week, that sort of thing.'

Bill reached for a crumpet and placed it on his plate. He crossed his legs and leant back in his chair, pleased to have escaped the home and gone up to Oxford but glad to be able to return at the end of term to find everything just as he had left it.

Not everything.

'I hope you have been attending church, Bill?' said Mrs Jarmyn.

'Of course, Mama,' he replied, irritated to be questioned about church-going when he was full of the tales of student life.

'Why do people end up in the pond?' asked Gus, frowning.

'It's tradition. You'll find out when you get there.'

Gus pondered this.

'And your studies?' asked his mother, doggedly sticking to her theme. 'Are your studies going well?'

'Yes, Mama. Well enough. I attend the required number of lectures and hand in the required number of papers. But university life is about much more than academic study. I have already been nominated for both the Templonians and the Unikorn Club and am a member of the Forum Society and have put my name down for the college boat club—'

'Have *you* ended up in the pond?' said Gus.

'No. Happily I have managed to avoid that fate thus far.'

'It sounds rather silly to me.'

And Dinah, sitting beside their mother on the sofa, looked down at her lap and smiled.

'Well, no doubt it does. When you're still residing at home with the womenfolk the life of the university student seems very mysterious and unknown.'

'Cousin Roger is on his way to the Transvaal,' said Jack. 'He is to join his regiment, the 58th, and then they are to fight Kruger.'

'Is he indeed? Well.' Bill nodded and forgot what he had been about to say. 'Why is it so devilishly cold in here?'

The only member of the family not present to mark Bill's return from Oxford was his father. Mr Jarmyn had gone away to the Midlands preparing for the accident inquiry but he returned in a cab that evening, direct from the station and bringing with him a blast of frozen London air and a coating of thick, clinging black dust. On being informed of Bill's arrival he summoned his eldest son to his study for a pre-dinner whisky.

He raised his glass. 'Here's to you, Bill. We are glad to have you back.'

Bill smiled politely and raised his own glass, noticing that his father did not also raise his eyes to meet Bill's but instead kept them on the empty fire grate. He looked tired, thought Bill, seeing lines on his father's forehead and around his eyes that had not been there before, or that he had not noticed, and streaks of grey at both temples. He had lost none of his stature or bearing though. He bent towards the empty grate and a frown shadowed his face. This is how he will look as an old man, thought Bill with a sudden and unsettling premonition: stooping over the fire, a rug over his knees, querulous and dogmatic with no one to order about except Mama. He pushed the thought away. His father had not changed that much. It was simply that, being away, one noticed things upon one's return.

'You probably find us somewhat . . . grim,' his father observed.

'Oh well. After Oxford, you know . . .'

'Ah yes. Oxford.' Lucas nodded as though remembering his own time there and, perhaps finding this a safe topic, turned now to face Bill. 'How is the old place? Are you drinking too much?'

'Not too much, no. Just the right amount I should think.'

'Ha. Good. Good answer.' Lucas returned to his contemplation of the grate. 'You've seen your mother?'

'Yes. We had afternoon tea. In the drawing room.'

'Afternoon tea, was it?' and he regarded Bill thoughtfully.

'Yes. Teapot. Crumpets. That sort of thing.'

Lucas nodded but said nothing.

'I say, it's jolly cold in here,' observed Bill. 'Can we not get the fire lit? Looks like it hasn't been lit since the summer. Unless Mrs Logan has taken to sweeping it out herself every morning? Wouldn't put it past her.'

'No.'

'I beg your pardon?'

'I said, no. We don't have the fires lit. Not now.'

There was a silence.

Bill stared at the grate then took a sip of the whisky. Of course, it was a rebuke, plain and simple. His father's somewhat clumsy way of saying, *You* seem to have forgotten what has happened here. *You* have been away and *you* can have no understanding of *us*, of how *we* are doing.

It was absurd! Refusing to light the fires was the most irrational, the most childish thing he had ever heard. And how long, exactly, did Father intend to keep this up? All winter? Until one of them—his other daughter perhaps?—caught cold and ended up with pneumonia? And why the Devil had they put up with it? Someone, Mama at least, or Mrs Logan, must surely have said something?

He knew they had not. Would *he* say something? He wouldn't have, a few months ago. But now he was at Oxford.

'And is that really the best course of action, Father?' he said, squaring his shoulders and lifting his chin, aware as he did so that this was some kind of milestone between them. The outcome almost did not matter.

'I would not be doing it if I did not believe that it was,' his father answered quietly.

Bill nodded slowly. 'And if Mama or Dinah or the boys are cold?'

'No one has complained to me of feeling the cold.'

Bill made no reply. He sipped his whisky and felt it burning his insides.

—⁓—

'I think Father has become some sort of tyrant,' said Bill as he shovelled coal into the empty grate in the drawing room.

'What are you doing?' said Dinah, aghast.

'I'm shovelling coal into the grate. Have you been without a fire in this house so long that you have all lost the ability to make one? Fat lot of use you would all be shipwrecked on a coral island with only your wits to help you and two sticks to rub together. You'd probably be forced to exist on nuts and berries.'

'Put it down. Now. Please, Bill.'

Bill stood up and regarded his sister with some consternation.

'Why? Because Father tells you to? Or because you've all suddenly stopped feeling the cold even though it's the same temperature in here as it is outside in the street—where, I might add, there is a frost on the ground? It's his idea isn't it? How long does he intend to insist on this barbaric decree?'

'You do not understand,' said Dinah quietly as she observed her brother doggedly stoking the fire. She went to the window. He was right: there was a frost on the ground. And yet she felt nothing. *Had* she stopped feeling it?

'I understand very well,' he countered. 'But I happen to believe this is not the way. And I simply do not believe Mama will stand by and allow this nonsense to continue.'

'You do not understand,' said Dinah a second time. 'You haven't been here, you've been away.'

'Yes, I have been away and I believe that being away allows me a certain . . . broader perspective on things that the rest of you do not have.'

'Perhaps,' she conceded though she did not really believe this.

'I believe Father has lost his perspective,' Bill continued. 'Why, he appeared barely interested to hear of Oxford and his old college.' He paused to hold a lighted spill to the coals to get them to catch.

'It has been a difficult time,' Dinah said. 'There was a dreadful railway accident a fortnight ago—'

'But you believe this change in him is acceptable? That there is nothing . . . strange, ghoulish, about it?'

'Acceptable?' Dinah regarded her brother in surprise. 'To whom? To God? Or to you? To Mama, perhaps?'

'Blast this thing!' Bill lit another spill and attempted, without success, to light the coals. 'Where is Annie?'

'You won't get the maid to light the fire. Certainly not in here. Besides, Annie has gone. Agnes too. There is a new girl.'

'Ah, there she goes!' The coals had caught alight and one or two now began to glow. 'Now, we shall have some warmth in this mausoleum. Come, warm your hands, Dinah.'

The fire flared up as though some pent-up force had been released and Dinah found the glow from the coals bewildering, mesmerising. It drew her in and she experienced an almost primeval need to reach out to embrace the fire, but another part of her, a no less instinctive part, shied away in horror. Her father had forbidden the lighting of all fires in the house and Bill had gone against him. But it was more than this. Was Father's decree so barbaric? She had seen what the fire could do to a child's flesh.

She could not stay in the room.

'Dinah! For God's—'

'You were *not here*, Bill. You were *not here* when it happened.'

And what she meant was, you are free of guilt, you cannot be blamed in any way for what happened. He was absolved and he did not even know it and the fact of it formed an impenetrable barrier between them.

She could see her words had stung him for he stoked the coals vigorously with the poker. A single lump of coal slipped off the pile and rolled off the grate towards the carpet. Bill made a grab for it with the tongs but only succeeded in dropping the coal onto the floor, where it burnt a small round patch on the new carpet.

—⁂—

After dinner, and in deference to Bill's homecoming, the family retired to the drawing room where—inexplicably—a small fire seemed to have been recently lit in the grate but was now out, the coals cold and grey and lifeless. No one mentioned this though they could hardly fail to see it or to notice how this room, even after the fire had gone out, was a few precious degrees warmer than every other room in the house, save Mrs Varley's kitchen.

Mrs Logan's team of tradesmen had come and then departed and a new Turkey carpet now covered the floor and new curtains of a plush deep red velvet hung from the large bay window at the end of the room. Otherwise the room was untouched. The same crimson flocked wallpaper covered the walls. The *Sistine Madonna* still hung above the fireplace. The same array of ottomans, upright chairs, easy chairs and stools still crowded around the various writing desks, console tables, occasional tables and the big round table in the centre of the room. The grand piano still stood in the corner of the room and the same palm in a brass pot nestled beside it.

The family, minus Gus and Jack whose bedtime had been passed, paused on the threshold and it was Mr Jarmyn who led the way, negotiating the various obstacles in the room, and sat down, adjusting one of the lamps so that the room became instantly lighter. It was the first time the family had sat together in the room since its recent transformation but no one remarked on the new carpet or on the plush new velvet curtains. And no one commented on the small round patch on the brand new carpet that looked like a burn mark. The fire was out yet still Mrs Jarmyn went straight to it and sat on the chair closest to the hearth, holding her hands out to the empty grate as though the fire burnt still, and it seemed to Dinah that her mother's hands shook.

Roger was four days into his voyage. Dinah had pushed the thought down and down for four days, and it had helped not knowing the exact hour of his departure, but the knowledge that he was, even now, sailing southwards was, somehow, quite awful.

'Dinah, why don't you play for us?' her father suggested.

Dinah gaped at him in mute horror. But they were all watching her. She moved over to the piano and arranged herself on the stool. For a moment she looked down at her hands as they rested on the lid of the piano and it occurred to her that her father had no particular desire to hear her play, it was simply a way of precluding conversation. A sheet of music lay on the music stand and it must have been there all this time as no one had played the piano in all these months. It was Mozart's Minuet No. 2 in F, an easy piece she had learnt years ago and had played over and over till she was note perfect. She laid her hands over the keys and after a moment's hesitation began to play.

Her fingers had not forgotten. They flew over the keys, no longer in need of the music, finding their own way and it was joyous!

When she came to the end she turned around smiling, and the faces of her mother, father and eldest brother were all turned towards her.

'Bravo,' said her father quietly. 'I had forgotten. I had quite forgotten . . .'

Dinah turned back to the piano and rummaged through the pile of sheet music, coming up with another old favourite, the first movement from the Sonata in D. Why did I ever stop? she wondered, amazed at herself. The piano had been here in this closed off, silent room all this time and she had simply forgotten its existence. A memory popped into her head: Sofia running into the room in her tiny silk slippers, so full of excitement.

'Dinah, I can play a duet with you! Let me show you!' And she had squeezed her slight frame onto the piano stool beside her sister and placed her small hands inexpertly onto the keys and begun to pick out a tune. Dinah had been scandalised. Her own piano teacher had been rigid in his enforcement of the seven-year rule: seven years of scales and finger exercises and then, and only then, should the student be allowed to play. But Sofia had a different teacher and the rule apparently no longer applied. The injustice of this had smarted and she had replied tartly, 'I certainly will not play a duet with you—you have only just begun practising scales!' and had pushed her sister off the stool and snapped shut the lid of the piano. There would be no duets.

And so it had proved.

Dinah's fingers floundered and struck the wrong chord, then slumped, lifeless, on the keys. She lowered her head.

'Ouch!' exclaimed Bill. 'Did you lose your place?'

But Dinah had closed the piano lid.

'Bravo! Bravo, Dinah . . .' said her father, his voice trailing off, and he stood up and went over to the window though the curtains had been drawn hours earlier. Perhaps he wanted to admire the new fittings.

'How lovely your playing is,' said her mother, turning momentarily away from the fireplace to smile. 'Lucas, isn't it lovely to hear the piano again?'

'Yes, yes. Lovely.'

We should not be in here, realised Dinah. It was a mistake. The room ought to have remained closed forever.

'I see we have new carpet,' Bill remarked then he sat up and looked around him. 'And the curtains are new too—'

'How is your uncle this evening, Aurora?' said their father, and Dinah could see Bill looking at him in surprise at being cut off.

'A little confused,' replied their mother. 'I think all the changes have, perhaps, made him more restless than usual.'

Dinah left the piano and took a seat beside her brother who, perhaps irritated by his parents' conversation, had picked up a book from the table and begun idly flipping through the pages. It was *Squires' Study of the Workings and Evolution of the Railway Steam Engine* and it was full of technical diagrams and specifications. Bill soon closed the book and returned it to its place on the table.

'Dinah, you are wearing your hair up,' he observed.

'Of course,' she replied. She had turned eighteen, though no one else appeared to have given it a thought.

She had given Bill a lock of her own hair, she remembered, on the day of Sofia's funeral. She had taken his hand and placed the lock of hair in it, closing his fingers over it and clasping his hand to her and saying, *'Put this in the grave, Bill, please do this for me.'* And he had given her his solemn word that he would do this for her. After the funeral she had asked if he had done it and he had assured her he had done exactly as she had bidden. Yet in the moment between her asking and his reply his eyes had slid from hers and she had known, as surely as if she had been there herself, that he had forgotten.

—◈—

Despite Bill's homecoming it was not a late night.

After so many months without practice, Aurora observed, Dinah seemed to have lost her skill on the piano and could not be enticed to play another piece. Lucas was lost in thought and was clearly having to make an effort to rouse himself to converse with his eldest son. Fortunately Bill was in a loquacious mood and regaled them with tales of undergraduate life and Aurora, watching her eldest child from her chair by the fireplace, thought: he has accepted what has happened, he alone, amongst us all. And as she watched him she could not decide whether this was a good thing or not. It was good for Bill, perhaps.

'Well, it would appear the old place does not change much,' said Lucas of his old college, twirling his tumbler of port on the armrest of his chair. 'Lord knows, everything else changes at a terrifying rate.'

No one replied to this and soon Dinah excused herself and went off to bed. Aurora followed soon after, though found she did not feel tired. Upstairs in her room she sat by the window and listened to the sounds of the house. Presently she heard footsteps and a door open and close; not her husband's door, Bill's.

She stood up and went silently back downstairs. A lamp still burnt in the drawing room so she presumed Lucas was in there. She hesitated outside the door, wondering if he was aware of her presence outside, if he had heard her come down the stairs. She would look foolish standing here without going in. Bill had accepted what had happened, why shouldn't Lucas and why shouldn't she? Was it right that she, his wife, should hesitate to go into a room where her husband was?

But Mrs Logan was there. Mrs Logan was—doing *what*? What could she be doing at this time? Were her duties so numerous she had to work till past midnight to finish them?

'Mrs Jarmyn.'

And why did her greeting always sound like a challenge?

'Mrs Logan. Don't let me keep you.' And Aurora waited till the housekeeper had gone.

Her parents had had a housekeeper at their Chelsea house, though that had been a much grander establishment, a house that required a housekeeper. She had been a child then but even so she had only the faintest recollection of the woman who had faithfully served the family for a decade or longer. She had been invisible. A housekeeper ought to be invisible but

Mrs Logan was not invisible and somehow she was becoming more opaque with every passing week.

Aurora opened the drawing room door and stood in the doorway. Lucas was standing in the middle of the room, and he turned to face her, cradling a glass of port in his hand. Perhaps he had heard the interaction with Mrs Logan. Three years earlier when Mrs Logan had first arrived she had reacted, as any wife would, with outrage: the home was her domain and she had been undermined. What did it say about his faith in her ability to run his household that he had brought this woman into the house to run it for him? It was a humiliation not to be borne! Aurora had departed at once on an extended visit to a distant relative. Lucas had been furious. But if he had anticipated her meek acquiescence, if he had expected her return after a day or two, he had been mistaken. He had waited two weeks then come after her, by which time his fury had been frightening—and a little thrilling. But he had not married a meek and acquiescent wife. They had fought but in the end he had brought her home with him, once more the master of his own house, and the new housekeeper, whose position in the house she did not understand and whose presence she resented, had remained. She had given him his victory because his love for her, his passion after this breach, had been as it had in those first intoxicating years of their marriage.

But that was three years ago and now he was frowning, and whether at her or at his glass of port she could not tell. Perhaps he might offer her a glass? But he placed his glass on the table without taking a sip and she had an idea he was not pleased that she had seen him drinking.

'My dear,' he said, and his greeting was not the sort of greeting a husband gave to his wife, to the mother of his children. It was a challenge. She ignored the challenge and took it the way he had not intended it: as an endearment. She came into the room, closing the door and smiling at him.

'It's so nice to have Bill home,' she observed warmly. 'Is it not?'

'Yes. Certainly,' he replied, facing the fireplace. 'I thought you had retired?'

'I was not tired. I think it is Bill's return. It has quite invigorated me.'

'I am delighted you find yourself invigorated.'

She closed her eyes for a moment. 'Lucas, is it not time we put the past behind us? That we try to look forward a little?'

'I did not realise I was not doing exactly that.'

She came forward and spoke in a low voice. 'I was referring to our marriage, Lucas. To you and me,' and she placed a hand on his arm.

Instantly she felt the muscles in his forearm tense and he reached across and with his other hand removed her hand from his arm.

'*How can you suggest such a thing?*' and he turned and left the room.

When he had gone, she stood alone in the room for a long time before turning off the gaslight and going upstairs. There was no light from her husband's room and she went directly to her own room and closed the door.

Bill had come home and that was a good thing.

—◆—

There was no light from her husband's room because her husband had not lit the lamp. Instead Lucas stood quite still in the middle of the room in darkness.

The imprint of her fingers on his arm felt like the brand of a hot iron and it was all he could do not to rub at it to relieve the sensation. Why had she come to him like that? What had been her intention? Could she really not sense his disgust, his loathing? He had tried so very hard to hide it but some part of him had thought she must surely sense it—how could she not?

He had a memory of her in the days following their wedding, laughing and lovely and coquettish, hardly the blushing bride he had somehow expected. They had taken a walk in Hyde Park, she on his arm, and he had seen the gazes of other men on her and he had seen her eyes fixed on him and he had felt like the luckiest man alive. In the years that followed she had turned his household into a home and had given him five splendid children, she had presided over his dinner parties and sat beside him at church. These things alone meant nothing: they were what any wife did. It was the place in his heart that she had inhabited that set her apart.

Now that place was empty. Desolate. Uninhabited. Now he had to steel himself to sit at the same table as her.

But he would not let her see it. He was still her husband and he would not say what burnt inside him, even though it cost him everything to say nothing when the words threatened to erupt from him at every moment. He would not say it. He would take it to his grave rather than utter those words: *You killed our daughter. It is your fault she is dead.*

CHAPTER NINE

May–June 1880

IN THE GREAT CITY OF London time went on as usual: Parliament sat and laws were passed. Business was conducted and a great many people made fortunes and an even greater number went hungry. Lives were started and lives ended—sometimes on the same day and to the same individual. May drifted into June with a promise of summer in the air.

Inside 19 Cadogan Mews time had ceased. It no longer existed, it had no meaning. A silence had fallen that no one felt willing to break. Footsteps were muffled and commands, if they were uttered at all, were given in muted whispers in the hallways and corridors. Doors were kept closed and before entering hands hesitated on doorknobs and deep breaths were taken. An excuse not to enter at all was often found.

On the fifth morning after the fire Lucas stood outside the drawing room door at a loss. He had not slept for days. He imagined that no one had. The doctor had returned each morning and had shaken his head a great deal. The boys, Gus and Jack, were to be sent away to stay with their aunt and uncle in Great Portland Street. Mrs Logan was to arrange it. Aurora had emerged from her stupor briefly, but was now sedated again. Lucas had sat with her for a long time when he had no longer been able to sit with Sofia, stroking his wife's hair and kissing her sleeping eyes because his heart broke each time he thought of her waking and remembering.

The burn on Aurora's arm was worse than he had first realised. It would heal but it would scar horribly. He had helped the doctor to change the dressing. There was normal untouched pink flesh around the wound—one could at least see what normal unburnt flesh looked like. He could not help the doctor change his daughter's dressings. He left the house rather than listen to her screams.

He had prayed with all his strength but in his heart he had argued, Why should God save my child and yet let so many others perish? The answer was simple: God would not save her.

He pushed open the drawing room door and surveyed the scene, though it broke his heart afresh to do so. Sticking out from under an armchair was a child's shoe, an outdoors shoe made of brown suede with a buckle. He picked it up and held the shoe tightly in both hands and poured out his soul in great sobs that, until that moment, he had not been able to release.

After a time he calmed himself and looked about him. The room was untouched since the afternoon of the fire. The air was still heavy with smoke and other odours that for a moment caused him to put out a hand to the wall to steady himself. The wall was coated with grime from the fire. The carpet was singed but only in a thin oval-shaped ring. In the centre, where the Persian rug had lain, the carpet was untouched. Chairs and tables had been knocked over and Lucas stooped and righted one or two then made himself stop. Amazingly the side table on which a sherry decanter and a glass had been placed lay undisturbed and unspilt. The decanter's glass stopper was out as if someone had been drinking, or pouring a drink, at the exact moment—

At the exact moment.

He picked up the stopper and replaced it slowly into the decanter.

'Who's there?'

He wheeled around to see the major standing motionless and silent in the doorway. For a moment both men regarded each other. Slowly, calmly, Lucas returned the decanter to the sideboard. The major responded better to slow, calm movements. And for the last five days he had been in a state of prolonged agitation and distress—so much so that Mrs Logan had begged more pills from Dr Frobisher, and that had seemed to do the trick.

'Come away now, Uncle, this is no place to dwell,' Lucas said gently, holding out his arm in a way suggestive of their departure from the room.

But the major made no move to leave. Lucas looked into the old man's eyes and, for a second, experienced a view of the world deeper, more intricate than he had known existed. A war was raging but it was not simply on a battlefield in the Crimean Peninsula a quarter of a century ago, it was right here and now. He lowered his eyes, deeply troubled.

'She oughtn't to have been drinking. She got too close to the fire and the pretty little girl tried to save her.' The major's voice had a curious youthful quality that was horribly at odds with the broken man who uttered these words.

'What did you say?'

Lucas advanced on the old man, his heart lurching inside him, but the major pressed the palms of his hands against his temples and began to rock back and forth.

'Uncle, *please*! What did you just say?'

'She tried to save her but her dress caught alight,' and the major began to weep, tears streaming down his face, and Lucas gazed at him, appalled.

'My wife? Are you referring to Aurora? Are you saying that she got too close to the fire and Sofia tried to save her? Is that what you are saying? Uncle?'

But the old man had gone, or the lucid part of him at any rate, and though Lucas shook the old soldier's shoulder vigorously he knew it was of no use.

'Father. Mama has awoken and is calling for you.'

Lucas came out of the room, leading the major, closing the door behind him and turning the key in the lock. Dinah was standing in the turn on the staircase waiting for him but his heart had turned as black as charcoal and, rather than go to this wife, he left the house without a word.

CHAPTER TEN

London and the Midlands: December 1880

THE FIRST SNOW FELL THE day before Christmas Eve and London at once became bright and muffled and mysterious where before it had been dark and noisy and all too familiar. Young ladies took carriages along Regent Street and walked arm-in-arm in Hyde Park, hands deep in fur muffs, and those who were old enough to remember it recalled the last time the Thames had frozen over and how they had skated from one bank to the other risking certain death should the ice crack and they fall through to it to the waters below.

At 19 Cadogan Mews, Cook sealed off the kitchen and prepared her Christmas pudding following an ancient recipe known only to herself. The preparations completed, the doors were thrown open and the family trooped down to each take a turn at stirring the batter. When it was stirred and a lucky silver threepenny dropped in, Cook pressed the batter into a mould, tied a cloth around it and boiled it for six hours, then it was hung in the larder to age.

On Christmas Eve, and in deference to Prince Albert, a tree was brought into the house and decorated. Gus questioned why they were observing a German tradition especially now Prince Albert was dead, and Bill observed that, if enough English people did it, then it became an English tradition, didn't it? In the evening they sat around the piano and Dinah was persuaded to play so that they could sing carols, though they did not sing 'God Rest Ye Merry Gentlemen', which had been Sofia's favourite.

On Christmas Day the family went to church and afterwards Mrs Jarmyn and Dinah distributed a basket of food at the infirmary in Bedford Street. For dinner they ate roast goose and applesauce and Jack got the silver threepenny bit which meant that he would marry within the year and Dinah felt a little lost and sad and wondered why she had not found the lucky penny herself.

On Boxing Day Mrs Logan packed two bags and Mr Jarmyn journeyed north.

The inquiry into the Lea's Crossing railway accident was set to commence the following day but the snowfalls of the last few days meant that there were no trains out of Birmingham and he was forced to take a room at the Railway Hotel. A telegram awaiting him there informed him that the Board of Trade officials had been similarly inconvenienced and the inquiry delayed. It was eventually convened, two days late, on the twenty-ninth.

The mood at Wolverhampton was menacing. The previous day a gentleman identified—wrongly—as an official of the railway company had been set upon and beaten and now lay senseless in the infirmary. Protestors had journeyed up from the capital and from all parts of the Kingdom in time for the hearing and could be seen haranguing from platforms and handing out tracts. The crowds outside the Town Hall had not been dampened by either the inclement weather nor the enforced delay in proceedings and, despite the local constabulary forming a solid ring around the building, Lucas had to run the gauntlet of the mob simply to reach the hall in time for the first session. One of the protestors threw a stone that bounced off his shoulder and another thrust a pamphlet in his face which he made the mistake of reading:

Staplehurst—Shipton-on-Cherwell—Abbots

Ripton—Wombourne

And now **Lea's Crossing!**

88 **DEAD!** 263 **INJURED!**

When will the **CARNAGE** end?

Demand action NOW!

Demand an **ACT OF PARLIAMENT** to regulate rail safety!

Staplehurst, Shipton-on-Cherwell, Abbots Ripton and, of course, Wombourne. Four horrific railway accidents forever imprinted in the public's consciousness; forever identified with malevolent, grasping black-hatted railway owners placing profit above human lives. Lucas screwed up the pamphlet and stuffed it into his pocket.

'Four days it has taken me to get to this wretched place,' remarked Kemp, who was waiting for him just inside the main entrance. 'Why do we build our railways in such distant and dismal locations?'

'So that we do not have to travel on them ourselves,' Lucas replied. He was not pleased that Kemp was here. He would have preferred Freebody or Hart or even Sinclair again, at a pinch. But not Kemp. 'Do we know who is chairing the inquiry?'

'Llewellyn.'

'Ah.'

Llewellyn was a retired colonel who had chaired the Wombourne inquiry three years earlier. His report on that occasion had laid the blame for the accident squarely with the railway and his summation of its directors and practices had been scathing and widely reported in the newspapers at the time.

'Well, this inquiry is not going to be quite so cut and dried, I trust,' said Kemp. 'Good luck to him trying to prove our signals froze. Even if he does, he can hardly hold the company responsible for a frost, can he?' he said, echoing the words of Standish, the locomotive superintendent.

'No doubt he can and will,' Lucas replied, finding Kemp's bullish manner irritating. 'Shall we go in?'

They followed the jostling crowds into the same chamber in which the inquest had been started and soon adjourned some three weeks earlier. They had arrived in good time but the hall was already packed to bursting and most of the public benches had been taken, some with entire families settling down with rugs and pipes and pies and bottles of ginger beer as though to attend some country fair. The air was so charged, the volume of voices and eating and drinking and smoking and spitting so great, that Colonel Llewellyn, on first taking his chair, at once stood up and ordered the marshals to remove all persons who were not sitting in an orderly and silent fashion. This created a stir and a delay that further put back proceedings by some quarter of an hour but did at least result in Lucas and Kemp finding themselves seats in the front row.

Llewellyn, who had been a substantial man three years earlier at the Wombourne inquiry, was now positively vast and the table at which he placed himself shuddered as he leant his bulk against it, and the scribes and other officials on either side of him were dwarfed like children beside him.

'A man who grows fat on the suffering and destruction of others,' observed Kemp in a low voice.

'This man does not cause that suffering and destruction, he merely tries to find out the truth behind it to ensure it does not happen again,' Lucas replied tersely, wishing Kemp were back in London.

'And if it did not happen again, he would be forced to find some other employ, would he not?'

'If there was no investigation then public confidence would not be restored and no one would dare to travel on our railway.'

'Yes they would. People would still need to travel. They would have no choice.'

'*Damn* you, Kemp! I happen to believe in this process, I am here to work *with* this inquiry not against it. We have nothing to hide: if we are at fault then let it be known.'

'Laudable words.'

'Ladies and gentlemen, it is high time we got these proceedings under way,' declared Llewellyn in a booming voice that silenced the chamber.

Lucas tried to settle himself in his seat as Llewellyn introduced himself and the other officials on the committee and proceeded to outline the scope and nature of the inquiry. He had made the same speech three years earlier at the Wombourne inquiry and Lucas had sat in the front row of that inquiry with Kemp beside him.

He looked down, wondering if Kemp were thinking the same thing. The horror of that fortnight of testimony from the survivors and the relatives of the dead was still there, three years later. And the company had introduced additional safety measures as a result of the inquiry. Yet here they were, three years later.

Kemp had smoked a cigar, he remembered, as they had stood outside the inquiry on the first day. No doubt he would do so again today.

—∞—

The inquiry into the Lea's Crossing railway accident was to run for some weeks: there were, after all, upwards of sixty witnesses to examine and sworn depositions to be made. Many of these witnesses waited now in a small, windowless antechamber off the main chamber. Some were employees of the railway company. The guard of the ill-fated train, an ageing man with mutton-chop whiskers and a resigned air, was called to make his statement first, followed by the stationmaster at Dawley Station, a worried-looking individual with round spectacles which he removed half a dozen times and polished with a large red handkerchief. After him came a number of other railway employees: foremen and guards and superintendents. Outside in the corridor a never-ending stream of clerks and officials in tall hats and black coats strode back and forth staggering under the weight of documents and ledgers and talking in low voices. They seemed unaware of the people waiting in the small, windowless antechamber.

Finally the first of the passengers was called: a farm worker, his hair thinning, his body stiffened by a lifetime of manual labour, a cap twisting between two huge hands, who told the inquiry, in a broken voice, 'My son's legs were crushed in't smash. He were to tek up an apprenticeship as a tanner. It were all arranged. We were travelling together t'Birmingham so he could begin his apprenticeship. Now what is to become of him? He cannot walk, much less take up his apprenticeship.'

The man's words were recorded but no one attempted to answer his question. Next came a pregnant woman, whose husband had been knocked insensible by the crash and who could now no longer speak nor feed himself. She had cried throughout her deposition, dabbing a sodden handkerchief to her eyes. Eventually she had been led, fainting, from the room by an official. Then came the man, Brinklow, whose child had been killed. Whilst what had gone before had unsettled the attendant crowd, the arrival of Brinklow sent a thrill of anticipation through the room.

Brinklow was tall though slightly built for a foundry worker. He wore a collarless shirt and a jacket and trousers that fit him badly and, like the man whose son's legs had been crushed, he held his cap tightly in his fists. Only those seated at the clerk's desks and in the front few rows of the chamber could see his face clearly. What they saw was a thin moustache and badly shaved chin, a flattish nose slightly awry as though once broken, grey expressionless eyes. They saw the lean, hollow look of a man who worked hard and never had quite enough to eat. They saw an unremarkable face where they had expected to see something else.

'Mr Brinklow, please state for the inquiry your name and profession.'

'Thomas Brinklow of Blackstone Cottages, Foundry Lane, Dawley, Shropshire. I am a foundry worker, second class, at Spendlow's Iron Company, Iron Works and Heating Engineers in Dawley.'

An unremarkable reply made in an unremarkable voice. Whether this was a God-fearing man or a drunk, or neither, the people listening could not tell.

'Mr Brinklow, you understand that this is not a court of law and that no one today is standing trial? You understand the purpose of this inquiry, that it is to investigate the events surrounding, to ascertain the cause of and, where possible, to make recommendations on, the terrible train crash that took place at Lea's Crossing on the fifth of this month?'

'Aye, sir.'

'Very well. Would you now please relate in your own words, and in as much detail as you are able, the events of that day from the point at which you boarded the train at Dawley.'

At this the man faltered but he took a breath and once he had begun he did not waver in his account and his account was all the more terrible for that:

'On that Sunday—the fifth day of December—I were travelling t'fair in Wolverhampton with my daughter, Alice, who was nine years old. Her ma did not come as she were unwell that day. We took the afternoon train from Dawley to Wolverhampton. We boarded a third-class carriage at the front of the train and I sat on a bench and my little girl sat on my lap. The train started out and it were late, maybe fifteen or twenty minutes late, I cannot say for sure and I do not know why the train was late. The carriage were full. A lot of folk were attending the fair and a great number of folk were crowded into the carriage. Any road, we went along and travelled quite fast, perhaps to make up time. Then we came alongside a canal at a place, I was told later, that folk call Lea's Crossing. This were about a quarter of an hour since we had left Dawley. There were nowt wrong then far as I could tell. The train jolted and some folk fell over and cried out but it did not seem to be anything worse than a slowing of the train, sudden-like. Then there was a second jolt straight after the first. This was more like a loud bang and we were all thrown about. There was a fearful alarm and panic and folk screaming and the like, and I were thrown out of my seat clear across the carriage. I had hold of my little girl, I think, though I cannot say for sure. We knew at once we had crashed. The train had stopped but folk were trapped and making a dreadful clamour. I was stunned at first and unable to get up but I soon did and went to look for my little girl. Folk were hurt, I could see, and I was very afraid. I found her, my little Alice, lying at some distance from me, and she had been thrown across the carriage and had hit something. I learnt later that a metal rod had pierced her straight through though at first I did not know this. I called to her but she did not answer. I went to her and thought at first she must be dead but she was breathing though she stopped soon after and she was dead.'

His words ended and in the silence that followed Kemp lit a cigar and took his first puff.

—⁘—

Naturally, Kemp was only too pleased to be called upon to address the inquiry but Lucas forestalled him, insisting that he himself take the stand and answer the committee's questions and present the company's case. Kemp's attitude towards the accident was hard enough to stomach as a fellow director. If the inquiry or the public or the banks of waiting newspapermen got wind of it, it could be explosive. So on the third day of the inquiry it was Lucas who faced Llewellyn across the chamber of the packed Town Hall.

'Could you please state for the purposes of this inquiry your name and position?'

'Certainly. I am Mr Lucas Jarmyn and I am a director of the North West Midlands Railway Company.'

'Thank you, Mr Jarmyn. Your father, I believe, built the railway?'

'That is correct.'

'*Bet he never travelled on it!*' quipped a male voice from the gallery and a number of people laughed.

'I would respectfully request that members of the public refrain from commenting,' said Llewellyn, fixing the gallery with a look over his spectacles, and the gallery fell silent. 'Mr Jarmyn, can you please outline for this inquiry your company's policy on safety?'

'Certainly. But with the inquiry's permission, I wish to express, on behalf of the company, our terrible grief and regret at this dreadful accident, to assure the committee that every request made by this inquiry will be met; and to reassure the public that every effort has been made to contact the relatives of the deceased and injured so that everything within our power could be done for them to ease their suffering.'

It was not the first time Lucas had delivered this speech. He had done so at the Wombourne inquiry. He trusted he would not have to do so again. But it was important that the committee and, most particularly, the public, understood the company's desire to help, to do all that it reasonably could.

'*Words! Empty words!*'

Lucas tried to identify the person who had called out but saw only a mass of faces, row upon row of them, and any one of them could have said it.

'*Your words mean nothing!*' A different voice this time.

'*Shame!*'

'*Boo!*'

'*One* more interjection of that nature and the perpetrators will be *ejected* from the chamber,' boomed Llewellyn, slamming an enormous leather-bound ledger down on the tabletop with a loud thud that startled the gallery into silence. '*Thank* you. Mr Jarmyn, this inquiry notes your company's words but is keen to hear its policy on safety?'

'Naturally we are only too happy to supply whatever information is required of us. This company has long followed a policy of safety first, profit second—'

'*He must be a very poor man, then,*' someone called out.

'*He don't look it!*' a second added.

'This company's safety record is second to *none*,' declared Lucas, addressing the gallery.

This only evoked jeers.

'*He means no other railway company has a record SO BAD!*' a man called out, rising to his feet and pointing an accusing finger.

'*Hear, hear!*'

'*You tell 'em, lad!*'

'*I'll wager he never travels on his own trains!*'

'*Too scared!*'

'Marshals, eject this man,' demanded Llewellyn, and the man who had stood up was man-handled out of the chamber to the derision of the crowd. 'Please continue, Mr Jarmyn.'

'Thank you. I— we—' Lucas consulted the notes he had brought with him. 'This company has, throughout its history, attempted to keep abreast of the latest developments in regard to passenger and employee safety. The company's rules and regulations are most specific regarding the various precautionary measures that must be taken prior to every train's departure. A copy of these rules and regulations has been made available to this inquiry. The committee will already be aware that as a result of an earlier investigation all our wheel fastenings were replaced with a sort recommended by the inquiry. Communication cords for the use of both crew and passengers have long been in use. A system of continuous brakes was adopted as early as 1868—'

'Thank you, Mr Jarmyn. The committee notes these laudable measures introduced by your railway to secure the safety of its passengers. However, none of the measures listed were enough to prevent this particular accident?'

'Surely that remains to be established?' Lucas countered.

'Indeed. We have heard at length from various employees of the company including the signalman on duty on that fateful day and, though the exact details of that day are still in dispute, it has been established that signals have a tendency to freeze and that, if frozen, they will default to the "clear" position, whether in fact the line ahead is clear or not, is that correct?'

'I understand there may have been cases where this has occurred, yes.'

'Indeed. And, this being so, what measures have your company taken to ensure against it?'

'*Nowt! They have taken nowt!*'

'It has *not* been proven that this was the case in this instance,' Lucas countered, yet his words sounded defensive even to his own ears. He had not anticipated this level of hostility. 'Nor has it been proven that any such incident has ever occurred on our lines—'

'*They care nowt about the folk who travel on their trains!*'

'*Nothing* has been proven. The cause of this accident could well have been driver error—' Lucas felt the blood rush to this face.

'*Murderers!*'

'Only three people died!' he countered, rising to his feet.

'*How many more have to die?*'

'The company can hardly be held responsible for a frost!' he shouted above the fury of the crowd, and in the front row Kemp calmly puffed at his cigar.

CHAPTER ELEVEN

London and the Transvaal: January 1881

FROM THE DECK OF THE steamer *Orion* Roger Brightside watched as the Cape coastline sailed smoothly and rapidly past the port side of the ship.

Loaded with twenty tons of ammunition, a battery of artillery and a hundred and fifty horses and men, they had departed from Portsmouth on the nine o'clock tide and it had been smooth sailing across the Channel, along the northern Spanish coast, wheeling around to strike southwards, docking briefly at Madeira, then due south again to the island of St Helena and finally southeast till they had hit the southern African coastline with its strange tropical sounds and smells, the air thick with a humidity foreign and unfamiliar to a Northern European man, where nameless and vividly hued birds circled and swooped overhead. They had rounded the Cape in thirty-foot seas and the ship had bucked and lurched for a day before finally forging a path through to calmer waters. Swinging north, they had continued to follow the coastline. Now, on this fine and tranquil first day of the New Year, and a mere eighteen days since their departure, their destination was in sight.

They had received no news of the war since leaving Madeira—had Colley marched on Kruger? Had Kruger already surrendered? Or was it all still to be decided?

God, let it be so! thought Roger, for would he not look rather foolish taking such solemn leave of everyone at home and sailing all this way only to find it had all been decided before he had even struck land!

The ship wheeled a degree or two to port and it seemed that they were making towards the shore.

'Durban,' said Lieutenant Graves, who had come to the rail to stand near him. Graves held a tiny brass spyglass to his eye, and he now held it out to Roger. Roger put it to his eye and could instantly make out a long bluff of rolling green hills thrusting out of the coastline and forming a natural harbour beyond which was a cluster of single-storey buildings on the distant shoreline. A port was now visible, with a series of wooden pontoons thrusting into the harbour and a great number of merchant and naval vessels of all sizes lined up side by side.

He removed the spyglass and the port vanished.

'How far would you say, Graves?'

'An hour's sailing, no more.'

Roger nodded and lifted the glass once more to his eye. It was too far away for him to make out any figures but the vessels, moored side by side, their sails lowered, appeared tranquil. At peace.

And oddly, he felt a flicker of fear.

'Here,' and he handed the glass back, anxious to smother the feeling, concerned lest Graves might sense it. He thought of the dinner with his cousins in Cadogan Mews. The boy who had sat at their table in his new uniform (could it really be only three weeks ago?) and spoken boastfully of his role in the coming war now seemed like another person. He thought of Dinah, who had sat silently throughout the meal barely listening to him talk about army life when the boys—Jack, in particular—had been eager for every detail and he had been eager to give it. She had got up and left the table and she had done so with relief it now seemed. Had he been such a bore, then? Had he been so boastful? She must have known he had only come that evening to see her.

He leant out over the ship's railings and a fine mist of sea spray covered his face. He tasted salt water on his lips and tongue.

He had waited for a word from her, a letter, but none had come. He had imagined a token being offered—a flower placed in his buttonhole that someone would later press and that he would henceforth carry in his pocket-book. Or a lock of her hair placed in the palm of his hand, no words spoken, just a look exchanged and her fingers closing urgently over his. But no token had been offered: no flower plucked, no lock of hair cut. No look exchanged.

Had it all been a dream then? Did she, in fact, not love him? The thought, once realised, would not be dislodged and he felt his face grow cold.

A seagull wheeled overhead, diving and squawking, and one of the other officers took a pot shot at it and missed.

It was News Year's Day. At midnight, the bells had rung out across London to herald the New Year. This morning's *Times* reported that the Queen, Princess Louise and Princess Beatrice had taken a drive in the Royal coach through Cowes and Newport and there was a lengthy and patriotic article detailing the steamships that were being hastily fitted out at Woolwich and loaded with troops, horses and supplies in preparation for their imminent departure for the war in the Transvaal.

And, though *The Times* did not see fit to report it, Mr (formerly the Reverend) Travers Brightside, following the disavowal of his only son, Roger, had written a tract and embarked on an anti-war lecture tour of the North. He was, according to Aunt Meredith's latest communication, currently at Oldham, where he had been met with jeering and a pelting of rotten fruit: the war was proving a tricky adversary. There had been no word from Cousin Roger since his departure and, with the Brightside men absent under such difficult circumstances Dinah and Bill had arranged to dine in Great Portland Street with their aunt and cousin to lend moral support.

Brother and sister had not said a great deal to each other since that first evening of Bill's return and they sat now in silence as the hansom cab made its way northwards along Gower Street, each lost in their own thoughts.

It seemed that, though you could have the same parents, live for almost the same number of years in the same house with the same people, it was no guarantee you would grow into the same type of person—or this was Bill's observation, at any rate.

It was not simply that Dinah was a girl: he very much doubted he had much in common with his younger brothers either. And he seemed to be constantly at odds with his father. Bill was annoyed and, yes, perhaps a little hurt though he could not have said why. He was impatient to return to Oxford. He smoked and frowned out of the window.

He caught Dinah's reflection in the glass of the cab's window, and that made him think of the lock of hair she had given him on the day of Sofia's funeral, asking him to place it in the grave. He had put the lock of hair for safety in the handkerchief in his pocket and had not thought about it again until he had been sitting in the carriage on the way back from the funeral, when he had taken his handkerchief out of his pocket and seen it still in there. He had felt badly about it at the time, particularly when Dinah had asked him that evening if he had done as she had asked. He had lied to her and later had disposed of the lock and not thought of it since. Now he shifted uneasily in the cab and wished he had not remembered the incident, for what was to be gained by chafing? The deed was done—or not done—and Dinah could not discover his deception. It was best forgotten.

With a burst of something he could not quite comprehend, he found he needed to unburden himself of this lie. 'Dinah—' he began, turning to her. But the driver had pulled up his horse, jumped down and thrown the cab door open and the moment was gone.

'I told Tilda we were having Dinah to dine with us,' their cousin Rhoda explained. (Tilda was the Brightsides' maid. She had been with them for only a month.) 'Of course, I ought to have said, We are having Miss Jarmyn to dine with us, but it sounded so much more amusing to say, We are having *Dinah* to *dine*. And poor Tilda had no idea at all to what I was referring! She was completely baffled,' and Rhoda laughed.

His cousin Rhoda, Bill observed, had not improved much. She dressed very well and had a very proper bearing and pretty manners which was all to the good, but really when she opened her mouth it was all undone and the truly breathtaking insipid stupidity that lay within was at once exposed. So it had always been; he ought not to be surprised.

'Really, Rhoda, teasing the servants is in very poor taste,' admonished Aunt Meredith and, regarding his aunt, Bill saw the woman that Rhoda would become in another twenty years: petty and a little querulous and certainly disappointed. He sat back in his chair and marvelled at how a few months away sharpened one's instincts and allowed a clarity about one's family that had previously been absent.

'All the more so in the circumstances,' his aunt went on. The 'circumstances' of course were Roger's feud with his father and his imminent part in a war on the other side of the world, and Uncle Travers' apparently fruitless lecture tour of the North.

'Have you heard from Roger?' Bill inquired, though he was fairly certain they had not. Beside him Dinah stirred as though he had said something he should not, but, damn it all, that was the reason they were here, wasn't it: Roger, the war, the feud? He decided to ignore his sister's sensibilities.

'We've heard nothing,' confirmed Aunt Meredith. 'They were to go via Madeira and St Helena and to arrive at Durban in three weeks—that is all we know. Indeed he may have arrived already, for all we know. He may be engaging the enemy this very minute.'

'Not at night, Mama, surely?' said Rhoda.

'It is war, Rhoda, not a tennis party,' her mother chided. 'These Boers have little concern for the niceties of civilised society.'

'And is there any more news of Uncle Travers?' Bill asked, keen to forestall his aunt's appraisal of the situation in the Transvaal.

'Not since he arrived at Oldham, no,' Aunt Meredith replied. 'He was to speak at the Methodist church hall this evening, I understand, though the hostile reception he received earlier may have prevented this.'

'The war is proving popular then?' said Dinah, who had remained silent throughout this discussion.

'Or Father is proving unpopular—it is difficult to say which,' said Rhoda.

They fell silent as the baffled Tilda entered and proceeded to serve the fish course. Bill watched the maid and thought about his cousin Roger who was on the far side of the world fighting a war whose purpose was unclear at best, and about his uncle who was giving a lecture tour of the North in opposition of this same war. Did they cancel each other out, he wondered? Which of them, his cousin or his uncle, would prevail?

'You have not thought of taking a commission and going to the Transvaal yourself, Bill?' inquired Rhoda, startling Bill out of his reverie.

'Certainly not! I should hope I have too much common sense for such an absurd course of action.'

His words, spoken in haste and without forethought, had the effect of dousing an already uncertain mood and they ate the remainder of the meal for the most part in silence.

CHAPTER TWELVE

London

IN THE THIRD HOUR OF the battle his troop charged the Russian lines and Austin found himself temporarily cut off from his men.

The smoke from the battery of guns up on the hillside and from the shot of the percussion muskets used by the Russian infantry created a fog that smothered everyone and everything, a fog that caught at your lungs and made you choke, reducing visibility down to an arm's length. It was disorienting, even for the most hardened soldier. Made you lose your way. Made you stumble into the enemy and not realise it until the fellow was right there on top of you with a sword a yard from your head. It muffled noise so that a voice on your left sounded like it was behind you, a shouted order to retreat sounded much like a command to advance. Even the bugles were distorted.

He had become cut off from his men, from his own side, and he was no longer mounted—his horse had been shot from under him. He could not recall when or where.

In the melee he had been aware only of the need to prevail. He had cut down two Cossack troopers—knocked them out of the battle at any rate: one with a slash of his sword that caught the fellow in the neck, and he had gone down in an arc of blood. The other he had slashed at across the chest and had not stopped to see the results of his strike, pushing ever onwards. And now he found himself alone.

He stood perfectly still and let the muffled noise, the fog, swirl around him. No point blundering about like a damned fool. More chaps killed that way. Stop for a moment, get your bearings.

He crouched down to make himself less of a target, rehousing his sword. His left hand was covered in blood, he saw with surprise, for he felt nothing. He reached with his right hand for his handkerchief and attempted to wrap it around his injured hand: it was his little finger. It had been cut clean off. He saw the bone. For a moment he felt faint. He clapped the dressing over the hand and rallied. The finger was no longer his concern. It was not his finger. He wondered why it did not hurt.

He reached for his sword and, as a brief gust of wind caused the fog to momentarily lift, thought he saw a dragoon from his own regiment over to his left just as the man fell, a dead weight, to the ground. Behind him, perhaps ten yards away, sat a Russian cavalryman, mounted, a rifle smoking in his hand.

He was a fine-looking fellow in his tall cylindrical peaked red cap, in a jacket and pelisse both of dark green, the braiding across his chest torn and stained with the blood of battle: a giant upon a great foaming chestnut horse. He sported a massive moustache, his face white, his eyes very black. As the smoke swirled about him Austin could see the nap of the man's tunic, the red stripe down the length of his breeches, the ridges of the man's knuckles as he held the rifle steady before him. He saw all this and more and he drank it in because he knew this was the man who would kill him.

But you didn't wait like a lame dog to be shot at.

Austin raised his sword and let out a shout, launching himself at the man.

When he opened his eyes the smoke had dispersed. He could see clearly. Even the smell of gunshot had gone. And there was an odd silence, aside from the slow and steady ticking of a clock.

He turned his head and saw a furnished room in daylight. Heavy curtains in red velvet hung beside a bay window, reaching to the carpeted floor. Through the window he could see sunlight, a patch of sky, rooftops, chimneys, smoke—but not gunpowder smoke.

The walls were papered in crimson flock and a painting of the Madonna and Child atop a cloud and observed by two pensive cherubs hung above the mantel. A confusing array of ottomans, upright chairs and easy chairs cluttered around a writing desk, a console table, an occasional table and a large round table in the centre of the room. A highly polished grand piano stood in the corner, a palm in a brass pot nestling beside it.

He knew this room though he could not recall how he knew it. He recognised the painting: it was Raphael's *Sistine Madonna* and it had hung on the wall of his father's house though this was not his father's house.

But his injuries did not hurt and that was the thing. What injuries had he sustained? Had the Russian fellow shot him?

Yes, he believed now that the fellow had indeed shot at him, he distinctly recalled the recoil of the weapon, the puff of smoke and an instant later the noise of the explosion.

Then . . . nothing.

Had the fellow missed? At that range? It seemed unlikely. And yet here he was.

Austin put up a hand instinctively to his head and his fingers found a face that was not quite as he remembered it: an indentation, a groove that had not been there before. He lowered his fingers thoughtfully. What must he look like, with this new face? He moved uneasily in the chair. There would be a mirror, surely, in a room like this (what room *was* this like? He did not know). But what did it matter what new face he had: he was not a vain man. There was no wife waiting for him back in England. He was a soldier.

He knew at that moment that he *was* in England, that this was no field hospital. This was not the Crimea. This was undoubtedly an English sitting room. He stirred uneasily again. How long, then, had it been since he had faced the Russian cavalry officer in the smoke?

He looked down at his hand, at once fearful. The little finger had been cut clean off and he had wrapped his handkerchief around it. Yes, it was gone and yet the skin had grown back over the wound, was as smooth and aged as the skin elsewhere on his hand.

He touched the stump of the amputated digit and felt nothing. No pain, no tenderness. The stump felt exactly the same as all his other fingers.

And now he saw that the skin on his hand was not as he remembered it at all. It was wrinkled, spotted. The fine hairs on the back of his hands were quite white. He looked at the other hand and it was the same.

At once the fear of standing on a confused, bloodied battlefield surrounded by an unseen enemy and armed only with a sword was as nothing to the fear that welled up inside him now. He gripped the arms of the chair with both hands to steady himself and watched in horror as the flesh puckered into deep ridges.

He pulled himself to his feet and staggered forward, only saving himself from falling by putting out his hands towards a long mahogany sideboard that ran the length of the room. He was injured, naturally he would be weak. Stiff. Yes, his limbs felt stiff. He waited, catching his breath, feeling his heart beating rapidly but feebly.

It was silent in the house, aside from the damnable ticking of that unseen clock. Where was everyone? Why had they brought him here? Why had they left him?

He turned slowly around. A young woman was standing in the doorway observing him. The woman—in fact, he saw now that she was not much more than a girl of perhaps eighteen—wore her hair up and was dressed in a long silk gown of an unusual style. Could ladies' fashions have changed so rapidly whilst he had been away at war? She had a sweet face, high cheekbones, clear grey eyes, a pale and unblemished complexion. He envied her.

She came into the room, smiling a little, and said something to him, then went over to the fireplace and stood quite motionless with an expression that spoke of so much yet told him nothing. There was no fire in the grate and the coals were lifeless but she reached for the poker and stirred the dead embers and it occurred to him that the girl was holding something tightly in, that she was shielding something from him. Or from herself. He found he no longer envied her.

She stooped then, as though she might light the fire.

In a moment of appalling clarity Austin knew exactly what was going to happen for he realised he had seen it once before: the coals would flare into life and the flames leap up as a wind rushed down the chimney. The swirling silk skirts of the girl's dress would brush against the flames and catch and with a whoosh the girl's hair would ignite until, in a horrifying instant, she was a column of fire.

But before it could happen Austin launched himself at her with a roar, intent on saving her. He could smell burning flesh and he knew it was not a smell from the battlefield: it was the smell inside this room.

From other parts of the house people came running.

—⁂—

Aurora stood outside her husband's study preparing her words carefully. She imagined Lucas sitting in his armchair, poring over some Board of Trade report and nursing a glass of port. He would not welcome her intrusion, but it could not be helped. She would make him listen. She knocked briefly on the door and opened it.

He was seated, not in the armchair but at his desk, papers spread before him, and he looked up as she appeared in the doorway. Aurora hesitated. She had intended to be strong but a fear suddenly gripped her and for a moment she could not catch her breath or form her words.

'Lucas, I must speak with you. I am sorry to report that I believe we can no longer maintain my uncle.'

She closed the door behind her and awaited his reply. He had turned away and now placed his elbows on the desktop, his fingers locked together, chin resting on his hands. He did not move for some moments. Finally he stirred.

'By "no longer maintain" I presume you mean no longer keep him here in our household?'

'Yes, I do. He is my uncle and I believe I know what is best.'

'For him?'

'Certainly. And for us.'

'And this, I presume, is because of the incident earlier?'

'I am afraid so, yes—he all but attacked Dinah!'

Lucas frowned. 'I have never known him violent before this, at least not towards others.'

'Nor have I and yet Dinah says when she entered the drawing room he appeared alarmed by her and he lunged at her. Dinah was very much frightened.'

Lucas considered this. 'I believe it takes much to frighten Dinah,' he said quietly.

'There you are then, is it not proof of how much distressed she was? I too was not a little disconcerted, for her safety as well as my own.'

Or was he unconcerned for her safety?

He did not agree nor disagree with this statement. Instead he replied:

'Where is he now?'

'Mrs Logan is with him. I believe she calmed him.'

For Mrs Logan could calm her uncle when she no longer could. The failing appalled her. And the way their housekeeper forced her presence into the room between them without even being here, that appalled her too. But she would not be put off. She would make Lucas react! She would force him to care!

'Lucas, I no longer feel safe. I no longer know what he is capable of.'

He made no reply. His fingers softly tapped on the desk. In the distance a horse clattered noisily across Cadogan Square, passing the end of the mews and away.

'What do you propose?' he said at last.

'He needs proper care and attention from people who know how to deal with his sort of problems.'

'The mad house.'

'An asylum, yes. Is there some alternative?'

Lucas turned back to his desk and reopened the report he had been reading.

'I will consider it.'

Aurora stood silently behind him as he began to read but clearly the interview was concluded. She turned and left the room.

—⚅—

No sooner had she gone than Lucas threw down the Board of Trade report in disgust. He was aware of the incident that afternoon and of Dinah's own recounting of the event: the major had been confused and disoriented, as he was much of the time, but something had frightened him. The fireplace, or her proximity to it, Dinah had guessed. Well, little wonder after what the old man had witnessed. And now Aurora wanted to rid herself of him—why?

He very well knew why and the reason sickened him: Austin had been the only witness to the drunkenness that had resulted in his daughter's horrific death. No wonder she could not face him. Or his secret. Well, he would be damned if he would agree to her wishes.

He crushed the papers in his hand.

Let her suffer.

—⁂—

A serving woman had assisted Austin back to his quarters and the major allowed himself to be partially undressed. He lay down on the bed. He felt so tired. His limbs appeared to have no strength in them. It was good to lie down. He would close his eyes, just for a moment. It was safe here. The battle was a long way off and in the meantime he was safe here.

He closed his eyes.

In the third hour of the battle his troop charged the Russian lines and Austin found himself temporarily cut off from his men. The smoke from the battery of guns up on the hillside and from the shot of the percussion muskets used by the Russian infantry created a fog that smothered everyone and everything, a fog that caught at your lungs and made you choke, reducing visibility down to an arm's length. It was disorienting, even for the most hardened soldier.

It made you lose your way.

CHAPTER THIRTEEN

'I AM AFRAID I HAVE some sad news,' said Mr Jarmyn, seated at the head of the table, and he nodded briefly to Hermione, who was hovering behind his chair with the soup tureen and a ladle.

Everyone paused, spoons poised midway to mouths. Dinah had just that moment lifted a glass to her mouth and she replaced it now on the table and waited. She was aware of an increase in her heart rate, of the slightest quickening of her pulse.

'Your cousin Roger has, I am sorry to relate, been reported killed.'

Gus, sitting opposite her and with his spoon still poised, looked to left and right as though in some confusion and after a moment placed the spoon back in his soup bowl. Jack, sitting to Gus's left, looked down at the table and shifted his position in his seat without looking up. Bill reached out a hand and moved the silver salt cellar an inch to the left then moved it back again. Their mother, sitting at the far end of the table, a crystal tumbler in her hands, smiled brightly and her eyes glistened in the gaslight. She took a sip from the glass then replaced it silently on the table.

Dinah saw all this very vividly yet from a great distance as though she were peering at them down the wrong end of a telescope.

Her father nodded again to Hermione who withdrew the tureen and her ladle and moved around the table till she reached Mrs Jarmyn. Mrs Jarmyn shook her head once, sharply, without looking at the girl.

'And are there any details, Father, about our cousin's death?' said Bill and his voice rang out very clear and brutal and Dinah thought she might faint or she might kill him. She took the silver napkin ring from the table and closed her fist around it until its edges cut into her flesh.

Her father did not look up from his plate. 'Other than the date upon which his death occurred, no, it appears there are not.'

To his left, Gus, again caught in the act of trying to sip his soup, once more paused in confusion, spoon midway to his mouth.

'What was that date?' said Bill, and Dinah squeezed harder until tiny red dots appeared in her vision.

This time Mr Jarmyn paused. He appeared to study the surface of the soup in his bowl. 'On New Year's Day, I believe. The day his troop-ship docked at Durban.'

New Year's Day. The news of his death had taken a week to reach them. He had been dead all this time. Into Dinah's head crowded all the things she had done, all the mornings she had awoken and dressed and breakfasted, all the lunches she had eaten and the walks she had taken and calls she had made, all the dinners she had sat down to and the conversations she had had, all the nights she had undressed and lain shivering in her bed. Now it turned out Roger had been dead all this time.

And it turned out that she herself had done very little in all that time.

They had all fallen silent, not just herself, and it seemed that they must all be thinking the same thing: Poor Roger—who had sat at this table less than a month earlier in his splendid scarlet lieutenant's tunic, talking importantly about the war and about his own important role in it—had died the day he docked. *How* had he died? Their father had not said. Quite likely no one yet knew. Bill, who had not been here for Roger's last dinner, who was seated where Roger had sat, who had too much common sense to take a commission and go to the Transvaal himself, moved the salt cellar an inch to the left and then back again.

'It is unlikely there will be a funeral,' said Mrs Jarmyn, slicing through the ice with a pickaxe. She meant: They will not return his body, Roger would be buried in the Transvaal. He would not be coming home.

'There will be a memorial service presumably,' replied her father curtly, picking up his spoon and dipping it into his soup, and in the silence that followed something hung heavily in the air stifling further conversation.

And Jack, who had sat in silence since their father's news, pushed back his chair and ran from the room.

For the briefest moment no one moved and it seemed to Dinah they were each holding their breath and she thought,

I cannot bear it, and her father said, 'Bill, pass me the salt, please.'

Then there was an almighty crash from outside.

—ɯ—

Jack flew through the dining room door and straight into Hermione, who had her hand on the dining room doorhandle and in her other hand was holding a large tureen of Cook's best salmon and basil bisque. The two collided so that Hermione was thrown backwards, the tureen was knocked from her hand and clattered to the floor and the bisque shot in an arc into the air and down onto the girl's dress and legs and across the cedar-panelled wall, narrowly missing the portrait of his mother that had been painted in 1872 by the Royal Academy artist E.G. Hunt, and ending up in a pink and green pool on the carpeted floor.

Hermione screamed: first when Jack collided into her and a second time, more loudly, as the hot liquid splashed onto her legs.

Jack, who had landed on his bottom at the foot of the stairs, stared dumbly at the havoc he had wreaked and, as the dining room door opened wider and various people spilt out, he scrambled to his feet and fled up the stairs.

He didn't stop until he had reached the bedroom on the upper floor that he shared with Gus. Once here he pushed shut the door and wedged a chair against it and sat down heavily on the floor.

He would not cry, he would not! He was going to be a soldier and soldiers did not cry. He was going to be a soldier just as soon as he was old enough and he would go away to an academy and wear a uniform and learn how to be an officer and how to drill and how to fire a rifle. He was going to go off to wars in far-off places and perhaps shoot at other soldiers and at natives in Africa and in India and in other places and he would win a medal for his courage and be mentioned in dispatches and he wouldn't have to live here in this house for one more day! He was going to be a soldier like Cousin Roger.

But Cousin Roger had been killed on his very first day.

Jack kicked out with his shoe, kicked the chair that was wedged against the door, until it became dislodged and fell with a thud to the floor and he stood up and continued to kick it until the wood splintered and the cross-bar connecting the legs sprung out.

Everyone *died*! *Why* did everyone die?

He could hear voices downstairs, his father ordering something to be done. Would Father be angry with him for running out like that? For upsetting the soup? Gus would say he was a cry-baby.

No, he realised, Gus would not say that—it was he who would have said it to Gus had their roles been reversed. There was bisque on his shoes and now on the carpet. Had he hurt Hermione? She ought not to have been in his way, it was stupid of her to be standing there, right in his way like that and carrying something hot. She would learn! It was a lesson for her. She would not make such a mistake again.

He pulled off his shoe and there was bisque on his hand.

They had not let him see Sofia, neither he nor Gus had seen her. They had kept her shut away in a room, hidden behind a

175

screen, and all he had seen was Father, Dinah, Mrs Logan, the doctor, going silently in and out carrying bandages and bowls of water and tubs of balms and ointments. He had watched them enter with tight smiles on their faces and leave with their faces grey and closed. And beyond the door he had heard muffled sounds, like an animal whimpering. He had run up to his room with his hands over his ears. Then they had been sent to stay with their aunt and uncle in Great Portland Street.

After ten days she had died and even then he had not been allowed to see her. It had been a closed coffin. Now, whenever he closed his eyes he imagined a blackened, disfigured face.

It had been seven months but the face would not disappear.

He wiped his hand on his shirt front and it was stained a pinky-orange. In a rage he tore at his shirt and picked up the shoe and hurled it at the door.

—⁓—

Cook was not impressed. First Mrs Logan had come downstairs to announce that Mr Brightside was killed and now that daft girl had gone and got herself scalded again.

'Ain't there enough ways to get yourself killed right 'ere in London, without a body taking itself all the way off to the Cape to do it?' Cook demanded of Mrs Logan.

'No doubt there are,' agreed Mrs Logan wearily as she bathed the sobbing girl's legs with cold water. 'Please keep still, Hermione, I cannot help you if you wriggle about so.'

'And that were me best salmon and basil bisque,' said Cook, throwing down her rolling pin in disgust. 'Took me all morning to make it. Now it's all over the floor without a livin' soul so much as tasting one morsel. I call it a downright shame, that's what it is,' and she cast a malevolent look at Hermione.

'It wasn't Hermione's fault,' said Mrs Logan.

'Oh, it's never anyone's fault!' grumbled Cook. ''Cept when it's *my* fault, then folk are fallin' over themselves to find someone to blame, leastways that's what I've always found.'

'Master Jack came out of the room in a great hurry,' Mrs Logan continued, ignoring this interruption, 'and he knocked straight into her.' She reached for the jar of balm that she had not got around to putting away since the last time the girl had been scalded. 'And to be fair I think the poor boy was upset—'

'*Upset!* I'll give you upset—'

'—on account of Mr Brightside's death.'

'Hmmph!' said Cook and stuck her hands one on each hip in readiness to launch herself into her favourite topic. 'If you ask me, Mrs Logan, there's a deal too much wailin' and gnashin' of teeth goes on in this house when folk die. I mean to say, it ain't as though we ain't all goin' to die at some time or other, is it? Me and you, Mrs Logan, have both seen it firsthand and we wasn't forever wringin' our hands and runnin' out of rooms knockin' into people—leastways *I* wasn't and I have a pretty fair guess you wasn't neither. And another thing—'

But Mrs Logan stood up, with an abruptness that caused the prostrate Hermione to stifle a cry, and faced Cook.

'I would prefer it, Mrs Varley, if you would refrain from speculating on my past life or making comment on my present circumstances. I believe they are no concern of yours, nor of any other living soul.'

Cook fairly bristled with indignation.

'Well! I'm sure I meant no offence by it and furthermore—'

'Good. Then let us attend to this poor girl.'

The poor girl, who had been weeping quietly during this exchange, now turned her tear-streaked face towards Mrs Logan. 'Shall I be able to walk again?' she asked tremulously and Cook rolled her eyes and Mrs Logan patted the girl's arm.

'Don't be silly, Hermione, of course you shall walk again— why, it's only a scald.'

'And you needn't think you're going to get out of any of your work, missy, neither!' added Cook with a scowl. 'I remember when I was in my very first position, just a slip of a girl I was, and I dropped one of them big old cauldrons on me foot coming down the scullery stairs. Broke a bone, it did, and the bruisin' were somefing awful. But never a word did I say to no one! Kept on workin', night and day, up and down them very stairs. Never a word of complaint. I'd have lost my position if I had. This foot has never been the same since that day,' and she hobbled across the kitchen as proof of this.

'I am sure you are an example to us all, Mrs Varley,' said Mrs Logan.

Cook had an idea Mrs Logan was not as impressed by this tale of heroic fortitude as she might have been and she returned to her rocking chair near the range.

'Well, I can't be standin' around here gossipin',' she announced. 'The dinner's ruined and I'm sure I don't know what's to be done about it at this late hour.'

'Is there no bisque left? It was all spilt?'

Cook sniffed. 'How should I know? Send the girl to find out.'

'She's hardly in a fit state. Mrs Varley, I would advise you go up and retrieve the tureen and ensure no one slips on the spillage.'

'I ain't goin' up them stairs for no one, thank you very much, certainly not when some damn fool of a girl gets herself burnt—'

'Then I shall go and you shall need to tend to Hermione. I believe you will make a very fine nurse—'

'I ain't no one's nurse! Not to some damn fool girl what's got herself burnt.'

There was a silent stand-off as Mrs Logan returned her look wordlessly and Cook decided on the lesser of two evils and took herself off and up the stairs.

Upstairs the signs of the recent calamity were still very much in evidence. The tureen lay on its side at the foot of the stairs where it had landed. Lumps of salmon and potato and leek lay like small islands in a vast ocean of soup and it broke Cook's heart to look on her work thus destroyed. But see! At the bottom of the tureen, though it lay on its side, was a few spoonfuls of unspoilt bisque and the ladle, miraculously, still inside. Cook observed the door to the dining room, which was firmly shut, and she observed the hallway and the stairs, which were similarly silent and deserted and, with a swiftness surprising in one so advanced in age and so wide of girth and who had displayed her lameness for all to see not two minutes earlier, she darted forward and scooped up the tureen, righting it and, grasping the ladle, she began to shovel the largest lumps into it.

What they don't know won't harm them, she thought as she scooped up a ladleful of the thick gravy. In a remarkably short time the tureen was half full and the vast ocean reduced to a smallish lake—though now it had a tell-tale criss-cross of large, flat footprints through it. Cook used the ladle to smooth out the footprints and, satisfied with her work, set off with the tureen back downstairs.

'Managed to save some of it,' she announced, returning triumphantly to the kitchen. 'Call it a miracle if you like, but the girl managed to drop the thing so as it landed right way up and most of the stuff still inside.'

The first aid having been administered, Mrs Logan was putting the ointments away and Hermione was attempting gingerly to stand up, holding her ruined skirts in one hand, leaning heavily on the kitchen table with the other. They both observed Cook in some surprise as she made this announcement.

'But—' began Hermione. She was silenced by a look from Mrs Logan.

'Whilst I do not call it a miracle, Mrs Varley, it is certainly most providential,' Mrs Logan remarked. 'Now, Hermione, go and change your apron then return to your duties. I shall go upstairs and report this piece of good news to the family. No doubt they are quite famished by now,' and she left.

Cook plumped herself down on the rocking chair to catch her breath and reached for her pipe, which had long gone out. She felt hot and out of breath but pleased with the rescue she had effected with the bisque.

'What a day!' she declared. 'And all because the young chap gets hisself killed! What did he die of, anyways? Was it a gunshot or a native spear or some jungle disease? They all die of disease in my experience. Come on, what was it?'

But Hermione, who had by now made it as far as the kitchen doorway, could not say and Cook was left to speculate on all the many and varied ways by which a young man could meet his death in Africa.

—⁓—

The dinner was over and Lucas had gone out. He had not said where.

Aurora had resolved to see her children. On this night, of all nights, they needed the love, the strength only a mother could provide. Dinah's room was silent and no light showed and that was as well for she had feared Dinah would feel it the most, but instead it had been Jack. She passed on by her daughter's room. A faint light flickered from beneath the door to the boys' room and now Mrs Logan emerged cradling a stub of candle which she shielded from the draught, and there was something of Florence Nightingale about her, a calm serenity that ought to have been soothing, reassuring.

Aurora felt a thin red veil cover her eyes. And so it had come to this. This slow, encroaching takeover of her duties that had begun three years ago so slow, so encroaching that it had gone all but unnoticed. It had seemed, at worst, a benign but unavoidable consequence of bringing a housekeeper into her home. Now it seemed planned. It seemed malignant. 'Why do we need a housekeeper?' she had demanded of Lucas three years ago. 'These are the duties I perform as your wife. Other people we know do not have a housekeeper.' It was an unnecessary expense, she had argued. And what, exactly, was she to do, his own wife, if this housekeeper oversaw the kitchen, the tradesmen, the bills, the weekly accounts, the other servants? What duties were left to her? But he had been adamant, and his wife would still oversee the accounts, if that was her wish. She would still oversee all duties performed in the house and Mrs Logan would organise the day-to-day running of tasks. Mrs Logan would consult her, naturally, on every point, at every turn. And at first Mrs Logan *had* consulted her—or had made a pretence of consulting her—but almost at once a new daily and a weekly routine was set in place and both maids retrained and redeployed. The tradesmen went directly to Mrs Logan and soon all that was left was the daily menus and the weekly accounts. And since May, even those had devolved to Mrs Logan. There was nothing left. Aurora no longer knew what they were to eat at lunch or dinner. She did not know the name of the boy who delivered the meat from the butcher's. She had not opened the various accounts ledgers since the summer.

'Mrs Logan,' and she spoke loudly and clearly into the gloom so that the housekeeper spun around, her candle flickering wildly. 'Would you mind telling me what you are doing?'

Mrs Logan steadied herself, regaining her composure, and her face, which for the briefest of moments had registered alarm, now resumed its more usual neutral countenance.

'Checking on Master Jack, Mrs Jarmyn. He is a little shaken still. Though he is calmer now, I believe.'

'Do you? And no doubt you are an expert in childhood upsets?'

Mrs Logan lowered her eyes but lifted her chin.

'I have been a child, if that is what you meant, Mrs Jarmyn.'

'No, Mrs Logan, that is not what I meant. I was alluding to the condition more commonly known as "motherhood".'

There was the slightest of pauses. 'It is quite true that I have not been a mother, no. If that is all, Mrs Jarmyn?'

'Yes that is all. I shall see my son.'

But she waited until Mrs Logan had made her way along the corridor and up the back stairs and the light from her candle was gone.

The boys' room was almost in darkness. A guttering candle set off a faint glow as the drops of wax fell away and the wick burnt itself out. She could hear the gentle snores of her children sleeping. Crossing to the window she eased the curtain open a few inches so that the moonlight fell in a long strip across the two beds and across the two sleeping forms. It was a clear night. It felt like it might snow again.

She sat on the chair between the two beds and looked first at Gus and then at Jack. They were so different. All her children were so very, very different and how could that be when they had the same parents, had grown up in the same house? She had no brothers and sisters so she could not imagine what they might have been like; a version of herself and yet not herself. But her own children: Bill, who was so like his father, so sure of himself, so full of his own self-importance. And Dinah, a sweet girl. So good, so fair. But something had changed in her since the accident. She had become at once harder and less sure of herself. And there was something else, some restlessness about her that was unsettling—

'Mama?'

'Gus. I thought you were asleep.'

'I think I was. I was dreaming.'

'What about?'

'I can't remember. It's gone . . . Mama, I believe Jack was very upset by Father's news.'

'I know, dear. We all were.'

Gus struggled to sit up, wide awake now and irritated by the sheet that enclosed him. 'Yes, but Jack especially was *very* upset.'

'I understand that. He does not need to fear Father being angry with him for leaving the table and knocking the maid over. Father is not angry.'

She did not know this to be true but it felt important to reassure the boys.

But Gus shook his head. 'It's not that. He wishes *so much* to be a soldier.'

'And now he believes that, after this, Father will never let him be one?'

Gus appeared to consider this. From the other bed Jack's steady breathing reassured them he was fast asleep.

'Yes, I suppose that must be it . . . But Mama, what if one should wish for something all one's life—to go to Oxford, for instance—and then, on the very day one gets there, one is killed?'

Aurora felt a chill settle across her shoulders. She made herself smile.

'Oh my dear. Nothing will happen to you at Oxford. Why, the worst that will happen is that you might find yourself tipped in the pond!'

Gus shook his head, dismissing this.

'But what if Jack becomes a soldier?' he said, and she smiled at him and patted his hand in the moonlight.

But what if Jack *did* become a soldier?

Aurora undressed hurriedly and got ready for bed. There was little that Lucas could do to prevent it if the boy's heart was set on it. Surely though, the events of this evening would give Jack pause for thought?

Perhaps—and perhaps not. Years would pass. He would forget his cousin's death. He would remember the scarlet tunics and the flashing swords and the bright rows of medals in his books. There was little one could do to guard against the future. It was all one could do to guard against the past.

Aurora got into bed, experiencing a moment of anxiety that in all the distress the maid had forgotten to warm the bed for her. No, the girl had done her job and her feet pressed themselves gratefully into the warmth of the mattress, craving its fleeting heat.

Another death. Pointless, untimely, utterly tragic. She could not judge if she was horrified by it or untouched.

The hour was late. The clock in the hallway was striking midnight and a moment later she heard Lucas's footsteps in the street below, now coming up the front steps and the front door opening. He had gone out directly after dinner. Did he ever visit their child's grave? she wondered. She had never asked him, and she wondered how she would answer if he asked her the same question for she had never visited the grave, not once. She was too frightened to. She was not certain that, if she did, she would return in one piece. Lucas had not been to their daughter's grave tonight, of that she was certain. To a mistress then?

Aurora got quickly out of bed, pulling a shawl about her thin shoulders against the oppressive cold, and went to the doorway and stood for a moment listening. Her heart was beating very fast and a memory—all but lost—now appeared to her of herself twenty years past, a girl of eighteen, standing at the window of her room in her mother's house on the evening she and Lucas had met, waiting for a glimpse of him in the street below. The staggering impropriety of it had made her giddy and daring. She had opened her window and allowed him to see her standing there. It had driven him mad, that glimpse of her in the moonlight, and he had paced like a crazed man up and down between the streetlamps, lost in shadow one moment, thrust into dazzling gaslight the next, then in an instant he had run at the balustrade and pulled himself up and in no time at all was clinging to the ironwork on the outside of her balcony, still in evening dress, a carnation in his buttonhole. Had she made him climb thus to her balcony? It seemed to her eighteen-year-old mind that she had made it so and that he had no choice but to acquiesce. She had kissed him and afterwards had wondered if other girls of her acquaintance behaved as she had done. If they did, they never said so.

The memory was gone but the impression it left was strong. She heard Lucas climb the stairs and her heart beat a little faster. In another moment the door of his study opened and softly closed. She leant her head against the door. Ought she to go to him in his study?

She knew she would not. He would be taking a glass of port. Did she want a glass of port? She pressed her forehead against the door and the surface was cold against her skin. She closed her eyes just for a moment. He might be fresh from his mistress. No, she did not want to see that: it was vulgar. Besides, Mrs Logan was bound to be about. Mrs Logan would, in fact, be serving him port. Mrs Logan might as well be his mistress.

She opened her eyes. The thought made her uneasy.

The clock in the hallway had struck two before, eventually, she slept.

—⁓—

The clock had struck two and the household, at last, slept. All but Dinah, who sat on the floor of her bedroom, and bit down hard onto her bedspread so that no one would hear her sobs.

CHAPTER FOURTEEN

COUSIN ROGER WAS DEAD AND a fresh snowfall covered London.

In Regent Street the snow lay in a thick carpet and, though it had fallen only the previous night, already the wheels of a hundred carriages and the hooves of two hundred horses and the feet of a thousand Londoners had rendered it a dirty brown slush that splashed over toes and crept over the sides of boots.

Cousin Roger was dead. Three days had passed and Dinah and Rhoda were shopping for mourning attire.

Dinah stopped outside the window of a shop and thought, here we are again: just seven months later. (Indeed, it was the very same shop, the words *'Dearly Departed—An Emporium for the Recently Bereaved: Est. 1805'* picked out in sympathetic gold lettering on a sign above the doorway.) Only now I am here with Rhoda and Roger is dead.

A very elderly lady emerged from the shop on the arm of a much younger lady, her face veiled, head bowed, her ageing frame already creaking beneath yards of thick bombazine. Her companion—her daughter perhaps—dabbed a handkerchief to her eyes but otherwise appeared unaffected by whatever tragedy had beset her mother.

Did we look like that, Dinah wondered?

Seven months ago she had been accompanied by her Aunt Meredith. Her mother had, for many weeks, been too ill to leave her room. Rhoda had wanted to come to support her cousin and privately Dinah had thought: Rhoda wants to come because she is excited, because she has never shopped for mourning before, because it is an adventure. But Rhoda had not been allowed to accompany them. And Roger had still been alive. Now Rhoda was here and Roger was dead and it was not so very exciting, was it? It was not, in the least, an adventure. Instead it was all rather horrid.

Beside her, Rhoda leant on her arm and at that moment her cousin seemed very slight and very alone. Dinah laid her own hand over Rhoda's and thought, she thinks me to be the strong one, after all it is her loss, not mine. But the ground was so flimsy and insubstantial beneath her feet that she felt if she let go of her cousin's arm she might float away. So they held on to each other very tightly and peered together through the black-draped window of the shop. The two faces reflected back at them were pale and dazed and Dinah did not recognise either of them.

'Bombazine,' whispered Rhoda, indicating the elderly lady and her daughter who were now boarding a waiting carriage. 'I don't think I can stand to wear bombazine.'

'You don't have to. You can wear crape. We wore crape. And after a week we took to wearing it only when we went out.

No one will know. And besides, you will have all the blinds and curtains drawn.'

'The servants will know,' Rhoda replied.

Dinah did not know what to say to this so she led the way inside.

The shop had been established in 1805 (Trafalgar, noted Dinah. No doubt 1805 was a good year to open an emporium for the recently bereaved) and, judging by his decrepit appearance, the proprietor who now greeted them could well have been the original owner.

'My dear ladies!' he exclaimed, coming at them, his hands clasped before him and producing an expression that somehow conveyed dismay at their recent bereavement tinged with just the correct amount of joy at their decision to enter his establishment. 'Allow me to offer my humblest condolences at this difficult time.'

They acknowledged his humblest condolences with a slight inclination of their heads. The man wore a stiff tailcoat of charcoal-grey, a sombre waistcoat of similar hue and a crisp, snow-white cravat of a style made popular by the Prince Regent some sixty years previously. His ancient frame was so bent and diminished, the flesh so shrunken—in places it appeared almost transparent—that it seemed to be the clothes alone that held him together.

'Might one inquire as to the relation of the deceased?' he continued in a voice that sounded as though it had been locked away in a trunk under the bed for many years. 'A dear mother, perhaps?'

No, it was not a mother.

'A father then? . . . No? A sibling—?'

'It's my brother,' Rhoda announced, clearly impatient with this guessing game.

The proprietor sighed. 'How touching. How sad,' he observed. 'A sister's grief for her brother. A riding accident?'

'My brother was killed in the Transvaal in the service of Her Majesty and the Empire.'

The proprietor almost swooned. 'Madam, there is no more honourable a way to die,' and launched into an elaborate bow that threatened to topple him right over, and Rhoda lifted her chin and straightened her back and acknowledged this accolade with a second inclination of her head. Dinah noticed how tiny flakes of dead skin shed from the decrepit man's hands and onto the carpet.

She left her cousin and walked over to the rolls of thick black material ranged against the counter. They had stood right here, herself and Aunt Meredith, seven months ago and Aunt Meredith had inspected various bolts of cloth and studied various patterns, then she had consulted various books and finally she had made various orders, and her niece had stood and mutely looked on. Roger, she remembered, had offered to accompany them.

'My brother's death was noted in today's *Times*,' Rhoda was explaining to the proprietor.

Sofia's death had also been noted in *The Times*, though the one was in a War Office list of casualties, the other a minor account of a tragic domestic accident. Did the shopkeeper remember, Dinah wondered? Was he secretly thinking, What a careless family—two losses in seven months! But here was a man who revelled in careless families, who must rub his hands together at a cholera outbreak, a high tide or a sudden winter frost, an incautious pedestrian and an impatient horse, a conflict in a distant corner of the Empire.

Rhoda was shown to a chair and offered a tiny glass of Spanish sherry. She was provided with a velvet-covered footrest by an assistant who had been summoned specifically to perform this necessary task. Dinah stood at the window and observed the snowy scene outside. A horse had slipped on the icy road and fallen awkwardly. Two men were attempting to disengage the stricken animal from the shaft of a carriage, a third man was holding the horse's head to prevent it from thrashing about. If they didn't move it soon someone would shoot the poor thing.

Are we punished, she wondered, here on Earth, for the bad things we do? and thought of herself and Roger in the garden on an afternoon in May.

'Dinah, what do you think of this black? It is called Darkest Night.'

Dinah rejoined her cousin and studied the bolt of cloth the proprietor was holding out to her.

'It is very black,' she agreed. 'Though I wonder . . . Do you perhaps have anything blacker?'

'Blacker?' repeated the proprietor.

'Do you think it not quite right, Dinah?' said Rhoda anxiously and Dinah instantly relented. She was here to support her cousin, was she not?

'Forgive me, now that I look again, I can see that it is indeed very black. I am certain this will do admirably.' Chastened, she returned to her place by the window. Already the horse had been removed and the carriage was gone.

The Jarmyns had been out of mourning for just over a month. Now it was the turn of the Brightsides. We will forget what we look like in colours, thought Dinah and she observed the ladies passing outside the window. Magenta, it appeared, was popular, and Empire-blue. So too vermilion. She could not imagine herself in vermilion.

'I do wish Mama were here, to make the purchases,' said Rhoda, joining her at the window. 'Normally Mama would make the arrangements, she would organise it all. She would have definite views about everything.' Her cousin bit her lip, clearly a little overwhelmed at the responsibility that death had thrust upon her.

Dinah pulled herself up and gave a little smile, reaching for her hand. 'I am sure you will make the right decisions,' she reassured her, though she was reasonably certain Aunt Meredith would baulk at the yards of Darkest Night her daughter had just ordered.

But Roger lay dead in a coffin in the Transvaal and their purchases, their presence in the shop, their very existence, seemed suddenly negligible. *Was* his body in a coffin? If he had died on the field of battle, he may lie anywhere. He may never be found.

She squeezed Rhoda's hand and for a moment they stood in silence.

'There! Look!' said Rhoda pointing, and in the street outside they saw Mrs Van Der Kuyt and Isabella Van Der Kuyt hurrying past in the snow, their hands thrust deep inside fur muffs.

Rhoda went quickly to the door and hurried out and, against all rules of propriety, called out to them.

Through the window Dinah could see first Mrs Van Der Kuyt then Isabella stop and turn. Rhoda went after them and an exchange took place during which the Van Der Kuyts, evidently already in possession of Rhoda's news, appeared to offer their condolences which Rhoda appeared to accept gracefully and with an almost serene composure. Isabella, rising to the occasion, placed a hand on her heart and made an anguished face as she spoke. Her mother placed a sympathetic hand on Rhoda's arm. And Rhoda responded with a stony-faced stoicism befitting the daughter of a family who had just lost their only son in the service of Queen and Empire.

'Will the young lady be requiring black-edged notepaper and black sealing wax?' inquired the proprietor, approaching Dinah, clearly anxious that his customer had run from his establishment before he could conduct all the necessary transactions.

'I don't doubt it,' Dinah replied, not turning around. We have some, she thought to herself, indeed we have boxes of both. The Brightsides were welcome to them . . . But somehow she knew Aunt Meredith, and Rhoda as Aunt Meredith's daughter, would not wish to borrow someone else's. This was their death, after all. One would not borrow someone else's ring to get married with, would one?

Rhoda re-entered the shop, her cheeks pink, and a rush of cold air came in with her.

'They had heard the news,' she reported. 'They had read it in this morning's *Times*. They have already called on Mama and left their cards. Mrs Van Der Kuyt said the Fairchilds and the

Larches were also leaving cards and two other parties whom she did not know. I think one must have been Dr and Mrs Fanning judging by their description of the carriage. Isabella said Roger is sure to get a medal. And Mrs Van Der Kuyt said that, if he does, we shall all be required to attend at the Palace to receive it on his behalf. From the Queen,' she added just in case this was not absolutely clear.

So, Cousin Roger's death was not in vain: his mother, father and sister would get a trip to the Palace. They would meet the Queen.

'I am sure Isabella is right,' Dinah replied with an encouraging smile, though why Isabella Van Der Kuyt should be considered an authority on military decoration or palace protocol was not immediately clear to her. 'Shall we continue with our purchases? I'm sure Aunt Meredith will be anxious to have you back home with her.'

'Oh yes . . .' agreed Rhoda vaguely, the excitement of purchasing mourning attire apparently now superseded by the thrill of the forthcoming presentation to Her Majesty.

They made the remainder of their purchases and arranged for the items to be delivered later that day to the house in Great Portland Street.

'This has been an honour, madam,' the proprietor commented as he held the door open for them, and Dinah looked into his face and saw death, a thousand deaths stretching back over decades, and she smothered a shudder.

The door closed behind them but Rhoda remained where she was, standing in the doorway beneath the sign with the sympathetic gold lettering, unmoving, and Dinah stood beside her but there was nothing to say.

'Dinah, we received a most extraordinary communication from a woman,' said Rhoda unexpectedly and Dinah felt a flicker of unease. She glanced about them and took her cousin's arm and led her away from the shop.

'What sort of communication?'

'It was most extraordinary. It was in the second post. Roger's death was reported in this morning's *Times*, of course, so anyone could know about it. Nevertheless my father received a letter from a woman. The letter said the woman had heard from Roger.'

Dinah looked away and nodded slowly, not wishing to hear more.

'It said she had heard from him *after his death*. That she was a spiritualist.'

They crossed Beak Street heading gradually south.

'We had one too,' Dinah replied. 'In the week after Sofia's death. Perhaps it was the same woman.'

Rhoda stared at her. 'What did you do?'

'I? Nothing. It was addressed to Father. He showed it to Bill. Then I believe Father threw it away and it was not mentioned again.'

'It was the same for us—Father received and read it though he did not read it out to us. And he got angry and threw it out. But when he had gone out Mama retrieved it. She came and showed it to me. We were both greatly upset by it. But also . . .' Rhoda looked down.

'But also you wanted to know if it could be true?'

'Yes. Of course. Did you not think the same thing?'

Dinah considered. Had she? She could not remember. If she had, she had quashed the thought at once. She knew she would not have allowed the faintest possibility to flicker even for an instant.

'Perhaps,' she said, in answer to Rhoda's question.

'Of course these people are all charlatans, everyone knows it. And yet—'

They had reached Piccadilly Circus and they paused now to watch the chaos of carriages and cabs.

Yes, everyone knew they were all charlatans. And yet.

—∿—

Roger's memorial service was held two days later.

The snow had turned to ice making the going treacherous for the large group of mourners who followed the elderly rector through the cemetery and towards the small marble stone that was to serve as Roger Brightside's memorial.

Lucas walked on one side of Travers, supporting his arm and feeling a tremble go through his brother-in-law, his fingers tighten around Lucas's forearm.

The ladies had remained at home. He had seen Meredith through the open front door of the house in Great Portland Street as he had arrived to take Travers to the church. He had not been able to see her face because of the veil she wore. They had boarded the carriage, himself, Travers and Bill, and travelled to the church. All three wore black armbands and black gloves and trailing bands tied around their hats. The horses had sported black ostrich plumes and the carriage was draped with black velvet. There was no casket; Roger would not be returning home.

The chief mourner—a man all in black and supplied by the funeral company—led the way and the procession had moved through the street at an agonising pace. Heads had turned to watch as they passed, conversations halted and a number of men removed their hats. There was no disguising a funeral.

Damn Roger for being such a fool, Lucas thought angrily. To put Meredith through this, and for what? So that some tiny outpost of humanity could be pink on the map? So that other young men in other families years from now could also lay down their lives in pointless defence of a worthless piece of land on the other side of the world? Was the Empire not big enough, important enough, did it not cover a vast enough portion of the world, did it not yet generate enough trade and goods and wealth to satisfy even the most demanding appetites?

He would like to give the boy a piece of his mind were he standing here now! He would like to ask Roger just what this pointless venture had achieved, what all that training, that irrevocable falling out with his father, that long sea voyage to some distant continent, what exactly had been achieved by it?

The Times that morning had reported that the garrison at Potchefstroom could hold out for a month, no longer. Meanwhile supplies, horses, troops, whole regiments from various parts of the Empire were being bundled into ships and sent, helter-skelter, to the Cape to come to their rescue. The garrison would be relieved, or it would not. What difference did it make? Roger would still be dead.

Sketchy details of Roger's death had been relayed to them via a letter from a fellow officer, a Lieutenant Graves, and they were details that offered little consolation to grieving parents. Roger had died within hours of disembarking, as a result of a gunshot wound to the neck. The troops had not, at that time, been engaged with the enemy; indeed they had barely completed their disembarkation and moved into the garrison's temporary quarters. Faulty equipment was suggested as the cause of the gunshot and, reading between the lines, it appeared that either someone had accidentally shot him or, worse, Roger had accidentally shot himself.

The boy had boasted of his prowess at marksmanship. Perhaps it was best to assume someone else had fired the fatal shot.

A crow cawed loudly right overhead, once, twice, and the rector, an ancient man in a long black coat and leaning heavily on a gnarled oak stick, stumbled on an open gravesite and would have slipped had Bill not put out a hand to steady the fellow.

Travers was grey this morning, his normally arrow-straight frame bent forward against the bitter chill and no doubt against other chills that had little to do with the weather. His hat was askew, as was his collar, and at one point he put his hands up to adjust it and his fingers shook. He walked with his eyes cast downwards and Lucas wondered if it was shame that made him walk thus, unable to meet the eyes of the other mourners, of the people who knew that his last act towards his son had been to disown him.

And yet his brother-in-law was guilty merely of trying to save the life of his only son. He alone, amongst a sickening clamour of patriotism, had sounded a cautious note, had tried to prevent what now seemed to have been inevitable.

They had reached the memorial, a small square of marble atop a plinth, and the words:

In memory of a beloved son
Roger Brightside, aged 19
whose body lies in a distant land
and who died in the service of Queen and Empire.

Lucas at once looked away. How exactly was the Queen or the Empire served by his death? No one had yet said. Perhaps it would be explained by the rector who had now come to a halt and was resting for a moment against his stick, wheezing painfully, his breath hanging in the frozen air. Lucas watched the man and did not hold out any great hope that he would be able to explain anything much to the waiting mourners. The rector was speaking, though the wind whipped his words away and they had to turn their heads to hear him.

'Man that is born of a woman hath but a short time to live, and is full of misery. He cometh up, and is cut down, like a flower; he fleeth as it were a shadow, and never continueth in one stay.'

Well, Roger had been cut down, though whether or not it was like a flower, Lucas could not say. He suspected not.

'We brought nothing into this world, and it is certain we can carry nothing out. The Lord gave, and the Lord hath taken away; blessed be the Name of the Lord.'

Lucas shut his ears to the words.

The man had finished speaking and he had not explained Roger's death and perhaps it was not his place to do so. Perhaps only God could do that.

The mourners made their way back along the little path through the cemetery. There were a handful of military men in attendance and Travers disengaged his arm and made his way unsteadily over to them. When Travers rejoined them, his face was stricken, though he said nothing. Once they were back inside the carriage and Bill had pulled up the windows and was slapping his gloved hands together to warm them, Travers spoke.

'They have every confidence of a swift victory,' he said, clearing his throat, and for a moment Lucas could not make sense of his words. 'Colley is in an unassailable position, it appears.'

The war.

Lucas nodded slowly. If this gave Travers some comfort, well so be it. There was precious little comfort to be had in the details of his son's death. Bill glanced at him, and seemed at a loss for how to reply.

'I am certain they will be proven right,' Lucas replied. And perhaps when they were the reason for this war would become clear.

—◦◦◦—

'My Godfather, the bishop, sent us his condolences,' Aunt Meredith, seated opposite her sister-in-law, announced, and beside her Rhoda seemed to stir restlessly.

The ladies were not attending Roger's memorial so they waited together in the drawing room of the Brightsides' house in Great Portland Street.

'How kind,' murmured Mrs Jarmyn, summoning a vague smile and Dinah thought, looking at her mother, these were the things one clung too, the small but important details, the rituals undertaken to fill an otherwise unfillable void. 'He is well, the bishop?' her mother added.

'Oh yes. Quite well. Though I understand he suffered a head cold earlier in the winter.'

'Oh dear. And at his age . . .'

'Yes, indeed,' agreed Aunt Meredith readily—but here she stalled. The question of the bishop's health and age and the nature of his condolences appeared to have been stretched as far as it could.

Dinah felt her mother's gaze upon her but she sat perfectly still and silent on the Brightsides' sofa, her hands folded in her lap, her face composed, every inch the dutiful daughter at her cousin's funeral. Opposite them Aunt Meredith shifted and her mourning gown rustled and rearranged itself into new folds.

'You went to Dearly Departed in Regent Street?' said her mother indicating Meredith's gown, though she knew very well that this was the establishment the Brightsides had patronised as Dinah had related the details of her and Rhoda's outing to her, including the meeting with the Van Der Kuyts.

Aunt Meredith nodded. 'Such a relief, crape,' she observed, leaning forward and speaking in a conspiratorial tone so that the maid might not overhear her. 'One is so restricted in bombazine.'

'I do so agree. We wore crape. And after a week we took to wearing it only when we went out. No one knew. And besides, we had the curtains drawn.'

'The servants would have known,' Aunt Meredith replied, with a significant glance over her shoulder.

And Rhoda, who had been sitting stiffly beside her mother, leapt to her feet with a sob and ran crying from the room.

A terrible silence followed as the three remaining women sat and waited. Rhoda's absence, her sob, seemed to echo and fill the room. But no one moved.

'I think I hear the carriage returning,' said Dinah, getting abruptly to her feet and going to the window. She tweaked the heavy drawing room curtain aside to look out at the street beyond. A dozen or more carriages were passing: hansoms and crowded omnibuses heading south towards Oxford Street or north towards Marylebone and the park: broughams, phaetons, a landau, even a barouche open to the weather driven by two young men buttoned up against the chill. But of the funeral procession there was no sign.

Of course they would not be returning yet, they had left barely more than an hour before; they would hardly have ended the service yet. But she had needed to stand up. Could no longer bear to remain seated in that horrid silence, with Rhoda gone upstairs.

It is their bereavement, not mine, she told herself. It is for Rhoda to run upstairs and Aunt Meredith to sit in state and receive condolences and Uncle Travers to lean on Father's arm.

We are not even immediate family and after the funeral we will remove our mourning clothes and no one would even know we have suffered a loss. Dinah waited by the window and the traffic did not cease.

'Is it them?' inquired her mother.

'No, Mama. It is not them. I was mistaken.'

She left the window, finding no reason to remain there, and returned to her mother's side on the sofa.

On the sideboard was a framed photograph of Roger. He was in uniform, standing very straight and proud, beside an opulent fern, its fronds brushing against the arm that held his officer's hat, so that he must be posing either in the very heart of an African jungle or in a photographic studio. Dinah assumed the latter. A black cloth lay beside the photograph as though it had covered the frame but someone had recently removed it. Who had covered it, Dinah wondered, and who had uncovered it? She turned her face away from the photograph.

'We are hopeful of further information,' said Aunt Meredith and Dinah realised her aunt was also regarding the photograph. 'Of Roger,' she clarified.

Of his death, she meant.

He wanted to marry me, Dinah said—but not out loud, inside her head where the words thundered and reverberated—but I turned him down. Dinah studied her hands in her lap. She had said yes but then she had turned him down. She looked up at her aunt who was casting about her, searching for something that would not be found.

'This Lieutenant Graves was very kind to write to us,' her aunt continued. 'To take the time to write. In such difficult circumstances. Of course, we know nothing about him, about his people, nor he us. But he was very kind, nevertheless. Even so, the details were sketchy. Naturally, he would not have the time to write at length but we are hopeful, once things are settled, that he will write to us again. Or perhaps pay us a visit upon his return. It would be such a comfort for Travers. For Rhoda. To hear. From someone who was there. From a fellow officer. Such a comfort.'

Dinah looked down again at her hands in her lap, hoping her mother could summon up a suitable reply. Instead, the door to the drawing room opened and Rhoda returned, her face pale but composed. She looked at no one but silently came and sat beside her mother.

'I had thought I had heard the carriage,' she said. It was perfectly clear to them all that she had not left the room because she thought she had heard the carriage.

'Yes, Dinah thought so too,' said Mrs Jarmyn. 'Though in the end it turned out not to be them.'

A silence fell that the clanging of pans in the kitchen below and the clatter of the constant traffic outside seemed to magnify.

There would be no medal, that much was clear, and no trip to the Palace. From the sideboard the Roger who regarded them from the photograph, so splendid in his dress uniform, was unaware he would die without ever facing the enemy.

'Did I mention my Godfather, the bishop, sent us his condolences?' said Aunt Meredith, and Dinah closed her eyes.

CHAPTER FIFTEEN

London and the Midlands

RIGHT UP UNTIL THE LAST possible moment Thomas Brinklow did not know whether or not he was going to board the train. The guard had blown his whistle and waved his flag and doors had slammed up and down the length of the train. The engine had let off a great whoosh of steam and the couplings had gone taut, shuddering as they began to take the strain of the carriages. Thomas chose that moment to grab the nearest door and fling it open and himself into the third-class carriage as the shouts of the furious guard rang in his ears. The train was already moving out of Dawley Station, heading south, as he righted himself and pulled the resisting door shut behind him.

The 11.55 a.m. local train to Birmingham was dead on time.

The irony of embarking on his journey by boarding a train of the North West Midlands Railway was not lost on him. Trains continued to run between the various northwestern Midlands towns and passengers continued to purchase tickets at the ticket offices and board the trains with their wives and children, and goods and livestock for the market, just as though they had every expectation of reaching their destination intact. Five weeks had passed since the accident yet people, for the most part, had forgotten. Or they found it prudent to forget, especially if they needed to take a train journey.

The inquiry into the railway continued but Mr Brinklow's attendance was no longer required. Instead he was taking the train to London.

A whistle blew and a sudden gush of steam from the engine deluged the fast-disappearing platform so that all he could see was the slate roof of the ticket office and the smoke billowing from the stationmaster's chimney. The train began to gather speed and instantly Thomas felt a pressure in his chest so that it was difficult to breathe. He reached up and pulled blindly at the window latch and a blast of steam, smuts and frozen air hit him. The woman opposite him reached over and slammed the window shut with a glare.

His palms were sweating. He stared down at them and thought: what kind of man am I that I cannot get on a train without fear?

He wiped his hands on his trousers, looking up at the faces of his fellow passengers. The woman opposite him returned his gaze unwaveringly. Beside her a man, a farmer by the look of his clothing, cradled a little girl on his lap. The little girl slept though the carriage rocked violently from side to side, and her father stared emptily over her head at nothing. Next to him was a family of four or five children and a mother in their midst, clutching a basket covered with a cloth. The children were silent, some standing, some sitting on their mother, some crouched at her feet wherever they could find a space.

The train continued on its way, leaving the town in its wake, flying through farmland and woodland, climbing and dropping, rattling over points and plunging into tunnels. Soon the farmer nodded off and his arm slid from the child's shoulders so that she was balanced precariously on his knee as he slept. The train rattled over more points and she swayed to left and right.

Thomas rubbed at his chest to relieve the constriction he felt. If the train braked sharply the girl would surely be tipped to the floor. He thrust out both hands to catch her and the little girl opened her eyes and viewed him with a look of terror, shying away, and he let his hands drop to his lap and turned to look out of the window.

His wife had stopped speaking to him. He hadn't realised it at first, as he had had little enough to say to her. But after a while, some days, he realised she no longer spoke to him. Or looked at him. As if he no longer existed. The silence was more than he could bear and he could not fill this silence himself—the Brinklows were not known for their skill at conversing. They left fancy talking to the union man and the local member of Parliament and the reverend in his Sunday sermon.

The train ran alongside fallow and overgrown fields, abandoned farm buildings, a rusting threshing machine left behind after some long-distant harvest.

The Brinklows were not talkers: they were farm labourers, nothing more and nothing less, going back generations—back to King John's time, Grandpa Brinklow had claimed, though how he could know this when the Brinklows' only mark in history was an occasional cross in a parish register was a mystery. Two dozen generations on the land. It had ended abruptly with Daniel Brinklow, Thomas's father, moving to the town for a job in a mill, marrying a factory girl and living in one room in the shadow of the mill, raising a family who grew up knowing no other life. Perhaps Daniel Brinklow would have fared better remaining on the land, though the work was itinerant and seasonal and famine was never far away. But Progress was a lure not easy to resist, particularly for a young man. Daniel Brinklow had not resisted and had paid the highest price: horribly mangled in a mill accident before he had reached his thirty-fifth year, leaving a widow and seven children. The family, without a breadwinner, had entered a workhouse where they were separated, the mother from her children, brothers from their sisters. Twelve-year-old Thomas was sent to work at the ironworks in Dawley where he had worked fifteen years, boy and man. He had not seen his mother since the day he had entered the workhouse and did not know the whereabouts of any of his four sisters or two brothers. He still thought of them, occasionally.

He had attended—all the local children attended—a Sunday school in a small unfurnished room above the Trades Hall run by a short-sighted spinster with a permanently red nose who had spoken of Jonah and Noah and Moses as though they were personally known to her. Thomas had not found God in that small unfurnished room but he had found Jenny Bythwaite.

She was a year older than he and he had never seen her without four or five younger brothers and sisters crowding about her knees and tugging her skirts and pulling at her hands. She sat always in the same chair in the second row at the Sunday school, and the four or five brothers and sisters arranged themselves in a noisy circle about her feet. When she quietened them they fell silent. When she read—and read she could, better than anyone, as good, nearly, as the short-sighted spinster—they listened in rapt awe. The whole class listened in rapt awe; certainly Thomas did. One Sunday he had arrived early and pleaded of the short-sighted spinster which Bible story they would be reading that day. Locating the particular passage, he had placed a single buttercup between the pages then left the Bible on Jenny's chair. When she came to open the Bible he could hardly bear to look at her face and watch as she laid her eyes on the gently pressed flower that lay between its pages. But he did look and when she opened the book the rich and heavenly yellow of the flower had bathed her angel's face in a rich and heavenly yellow light and he had thought in that moment he was watching the Word of God come to life.

They had wed four years later and there was Progress, right there, for Thomas had signed the marriage register with his own name—the first Brinklow ever to do so. Alice had come along a few months after. There had been no other children but Jenny's lying in had been so arduous—three days, with her and the unborn baby in mortal danger the whole time—he had been glad. He had wondered if something had broken inside her that meant she could have no more children but they had never minded it for they had Alice and she was everything and more.

The train rattled over another set of points and a branch line veered off to the east.

And now Jenny would not speak to him because he had taken their only child to the fair on his day off and she had been killed. Perhaps she believed it to be God's punishment. He himself did not think it was God's punishment. He thought it was the railway company that had caused his child's death. God had had nothing to do with it. God had nothing to do with anything, it now appeared.

He had received a letter of condolence from the railway company. The letter had been sent a week after the funeral with a third-class stamp. It was postmarked London and the notepaper was headed with the emblem of the railway company and an address in the City. The letter was addressed to *Mr Thomas Brinklow, Esq.*

Nothing good could ever come from a letter such as this and he had torn the letter in half and thrown it away.

He had lost his job at the foundry because he had taken time off work for the accident and the inquest and then for the funeral and finally the inquiry. He had retrieved the letter of condolence and opened it: the railway, he read, expressed their grief and regret; they were desirous to make every effort possible to contact the relatives of the deceased and injured so that everything might be done for them as lay within their power.

Paying for the cost of the funeral was within their power and yet they had not done so.

And now he was on a train heading south and the letter from the railway company and the bill from the undertaker were in his pocket, burning a hole in his flesh. He did not have four pounds but it was more than that—he wanted someone to explain *why* they had failed to pay it, even if it meant travelling all the way to London.

A blast from the engine's whistle startled the little girl on her dad's lap and a moment later the train plunged into a cutting. It emerged almost at once and they were soon running alongside a canal. The line began to climb slightly and he could just make out the remains of a bridge up ahead, its recently smashed brickwork replaced by temporary wooden fences—

He felt the blood drain from his face. His entire body turned cold. Perspiration formed on his forehead and upper lip. This was the place: the cutting, the canal, a lock approaching on the left-hand side, a white-painted lock-keeper's lodge with horse brasses over the door and a broken-down cart in the yard; a barge, tethered and derelict; the bridge—

The train rattled onwards, over a set of points and past a signal, passing the lock and the lodge and the broken-down cart, then up and over the bridge and Thomas started up, half leaving his seat, clutching the handrail above his head.

The toll-path and a paddock of tall grass beside the railway line were still littered with broken bricks from the bridge and twisted bits of metal from the carriages but that was all. They approached and sailed past.

Thomas sank down again into his seat and rubbed his face hard with his hands. His face felt clammy. He had wanted there to be some sign. Something by which people would know a little girl had died just here.

He lowered his hands and looked at the farmer, who was now awake and regarding him warily.

'A little girl died,' said Thomas. 'Just here. We've passed it now. Back there. A little girl.'

The farmer made no reply and the train continued on its journey.

—✺—

'It will be only a small dinner. There is no question now of a larger party,' Mrs Jarmyn announced in the drawing room of 19 Cadogan Mews, and what she meant was, Now that Roger is dead and the Brightsides in mourning and no longer able to attend.

'Yes Mama,' said Dinah, seated in the chair opposite and numbed by the idea of the dinner. But her mother seemed resolved to press ahead.

'I have invited the Eberhardts and Captain Palmer,' she went on. 'And the Duvalls, the Miss Courtaulds, of course, Dr and Mrs Gant, Professor Dallinger, and Mr Freebody and his wife and Mr Hart from your father's railway.' Here she tapped her dinner table plan irritably. 'Bill clearly said he was not able to attend and now he is—that means we have unequal numbers!'

'So I may be excused from attending?' offered Dinah.

'Certainly not! We already have more gentlemen than ladies. Your attendance now is critical.'

'And I am to partner Mr Hart?' asked Dinah, hardly bothering to mask her dismay. Mr Hart, one of the directors of the railway, was a long-term bachelor though still of an age when the possibility of a wife was not entirely out of the question—or so, at least, her mother's dinner invitation appeared to suggest.

'It is a dinner, not a marriage proposal,' replied her mother. 'Besides, one never knows whom one might meet and what might occur,' she added mysteriously, as though remembering her own first meeting with her future husband, and Dinah despaired. But here Mrs Jarmyn's smile faded and she turned to study the seating plan on the table before her. Indeed she stared at the seating plan for so long she must surely have come up with every conceivable combination of who was to sit where. Dinah shifted restlessly, wondering if she could make her excuses and leave.

'Mama?'

Her mother looked up and inconceivably, appallingly, there were tears in her eyes. 'Dinah, do please lower the lamp,' she said. 'The light is affecting my eyes.'

Dismayed, Dinah reached up and adjusted the lamp that was fixed to the wall above their heads. Roger had died and in the pit of her own grief she had given no thought at all to how others might feel.

But perhaps she had been mistaken for already her mother was applying herself once more to the knotty problem of the seating plan, and she pursed her lips and frowned and tapped her pen against the tabletop as though she were the Prime Minister reorganising his Cabinet.

'Roderick Duvall has no connections or family at all of course and he made his money in South African diamond mines so he will end up in the centre of the table. Yet Emily Duvall is the daughter of the Bishop of St Albans so that puts her on Lucas's right-hand side . . . Though now that she is married to Roderick that perhaps takes precedence, so ought she to be directly to

Lucas's right, after all? Do you know, Dinah, I cannot remember the last time we had the Duvalls over—and now I recall: they are dreadfully difficult to seat. When we had dinner at your aunt and uncle's last year your aunt seated Mrs Duvall beside the Member of Parliament for Croydon which seemed like a snub at the time until it came out that the member had been offered a Cabinet post. (I remember thinking at the time Meredith appeared quite smug.) The Miss Courtaulds will be offended wherever I seat them so one might as well not worry too much. I could seat Aunt Fresia beside Mr Freebody—that will annoy them both.' Mrs Jarmyn seemed to enjoy this prospect, then she paused, frowning. 'I have an idea *Mrs* Freebody is related, though distantly, to the Beauchamps of Northamptonshire and they have land. I shall have to ask Lucas. That will make a difference. I'm afraid it does not bode well for Mrs Duvall.'

'What about the Eberhardts?' said Dinah, feeling some response was called for. 'They are very wealthy.'

'Of course, dear. They are American. But that makes no odds here,' and by 'here', her mother was referring to the etiquette book that lay open on the table before her and over which she was now poring. 'Dr Gant and therefore Mrs Gant will take precedence. Captain Palmer, by dint of his commission in the Royal Horse Guards, and Professor Dallinger, by dint of his being Chair of Divinity at University College, will similarly take precedence. I am afraid to say the Eberhardts outrank only Mr Duvall and Bill and poor Mr Hart. And you, Dinah.'

'Poor me,' sighed Dinah. She ought to feel peeved at finding herself lumped in with the owner of a South African diamond mine and Mr Hart but she felt nothing. 'Perhaps it would be better if I did not attend?' she suggested.

'Don't be absurd,' replied her mother, not looking up. 'You are a young lady of the house now. It would be unseemly if you did not attend. Now, the menu: we'll start with artichoke soup and a clear turtle soup, then . . . I wonder, herring roe or anchovy toast?'

Dinah tried to apply her mind to this conundrum but found that she could not.

'No, on the whole I think it better we go with the anchovy toast,' her mother decided, answering her own question, though why it was best to go with the anchovy toast rather than the herring roe she did not say. 'Fillet of turbot, broiled lobster, medallions of veal, roast leg of lamb, boiled venison, wild duck. We need one more fowl dish . . . I would suggest pigeon but Cook has a morbid aversion to it, the origin of which one can only speculate.'

Dinah nodded, recalling the scene the last time Cook had been asked to prepare pigeon.

'I do not believe Cook realised what it was until Jack told her,' said Dinah, remembering. 'Perhaps if we do not tell her what they are, she may not take umbrage?'

'Excellent idea, Dinah. I shall tell her they are Prussian fowls, a delicacy served in Potsdam and enjoyed by the Kaiser. So, we have fillet of turbot, broiled lobster, medallions of veal, roast leg of lamb, boiled venison, wild duck and Prussian fowl pie. Now: watercress, stewed celery, new potatoes, peas and a Hannover salad. Then to follow, a Sandringham pudding, a greengage pudding, pineapple creams and raspberry water ices . . . Will it be enough?'

Dinah did not know if it would be enough. She did know that she had a secret and growing dread of the forthcoming dinner party that was, surely, out of all proportion to the event itself.

—∽—

Arriving at London's great Euston terminus, armed only with an address on a letter, an overdue bill from an undertaker and the clothes he was wearing, Thomas Brinklow set off at once, making his way eastwards, and almost immediately got lost.

The congested thoroughfares clogged with hansom cabs and over-laden omnibuses quickly gave way to steeply sided passages and alleyways where narrow buildings crowded over each other almost meeting above his head, and where carriages could only travel single-file. The people—so many people!—surged and jostled so close a man had to watch his every step or risk theft or worse. After an hour the passages at last opened up to allow some daylight to penetrate and he found himself at the steps of St Paul's, where he sank down to rest, too demoralised and exhausted even to marvel at its greatness. He already hated London with a fervour that took his breath away and the great cathedral seemed to him a monument of all that was hateful: something so grand and immense yet surrounded by such poverty and degradation was monstrous and he would not deign to gaze up at its fabled dome.

He stood up. But which direction? He was no longer even certain from which direction he had come, and he could no more seek directions from these folk swarming every which way than he could from a Frenchman, as he could not fathom a word they said.

Had it not been for the protestors it is doubtful Thomas would have found the place at all. As it was, he stumbled in sheer exhaustion right past the turning, and the gradual realisation that the sound he could now hear was not the rabble of Cockney voices he had already come to loathe, but was in fact chanting, caused him to pause. He found himself standing at the entrance to a street as narrow and confined as those around it, curving sharply to the south halfway along its length and bordered on both sides by dingy clerks' offices and shops with dusty windows and closed doors. Looking up he saw a street sign nailed high up on the corner of a building that announced itself as Half Mitre Street, and if the name of the street suggested some ecclesiastical connection, this was not reflected in the commercial premises housed along it, most of which appeared to be pen and ink and paper suppliers. In the middle of the street, at the point at which it veered to the south, was a prominent six-storey building, gabled and imposing, and it was from outside this building that the chanting came: a motley collection of perhaps eight to ten individuals—at least three of them young women—stood in a loose semicircle waving handmade placards and proclaiming their outrage in no uncertain terms.

'*People first! Profit last!*' appeared to be the gist of the chant. There was little doubt he had come to the right place, and as confirmation he now saw beside the doorway a discreet engraved sign announcing in ornate lettering that this was the offices of the North West Midlands Railway Company.

Protestors he had not anticipated. There had been a crowd outside the inquest—more of an angry mob, really—and again on the first day of the inquiry, but that was folk directly affected by the accident, folk that lived and worked and travelled daily on the railway. These people here, they were another kind of folk altogether. One or two of the men wore cheaply made suits and dressed like they themselves worked in an office; the others—apart from the three young women, whose presence he could not fathom—were dressed in a way he was unfamiliar with: unkempt and bearded, their clothes ill-fitting and shabby, yet they did not look like the kind of working folk he knew.

As he stood there the door of the office opened and a gentleman in a black coat and a tall hat emerged. The gentleman carried an umbrella and as he stepped through the doorway he peered suspiciously upwards at the gathering clouds. Then he peered suspiciously at Thomas and Thomas saw that it was the man who had attended Alice's funeral and who had left in a carriage. The gentleman appeared not to recognise him and similarly dismissed the small crowd who now surged towards him, their chanting rising a notch, their placards waving furiously about his head. One of the young men, the most unkempt, wearing the shabbiest coat, now thrust himself directly in the gentleman's way.

'We have your name, Sinclair!' he declared, jabbing a finger into the man's chest. 'The days when you can hide behind corrupt public officials and apathetic government ministers are ended!'

At this the gentleman angrily thrust his accuser's arm aside and strode off with a loud 'Tshk!' amidst a chorus of '*Shame! Shame!*' from the gathered protestors.

'*You will be held accountable!*' the shabby man shouted.

After this excitement everyone appeared a little ruffled, particularly the three women, who were flushed and out of breath. The man who had shouted strutted back and forth, then he stopped when he saw Thomas.

'What's your business here?' he demanded as though his part in the protest gave him some position of authority.

'No business of yours,' Thomas replied brusquely pushing past the man and, though he had not entirely resolved his own course of action, he entered the office.

He found himself in a sort of antechamber framed with dark panelled walls that muffled the sounds from the street outside so effectively Thomas was disconcerted. The room contained a number of upright leather chairs around a low, green baize-covered table and an imposing and highly polished counter behind which a clerk sat, with a number of closed doors ranged behind him. The clerk, a white-haired, extremely elderly gentleman in a tight black coat and waistcoat and very high stiff collar, was scratching figures into a voluminous ledger opened on the desk before him. He paused at Thomas's entrance, his pen poised mid-stroke, and slowly regarded the unlikely intruder from his mud-splattered workman's boots to the cap on his head as he might a new specimen at the zoological gardens.

'Take one more step inside these premises and I shall be forced to summon a constable!' he declared in a voice as truculent as it was feeble with age, clutching his pen in a gnarled hand as though it were a weapon with which he was prepared to defend both himself and his employers to the death.

Thomas had been prepared to be civil but the man's words enflamed him. 'Summon a constable! I shall not care. I shall tell the man your railway killed my child!'

The man did at least have the grace to look startled at these words.

'Here!' Thomas went on, producing the torn letter of condolence from his pocket and pointing to the relevant passage: 'The railway is desirous to make every effort possible to contact the relatives of the deceased and injured *so that everything might be done for them as lies within their power!*' And here—' he brandished his second document—'is the bill from for the funeral *which they did not pay!*'

The clerk regarded the letter and then the unpaid bill down the length of his nose. He squinted at them, he even went so far as to pick up both documents and inspect them much as a detective of police might inspect a bloodied footprint at the scene of a crime. Then he replaced them and slid them back across the counter with the tip of his pen.

'If you have a complaint it must be made in writing.'

'You do not seem to understand—I have journeyed here from the Midlands! Through this company's actions I have lost my job! I have the bill for the funeral which they did not pay—" and Thomas snatched up both documents and crushed them in his fist under the man's nose.

At this the old man leapt to his feet, producing from beneath his desk an ancient bone-handled silver duelling pistol which he brandished menacingly at the intruder. *'Leave at once or I shall send for the constable! Be gone!'*

Considerably startled, Thomas stumbled backwards out of the office where he stood in a daze so that for a heartbeat, two heartbeats, he did not move or even think. When he did move it was to snatch a placard from the nearest protestor—a young woman soberly dressed in black with a lace bonnet on her head and a Bible clasped in her free hand—and with a cry he swung it, cricket-bat style at the window of the office. The young woman whose placard he had appropriated screamed and two men whom he had not observed before and who did not appear to be part of the protest now darted out and grabbed both his arms just at the critical moment that the placard hit the plate glass window, and the window survived, intact, though the placard was broken beyond repair. The elderly clerk had somehow scrambled down from his very high stool and now appeared in the office doorway shaking his fist in fury, and shouting for a constable. He was instantly surrounded by angry protestors who, though not condoning of the newcomer's violent methods nevertheless instinctively sympathised with his sentiment, and the elderly clerk was forced to beat a hasty retreat, locking the front door behind him.

'Leave me! Leave me be!' Thomas shouted, struggling against the two men, who had a firm hold of both his arms. They did not let go and, as he was dragged into the gutter and a fist landed in his gut and a boot thudded into his ribs and another into his lower back, he understood that these men were employed by the railway company to keep the peace. They kept the peace now, thoroughly and methodically, and by the

time they had finished Thomas's protest had ended and he lay curled up in a ball.

When he came to himself it was to find that the thugs had long since melted away and the protestors were crowded around him, offering him a hand up and a handkerchief to douse his bleeding face and another to mop the blood from his shirt. But he wanted none of their assistance; they sickened him as much as the men who had beaten him did, as much as the clerk behind his desk. He fought them off furiously, struggling to his feet, retrieving his cap and pulling on his boot that had come off in the skirmish.

As he did so a second gentleman now emerged from the offices of the railway company. This gentleman, younger than the first, in early middle-age, carrying his top hat and a furled black silk umbrella and wearing gloves, stepped through the doorway and paused only long enough to place his hat on his head and offer a cordial 'Good day' before making off at a smart pace westwards. The ancient clerk followed him to the door, still brandishing the archaic sidearm with which he clearly felt he could protect his departing master. It was enough to distract the small crowd who, enraged, now gave pursuit at a run, the young women hitching up their skirts and showing their ankles to the whole world just as though they cared nothing for what folk might think.

Thomas followed too, as swiftly as his injuries would allow. His anger was a hard bitter knot at his core. It seemed to narrow his focus and provide a clarity that was stark and vivid and bright.

'That gentleman that just now left, what be his name?'

he inquired, out of breath and grabbing one of the protestors by the arm to get his attention.

'That one's Jarmyn,' the man replied. 'Mr Lucas Jarmyn. It was his father—Mr Jarmyn Senior, that is—who built the railway in the first place. He's got a lot to answer for, I fancy.' He paused to fix Thomas with a shrewd eye. 'What's your grievance, friend?'

Thomas ignored the question, partly because he had no answer for it and partly because his head was swimming and his vision blurred, but mainly because ahead of him was the man whose father had built the railway, walking briskly along Half Mitre Street, neatly side-stepping the various human and non-human obstacles in his way, his umbrella clicking on the road, and Thomas Brinklow set off after him.

CHAPTER SIXTEEN

FOUR DAYS LATER, AND IN the hours immediately before her mother's dinner party, Dinah went up to her room and, in a desperate act of subversion, pulled all the bones out of her corset.

She had not planned it as a desperate act of subversion, indeed she had not planned it at all. She had merely gone up to her room, retrieved the corset she was likely to be wearing that evening, taken up a pair of sewing scissors and cut through the threads holding the bones in place. She had then laid down the scissors, pulled out each piece of whalebone in turn and laid them in a circle at her feet. When she had done so, the corset had flopped into a helpless heap on the bed and Dinah had stood in the centre of the circle surrounded by the collection of bones that now resembled less an item of ladies' intimate apparel and more an exhibit at the newly completed Museum of Natural History.

Afterwards she wondered at herself. One minute she had been sitting in the drawing room working on her embroidery

and listening to her mother explain to Mrs Logan some necessary adjustment to the seating plan, the next she had found
herself up in her room assailing her undergarments with a pair
of scissors. She did not know herself.

She picked up the floppy remains of the corset and inspected
it thoughtfully. It was still fully functional, except that it would
no longer cut her in half and restrict her breathing and prevent
her from eating more than three mouthfuls at dinner. Well, all
to the good. It had, then, been a profitable five minutes—more
profitable, at any rate, than working away at an endless piece of
embroidery that she had begun on her twelfth birthday and that
it seemed likely she would not complete by her twenty-second.

When Bill knocked and went into his sister's room a few
minutes later seeking assistance with his black tie, it was to
find her seated on the floor surrounded by the internal organs
of her most expensive corset. He raised a curious eyebrow but
otherwise did not remark on it.

'Help me with this blasted thing, can you, Dinah?'

For a moment she did not move, then she got up and came
to his aid.

'Why do you not get Father to help you?' she asked, to which
Bill offered no reply. She had tied her father's black tie on
occasion but it was the first time Bill had asked her and her
fingers seemed unable to make sense of the task. Eventually
she gave up on the tie and her arms fell limply to her sides.

'Bill, do you think that people get punished whilst they are
still on Earth—by God, I mean—if they do something bad?'

The words sounded odd, even to herself—not the sort of
words she would usually speak—but they had grown and grown

inside her like a balloon that someone was inflating, until she could no longer breathe. Until she had had to cut open her own corset to survive.

'No,' said Bill, fiddling with the tie.

His reply—so short, so utterly unequivocal—silenced her and she felt a kind of despair at them. 'Well, but how can you be so certain?' she pleaded.

He did not reply at once, then he turned around and said briskly, 'Dinah, you are hardly ready yet! If you do not hurry Mama will be after you.' And he left.

—⁂—

A light had gone out in the upstairs window of the house and Thomas Brinklow, watching from the mews below, imagined that a life had been extinguished. Not his own, for that had been extinguished six weeks ago, the very moment Alice had gone—her small, child's body horribly mutilated—in his arms.

He closed his eyes and felt the pavement sink beneath him. It was a bitterly cold evening yet the moisture stood out on his forehead and upper lip and on the palms of both hands. He felt feverish and his head throbbed white hot like the molten iron that oozed from the blast furnace where he had worked since his thirteenth year but where he worked no more. He had to shake himself to clear his head of it.

He had been strong but some of that strength had deserted him. It was this city: it was a poison that got into his lungs and his bloodstream and into his very soul. It laid a veil over his eyes.

He had followed the gentleman whose father had built the railway, along crowded lanes and down into a brightly lit station beneath the street where he had bought a ticket so Thomas had bought a ticket too and he had travelled through a tunnel in an underground steam train, four stations, popping up, dazed and shaken, onto a quiet and tree-lined square. They had eventually come to this street: lined by narrow white-fronted, five-storey dwellings with black railings and blue front doors bordered on either side by pillars that ought to have fronted a municipal building or a railway terminus but here in London meant a rich gentleman's house. Into one of these houses Mr Jarmyn had gone. Thomas had remained across the street and out of sight until nightfall, when hunger and despair had forced him back to the crowded streets and the omnibuses, where he had found a bed in a lodging house in the Temple, a nightmarish place, but it had meant he could write to his wife. There had not been much to report and he was not a letter-writer so he had barely filled a page relating an abridged version of his meeting with the railway people. He had provided her with his lodging house address, too, in case she felt moved to write back to him. He had written on Thursday night and posted the letter the following morning. Now it was Monday evening and he had returned each day to this quiet street off the quiet tree-lined square and watched the rich gentleman's house, his bill from the funeral company in his pocket, the letter of condolence in his hand, but after four days he had done nothing and was no closer to knowing what he would do. Each day at nightfall he had left. But not tonight. Tonight he had remained.

When he opened his eyes the street and the house across the street were bathed red: a vivid, blood-streaked red, the same shade of red as the blood that had streamed from Alice's tiny body as she had lain in his arms, the same red that had spilt from her mouth and down the front of her dress. He saw it when he slept. It was the colour of his dreams as though every day, now, was a spectacular scarlet sunset. But it was not spectacular; it was a vision of Hell.

He blinked, two, three times and the red subsided.

He had lost his job. There were plenty of other men, they had said, ready and waiting to take his place. So let them take his place. What was he working for, anyway, if it was not to put bread on the table for his wife and child?

The flickering glow of a candle was visible in one of the upstairs rooms of the house opposite and Thomas stirred, imagining Mr Jarmyn sitting in his study, or perhaps taking a glass of port wine or reading that morning's *Times*. Reading, perhaps, of another railway accident on his railway line, shaking his head and turning over the page and taking a sip from his glass.

No, it was not a study. The light came from a bedroom for he could see a young lady, no more than seventeen or eighteen, standing in the window. She stood perfectly still, and the candle lit up her face and hair. She wore a gown of some soft grey shade that must surely be silk for the candlelight flickered and was reflected off it. Her arms hung loosely by her sides and she gazed ahead rather than down at the street, though what she could see in the distance on such a night, he could not imagine.

Like an angel.

The notion made him uneasy. It was not a word, an idea,

that he had thought he had a use for any longer. He pushed the thought away and waited, for surely she could not stand there very long, but she remained in the window, unmoving, and Thomas remained in the street below, watching.

The day had darkened into night and the street was utterly still and silent, no soul stirred in any of the white-fronted houses, and yet there was something, some expectation in the air. All day deliveries had been made to the house.

At last the young lady in the window turned her head and blew out the candle, throwing the room into darkness. Thomas started forward then checked himself. How long had he—had she—been standing there? He did not know. It seemed an eternity had passed.

The railway company had refused him an interview; they had offered no assurances that safety would be improved, that such a tragedy could never happen again; its hired thugs had beaten him nearly senseless. They had failed to pay for Alice's funeral—though perhaps this was merely an oversight? Everyone said that, in a case like this, it was usual for the railway company to pay for the funeral. But they had not done so. The bill was unpaid so now he was in debt on top of everything else—

A carriage swung into the mews at full pelt, though the corner was a tight one and the mews very narrow, led by two sweating black horses tossing their heads restlessly and snorting in the freezing air, their hooves on the cobbles shattering the silence, and the liveried coachman on his perch cursed and cracked his whip at the fool who was standing in his way.

—∾—

The first dinner guests arrived promptly at seven thirty and Dinah knew it was the Miss Courtaulds without even having to look out of her bedroom window. The Miss Courtaulds were second cousins of her mother, unmarried sisters in their seventieth year who resided in a house in Onslow Square that had not been redecorated since the Regency and who spoke of the Duke of Wellington as though he were still alive. They were from an era when a seven thirty appointment meant you arrived at seven thirty. The new fashion of arriving anything up to fifteen minutes after the appointed hour they considered scandalous and were not reticent in saying so.

Dinah moved rapidly down the stairs, and it turned out one could move quite rapidly indeed, once one was no longer penned in with a lot of bones. She moved, she glided, she flew down the stairs, feeling the fabric of her gown ripple across her body in a way that positively encouraged movement. She was free! She was liberated! She could leave the house and fly out into the night! She reached the bottom of the stairs and ran straight into her father.

He paused, adjusting his collar, and smiled at her and Dinah thought, But he is happy, right at this moment Father is happy.

'I do not believe I have seen you in this gown before, Dinah,' he said. 'Is it new?'

The gown was not new. It had been purchased seven months ago but this was the first time she had had a chance to wear it.

She faltered and for a moment could not speak.

She was aware of Bill standing behind her and of her father frowning at Bill's botched black tie. 'It is quite new, Father, though I think it is a little large for me now. I believe I was a different size when it was fitted.'

'Then we shall have to fatten you up a bit. Come, your mother has ordered enough food for a regiment.' It was an unfortunate analogy, with Roger's memorial only five days earlier, but he appeared not to notice it for he took her arm with a smile and together they entered the drawing room. Mrs Jarmyn had preceded them and Dinah sensed the change that now came over her father as the lightness fell away from him.

'Aurora,' he said, giving his wife a brief nod.

'Lucas. Dinah, how lovely you look,' said her mother. 'And what an unusual shape that gown is . . .' she added, appraising the bodice of the gown with a curious frown, and Dinah replied with a challenging smile.

'Miss Fresia Courtauld and Miss Adelaide Courtauld,' announced Hermione, curtseying awkwardly then standing back to allow the ladies to enter.

'Aunt Adelaide. How well you look. Aunt Fresia. What a delightful hat,' said Mrs Jarmyn, going forward to greet her cousins.

'Oh, are we the first?' exclaimed Aunt Adelaide. 'I am certain the invitation said seven thirty.'

'We arrived at seven twenty-five and had our driver make two laps of the square,' Aunt Fresia confided to Dinah. 'I must say, I expected to see one or two others doing the same?'

Mrs Jarmyn laughed. 'How amusing you are, Aunt.'

'I recall a dinner we attended at the Hardinges' in '51 or '52,' continued Adelaide, 'do you remember, Fresia, when Papa made us arrive so early we had to do twelve laps of Grosvenor Square before we could announce our arrival? The poor horse was so giddy by the time we stopped, it collapsed and had to be shot.'

'Fortunately Papa always carried a sidearm with him in those days so it was all managed most discreetly,' Fresia explained.

'It was a problem, though, my dear, when it came time to return home,' her sister reminded her.

'What a delightful anecdote, Miss Courtauld,' said Mr Jarmyn, neatly cutting her off. 'Hart, do please come in.'

Dinah's shoulders dropped and a little sigh escaped her but she summoned a smile as her father brought Mr Hart over who was to be her partner for the evening. She had been a child the last time they had met, upon which occasion he had not so much as nodded at her. Now she was a young lady of eighteen and Mr Hart, who was surely forty years of age if not more and whose hair was greying at the temples, turned his gaze fully upon her and made a gallant little bow that seemed excessive and was, therefore, somewhat irritating.

'Miss Jarmyn, how lovely you look. And may I say what a most elegant gown you are wearing.'

Dinah gave him a tight smile. Would he think her quite so lovely, her gown quite so elegant, had he witnessed her in her room butchering her corset not half an hour earlier?

The Eberhardts arrived next, and just behind them, Dr and Mrs Gant and Captain Palmer, so that now the room appeared quite full. Dinah smiled at her partner then ignored him so that when the Freebodys arrived, Mr Hart, whose small talk had begun to flag, appeared visibly relieved. The Duvalls arrival causing a little stir as Mrs Duvall insisted a man had been hiding in the street below, watching her, and Mr Duvall—who had recently returned from a disastrous commercial venture in Durban—just as vehemently insisted she had imagined the whole thing. What threatened to strike a disagreeable note was fortunately diverted by the late and rather dishevelled arrival of the final guest, Professor Dallinger, whose cab had gone to the wrong address.

Dinah listened and smiled and nodded but found she had nothing to contribute. Her mother, by contrast, was dazzling: flitting from couple to couple, producing a brilliant witticism one moment, and a droll observation the next, finding a compliment for the ugliest gown and amusement in the dullest anecdote. She intervened to prevent Mr Freebody from summarising to Mrs Gant the findings of a Board of Trade inquiry; she praised the plunging neckline of Mrs Duvall's gown even as the Miss Courtaulds gasped at its immodesty; she expressed admiration for Captain Palmer's military prowess whilst having not the slightest idea of what his role in the military was; she sympathised with Mr Duvall over the recent loss of his diamond mine and she complimented Mrs Freebody on the acquisition of an exquisite and staggeringly expensive necklace made from diamonds cut from the very mine Mr Duvall had just lost. And lastly—though unquestionably it was her finest moment—she forestalled Sissy Eberhardt when she seemed on the verge of inadvertently insulting the Royal Family.

As Mr Hart attempted to engage her in small talk, Dinah observed her mother silently. She recognised that she was witnessing an artist at work. Why then was her father watching on with such a black look on his face?

But now he had caught Dinah watching him and he re-arranged his features into a pleasant smile. She smiled back at him automatically. Perhaps she had imagined it. Perhaps he had been thinking of something that had made him angry and he was not actually angry with Mama. Yes, surely she had been mistaken for now he was making some charming remark to Mrs Freebody that caused Mrs Freebody, who was not a day under fifty-five, to bat his arm and blush prettily.

Mr Hart, who had been so valiantly carrying on their conversation on his own all this time, had asked her a question.

'I'm so sorry, Mr Hart. What did you say?'

'I inquired whether you had been out much of late,' he repeated. 'I mean to the park, or to the opera? Or to your committees? I understand from your father that you are involved with a number of committees,' and he gave an encouraging smile.

'One committee,' she corrected him, 'which I believe I may have now resigned from. I have not been to the park or to the opera as we have been in deepest mourning for my sister.'

'Yes, of course. How remiss—do forgive me,' replied Mr Hart, offering another of his odd little bows.

But she *had* gone out the previous Wednesday on the occasion of her cousin's memorial service following his tragic and, it would appear, utterly pointless death in the Transvaal a fortnight ago, and though she heard these words quite clearly in her head she could not speak them. Beside her Mr Hart had fallen silent.

The conversation around them had now divided itself roughly into two camps, delineated solely by gender: the gentlemen noted that the situation in the Transvaal was escalating ominously and that the sooner the flotilla of ships containing troops and supplies arrived at the Cape the sooner the insurgency could be put down. The ladies noted that Her Majesty and the Royal Family were still resident at Osborne House on the Isle of Wight and had, the previous day, attended a church service. Dinah found herself a party to neither camp. Bill, who at the start of the evening had seemed almost as unenthusiastic about the dinner as herself, was standing very close to the extraordinarily lovely Mrs Eberhardt and appeared to be enjoying himself immensely. Before Dinah could decide if this was a betrayal of what slim sibling affinity remained between them, she noticed Mrs Logan standing in the doorway and she began to realise that something was wrong.

—∞—

The kitchen was in uproar.

Cook had got up before dawn to start preparations for the dinner. The delivery from the butcher's had arrived late and they had forgotten to include the legs of lamb. The vegetables had been put on late and had only been boiling for an hour. A miscalculation with the icebox meant that the pineapple creams had frozen into a solid mass whereas the raspberry ices had melted into a single pool of crimson liquid. The venison, a whole carcass that had been delivered the previous day and had spent the night hanging from a hook in the scullery, had been got at by Mr Gladstone and Hermione had been put to work removing the more obviously savaged bits of flesh. Mr Gladstone had been booted outside and was now yowling indignantly even as he licked his paws and cleaned his bloodied whiskers.

'I was led to understand you were a professional, Mrs Varley,' Mrs Logan had declared, surveying this chaos an hour or so before the first guests were due to arrive.

'And so I am, Mrs Logan. But I have to work with amatoors, don't I? And if you think this is a disaster you shoulda seen the dinner I prepared at me last house. On that occasion, a rat got into the pigeon pie and no one noticed till it was served up. Now that was a sight to behold, and no mistake!'

'You certainly instil confidence, Mrs Varley.'

'Can't abide pigeons ever since,' Cook had continued, lighting her pipe and clearly warming to her subject. 'It quite turns me stomach to see one. And I won't cook wiv 'em, neither.'

'Then it is a good thing we are not having pigeon pie this evening,' observed Mrs Logan, who was a party to the Prussian fowl deception and who had already taken delivery of the pigeons—ready-plucked and minus their feet—from the butcher's that morning.

She had left the chaos of the kitchen for the relative calm of the cellar, where she had passed a solitary but not unpleasant half-hour digging out the appropriate bottles for the dinner. She had just located the Cheval Blanc when she heard a commotion in the kitchen. Assuming the worst she ran along the passage to the kitchen, almost tripping over Mr Gladstone, who had somehow found his way back inside and was now positioned on the stone-flagged hallway with his tail stuck up straight, his ears pinned back, his teeth bared and his orange fur standing up on end. He jumped at Mrs Logan's arrival and hissed at her.

In the kitchen Hermione stood in the middle of the room, quivering from head to foot, the palms of her hands pressed against the sides of her head, moaning softly.

'What is it? What's going on?' Mrs Logan demanded, coming swiftly over to the distressed maid. 'Oh, get out of the way, cat,' and she pushed the furious orange beast with her foot.

'I *seen* it! And I *'eard* it, too!' exclaimed Hermione, reeling around, her face as white as Cook's shortcrust pastry and about as appealing.

'She seen the ghost!' said Cook, chortling with delight. She turned away, wielding the chopping knife, which she now brought down with a thud upon the necks of the first two Prussian fowls.

Mrs Logan took things in hand. First she slapped the girl smartly on her left cheek, then she shook her by both shoulders. Then she said, 'Don't be so daft, girl. There isn't any such thing as ghosts.' Finally she sat the girl down and handed her a small nip of Cook's gin.

''Ere, don't you be too generous wiv that!' Cook warned and she beheaded two more of the fowls.

Mrs Logan ignored her.

'Hermione, the silver still has not been cleaned, the carpet in the dining room needs to be swept and the lamps lit, the tablecloth needs to be laid, the places need to be set, the curtains in all the rooms need to be drawn, and in the drawing room the carpet swept and lamps lit.'

She was certain she had forgotten something but that would keep the girl busy for the time being.

But Hermione had not moved.

'*That's where I 'eard it!*' she said in a terrified voice. 'The ghost! In the drawin' room, just like you said, Mrs Varley.'

'You told her about the little girl?' Mrs Logan demanded, rounding furiously on Cook.

'Ain't no secret,' replied Cook, picking up one of the headless Prussian fowls and regarding it suspiciously.

'Hermione, what exactly did you see or hear?'

'*It*. The *ghost*.'

'Yes. Now describe to me, as precisely as you are able, the noise the ghost made.'

'A child cryin'. Sobbin', like it were in terrible pain. 'Orrible, it were. Turned the blood cold in me veins. And then *clothes rustlin'*, like it were *movin'*, like it were *comin' towards me—*'

'And you were in the drawing room at the time that you heard this noise?' interrupted Mrs Logan.

'No! I was right outside. I was goin' in to sweep the carpet and do them other things when I 'eard it through the door. I couldn't move. I knew if I went in, if I saw it, if *it* saw *me*, I'd be turned to stone.'

'How'd you know that then?' demanded Cook, putting down the bird carcass. ''Appened to you before, has it—bein' turned to stone?'

'No. Never. But I know others what 'ave.'

'You know folk what 'ave turned to stone?' said Cook, ceasing her work completely to stand with her hands on her hips.

Mrs Logan had a sense of things getting out of hand.

'Hermione, come with me and we will go up to the drawing room together and—'

'*No!*' refused the girl, shaking her head, her eyes wide with terror. 'Don't make me do it, Mrs Logan, I'd as soon quit.'

'I can arrange that,' observed Cook. 'Plenty more girls in the orphanage.'

'Thank you, Mrs Varley. As always your observations are pithy though of no help whatsoever. Hermione, for this evening only, you will do the jobs in the dining room and elsewhere in the house and I shall do the drawing room. Now, get back to work or I will follow Cook's advice.'

Hermione got shakily to her feet, seemed for one agonised moment to consider her future in the household, then grabbed a bucket and a broom and left the kitchen.

'Don't think much of these 'ere Prussian fowls,' said Cook, nudging one with her knife. 'Can't think what the Kaiser wants with 'em. Look no better than pigeons to me.'

'Nonsense, Mrs Varley. They look nothing like pigeons.'

Mrs Logan had set to work in the drawing room, aware that they were behind schedule and that the family would be coming downstairs in a matter of minutes and the first guests arriving not long after. A cursory glance around the room before she set to work confirmed that no ghost was currently in residence and she snorted and shook her head at the girl's foolishness and Cook's unhelpful goading. Having completed the drawing room, she prepared to withdraw, backing straight into Mrs Jarmyn.

'Oh. Is the room not ready, Mrs Logan?' she asked, both eyebrows climbing delicately up her forehead.

'Certainly it is, Mrs Jarmyn. I was just giving it one final check.'

'Did it require one final check? Or do you not trust the maid to do her job?'

Mrs Logan did not trust the maid to do her job, particularly when the maid believed she had just seen a ghost, but she was certainly not going to admit this to her employer.

'It is customary to make one final round of checks prior to guests arriving,' she replied.

'A custom I am not familiar with. But no doubt you know your business. Thank you, Mrs Logan,' and Mrs Jarmyn swept icily out of the drawing room and closed the door firmly behind her.

After her mistress had gone Mrs Logan stayed for a time in the room calming herself. For the best part of the three years they had existed, herself and Mrs Jarmyn, if not exactly side by side, then certainly with a single purpose: the good running of the house. After Sofia's death Mrs Jarmyn's interest in the good running of the house had, perhaps not unnaturally, waned. But since the family had emerged from mourning the atmosphere had altered markedly and Mrs Jarmyn's antagonism, never far from the surface, appeared to be escalating. Oddly she had not attempted to wrestle back duties that for the most part now fell to her housekeeper and that her housekeeper would willingly have handed back. No, instead she seemed intent on undermining her.

Am I *afraid* of her? Mrs Logan wondered, uneasily. It was not a pleasant thought. No, she decided after a moment's reflection, she was not afraid. But the balance had definitely changed.

A sound outside the room, a floorboard creaking followed a moment later by light footsteps retreating up the stairs, made it clear Mrs Jarmyn had been standing just the other side of the door.

Is *she* afraid of *me*? Mrs Logan wondered, and the thought stunned her.

She left the room and hurried down to the dining room on the ground floor to see where Hermione was up to and for the next half hour they prepared the room. Only about half the plates had been cleaned but if they rotated the cleaned items quickly enough during dinner it was likely no one would notice.

'Fingerbowls,' said Mrs Logan, signalling Hermione with a click of her fingers. 'In the sideboard. Quickly. Fill them up.'

Hermione found the bowls and laid them at intervals on the table, then she filled them up with water from the jug.

'Rosewater. We need rosewater,' said Mrs Logan and Hermione gaped at her. 'We ain't got no roses, Mrs Logan! It's winter!'

'Then we improvise! Coloured paper. Go on, girl, to one of the children's rooms. It must be red or pink or yellow, and scissors, hurry!'

Whilst Hermione was gone she surveyed the table, adjusting one or two pieces, rearranging the chairs. When Hermione returned, triumphantly waving a sheet of pink notepaper and some sewing scissors, they set busily to work cutting out rose-petal-shaped pieces and dropping them into the fingerbowls.

'Looks like bits of coloured paper,' Hermione concluded as they stood back to survey their handiwork.

'Don't be defeatist. The guests may think that but no one will say so. We will say it is a new variety of rose. A Prussian rose. Now, go and help Cook and keep a lookout for the first

guests. It will be the Miss Courtaulds and they'll be here in
. . . four minutes.'

By a quarter to eight all of the guests had arrived and had
congregated in the drawing room.

By eight o'clock a drunken man had turned up outside the
house threatening violence to all those within.

CHAPTER SEVENTEEN

IT WAS HERMIONE WHO SPOTTED him first. She came running along the hallway, skidding to a halt in the dining room doorway, her cap askew, eyes wide, and Mrs Logan, who had been making final adjustments to the table settings, paused, hands on hips.

'Hermione, if you're about to tell me you've seen the ghost—'

'No, Mrs Logan, I ain't. It's a *man* and he's outside the house, shoutin' and carryin' on and threatenin' all sorts!'

They picked up their skirts and ran together back down the hallway. Mrs Logan could hear the rumble of voices and the occasional laugh coming from the drawing room. She also heard what sounded like an explosion coming from below stairs, but she chose to ignore that and to concentrate on the immediate danger: to wit, a man threatening violence and, more to the point, potentially disrupting the dinner party.

The hallway was illuminated by a single lamp halfway along its length and neither she nor Hermione carried a candle, whilst outside Cadogan Mews was flooded with street gaslighting. Consequently they could clearly make out, silhouetted against the stained glass panels in the front door, a man's figure, looming and grotesque, and a moment later, a thud as something hit the door.

'*Oh, he's comin' in!*' shrieked Hermione, cowering behind Mrs Logan as they both stopped.

'Oh, no he's not!' said Mrs Logan, marching up to the front door and opening it.

The man, whoever he was, seemed for a moment to fill the doorway and Mrs Logan was aware of her heart pounding painfully. A second later the man staggered backwards, appearing to have been thrown off balance by the door unexpectedly opening and an angry housekeeper standing before him. She could make him out more clearly now and she saw that this was a working man, a young man with a limp moustache but with a usually clean-shaven chin, though he clearly had not shaved for some days or longer. He wore a shabby jacket with a collarless shirt beneath it—ripped and bloodied, she noted—and a cap of some sort on his head and working men's boots on his feet. He was evidently taken with the drink for he stared at her uncomprehendingly, then blinked through swollen and bruised eyes, and he swayed for a moment, almost falling over the doorstep so that she got a faceful of alcoholic fumes.

'What do you mean by coming to this house in this manner?' she demanded.

'Mr Jarmyn—that's the gentleman's name, in't it? That's the gentleman whose father built the railway?' he replied, swaying towards her and catching at the doorframe to steady himself so that his face was briefly lit by the streetlight, and it was a terrible face—bruised and swollen and cut up.

'Mr Jarmyn? Mr Jarmyn will not see you. What do you mean by coming here at this hour? What is your business?'

'He knows! He knows why I'm here! Tell 'im it's Thomas Brinklow of Dawley.' The man's voice rose as he said these words and Mrs Logan cast a glance upwards where the voices from the drawing room could be clearly heard. Perhaps seeing she had momentarily taken her eyes off him, he made a move towards the front door, pushing against it and almost succeeding in getting in but Mrs Logan held him back and, after a brief tussle, managed to close the door. A moment later she saw him throw himself against the door with a curse.

Mrs Logan turned and walked quickly back towards the cowering Hermione.

'Wait here. Do not let this man get in—' (Hermione gaped at her) '—and I shall go and consult Mr Jarmyn. And it may be that someone will need to be dispatched to get the constable.' Hermione's eyes widened and she paled visibly.

Mrs Logan ascended to the drawing room, her steps slowing as she approached. Here she paused, remaining unobtrusively in the doorway, trying to catch Mr Jarmyn's eye but seeing instead Mrs Jarmyn, who flashed her an irritated glance. Mrs Logan had no wish to consult Mrs Jarmyn on this matter but Mrs Jarmyn came directly over.

'What is it, Mrs Logan? Is there a problem?'

'There is a young man—a working man—outside, asking to speak to Mr Jarmyn.'

Mrs Jarmyn looked a little bemused. 'Then I suggest you inform the young man that Mr Jarmyn is not available.'

'Indeed, I have done so however he is most insistent, to the point of—'

But Mrs Jarmyn had turned away to catch something someone had said. Now she turned back and appeared surprised Mrs Logan was still standing there.

'I feel certain you can deal with the matter, Mrs Logan,' she said, and she rejoined her guests.

And so I shall, thought Mrs Logan, picking up her skirts and heading quickly back downstairs. Hermione had not moved, and neither had the drunken young man for she could make out his darkened form leaning against the front door.

If she had thought he had called off his assault Mrs Logan was disappointed, for Mr Brinklow, with an intoxicated roar, began to pummel himself bodily against the door. Mrs Logan, who had momentarily placed herself just on the other side of the door in order to draw breath, jumped with fright but the front door was a solid one and no drunken working man in a soiled cap was going to knock it down anytime soon. Still, the guests would be descending to the dining room imminently and a drunkard attempting to batter down the front door was not a sight they should be confronted with.

Another explosion—muffled, but an explosion nonetheless—could be heard from below stairs. Mrs Logan took a deep breath.

'Get Cook, Hermione, hurry. Tell her to come upstairs.'

'Upstairs?' repeated Hermione. 'Cook?'

'Yes! Oh, for Heaven's sake!' and she pushed the girl aside and plunged down the stairs, tripping over Mr Gladstone and narrowly avoiding a nasty fall.

She paused in the kitchen doorway, confronted with a fog of thick smoke that instantly made her choke. Out of the fog, Cook appeared.

'These Prussian fowls go off like firecrackers if you cover 'em in brandy and hang 'em from a roastin'-jack for 'alf an hour,' Cook observed, wiping exploded fowl from her hands onto her apron and smoothing down her singed eyebrows.

'I'm sure it will make a most amusing party trick. In the meantime, Mrs Varley, I require your urgent assistance upstairs!'

'Upstairs?!' repeated Cook, aghast.

'Yes. Now please.'

Cook shook her head but nevertheless followed Mrs Logan back up the stairs.

'I ain't been upstairs since the business of the spilt bisque and before that, last May,' she muttered, 'and look what happened then,' she added darkly.

'This is not a time for reminiscences, Mrs Varley. There is a drunken young man attempting to break down the front door and I require him to be removed before the guests come down to dinner. As you have considerably more . . . presence than myself or Hermione, I would be much obliged if you would kindly remove him.'

Cook gave a second bewildered shake of the head. 'Right you are, Mrs Logan,' she replied, pushing up her sleeves and getting into the spirit of the thing, and she set off down the hallway in what could only be described as a businesslike waddle. Upstairs the rumble of voices got louder and Mrs Logan realised the guests were on their way downstairs.

'Hermione, there is nothing for it, I'm afraid.' And Hermione, who had not moved from her position behind the potted fern, gazed up at her with a look of dismay.

—⁂—

How futile it all was, thought Dinah, feeling the weight of a hundred dinner parties pressing down upon her shoulders.

They were preparing to go down to dinner. Her mother had marshalled each of the couples into their correct formation in the procession and now they were ready to set off. Father and Mrs Freebody, as host and most important lady, were first, followed by Emily Duvall who had been trumped by Mrs Freebody and now found herself being led to dinner by Mr Freebody, then came Miss Fresia Courtauld and Captain Palmer, Miss Adelaide and Dr Gant, Mr Eberhardt and Mrs Gant, Mrs Eberhardt and Mr Duvall, then her mother, as hostess, with Professor Dallinger as the most important gentlemen. Herself and Mr Hart, as single and (on one side, at least) youngest, brought up the rear. The Eberhardts, who were American, had embraced the idea of a procession with an enthusiasm that did not falter when their own lowly position in it became evident. Bill, with no partner of his own and strictly against the rules of protocol, took Sissy Eberhardt's other arm and looked very pleased with himself.

Mr Hart, by contrast, was clearly miffed. He had been part-nered with the youngest, the prettiest, the only eligible young lady of the evening but she had proven to be uncommunicative, her interest in him limited at best, and now he found himself bringing up the rear as they prepared to make their way down to dinner. To compensate, Dinah gave him her most—indeed, her only—encouraging smile of the evening, which meant he was forced to smile back when he clearly would have preferred to frown.

The procession set off and Dinah closed her eyes.

'Have you a headache, Miss Jarmyn?' inquired Mr Hart.

'Not yet,' she replied and they both lapsed into silence.

The front couple had reached the stairwell and begun to descend. They must have been about halfway down the stairs, with the rear couple still at the top, when they heard a tremendous crash down below followed immediately by a shriek. Instantly the procession broke ranks, the gentlemen clattering down the remaining stairs to investigate, the ladies standing where they had stopped, and clapping their hands to their faces.

'It's the maid,' said someone.

'The maid's come a cropper,' someone else confirmed.

By the time Dinah reached the scene, Hermione was standing surrounded by the remnants of a rather ugly vase that had once stood on the table in the hallway containing dried flowers, and by a semi-circle of guests. Hermione had a rather odd, almost frozen, look on her face, no doubt caused by the shock of the crash and by the sudden arrival on the scene of eight breathless gentlemen followed a moment later by eight shaken ladies.

'Is the girl all right?' someone asked.

'Yes, she's perfectly fine. No harm done,' said Mrs Jarmyn, assuming control of the situation, but she looked over the gentlemen's heads seeking out Mrs Logan as she said this.

Mrs Logan appeared from nowhere, smiling brightly. 'Yes, no harm done, a little domestic accident. Poor girl tripped over Mr Gladstone. He does have a tendency to get underfoot.'

'Good. Well, so long as no one is hurt, I suggest we remove at once to the dining room,' said Mr Jarmyn and, casting a thoughtful glance at his housekeeper, he began to shepherd the guests inside.

'Tripped over Mr Gladstone? Whatever can she mean?' said Mrs Eberhardt as she followed Mr Jarmyn into the dining room.

—✺—

Once the last guest had gone inside, Mrs Logan grabbed Hermione and brushed her down.

'That was very well done, Hermione. I shall not forget your sacrifice. Now, hurry and serve the soup—the clear soup first. I must check on things outside.'

'Things' had gone ominously quiet outside, so much so that Hermione's heroics with the ugly vase had almost not been warranted, but Mrs Logan had taken no chances in creating her little diversion. She made her way up the hallway and, after putting her head against the front door to listen, opened the door wide.

There was no one in sight.

She stepped out into the cold night, looking up and down the mews, and found Cook standing over a slumped figure some little way off, hands on hips.

'And let that be a lesson to you,' Cook said, and she spat on the ground. Then she turned and, rubbing her hands briskly together, waddled back up towards the house.

'Don't think you'll be having no more trouble from that one,' she announced but Mrs Logan, who could see the slumped figure stagger to its feet, wobble for a moment, then reach down for a large rock that seemed to have been placed there for just this eventuality, disagreed with her.

—⚬—

'Always a mistake, in my experience,' declared Professor Dallinger, 'naming a cat after a prime minister. Bound to lead to confusion.' He paused to bring his mouth closer to his soup spoon.

'No doubt you are correct, sir,' Bill replied, 'but, in point of fact, it was the other way around: we named Mr Gladstone Mr Gladstone before Mr Gladstone became Prime Minister, so we can hardly be held to blame in this instance.' He sat back rather satisfied with himself and Dinah, studying her brother from across the table, saw that he was utterly untouched by the two recent bereavements and for a moment she hated him.

'Ah well, not a great deal one can do in that circumstance,' the professor conceded.

'Except vote for Mr Disraeli,' suggested her father.

'Oh dear, I trust the men are not going to discuss politics,' said Mrs Duvall with a pretty smile.

'Politics? Who's discussing politics? I was talking about cats,' replied the professor.

'It is confusing, though, isn't it,' said Mrs Freebody, 'having a cat with the same name as the Prime Minister.'

'Yes, I believe we have already established that, Evelyn,' said her husband in a curt aside.

'Actually it's not confusing at all,' said Mrs Jarmyn, jumping into the slight pause caused by Mr Freebody's remark. 'For instance, if one hears that someone has tripped over Mr Gladstone or that Mr Gladstone has got at the milk, we usually assume it is the cat. On the other hand, if we hear that Mr Gladstone has made a great speech in Parliament on the Irish Question, then we are likely to assume it is Mr Gladstone, the Prime Minister.'

'Yes, yes, I take your point,' said Professor Dallinger, and Dinah thought: I cannot bear it.

—∾—

'Run, Mrs Varley!'

'*Run?*' said Cook. 'These legs ain't doin' no runnin'. It's a wonder they got up them stairs at all. Now you want me to *run?*'

And indeed the crazed young man was even now careering towards them, his arm raised, the slab of stone clasped in his right hand and a menacing look in his eye. He let out a great bellow of rage and at this, Mrs Varley picked up her skirts and fairly sprinted up the front steps, without so much as a backward glance to see what was occurring.

With the deranged man barely two yards behind her, Cook plunged through the door, aided by Mrs Logan who reached out and grabbed her arm, bundling her inside and slamming the front door in the young man's face.

They both collapsed against the door, the one breathing heavily, the other wheezing and clasping one hand to her bosom, and flapping her face with the other.

A second later the young man, or the rock with which he was armed, or possibly both, slammed against the door with a thud that made the door shudder, and the housekeeper and the cook hurled themselves to the floor, their hands over their heads as though the Heavens were falling in upon them.

—⁂—

The thud reverberated down the length of the hallway and could clearly be heard in the dining room, interrupting Dr Gant's fascinating anecdote concerning an item of rare fifteenth-century glassware he had almost, but at the last minute failed, to purchase in an auction room in Umbria the previous year.

'Oh, the maid has come a cropper again!' announced Captain Palmer, clearly relieved at the interruption.

'Perhaps she has tripped over Mr Gladstone again,' suggested Mrs Duvall. 'I mean the cat, not the Prime Minister,' she added lest there was any lingering confusion.

'Prussian fowl, madam?' said Hermione, offering the silver dish to her, and everyone at once realised that the maid had not, in fact, come a cropper as she was, at that very moment, in the room with them.

'Hermione, do you know what is occurring outside?' inquired Mr Jarmyn, mildly.

Hermione froze. 'Outside?'

'Yes. Outside.'

It seemed to Dinah, silently watching Hermione from her place at the table, that various responses flashed across the girl's face and were as swiftly dismissed. In the end Hermione went for the simplest option and merely shook her head. 'I really couldn't say, sir.'

'Then, if I may be excused for a brief moment, I shall take it upon myself to investigate and report back,' announced Mr Jarmyn, pushing back his chair and standing up. He paused to dip his fingers into the nearest fingerbowl, frowned for a moment at the rose petal that was stuck to his thumb, then with a bow to the ladies, left the room.

—◊—

'We require the services of a police constable, Mrs Varley,' said Mrs Logan as a second thud caused the front door to shudder again.

'I don't need no police constable. I need Mr Mappin and Mr Webb. You 'old the fort, Mrs L. I'll sort this,' and Cook set off at a brisk waddle downstairs.

Mrs Logan wasted no time speculating on who Mr Mappin or Mr Webb were and why they were resident in Mrs Varley's kitchen. Instead she grabbed the occasional table that stood just inside the front door and began to manoeuvre it against the door. Then she heaved the massive potted fern into place beside it and had just completed this task as Mr Jarmyn emerged from the dining room.

'Mrs Logan,' he called. 'I trust everything is all right?'

'Good evening, Mr Jarmyn. It would appear that we are under siege.'

'Under siege? Good Lord.' He came quickly down the hallway just as the young man made his third attempt on the front door. 'Who the Devil is it? What does he want?'

Mrs Logan briefly described the man's arrival and relayed the details of her short conversation with him.

'But he wants me? He desires to speak with me?'

'It would appear so. He did not explain the reason for his request.'

'Then I must speak with him.'

Mrs Logan at once thrust herself between her employer and the door. 'I do not believe that is a good idea, Mr Jarmyn. The man is armed and, in my opinion, clearly mad. You will only get harmed—or worse!'

Mr Jarmyn bowed his head and spoke in a quiet voice.

'I heed your warning, Mrs Logan, however I have a good idea of why this fellow is upset. I think it better if I speak with him.'

Mrs Logan faced him and for a moment they stood so close the cuffs of his coat brushed the sleeve of her gown. She closed her eyes for a moment then stepped aside. Mr Jarmyn calmly removed her makeshift barricade and faced the front door. At the final moment he turned to her and they exchanged a silent look.

'I believe it would be better if you were to beat a retreat, Mrs Logan.'

'I shall wait right here,' she replied. She would face the danger with him.

'As you wish,' and Mr Jarmyn flung open the door.

The young man stood before them, silhouetted as before and looking massive in the gaslight, his right arm raised and his face in shadow.

'Mr Brinklow? Is it Mr Brinklow? Would you like to come in? We can talk, if you would like to.'

The man had frozen, his arm still aloft. Mrs Logan, standing just inside the doorway, could feel her heart in her mouth and she knew, in an instant, that if the arm came down, if the madman struck, that she would spring forward and push Mr Jarmyn aside. That she would take the blow herself, if need be. She braced herself.

No one moved.

A sound like one might imagine a wounded bull to make, or perhaps a banshee at the gates of Hell, filled the night air and, seemingly out of the ground, a figure arose, giant and grotesque with a glinting flash of metal. The madman spun around, the rock falling from his hand, and he cried out, staggered and fell backwards down the front steps. Picking himself up he ran, in a dazed zigzagging path across the mews and around the corner into Cadogan Square.

'That fixed 'im good,' announced Cook, standing at the top of the basement steps with her best chopping knife in her hand. 'Evenin', Mr Jarmyn,' and she spat on the ground and descended the steps once more.

There was a moment when, left alone in the now empty doorway, neither Mrs Logan nor Mr Jarmyn spoke. Finally Mr Jarmyn turned to her.

'I had no idea I had such a formidable team below stairs. Shall we put these back?' and together they shifted the table and the fern back to their proper places.

'I think I had better return to my guests,' said Mr Jarmyn once they had removed all signs of the siege. Yet he made no move to return to the dining room. Instead he turned back to her, a look of bemused admiration on his face. 'A formidable team,' he repeated. Then he left and headed off down the hallway. As he reached the table where the ugly vase had until recently stood, he paused and turned back. 'Good choice, Mrs Logan. I never liked that vase,' and he disappeared into the dining room.

Mrs Logan stood in the gloom of the hallway for a long moment and was surprised to find she had an overwhelming urge to burst into tears.

—⁓—

'Curious. It tastes a little like pigeon,' said Nathan Eberhardt. 'It's not a delicacy we have in the States.'

'Birds are generally larger in the States,' Sissy Eberhardt observed to Mr Duvall, who was seated beside her.

'I do not believe we have had Prussian fowl before, have we, Fresia?' said the younger Miss Courtauld.

'I do not believe so, Adelaide, no,' her sister confirmed.

'Oh, but I feel certain it was served at the Dempsey-Bowes' last year,' said Mrs Jarmyn and Dinah looked at her mother and her mother returned her gaze impassively.

'Yes, yes I do believe you are right, Aurora,' said Miss Adelaide, nodding. 'Do you not remember, Fresia? We had it at the Dempsey-Bowes' last year?'

'And Mama, didn't Cook mention that they serve it to Her Majesty when she is staying at Balmoral?' said Dinah.

The dining room door opened and Mr Jarmyn came back in, resuming his place at the table with a bright smile.

'I do beg everyone's pardon. Dr Gant, you were telling us about that fascinating item of fifteenth-century glassware. I am impatient to discover whether your bid was successful or not?'

—⁓—

Much, much later, Dinah removed her gloves and her boots and unfastened her gown—the corset, unfettered now by whalebone, simply glided to the floor—and blew out the candle and went and stood by the window in her bedroom. She pulled the curtains aside and looked down on the deserted mews below. A single gaslight burnt and in the distance a clock struck the quarter hour. It was after midnight.

At least, she thought as she stood gazing out of the window, at least Mr Hart had not attempted to propose to her. She could not have borne that.

—⁓—

Much later still, when the army of pots and pans and cutlery and utensils and implements had been cleaned and polished and put away, when the tables had been scrubbed and the range had been cleaned in readiness for tomorrow, and Hermione had finally dragged herself up to her attic room and Mrs Logan had done her final inspection and gone up to her own room, Cook sat up late in her rocking chair, thoughtfully smoking her pipe and gnawing on the bones of the remaining Prussian fowls.

The house was silent but for the puff of her pipe and the sucking of her gums on the tiny bird bones.

And the smothered sobbing of a child above.

Cook stopped gnawing and removed the pipe from her mouth and listened. She heaved herself to her feet, picked up the guttering candle and went along the passage to stand at the bottom of the stairs. After a moment she returned to the kitchen, closing the door behind her and, pausing only briefly, she picked up a wooden chair and wedged it beneath the doorhandle. Then she resumed her position in the rocking chair but her pipe had gone out and she did not relight it.

CHAPTER EIGHTEEN

'FATHER, WHY WAS THAT MAN trying to break down our front door last night?' asked Jack, over breakfast.

Mr Jarmyn looked up from his morning kidneys and regarded his youngest son in some surprise. '*Was* there a man trying to break down our front door last night?' He sat back in his chair facing the other members of the family who were seated around the breakfast table. 'Did anyone else witness this extraordinary phenomenon?'

He was relieved that neither the maid nor Mrs Logan were in attendance at that moment. He had no wish for either of them to observe him lying to his entire family.

'Not I,' said his wife, casting a surprised glance at her son. 'When did this alleged atrocity occur, Jack?'

'Last night! Whilst you were all at dinner! And it's not "alleged"!

'And yet, oddly, I saw nothing of it at all,' remarked Gus, fastidiously cutting up the slice of cold tongue on his plate.

'Dinah, did you witness anything?' asked Mr Jarmyn.

Dinah shook her head. 'I'm afraid I was too busy discussing rare Venetian glassware and suitable names for cats to have noticed anything, Father.'

'Yes, they *were* high points in the conversation, were they not?' Mr Jarmyn turned back to Jack, who was looking increasingly agitated, and gave him an apologetic shrug. 'Sorry, old man.'

'But I *saw* him!' Jack insisted, getting indignantly up from his seat then noting his father's frown and sitting down again. 'I really did,' he repeated, though in a quieter voice.

As he said this, Mrs Logan entered the morning room carrying a vase with dried flowers in it. She looked at no one as she arranged the vase on the sideboard. Indeed it was almost as if she was avoiding everyone's gaze. Then she turned and left the room.

Lucas placed his napkin on his chair and stood up. 'I have work to do, so if you will excuse me,' and he followed Mrs Logan out, closing the door firmly behind him. Mrs Logan was waiting just outside.

'What is it?' he asked. 'Is the fellow back?'

'No, Mr Jarmyn, but there is a police constable outside. I wondered if you wished to speak to him?'

He hesitated, thinking. Having just lied to his family he did not now wish them to see him in discussion with a police constable. Did he wish this to become a police matter? But there had been an attempted assault on his house; one could not justify placing one's family at risk of further attack. Mrs Logan was watching him.

'I thought, if you did wish to talk to the man, I could put him in the front reception room,' she suggested, and it was clear that what she meant was, I could ensure no one sees him.

He smiled gratefully. 'Thank you, Mrs Logan, as always you have a solution to everything. I shall see the man in the front reception room.'

Police Constable Matlock took the news that a madman had attempted to break down the door of an establishment in Cadogan Mews in his stride, licking the end of his pencil and recording the details in his notebook with no more than the occasional nod of his head and Lucas, pausing in his story to observe the man, wondered how he would react to the report of a grisly murder.

'And you say you knew the man, sir?'

'I believe I may have seen this man, yes. Briefly. At my offices a few days ago. There have been some minor disturbances there recently. Protestors angry about a railway accident. It's possible this is connected.'

'It would seem likely, sir. However we try to avoid assumptions in our line of work. How many casualties did you say there were, sir, in this railway accident?'

Lucas stood up and walked around the chair to the window. 'Three. That is, three fatalities. Twenty-nine injured.'

'Taking into account wives, husbands, parents, children of the dead plus survivors and *their* wives, husbands, parents, children . . .' the constable paused as though doing some enormous calculation in his head '. . . potential for quite a large number of aggrieved people, I would suggest.'

Lucas made no reply.

'Well, your bloke's probably long gone by now,' the man sighed. 'Still, to be on the safe side, we'll keep this place under observation for the next few days. Might be as well to let your family know to be vigilant, not go out alone if they can possibly help it.'

'You can't believe the man will try it again?'

'Can't be too careful, sir. He's tried it once. Why not a second time?'

'Because my cook went at him with a meat cleaver. That would be reason enough, one would have thought.'

The constable rubbed the bristles on his chin. 'I have had occasion to meet the lady in question, sir, and I can testify that such an encounter would not be one any man would wish to repeat. But this fellow sounds like a madman. Can't predict 'em, sir. Irrational,' and Constable Matlock tapped the side of his head.

'I am sure you are right, Constable, nevertheless I would prefer to keep this . . . incident quiet, at least from my wife and children. By all means patrol the street and keep an eye on the house but please do so unobtrusively.'

After the man had gone, Lucas stood by the window thinking. The other directors should be told, they had a right to know in case the man came to their homes. He would go into the office and call a meeting for later that afternoon. As for Aurora and the children, no, he would not tell them. He had no wish to alarm them. He had already told them nothing had happened, how could he now go to them and say that he had lied? Besides, it was surely unlikely the man would return. And if he did, the constable would be on hand to deal with him.

If he could just have spoken to Brinklow. If he could have had ten minutes with the man . . . And said what, exactly? I understand your pain—

There was a soft tap at the door.

'Mrs Logan. Come in. Close the door. Has the constable been shown out?'

She nodded. 'Yes, Mr Jarmyn. It was managed . . . discreetly.' She touched the surface of the table with her fingers and looked down as she said this.

'Good. Good, thank you.' Lucas paused. It was important now to phrase his words carefully. 'As you will have ascertained, I have decided not to tell Mrs Jarmyn or the children what has occurred. I have no wish to alarm them. The constable seemed fairly certain that the man will have long absconded and as a precaution the police are to keep the house under observation so I feel justified in keeping this from my family.'

He stood at the window with his back to her. What must she think of him, lying to his family? What must her opinion of him be now, after this?

'No doubt that is the wisest course, Mr Jarmyn,' she replied, which told him nothing. He imagined himself turning around and searching her face to see her thoughts, imagined himself saying, But *is* it? Do you really believe so? What do you really *think*, Mrs Logan? But instead he said:

'And I am sure I can rely on you to ensure the discretion of the staff in this matter?'

He was asking her to make the servants keep a secret from the mistress of the house. He was asking her to collude in a deception.

'Their discretion is assured,' she replied.

He nodded, not turning around. 'Thank you. That will be all.'

He waited until he heard the door open then close behind her before going over to the spot where she had stood. He reached out and traced the place on the table that her fingers had touched and this simple act meant more, at that moment, than the railway accident and the deranged man and the lies he had told to his family.

Something, he realised with a growing sense of unease, had gone very awry.

—⁂—

Jack knew what he had seen and he was not going to be fobbed off. That no one else in the family admitted having seen it or appeared to believe him only spurred him on. Something had happened and it was being deliberately kept from him. This did not, in itself, surprise him. Things happened all the time in the adult world that he was simply not a party to. Sofia was kept alive in a darkened room for ten days and neither he nor Gus were allowed to see her. Her funeral happened and they did not attend. Cousin Roger came to dinner then a telegram arrived to say he was dead. There was no body, and they did not attend the memorial service or the gathering afterwards. People came to make calls, other people came for dinner. They arrived, they stayed a while, they left. He and Gus saw none of it. And now a man had attempted to batter down the door and everyone was pretending nothing had happened.

He left the morning room and instead of going up to the schoolroom to join Gus for lessons he went downstairs to investigate the front door. Before he had even reached the door he paused, noticing, with mounting excitement, the scuff marks on the hallway carpet. It looked just as though the table had been dragged out of position and moved to a spot in front of the door! And yes, the big fern had similarly been moved and then moved back! The marks were unmistakable.

Exhilarated by his discovery he turned triumphantly to tell someone and ran smack into Hermione, who had appeared out of nowhere and was armed with a rug beater, a dustpan and a broom.

Averting her eyes, Hermione curtsied then she swung the broom around and began to sweep it across the hallway carpet.

'No! Wait! Stop!' cried Jack and Hermione jumped and stared at him in alarm. But it was too late! The scuffs on the carpet had gone. It was as though they had never been there.

Jack stared in dismay and Hermione stared too, though she clearly had no idea what they were looking at. Or did she?

Jack looked up and studied the maid, who realised she was being studied and at once cast her eyes down and took a step backwards so that she was flat against the wall. Did she know? Was she party to the conspiracy? How likely was it that the girl would decide to sweep this part of the carpet at this particular moment? Not very likely!

'Who was the man who came to the door last night, Hermione?' he demanded, determined to force the issue.

'I couldn't really say, sir. There was lots of gentlemen come to dinner.'

Oh, she was clever. Too clever by half.

'I *mean* the man who tried to come in, who tried to batter the door down, that's who I mean.'

'Hermione, the laundry still has not been collected and packaged up. Please leave the carpets till afterwards. Good day, Master Jack,' and Mrs Logan appeared, signalling to the maid to hurry along, which she did—gratefully, it appeared to Jack.

He stood his ground, furious, as Hermione moved swiftly away.

'Mrs Logan, wait. Who was the man who tried to break the door down last night?'

'I'm afraid I was too busy with the dinner to see what was going on outside. Did you fancy that you saw something?'

'*No*, I did not *fancy*, I *did* see something! Only everyone is pretending nothing happened.'

'How extraordinary. Why do you think they would do that?'

'Because they always keep things from me.' Jack kicked angrily at the wall. 'There were marks, here on the carpet, you could clearly see it, where things had been moved around, probably to stop the man getting in . . . But now they are gone and no one will believe me!'

Mrs Logan took a step towards him, paused, looked cautiously down the length of the hallway, then leant down to whisper in his ear. 'I know. I saw them too. But now they are gone no one will ever believe us. I think it had better be our little secret. What do you think?'

Jack was astonished. 'Yes,' he said slowly. 'Yes, I see. And we will know something that no one else knows! Not even Gus!'

'No one,' and she put her finger up to her lips.

———

When he had gone, Mrs Logan studied the carpet and the two items of furniture that she and Mr Jarmyn had positioned and replaced but there was no evidence at all now that anything untoward had happened here. Next she opened the front door and, with a cloth, removed the dirty marks left by the man's fists. The dents in the door caused by the rock she could do nothing about but unless the sunlight was directly upon them they were not too noticeable.

Poor Jack, she thought, standing on the front step for a moment to rub her hands briskly together in the chilly morning air. He so desperately wanted something . . . but what that something was she did not know, and she doubted that he did either. ·

———

In the afternoon, Mr Jarmyn went off to a hastily convened meeting of the board of directors.

In the schoolroom, the boys worked silently on a Greek translation, Gus thoughtfully chewing the end of his pencil, Jack going over in his mind the extraordinary sight of the unknown man at the door and smiling to himself at the secret he now shared with Mrs Logan.

Dinah and Mrs Jarmyn called on Aunt Meredith and cousin Rhoda. They returned a little after four o'clock, when the sun was already sinking below the Bloomsbury rooftops and ice was beginning to form in the windows of the houses.

As their cab drew up outside the house and the two ladies alighted, they were observed, from two storeys up, by Uncle Austin.

The major was enjoying a rare moment of clarity. He understood that he was in a house in London and that the war was many years over. He knew that the lady in the dove-grey cloak on the street below who was turning to address the cab driver was his niece and that the younger lady in a lighter shade of grey, her hands snug inside a fur muff, was that lady's daughter. And he recognised the neatly dressed serving woman who now knocked on his door and entered his room, carrying a pile of newly laundered sheets.

'Good afternoon, Major,' she said.

'Good afternoon, madam,' he replied with a stiff bow. He knew she was a serving woman and yet he did not like to address her as such. There was something in her manner that prevented it.

He watched as she stripped the sheets from his bed and replaced them with clean sheets. She worked efficiently, making her way around his room with the minimum of fuss, shaking out the clean bedding and tucking in the corners with deft fingers. She pulled the massive oak-framed bed out from the wall to reach the corners, and he wished very much to go to her assistance but he remembered that he was an old man and that she was doing her job. He remembered that his hand was missing a finger and that the face that watched her was hideously scarred. He remembered that the war had been over a long time.

He lowered himself into a chair, the better to observe her and she looked up and gave him a smile.

'You are looking well today, Major,' she observed and he flapped his hand at her, pleased that she had taken the time to notice and to make her comment.

He wanted to tell her that he *was* well today, that he *did* indeed feel well. But he remembered the crazed man outside the house the previous evening, cursing and hurling himself at the front door, and he remembered the demonic being with a chopping knife who had come at the man with a terrifying roar and chased him off, and he realised he could not tell her these things and that the worst part of being 'well' was that one realised just how unwell one was most of the time.

He turned away and watched the pigeons on the sill outside his window until she had finished her work and he had heard her depart, softly closing the door behind her.

—◊—

'I'm tellin' you, Mrs Logan, I 'eard it!'

Mrs Logan stood in the kitchen doorway and regarded Cook with some consternation.

'Heard what, exactly?'

'The *ghost*!' hissed Cook, and she glanced to left and right as though fearing the apparition were amongst them and might overhear and strike her down this very minute.

'Oh Mrs Varley!' Mrs Logan stared at her in speechless disbelief.

'You may very well roll your eyes, Mrs Logan, but I know what I 'eard and I 'eard the ghost. Same as the girl did. Same sound, just like she told it.'

'Hermione heard exactly what *you* told her to hear. You put the idea in her head and she believed it so much she thought she heard it. Now *she's* making *you* think *you've* heard it!' retorted Mrs Logan. Really, the weak-mindedness of her colleagues was both astonishing and disappointing.

'That's as may be but I know what I 'eard!'

Mrs Logan sighed. It was gone midnight. They had eaten a late supper because the family had eaten a late dinner. Bill was dining out, the boys had been given an early tea and Mrs Jarmyn had not appeared at all, so it was only Mr Jarmyn, the major and Dinah and they had eaten little and, if Hermione's report was to be believed, said nothing to each other.

Now the house was still, a clock in the distance struck midnight and cook and housekeeper faced each other in a silent stand-off.

'Then, Mrs Varley, I propose we go and find this ghost and settle the question once and for all.'

And Cook, who a day earlier had chased a madman off the premises with a chopping knife, turned pale and gaped at her.

'I ain't goin' up them stairs to find no ghost and that's that!' she replied.

'And I say there *is* no ghost! Come, Mrs Varley, where is your spirit of adventure?'

Cook regarded her the same way she had regarded the madman yesterday.

'Right!' And she spat in a handily placed bucket and grabbed a meat cleaver in her fist. 'We'll see, and it will be the worse for us, just you wait!' she prophesied darkly. But she let Mrs Logan lead the way as, for the second time in as many days, Cook ascended the stairs.

Mrs Logan cradled a guttering candle to light their way, shielding the flame from the sudden breeze that shot down the stairs. They set off from the kitchen and climbed up the basement stairs, taking each step carefully, and Mrs Logan was aware of the creak of each floorboard, of the vast bulk of Cook half a step behind her, of Cook's breath rapidly turning to a wheeze as they ascended to the hallway. Here they paused and looked up and down the deserted passage. A scurrying below suggested a mouse. From the street outside they heard the sharp click of a man's boots on the pavement, a shout in the distance then nothing. They set off once more, going up the main staircase, and now that they were on carpet they moved more easily, their footsteps deadened by the thick pile.

They paused again, halfway up to the first floor, but no sound came to them. Mrs Logan was aware that, for the second night in a row, her heart was thudding very loudly in her chest—though last night it had been Mr Jarmyn who had stood beside her.

She smothered the thought. Tonight it was just herself and Cook and the guttering candle, whose flame darted about in every direction because her hand shook so much. How ridiculous! Didn't she walk up and down this staircase a dozen or more times each day, and yet now, because it was dark, because Cook was standing at her heels gripping a meat cleaver, because the light from the candle flickered around them, grotesquely distorting their shadows one moment and threatening to blow out the next, her heart was knocking painfully against her ribcage.

Ridiculous.

They started off once more, reaching the first floor landing, which was when they heard it.

A sobbing, a single gulping sob, and it came from the drawing room.

As one, they froze and the candle went out. Thrown into darkness, Mrs Logan knew a moment of sheer panic. Behind her, Cook stifled a gasp and clutched her arm so tightly they seemed fused together. Slowly the panic cleared enough for Mrs Logan to notice that it was not quite pitch dark. The door to the drawing room was very slightly ajar and through it an eerie light could be seen; not a light from a fire or a lamp or a candle, but a faint, pale, ghostly light.

Behind her, Cook moaned softly.

But they could now see their way forward, or at least Mrs Logan could, and she took a tiny, terrifying step towards the door. Cook, at once realising her intent, tried to pull her back. But Mrs Logan pressed onwards, one agonising step at a time until she had arrived outside the door.

A second sob followed the first.

Behind her, Cook had frozen, unable to move forwards or backwards, and Mrs Logan knew that if she made a sound now they would be heard. She stood directly before the door, her eyes fixed on the unearthly light that seeped beneath it and through the thin crack where the door was ajar.

Did this door creak when one opened it? She could not remember. Think! Think! *She could not remember.* Probably, in the daytime, if it did creak you would not notice it. Here, now, if she so much as breathed the sound would shatter the silence.

She reached out her hand towards the door and touched it. The hand shook. With her forefinger she pushed the door and it noiselessly moved an inch. The light from inside increased just a fraction. She had no thoughts now but to push the door again, and a third time and finally her head, seemingly of its own accord, leant forward and peered inside.

The pale, ghostly light was the moonlight. The curtains had been pulled back and moonlight streamed into the drawing room. No lamps or candles burnt. A solitary figure knelt on the floor before the hearth, bent forward, forehead almost touching the carpet, hands covering the face. The figure let out a sound—part sob, part gasp, part animal howl—such as Mrs Logan had never heard before. The blood seemed to slow in her veins as, watching from the doorway, she saw that it was Mrs Jarmyn.

She would have been less shocked had she seen an actual ghost. As it was, Mrs Jarmyn's was a ghostly figure, an apparition, a cruel facsimile of the woman she normally was. And for a fleeting, a horrifying, moment Mrs Logan stared into the chasm that her mistress daily endured. The loss of her child—how was such a thing to be borne? But the sensation was fleeting. It came and went in an instant and she was left feeling—nothing.

She had no recollection of turning away, of pulling the door to behind her, of rejoining Cook in the passage. She found herself grabbing Mrs Varley's arm, aware that Cook was gaping at her in terrified silence, but allowing herself to be pulled quickly away. Together, they hurried down the stairs, along the hallway, picking up speed as they dived down the uncarpeted back stairs and not stopping until they were back in the kitchen. Here, they collapsed against the doorframe, Cook purple and wheezing, bent double and clutching her sides, but lifting her head to ask the question:

'Was it . . . there? Was . . . it?' she gasped and Mrs Logan nodded, giving the confirmation Cook clearly dreaded to hear.

'Yes, Mrs Varley. You were right. Hermione was right. It was the ghost,' and Cook, who wasn't a Catholic and had no truck with religion, crossed herself.

CHAPTER NINETEEN

DINAH HAD RECEIVED A LETTER from Miss Parson of the committee. *'My Dear Miss Jarmyn,'* the letter said, *'You will have heard by now that the soup kitchen in Commercial Road is to <u>finally open</u>. Both Miss Joseph and I know how active you were in fighting for its establishment. It is—I need hardly tell you—a <u>triumph</u> for the Society and you, Miss Jarmyn, were <u>instrumental!'</u>*

Dinah paused. She *had* been instrumental. She had gone with Mr Briers and Miss Parson to Whitechapel a year ago to find a premises for the Society's first soup kitchen, holding up her skirts and pressing a lavender-scented handkerchief to her nose as they had traipsed through one dilapidated and infested building after another. And when they had finally located a suitable place only to learn that the Virtue and Temperance League had got there before them and intended to turn it into a reformatory for wayward girls, she had thrown herself into a frenzy of ardent letter-writing, lobbying, placard-making and meeting attendance and had even, on one heady occasion, thrown an egg—though it had missed its target. She had been not only instrumental, she had been impassioned!

'*You will, I am sure, wish to witness the <u>fruits of your labour</u>*,' Miss Parson's letter went on and it was plain—with or without her indiscriminate use of underlining—that the soup kitchen was the ace up Miss Parson's sleeve and with it she clearly expected to trump Dinah's desire to quit the committee.

In truth Dinah had received the letter from Miss Parson five days ago but thus far had not seen fit to reply, which was tardy of her if not downright discourteous. She would have liked not to reply at all, to simply ignore the letter, to ignore every letter. But if one gave up on the social niceties what else was there? She thought of her mother choosing just the right mourning notepaper and poring over her seating plans and studying the cards left by callers, and she understood, at last.

She went to her drawer and took up a clean sheet of note-paper (the paper, she observed, had an unusual purple border) and composed a brief reply stating that she would reconsider her resignation from the committee. There. It was done and it had not, in the end, cost her so very much.

Or had it? Is this the limit, then, of our choices? she wondered, a feeling of helplessness almost overwhelming her: whether to choose one gown or another, one style of notepaper or another, one dinner menu or another, to reply to a letter or not to reply—and even in this it seemed one did not really have a choice.

Whether to marry or not to marry.

But there was one thing she could do, of her own volition and without anyone's interference, and her cousin, Rhoda, was to be her confederate.

She took up a second sheet of paper and wrote a note to her cousin in Great Portland Street proposing they seize the initiative and contact the spiritualist woman to arrange a meeting. The meeting, Dinah proposed, should take place on the twenty-eighth, a Friday six days hence and she, Dinah, would undertake to write to the woman herself to make the arrangement. Did her cousin agree to this course of action?

She sealed the envelope at once before she could change her mind and pulled on her shawl and gloves to take the two letters to the post-box on the corner rather than place them in the silver tray in the hallway. Well, it is done, she thought, the scheme has been devised and its execution begun. It was to take place in six days' time. They would make their way to an unknown location in an unknown part of the city by themselves, alone and unsupervised. No one would know their destination nor their objective. And if this meant covertly, if temporarily, releasing her cousin from her uncle and aunt's house whilst she was in deepest mourning that was all to the good.

And when they met the spiritualist woman—

But she had not quite considered this part of the scheme.

—⚬—

'Let me take that to the post for you,' said Bill, coming downstairs, and if his sister had looked at him as if to ask whether he had been waiting there all this time for her to appear, he would have lied and said no.

'I can manage,' she said; his presence clearly not welcomed.

'Then let me walk with you,' and he took up his coat and hat and held open the door, ignoring her obvious unwillingness for company.

'I return to Oxford tomorrow,' he said once they had come down the front steps and had walked almost halfway along the mews.

'Yes. I know.'

Of course she knew. And this was not the reason he had waylaid her. The post-box on the corner loomed into sight and he slowed, eventually coming to a halt. 'Look here, Dinah.' But now that he had her attention he did not know how to begin, or even what it was he wished to say.

They had not spoken together for any length of time since the awkward conversation in the drawing room on his first day back. It troubled him though he could not put his finger on why. Her odd question to him before their mother's dinner party was a part of it, so too his unguarded, perhaps rather thoughtless, observation at their aunt's house about Roger's decision to go to war—though one could not have known at the time of saying it that Roger had been killed. If one had, obviously one would not have dreamt of saying such a thing. But it had been unguarded, certainly, and yes, perhaps a little thoughtless.

This then was what he wanted to say to Dinah.

'Look here, I think it was incredibly brave. Roger, I mean. Going off to war like that. Defending the Empire and everything.'

Dinah rounded on him and her eyes were furious. '*No* it wasn't brave. It was *stupid*. Stupid and utterly *pointless* and nothing will come of it, nothing whatsoever. It was all for *nothing*.'

Her words and the fury in her face shocked him. 'Well, but. Come on! I mean to say—'

'And you don't even mean what you say. You *don't* think it was defending the Empire and you *don't* think it was brave! You think it was *stupid*. And you are *right*! YOU ARE RIGHT!'

Dinah turned away from him and set off back the way they had come, her arms held tightly around her slender frame, almost running, and though he could not see it he knew she was crying. And she had not even posted her letters.

Bill waited for a time at the post-box in case she returned but she did not. Clearly her letters were not urgent. But it hardly mattered as tomorrow he returned to Oxford, though it seemed his departure was of no consequence to any member of his family except himself. Well, so be it. Oxford awaited him. That was where he belonged now. In the meantime he was unsure how he would pass the time.

—⁂—

At a very late hour that same evening, and long after the last curtain had fallen in the theatres of Shaftesbury Avenue and Drury Lane and the last carriage had returned its occupants to their homes at Chelsea and Mayfair, the dingy passages and mean little laneways of the City crawled with nocturnal life, though only those who had business at this late hour chose to be out in it.

In Half Mitre Street one man had business though he did not advertise the fact, almost striking a match to provide a moment's illumination then thinking better of it, so that his presence, one shadow in a much large shadow on a moonless night, remained undetected. The offices of a large railway company opposite which he crouched were dark and silent and had been so since he had arrived perhaps a half hour earlier. As he waited and watched, in the spot where the railway company thugs had beaten him senseless and some of his blood still stained the pavement, he felt nothing, thought nothing.

Earlier that night, a Saturday night, in the public bar of the Green Bear at Whitefriars Street, in the shadow of St Paul's and close enough to the river that you could hear the cries of the wherrymen, Thomas Brinklow had looked on as a cloudy brown solution in a tankard was slammed onto the pitted wooden bench before him.

'Dodger's Double Porter. Best in the borough,' declared the landlord in a tone that discouraged disagreement.

Thomas regarded the liquid with suspicion but as the landlord was a bristling hulk of a man with a pugilist's nose and blackened teeth and who spat onto the sawdust at his feet, he kept his opinions to himself.

His senseless, one-man assault on the house of the railway gentleman five nights ago had failed and he had fled moments before a police constable had arrived. He had not returned to the street nor dared show his face much outside of his lodgings. What he had hoped to gain by his drunken incursion on the gentleman's house he still did not know, indeed he was not at all sure he knew who this man was who had done such a thing. It was not the Thomas Brinklow who had boarded a train with his little girl to travel to the fair that distant Sunday afternoon. He had a thought to throw it all up and return home. But there had been no word from his wife and without that he stalled. He was too ashamed to return with his failure weighing so heavily. And with his face looking like this.

Then a letter had come this afternoon. The letter was from his wife and said she had gone to a neighbouring town to stay with her brother and his wife, and when he looked—because up to that point he did not quite believe it—the letter was postmarked Shrewsbury. She would stay with her brother and his wife, she said, for a time. For a time? He had not known what this meant. Jenny was better at writing than he and had been since the days of the Sunday school. Her thoughts and ideas became words on the page in the way his never did. But he did not know what she meant now. He understood only that his wife blamed him for their child's death.

The letter had come third post and now he found himself seated in the public bar of the Green Bear. It was a Hellish sort of place: spit and sawdust on the floor and gin-soaked harlots who stank of the gutter, and swaggering, tattooed mariners with scarred faces and missing limbs who pulled a knife on you as soon as looked at you. Its very name was a warning to him: what kind of place was it, he wondered, that had green bears? It was fantastical. It was frightening. He did not know why he was here.

He pulled the tankard towards him and poured half of it down his throat in a single swallow. The beer choked him and turned sour in his stomach.

'Not to your likin', duckie?' inquired a woman sliding into the bench beside him.

'Tastes like badgers' piss.'

The woman snorted and her breath came straight from the bottom of a gin bottle. 'They must have rum badgers where you're from,' she replied and she peered knowingly at him. 'And where *are* you from, handsome?'

He was not handsome, not with this face, and he knew exactly what she was. 'I'll thank you to leave me be and mind your own business.'

Instead of being put off the woman leant closer and leered at him. 'You're a long way from home, ain't you? Lookin' for work? Or somefing else?' and her hand reached beneath the bench, finding his knee and sliding up his thigh.

Her touch sickened him but it forced him to raise his eyes to meet hers. He saw a sharp little face framed by tight curls that cascaded untidily over bare shoulders inadequately covered by her gown. The gown was of indistinct colour, cut very low at her neck and showing skin reddened by firelight and drink. He saw a hard-lived face but not the hard living of the mill girls and the factory girls of his home. This was another kind of hard living that he did not know and did not wish to know. He thought of the Sunday school he had attended so many years ago and of the short-sighted spinster who had read them stories of Noah and Moses and Jonah. This woman made him feel unclean. He wished she would leave.

She did not leave and Thomas swallowed more of the foul beer as a way to avoid her gaze. He had made a fool of himself coming to London and he had made a fool of himself five nights ago at the gentleman's house and his scratched and bruised face and hands showed the evidence of his stupidity—of his failure—and he slid his hands beneath the table. He could do nothing about his face.

In his pocket the letter from his wife burnt a hole in his jacket and in his heart.

'You know nowt about me or my life,' he responded roughly to the woman's suggestion, pushing her hand away.

'Perhaps I don't.' She gave a little shrug and fell silent and seemed to give him up as a bad job. He saw in her face a flicker of despair and then of relief and it occurred to him she was much younger than he had first thought, much younger than he, though she spoke to him as though he were a boy. These contradictions unsettled him and he stood up, knocking back the remaining porter in a rush that made his head spin, and left.

Outside a foul mist that had risen up from the river and the smoke from a thousand, perhaps a million, hearths had turned the London street into a landscape dense with shadows and terrors and Thomas wavered on the doorstep of the public house.

'Off back to your wife and your job, then, are you?'

The woman—she was really just a girl—had not given him up or she had decided it was time for herself, too, to depart. Either way, here she was. He had made no mention of a wife or a job and he had no wish to divulge details of either to her. Her presence, so close to him in the doorway of a public house, turned his stomach though there was not, he realised, so very much that separated them in the eyes of God.

He would make his way back to the lodging house and in the morning he would make a decision. He would decide what to do.

The woman pulled him into a passageway and began to fumble with his trousers. The porter, he realised, had been stronger than he had given it credit for.

'My wife has left me and I have lost my job,' he said, in answer to her question, but she no longer seemed concerned with his personal life.

On the street outside the railway company offices at a very late hour that same night, Thomas decided he had waited long enough—was unsure what it was he waited for—and began, now, to get to his feet only to duck back down again as the nightwatchman shuffled into sight swinging a lantern that cast crazy shadows from one side of the street to the other. The man shuffled past and his light grazed Thomas, then it was gone and after a while his footsteps faded too.

Minutes past but the man did not return and Thomas slid out of the shadows and moved on silent feet towards the office, reaching the doorway and bracing himself. With his jacket protecting his arm he smashed the small leadlight pane above the lock on the door with his elbow and in the choking and dense London night air the sound was muffled. He reached through the broken pane and undid the lock, flung the door open and wedged it with his foot.

At his feet was the bottle that was to be his instrument of destruction: a squat brown beer bottle, Dodger's Double Porter, retrieved from the passageway behind the pub and still a third full. He picked it up and struck a match to light the spill of twisted paper that was wedged in the neck of the bottle. The match flared and for a moment Thomas saw his own hands, pale and ghostly, the hands of some awful apparition. The spill caught at once—it was fashioned from cheaply made notepaper: the letter his wife had written him—and it burnt with a whoosh that took Thomas by surprise, and he flung his head back instinctively. Regaining his wits he lobbed the bottle through the open doorway into the office, where it landed and exploded.

At once carpet and window drapes burst into flames, illuminating the room. At the rear of the office a door was flung open and a middle-aged man—the gentleman in the tall hat and frock-coat who had attended his daughter's funeral, though now the man was hatless and in his shirtsleeves—came out, only to stop with a cry, throwing up his arms to shield his eyes. Another figure was behind him in the doorway: a very young woman, her face aghast, clasping a dress to her breast because she was otherwise entirely unclothed. The man leapt forward, dragging the drapes from their runners and stamping on them to put out the flames, and the girl put a hand to her face, which had been ripped open by a shard of exploding glass.

Thomas saw all this though it must have passed before his eyes in a second, two seconds, no more.

It had not occurred to him there might be folk in the office at this hour.

The girl began to scream, the blood spilling from her cut face, and she pointed straight at Thomas. The man saw him too so that for an instant their eyes met before Thomas turned and ran from the building. He ran full-pelt down one passage after another, tripping and falling and getting back up. The throwing of the firebomb was where his plan ended; he had not thought out an escape route. He had not, in fact, imagined the time after the attack at all.

He saw before his eyes the naked girl—a whore, of course—with blood spilling down her face, and he ran.

CHAPTER TWENTY

SUNDAY DAWNED SLUGGISHLY AND RELUCTANTLY, a faint greyish glow in the east being the only indication of the new day. The lamps in Cadogan Square were extinguished one by one by the elderly lamplighter, who now began the long journey home to his lodgings south of the river, and a muffled and solitary flower seller set up her pitch in the centre of the square. Just around the corner in the mews a few hardy robins squabbled for scraps and outside number 19 the kitchen cat yowled indignantly until someone grumblingly let him in. The church bells across the city had begun the call to Morning Prayer and Mr Jarmyn learnt that his office had been firebombed.

He listened in silence as an inspector of police in a damp coat which he had refused to remove and a limp moustache that seemed better suited to a vaudeville villain stood in his study solemnly relating the events.

'Happened late last evening, sir. No one has as yet been apprehended, sorry to say.' Here he paused. 'I understand there has been unrest outside your offices in recent weeks? And that there was some kind of a disturbance right here at your house just a few nights ago?'

'There was some unpleasantness on Monday evening, yes. My housekeeper dealt with it. And it is true we do appear to have attracted the attention of various public-spirited bodies at our offices. It is a fact of life, Inspector, that people will protest. And the factory owners, the mill owners, the directors of railway companies—the men, in short, who built this country, who created its wealth, who give these people their employ-ment—we are, sad to say, an easy target for any grievance, real or imagined.'

'I see.' The inspector consulted a small pocket-book.

Here the conversation was temporarily halted as Mrs Logan came in carrying coffee on a tray, just as though the visitor were some acquaintance come to discuss an investment opportunity in the Americas and not an inspector of the Metropolitan Police here to announce that a man had firebombed the office. Lucas welcomed the interruption for it seemed commonplace, comforting, when the rest of his Sunday morning suddenly seemed neither. At a nod from him, Mrs Logan placed the tray on the table and wordlessly withdrew. He ignored the part of him that wished she would remain.

The coffee in a small silver pot steamed gently, releasing a delicate aroma but Lucas made no move to pour it out. The inspector's coat, he noted, gave out a dank, wintery odour mingled unpleasantly with coal smoke and horses. He suspected that the coat and the limp moustache was a façade, that the eyes that watched him saw everything and his tirade earlier about the protestors now appeared faintly ridiculous.

'There was a recent train crash, was there not, Mr Jarmyn,' the inspector prompted, 'on your own railway line, I believe?'

'Certainly,' Lucas acknowledged. The inspector was clearly pleased with himself for knowing about the train accident, though it was hardly a feat of detection, was it?—the crash and subsequent inquiry having been widely reported in all the newspapers. 'Am I to understand that you believe the men responsible for this incident harbour some sort of personal grievance against us—against *me*? That they were deliberately targeting our office because of this accident?'

'This is my belief, yes, sir. In my experience these things are rarely random events. There is always a reason. A rational man tends not to go to the trouble of making a home-made bomb and letting it off in a busy office building unless he has reason to.'

'A rational man? You think this the act of a rational man?'

'I do not presume to think either way, sir. My job is merely to apprehend the offender and ensure he is handed over to a court of law so that he can receive a fair trial. The rest is up to a jury. And perhaps a couple of the right sort of doctors.'

Lucas reached behind for a chair and sat down.

'I find all this a little hard to take in,' he said.

'I dare say you do, sir,' remarked the inspector in his tiresome world-weary way. 'And you can think of nothing that might have led to this action? No injustice done? No affront or slight—no matter how small it may seem to you?'

'It—no. As I have said, I am aware of nothing.'

'I see, sir. Then no doubt whoever did this act is a madman, as you suggest, and it is simply bad luck he chose your premises on which to unleash his madness.'

'But what of the damage? Was anyone hurt? I should go there at once.' Lucas stood up, filled with a sense of urgency that had been curiously lacking when the inspector had first made his announcement.

'As you wish, sir, though the place remains a crime scene for the time being. No one hurt so far as we can ascertain.' The inspector took one last glance at his notebook then flipped it shut and put it away in his pocket. 'A nasty business,' he observed as though he wished to somehow prolong the interview when Lucas was anxious now to depart. 'If you think of anything that might assist I'd be obliged if you'd let me know. Otherwise, thank you for your time, Mr Jarmyn, and I am sorry I had to disturb you on a Sunday with such unsettling news.'

And though he was impatient now to be off Lucas made himself wait at the window till the man had departed, which he did, though not without pausing to look up at the house for a long moment. A caped constable held open the door of a waiting carriage, the two horses stamping their feet and snorting restlessly, and then they did, at last, leave.

Someone had firebombed his office. The office his father had worked in, the railway his father had built. Lucas sat down again. He ought to feel outrage but instead he felt a flicker of fear. Someone had wanted to hurt him, had wanted to hurt his business, had targeted his family. He thought about the man who had come to the house demanding to see him the night of the dinner. Brinklow. Was it the same man? If he had spoken to the fellow that night might he have prevented what had happened? He ought to have given the man's name to the inspector.

'Lucas, why did you say such a thing to that man? It was untrue.'

Aurora stood in the doorway, in a gown of forest-green. The plush velvet hugged her thighs then flared out behind to a discreet train. It was a trick of the dress, surely—the styles changed so rapidly—but this woman was not the same person as the young bride who had stood at his side twenty years earlier. Her hand rested on the doorknob, lingering there, as though she had some business to be standing thus in his study, and he felt the fury rise in him.

'Aurora. How long have you been standing there?'

She laughed, a little oddly. 'Am I to announce my presence like a housemaid, in my own home?'

She came into the room, her eyes flickering from place to place as though seeing nothing and everything at once. A report was open on the desk and he fought the urge to close it and put it away somewhere.

He ignored her question.

'And am *I* to be accused of lying in my own home?' he said. She flinched at this but he turned away to face the window rather than look at her. Once he would have flayed his own skin rather than tell her a falsehood. Now it seemed that every second thing he told her was untrue.

In the street below the family from the house at the end of the mews were returning home from church, the husband tenderly holding his wife's arm to guide her around a frozen puddle. Lucas averted his eyes, finding the scene distasteful. 'And what exactly is this lie of which you accuse me?'

'My dear, I was merely pointing out that a man attacks your office and you say you can think of no reason for it, you say you can think of nothing that might have led to this action—'

Her words mocked him whether she intended it or not and his fury doubled. 'You believe I absolve myself of any guilt whatsoever? You think I am unaware that people were killed in that latest accident? That I do not know how many were injured?' At the window Lucas observed the sunlight diminish before his eyes into a tiny white dot surrounded by dark and impenetrable mist. 'You think I have, perhaps, forgotten?'

Still she remained silent. They had never, in twenty years of marriage, discussed his business affairs before—though she had no qualms about enjoying his prosperity—and now she thought it appropriate to censure him! Her hypocrisy turned his stomach.

'My father purchased this house,' he went on, softly, making this remark to the street outside the window as he could no longer bear to look on the face that had once made him feel like the luckiest man alive.

'My dear, I did not mean to suggest—'

'His father—my grandfather—was an itinerant weaver who died in an East London slum. He died in poverty. My father was self-taught. An illiterate child from a workhouse who taught himself to read and write, who became a clerk in an office, who rose to be owner of a railway company. A boy from the workhouse!'

He paused. She knew the story but she listened silently.

'And he made his fortune despite that. He purchased this house. And now we live in it. Our children have a tutor and attend lectures at Oxford University. Our daughter sits on committees and discusses ways to help the poor. My wife pays calls and takes afternoon tea. We are fortunate, are we not?' He did not wait for her reply. 'And it is the railway whence our wealth derives. No doubt you think I should close the railway? That I should lay off all those whose livelihood depends on it?'

She was shaken, he could see that. 'You misrepresent me. I do not presume to understand the world of business. I merely observed that what you said to the policeman was not true and I wondered why that was—'

'My *honour*—my *family's* honour—is not in question. It is above reproach!'

He turned around at last to face her and saw her shock. It was there in the whiteness of her face, in the tremor that rippled through her, for she knew, of course, that his words were a reference to her own family, to the Kolarov Affair, a bungled Foreign Office incident involving the Bulgarian Embassy, some crucially mislaid ministry papers and an unfortunate leader in *The Times* that had put an untimely end to her father's political career some thirty years earlier. The scandal had sent the Hon. Griffin to an early grave and plunged his widow and young daughter into a social abyss.

Aurora made no reply. Lucas was aware that her father's downfall still shamed and embittered her and for this reason he never made reference to it. It was unworthy of him now to bring it up, cruel even, yet he felt nothing.

He did not see her leave as he was again studying the street below but he felt her absence in the room. After a long moment he quit the study and went downstairs, fetching his coat but, on failing to immediately locate his hat and gloves, he left the house without them.

Outside, yesterday's snow had mostly melted but what was left had turned to ice and a wind was whistling down the mews. He paused on the doorstep as the wind whipped his face and stung his eyes and for a moment filled his senses so that he could no longer think.

'Mr Jarmyn. Your gloves and hat!'

He turned around, dazed, to find Mrs Logan standing at the doorway. He looked down and saw the gloves and hat that she was holding out to him. He could think of no reply.

'Your gloves and hat,' she repeated, more gently this time. 'You ought not go out in this weather without them.'

'No. Indeed, Mrs Logan, you are quite right,' and he allowed her to put them into his hands.

'It might snow again,' she added.

'Yes. Yes, I believe it might.' He smiled rather vaguely at her and placed the hat on his head and the gloves on his hands, then a slight frown creased his face as for a moment he was unable to recall exactly where he was going or with what purpose.

'You were perhaps going to your club, Mr Jarmyn?'

His face cleared and he nodded.

'Of course. My club. Thank you, Mrs Logan. Thank you,' and he set off.

Only when he had walked the length of Cadogan Mews and turned the corner into the square and out of sight did

Mrs Logan close the front door, smothering a shiver. She went silently up the stairs to his study and when she came down she was carrying Mr Jarmyn's ivory-topped cane, which he had left behind. She brought it downstairs to the hallway and placed it carefully in the cane rack, giving the ivory handle a little polish with her apron then rearranging it so that it stood more upright. She stood back and, satisfied it was secured, returned to her duties.

And Dinah, who was standing at the far end of the hallway in the shadow of the staircase and who had watched, felt a flicker of unease in the pit of her stomach.

Mr Jarmyn did not, in fact, go to his club. When he reached the end of Cadogan Mews he hailed a passing hansom and instructed the driver to take him to Half Mitre Street in the City.

It was a bitterly cold morning and he was grateful to Mrs Logan for forcing his gloves and hat on him. Inside the hansom the windows were drawn up firmly yet his breath hung in the air before him. Ice had formed on the inside of the windows so that he could not see out without scraping a small hole with his gloved finger.

His cane. He had forgotten to bring his cane.

The hansom moved swiftly through Holborn and was soon turning into Half Mitre Street, at which moment the horse shied violently and Lucas was thrown forwards out of the seat, jarring his knee and cracking his elbow painfully. Outside he heard the crack of a whip and a curse from the driver as they were both flung about. A man's shout followed and Lucas heard the panicked clatter of the horse's hooves on the cobbles as someone attempted to calm it. It was eventually stilled and the door to the hansom was flung open and Kemp's head was thrust in.

'Jarmyn! Good Lord! Didn't see it was you in there. Are you all right? A girl ran out in front of the horse and that damn-fool driver couldn't control it.'

Lucas had by now righted himself. He retrieved his hat which had been knocked off and dusted himself off. His left knee throbbed painfully.

'Quite all right, thank you, Kemp. The girl—'

'Oh, not a scratch on her. Scooted off with never a backward glance. The urchins that inhabit these streets have as many lives as an alley cat, you know. They're indestructible. Come, let us go inside, this cold air cannot be healthy.'

A constable was standing near the horse, loudly admonishing the driver of the cab.

'A somewhat providential presence,' Lucas observed, indicating the policeman.

'Not at all. The fellow is stationed here. On duty outside our offices,' and Kemp nodded to the constable, who returned his nod with a stiff salute.

He led the way up the front steps and, following him, Lucas paused and saw for the first time that the front door was smashed to pieces and that scorch marks surrounded the doorway and steps. Inside the front office walls and carpet were similarly marked and a powerful smell of smoke and burnt fittings assailed him. The drapes lay blackened and smouldering in a corner of the room. There was water damage too, where someone had attempted to quench the fire, and his foot squelched into the sodden carpet.

Good God, he thought as the realisation began to sink in that someone had wanted to burn his father's company down.

Kemp gave the damage no more than a cursory glance as he led them up the stairs to the directors' offices. It was only when they had gone through to his own office and he had closed the door behind them that he addressed his fellow director. 'I presume, Jarmyn, that you have been visited by a representative of Her Majesty's Metropolitan Police and are fully informed of the incident?'

'I have been and I am.'

'Sinclair was here, you know, when it happened.'

'I did not know, no.'

'Well, I gather the miscreant posed less of a threat than the police would have us believe. According to Sinclair it was little more than a disagreement.'

'Dear God, Kemp, our doorway has been torched. Somewhat more than a disagreement, wouldn't you say?'

'I believe it is a question of relativity. Context.'

Lucas raised both eyebrows incredulously. 'By which you mean that a firebombing of our office hardly compares to, say, an explosion in a factory resulting in the deaths of countless workers? Or indeed, to a railway accident with a similar outcome?'

'Quite so.'

'By the same token, then, a firebombing can hardly be compared to a dispute over an unpaid bill nor, indeed, to a near-accident in a hansom resulting in a slightly bruised knee? It is, in point of fact, a damned sight more significant.'

'Don't split hairs, Jarmyn. And I'm sorry about your knee. Do you require medical assistance?'

'No, I do not. The knee—though undoubtedly it is bruised—was merely used to illustrate my point. You do *take* my point?'

'Of course.' Kemp perched on the edge of his desk and reached for the box of cigars that resided there, and procured two. He tore the end off of one and placed it in his mouth, offering the other to his colleague, who irritably shook his head. 'Of course I take your point, Jarmyn,' Kemp resumed. 'There is no doubt as to that. But do you, I wonder, take mine? Which, in point of fact, is Sinclair's.' He lit the cigar and puffed contentedly once or twice. 'The facts are these: Sinclair was here on his own working late, on measures, you understand, to improve the safety of the railway—'

'What measures?

Kemp ignored this interruption, '—when he heard a commotion outside. Sparing little thought for his own safety, Sinclair ran out to discover the cause of the disturbance and found the front door smashed open, a lighted device burning on the carpet, drapes alight and the whole place filled with smoke. It was dark of course so no way to see anyone but he said there was merry hell going on outside in the street: shouts and running and he thought he was under attack.'

'Good God, man, he *was* under attack!'

'Sinclair did what he could to deaden the flames and a couple of constables turned up—too late to be of any use—and he was obliged to go off down to the police station and make a statement,' Kemp went on, sitting back and puffing a number of times in silence. 'And I should say that this so-called "bomb" was little more than a home-made affair consisting of a bottle of alcohol and a spill. Very primitive. It is entirely likely it would have caused no damage whatsoever.'

'On the other hand it might have set the entire building alight and killed sundry innocent persons.'

'It was a child's firework, no more. Hardly the Gunpowder Plot. And no point playing "what if" either. Your cab might have overturned just now and killed you outright. But it didn't.' Kemp regarded him over his cigar. 'Sure you won't have one of these?'

Lucas turned away from Kemp and stood by the window. The hansom, which might have overturned killing him outright, had long gone, and another passenger was no doubt already seated inside it thinking about his life. The girl who had run out in front of the horse was also, one imagined, long gone and he had not so much as caught a glimpse of her. It was as though she did not quite exist. And yet she might have caused his death.

He turned to face Kemp.

'Is Sinclair shaken by it?'

'Not a bit of it. Annoyed mostly. Told this inspector fellow they should think no more about it. He's a good man, Sinclair, nothing shakes him. And he bears no ill feeling towards this undoubted lunatic. He's an example to us all, Jarmyn.'

'The lunatic?'

'No. Sinclair.'

'No doubt he is. And his motives are in no way driven by his desire to protect the company,' observed Lucas. 'To avoid any more bad publicity in *The Times*.'

MAGGIE JOEL

Kemp frowned and crushed the stub of his cigar on the ashtray. 'Damn it, it is *your* company, Jarmyn. *Your* father created it. Do you absolve yourself from all responsibility for its future?'

'On the contrary, I think I am the only one of us who *does* feel responsible.'

—⁓—

About one thing, at least, Mr Jarmyn was quite mistaken. The girl who had run out into the street in front of the oncoming cab was not long gone. And contrary to Mr Kemp's assertion, she was not indestructible. Far from it. It was Annie who had once worked in Mr Jarmyn's household until a terrible accident and its aftermath had driven her, only a few short weeks ago, to flee.

On leaving his household Annie had made for Bethnal Green in the east to find Agnes. But Agnes had left no forwarding address and Annie, wandering the unfamiliar and frightening streets alone, had not reckoned on so many endless, identical broken-down houses or so many unfriendly, desperate faces. She had fled once more, this time back into the City, and had slept a night in a doorway and another beneath a railway viaduct where a man had tried to force himself on her and a woman, to whom she had turned for help, had taken her belongings and tried to cut her face. She had panicked, then. No job and no place to stay and no one to help her. When she had seen her old mistress outside a shop in Bond Street it had seemed a miracle, like God Himself was telling her to go back and, in her desperation and despite the ghost, she had asked for her job back. The interview had not gone well. Annie had an idea she had mentioned the ghost. She had not been given her job back.

302

She had become weak with hunger and thirst and despair and out of her despair had come here, to Half Mitre Street. The master worked here. He was no longer her master but he was a kind man; Annie knew this instinctively when every other instinct had let her down.

Annie had crouched, waiting, with no real thought for what she might do next, when a black cab had swung around the corner and in the window of the cab was Mr Jarmyn. Afterwards she wondered if the ghost had made her do it. Something, at any rate, had made her career into the street and into the path of the oncoming cab. She didn't know much but what she did know was that, no matter what happened next, the cab would stop and if she was badly hurt they would help her and in all likelihood and out of pity, if nothing else, give her back her old job.

She had screamed, ducked and thrown up her hands too late to avoid the flying hooves, which had caught her a glancing blow to the head. Stars had exploded before her eyes and she had stumbled away, arms shielding her head, staggering and blundering into a wall where she had slid to the ground and sat clutching her head, from which a trickle of blood seeped. She had rocked back and forth. She had felt sick.

She had remained in this position as Mr Jarmyn and Mr Kemp discussed the deranged man and debated the significance of the event. Now she cried a little. After a long while she looked up, blinking as a black fog swam before her eyes, pressing her hand tighter to her temple, which only caused the wound to bleed more copiously. The cab had stopped but no one had come to her help.

CHAPTER TWENTY-ONE

THE OFFICES OF THE NORTH West Midlands Railway Company had been firebombed and now, only three days later, there had been another train accident. *The Times*, having missed the first incident, had not been reticent to record the second:

> *The express train is reported to have gone into the rear of a stationary goods train at a place called Prior's Marsh Junction some five miles southeast of Wolverhampton. The driver of the passenger train, seeing the danger early, had applied his brakes so that the express only clipped the last car of the goods train and the resulting casualties were limited to a few bruises, sprains and minor lacerations. The cause of the accident is yet to be determined but will, no doubt, form the subject of an inquiry.*

On Thursday morning—and for the second time that week—a meeting of the board of directors had been hastily convened.

'As usual, an incident occurs and we—not to mention the public, the shareholders, the newspapers—fly into a panic!' said Kemp, standing up and walking around the large oval table that dominated the board room, his hands behind his back in a way that reminded Lucas of one of his old Latin masters at Harrow.

'I don't see anyone panicking, Kemp,' Sinclair replied mildly, lighting a cigar, and for a man who had recently survived a firebomb he did indeed appear remarkably calm.

'Would you prefer not to have been told about the madman at Jarmyn's house? And have you already wiped from your mind the firebombing of our own office, Kemp? Or is your concern for your family's safety as cursory as your concern for that of our passengers'?' snapped Hart.

'Don't be ridiculous!' exploded Kemp, coming back to the table, thumping his hands down on its surface and leaning over it at Hart.

'Gentlemen! This is unhelpful,' interrupted Sinclair. 'We are all cognisant of the distressing events that occurred at Jarmyn's house and we have discussed already the outrage here on Saturday evening. Let us say no more about that—the matter is now in the hands of the police. Our immediate concern must be the incident that occurred this morning on our own railway line and we are here to decide what action, if any, is required of us.' He paused to allow his words time to sink in. 'We are all acquainted with the facts as they currently stand. It would appear there is little room for doubt that frozen signals were again to blame—'

'That is supposition,' countered Kemp at once.

'Be that as it may—'

'No. Not "be that as it may". There is a procedure: an inquest, a public inquiry, a report.'

'Not an inquest,' Hart pointed out. 'No one died.'

'Yes, indeed. That is so, I had quite forgotten,' Kemp conceded. 'Nevertheless, there is little to be gained by pre-empting the report.'

'I believe, and the minutes will bear me out, we will find that you stated the exact same thing at the meeting following the Lea's Crossing accident in December, Kemp,' observed Freebody.

'Yes, and I stand by it.'

'And in the meantime, another accident with the exact same cause has happened!' Hart retorted, pushing his chair back in disgust.

'How do we know it is the exact same cause?' Kemp replied, speaking slowly and patiently as though to an imbecile. 'And, as you have just pointed out, there were no fatalities. I think, therefore, that my policy of no action has been fully and finally borne out.'

'Preposterous!' declared Hart, leaning back in his chair and looking to his fellow directors for their opinions.

'The report of the Board of Trade's inquiry into the Lea's Crossing accident is scheduled for release on the 1st of March,' said Sinclair. 'It would be imprudent of us to act prior to that time.'

'I would prefer that we had acted in December,' said Lucas, stirring uneasily in his chair. 'It is surely only due to good fortune that we have suffered no further fatalities since that time. However, as we have made it this far, perhaps Sinclair is right, perhaps it is prudent to await the report's findings before acting.'

He was aware he had contradicted himself but his mind was so foggy he could do nothing about it.

'I disagree,' said Hart instantly. 'We already have a proposal on the table for measures that will radically improve safety for both employees and passengers and we know the costs involved. Indeed, we have had such a proposal for some months though we have, thus far, entirely failed to act on it. The technology exists, other lines have used it, the work can begin at once. It is merely a question of approving these measures, is it not?'

'Well said, Hart,' nodded Freebody.

'We know the costs and that is the issue,' replied Kemp, lifting up the proposal that lay before them then letting it drop disdainfully back onto the table. 'The cost of changing every single signal is prohibitive. We will find ourselves having to lay off employees and cut services in order to fund it. And it will take months, even if we commence straight away. We know the impact this will have on the shareholders. The result could be . . .' he paused, looking for the right word, 'catastrophic.'

The other directors said nothing and Kemp went on.

'It is almost February. The winter is drawing to an end. How many more frosts will there be before the spring? I say let us wait till next winter before rushing into these costly and potentially calamitous improvements.'

'What you are proposing is nothing short of manslaughter, Kemp.'

'And what you are proposing will bring this railway down!'

'Gentlemen, let us put the proposed measures to a formal vote,' said Sinclair. 'I believe we are all familiar with the suggestions that have been made and the projected costs involved? Good. Freebody and Hart, I take it you are both in favour?' Both men nodded. 'Kemp, you, I understand, are against it?' Kemp gave a sharp single nod. 'And I am inclined to vote against it myself, at least at the present time. Jarmyn, it would appear that you have the deciding vote.'

—◇—

'Mrs Logan, is Mr Jarmyn home yet?'

'Not yet, Mrs Jarmyn.'

Aurora stood at the window in the drawing room and regarded the street below. She had been watching for his return for some time, uncertain if he had somehow slipped in without her knowledge. Mrs Logan knew, of course. It irritated her that Mrs Logan would know if her husband had returned and she would not.

'Will that be all, Mrs Jarmyn?'

'Yes, that is all.'

She did not turn around as the housekeeper withdrew. It was only once she heard Mrs Logan make her way down the hallway that she moved. She glanced at the door to see if it was shut then went silently to the cabinet on the far side of the drawing room that housed the decanted liquors.

It was locked. This surprised her. In the first years of their marriage they had dismissed a housemaid for secretly helping herself to the sherry, and for a time after that the cabinet had been kept locked. But not for many years. Aurora pulled on the handle a second time to make sure it was not merely stuck. It was certainly locked. Well, then someone had erred. She could not think who: Mrs Logan held the keys to all the cabinets and cupboards in the family rooms but she felt certain Mrs Logan would not take it upon herself to suddenly, after three years, start locking this particular cabinet. A mistake then. Or she had been instructed to do so.

And if she had been instructed, who had done the instructing and who was being locked out?

She stood in the middle of the room, staring straight ahead, unseeing. She was no longer in the drawing room at Cadogan Mews: she was at her mother's house in Cheyne Walk. Poor Mama—wife of the late and once Hon. Griffin Randle, MP—had been a drunk. A discreet drunk, it was true, but a drunk nonetheless. Not even the servants had known it. Indeed her own daughter had never had so much as an inkling until she had begun that unenviable task of going through her mother's belongings in the months following her death. And there they were: Andalusian sherries and vintage Iberian ports, Armagnacs, Calvados, and Tyrolean schnapps—indeed every variety of strong liquor one could conceive—hidden in drawers and on the tops of cupboards and at the backs of wardrobes for all the world like a sort of morbid distillery treasure hunt. It had been an appalling discovery.

And she had made the mistake of telling Lucas.

It had not seemed like a mistake at first—he was her husband, wasn't he?—and he had been very tactful about it but as the years had passed she had come to realise that he watched her each and every time she drank. It was so subtle she had convinced herself, at first, that she imagined it. Yet the realisation would not go away. Lucas had enthusiastically read Mr Darwin's *Origin of Species* early on in their marriage—indeed it had been published the year they had met—and though she had not read the book herself she felt certain Mr Darwin did not assert that should the parent of the species be a drunk, then it followed that the offspring would be too. This, however, was what Lucas appeared to believe. In the months following Sofia's death his eyes had never left hers whenever she poured a glass of wine or accepted a sherry after dinner. She no longer thought she was imagining it. And now the liquor cabinet was locked against her.

She paused, listening again for Mrs Logan's footfall on the carpet but hearing nothing.

The efficient, the estimable, the loyal Mrs Logan. Could she . . . was it possible she was a confederate in this scheme against her?

She moved back to her place by the window. Outside, a police constable was strolling past the house on the opposite side of the mews, whistling and twirling his truncheon. He glanced up, almost as though he was aware she was watching him, and tipped the end of his truncheon to his helmet in a salute. Aurora stepped back from the window and let the curtain fall back into place.

She shivered, pulling her shawl closer about her shoulders.

At the sound of hooves on the road below, she pulled the curtain aside again. A cab had turned into the mews from Cadogan Square and she watched its progress as it approached the house. As it passed him the police constable stopped to nod his head at the occupant of the cab. A moment later the cab pulled up outside the house and Lucas got out, though all she could see of him was the top of his hat, the tips of his shoes and the black cape thrown over his shoulders. It could have been any gentleman alighting from any cab in London yet the manner in which he flung open the door of the cab and stepped down, rummaging in his coat pocket for coins, flicking the cape aside then turning towards the house and hurrying, his shoulders hunched against the cold air, up the front steps—it was all him. One could not be married to a man for twenty years and not know every part of him and he, you.

He had not dined at home for the last four evenings, ever since, in fact, the Sunday morning visit from the police inspector. But he was home now though he would not come up to see her, of that she was certain. So be it. She would see him later, if he stayed for dinner.

She dressed carefully for dinner, choosing a gown of the best shot silk in the richest purple and the lowest neckline. She wore her pearls though it would be just the family dining, and she pulled on a pair of slender dove-grey silk gloves that came up beyond her elbow and so covered the vivid white scar on her arm. Tonight she did not look at the scar. She regarded herself unflinchingly in the mirror: no one had ever said Aurora Jarmyn was once considered a great beauty because one only said such things about a woman whose beauty had faded.

She waited patiently at her dressing table thinking about her mother, who had been so strong in the weeks and months following the Hon. Griffin's spectacular political downfall and his physical demise not long after. She had rebuffed the most brutal social slights, forestalling, with sheer force of will, the catastrophic social plummet that seemed—so suddenly—to be their fate. Indeed she had held onto the house and their social position with a tenacity that had seemed nothing short of heroic so that, there they were, mother and daughter, less than nine years later, playing host to ministers and industrialists and foreign dignitaries and their wives in the very room where the Hon. Griffin had collapsed and died of apoplexy. The very room, it had later transpired, where two bottles of Colombard Armagnac were hidden in the piano stool.

Oh Mama, sighed Aurora. She had appeared strong yet she had not been strong. Do I appear strong? she wondered now, studying her reflection. But there was the dinner gong and she rose and descended to the dining room.

Lucas was there, already seated, and he looked up upon her arrival.

'Aurora,' he said, getting up and moving to pull out her chair, all without once looking at her, without seeing the gown or the pearls or the dove-grey gloves, or the face that had once been painted by Royal Academy artist E. G. Hunt. Her beauty irritated him, she felt. More, it made him furious. She seated herself and allowed him to move her chair under the table. He thundered back to his own end of the table and angrily shook out a napkin. A place was set for Dinah but so far she had failed to appear and Bill had returned to Oxford on Sunday.

'We are dining alone tonight,' she observed.

'It would appear so.'

She nodded. Well, so be it. If they were to have this little interlude together, just the two of them, she would not waste her time. 'Lucas. Have you given any further thought to the situation regarding my uncle? It is not my own safety I am concerned with,' she went on before he could answer, 'it is the children. It is the servants. It is the people visiting our home. I am afraid he has become a risk. A liability. I realise that you made this point when we were first married and I argued strongly in his favour. I believe now that I was wrong. Or rather, that things have now reached a point where we can no longer manage him.'

She met his gaze and saw his brow crease.

'You are still set on removing him to an asylum?'

'I believe it would be best. And I understand that such places are quite different now than they were when I initially looked into this option. Twenty years have passed. I believe the more exclusive, private places are considered to be not dissimilar to the resorts one visits for a health cure in Switzerland.'

'To be paid for by the railway company profits?'

For the first time she felt her mask crack but she kept her voice steady: 'I brought my own money into this marriage, or had you forgotten?'

The maid came in at this point, carrying the soup tureen. She paused, appearing perplexed by Dinah's absence from the table.

'Hermione, do you know if Miss Jarmyn will be joining us for dinner?' inquired Lucas.

'I couldn't really say, sir,' was the reply.

'Then I propose you serve the soup and we shall await developments.'

They both fell silent as the girl ladled a clear soup into their bowls and withdrew.

Lucas had not given her an answer regarding her uncle's future. The question lay unresolved—one of many such questions—and it threatened to get lost in the crowded space between them.

Aurora tried once more to cross that space. 'And what news of this second railway accident?' she inquired. It was, perhaps, an unfortunate choice of topic.

'That is hardly dinner conversation, I would have thought,' he replied, not looking up.

'Indeed? And when do you propose we discuss it? Are we to be the victims of further reprisals, do you think? Or do you consider your family's safety not worth discussing with your wife?'

'*Enough!*'

He stood up and the door opened and Dinah hurried in, two spots of colour on her cheeks.

'So sorry,' she said, glancing at both her parents, then dipping her head and taking her seat. Lucas sat down again and picked up his soup spoon, but a vein stood out in his neck. Dinah gave no explanation for her tardiness and for a time did not lift her gaze from her lap. When she did, her eyes were a little reddened and Aurora thought, *But she has been crying!* The realisation astonished her and she almost exclaimed out loud, but the maid had come in to remove the soup bowls so she said nothing. When she did manage to catch her daughter's eye, Dinah returned her gaze with a face that was composed and expressionless so that she wondered if she had imagined it.

'Hermione,' (Aurora had learnt the girl's name), 'why do we have no wine with our dinner? Please fetch a bottle of the '71 claret from the cellar. Mrs Logan will show you where it is.'

'Very go—'

'*No.*'

Hermione jumped, a look of terror on her face. No one moved so that for a moment they were a frozen tableau.

'There will be no wine with dinner. Hermione, you may leave us now.'

Hermione left but in the shadow of the doorway stood Mrs Logan and Aurora saw her, silent and triumphant, as though she had somehow planned the whole scene.

—⚇—

As the Jarmyns shared an uncomfortable meal in Bloomsbury, just a mile or so to the north beneath the great domed entrance of Euston Station Thomas Brinklow stood in the frozen night air, his collar turned up and his hands deep in his pockets.

Everything had turned out badly. The madness that had taken over him the first morning he had gone to Half Mitre Street and had eventually carried him back to the very same place five nights ago so that he had found himself firebombing an office, which had almost burnt down a building and nearly killed two people, had deserted him, leaving him sick and empty yet filled with a loathing that turned his stomach.

He had been too afraid to return to his lodgings and for five days and nights he had walked the streets, sleeping rough in corners and in doorways, certain that if he attempted to leave the city there would be constables stationed at all the main railway termini, that his likeness would have been distributed as far and wide as Whitechapel and Kensington, though he had only the vaguest notion where either of these places were. After five days he was wretched beyond anything he could imagine and, in his delirium, a cell in a police station no longer seemed the worst option. But no constable had stopped him and no mention of the bombing had been made in any newspaper that he could see and he had marvelled that here was a city where a man might firebomb an office and it not warrant a mention in the paper. There was a war going on, he saw, in some foreign place, and that took up a great many columns in some newspapers and a great many illustrations in others.

He had escaped but he had brought the loathing and sickness with him.

Drunks and beggars crowded the station entrance and there was nothing now to distinguish him from them. The street girls who plied their trade for a few pennies in the dark places that surrounded the station avoided him. He had fallen lower, even, than they and as he watched the trains come in from the North and depart for there again an hour or so later, he despaired of ever seeing his home again.

The girl at the public house had taken his money. She had rifled through his pockets and taken everything and in his drunken and confused state he had let her. The memory of it sickened him. His attempt to destroy the railway company office later that night had been nothing but an attempt to destroy the fact of his encounter with the girl in the dingy passage behind the public bar. He had not destroyed the office and he had not destroyed the memory of that encounter. Each step he took caused him to slip further into this pit and at each slip his soul became blacker. The thought of his wife was as painful to him now as the thought of his dead little girl. He could not return home and the fact he had no money was not the reason.

From this place, very far away at the bottom of a deep, dark pit, it had been a day or more before Thomas had become aware of some change around him—indeed it was impossible to miss for everyone at the station was agog with the news: there had been another train accident. An express train had gone into the rear of a stationary goods train at a place called Prior's Marsh Junction. The train was a North West Midlands line train.

Another accident? Thomas reeled. It was murder and no one did a thing to stop it.

—ɯ—

'That police constable has walked past the house six times in the last hour,' observed Dinah, who was standing by the window in the drawing room, where they had retired after dinner.

'Six?' said her father. 'Really?'

'Yes. I have counted.'

It was clear to Aurora—though apparently not so to Dinah— that Lucas had no wish to discuss the police constable. His angry outburst at dinner hung over them, creating a sort of fog that it was difficult to see through. Her own anger and the humiliation she felt at being spoken to in such a way before the servants, before her own daughter, seemed a lesser thing. She had said nothing since they had retired to the drawing room but she spoke now: 'Perhaps he believes there is to be a robbery,' she suggested, not lifting her head from her embroidery.

'Then he must believe it is to happen here,' replied Dinah, 'because it is at our house that he keeps looking.'

The maid came in with the tray of coffee and Lucas looked up from his newspaper.

'Ah, Hermione. There is to be a robbery. Can you confirm that the plate is securely locked up?' The girl, unskilled at recognising mockery, looked up and opened her mouth to speak but Lucas held up a hand, forestalling her. 'That's fine. You couldn't really say—is that right?'

'I was going to say, sir, that yes it is. Mrs Logan checks it personally herself every night, last thing.'

'Oh. Well, very good,' said Lucas, and he returned to his paper.

'If you please, sir, when is the robbery to 'appen?'

'Mr Jarmyn was making a joke, Hermione. There is to be no robbery.'

'Very good, madam.' The girl turned to go.

'And, Hermione, would you advise Mrs Logan I wish to conduct an inventory of the cellar tomorrow morning. First thing. Directly after breakfast.'

'Yes, madam,' and the girl left. Aurora returned to her sewing, aware that Lucas had looked up, but what could he say; the household was still her domain, was it not? She knew he would say nothing.

'Do you remember that housemaid, Lucas,' she said, addressing him as though he had not rebuked her in front of them all at dinner, 'when we were first married—Clarice? Clara? She was dismissed when we found her syphoning the sherry. We had to put a lock on the liquor cabinet. I wonder what became of her?'

'I cannot possibly imagine,' he replied and she saw the consternation in his face.

'I wonder if we should not have called the police instead of simply letting her go. One cannot imagine any good coming of someone like that. It is such a relief to have servants one can trust.'

Aurora found her fingers were numb with the cold and, as she thought this, her needle slipped and the point went straight into her thumb, piercing the skin. A bright red bead of blood immediately welled up and she stared at it, feeling nothing. When would the house be warm again? When would *she* be warm again?

'Here he is again,' said Dinah, from the window. 'That makes seven.' She moved away from the window but instead of taking a seat, stood restlessly for a moment. 'Mama, I think I shall retire to my room,' she said, and having made this decision she kissed them both and left the room abruptly as though to remove herself before the constable could return for an eighth time.

Had Dinah been crying earlier? There was nothing now in her countenance to suggest it. She had mentioned an intention of going to her committee in the morning—though she had, surely, resigned, from this very committee only a few weeks earlier, it occurred now to Aurora. Dinah had mentioned her intention after dinner but before Lucas had come into the room and this, too, now appeared significant, though why it should appear so Aurora could not say.

She looked down at her lap. The pin-prick on her thumb would not stop bleeding. She reached inside her sewing bag for a handkerchief, wrapped it around her thumb and held it tightly.

'An inventory of the cellar?'

She did not look up at her husband's words. There was an iciness to his tone that had not thawed one iota since dinner. She had thought he would say nothing.

'Certainly. Do you not approve?' she asked lightly, determined not to be unsettled.

'Approve? It is no concern of mine what you undertake in the way of household duties. I am merely curious to know what it is you hope to achieve by it.'

'I would have thought that to be obvious. As with any inventory, it is to provide a detailed record of our stock. And if we find we are deficient then we shall be in a position to rectify the situation. Do you not undertake such inventory of the rolling stock on your railway?'

'It is hardly necessary. Our rolling stock does not require replacing quite as readily as our cellar does, it would appear.'

Lucas stood up, brushing from his lap the newspaper he had been reading so that it fell to the floor. He took two steps then paused, standing in the centre of the room, his fists clenched by his sides.

'Perhaps it is easier to steal a bottle of sherry than a train,' Aurora observed and saw at once she had made a mistake.

'*Do you think I am not aware?*' Lucas demanded, rounding on her. '*Do you really believe a husband does not know when his wife is a drunk?*'

Aurora continued with her embroidery and with her thumb immobilised it was no easy task to push the needle through the thick material; indeed the part she now worked on was particularly stubborn and the needle would not—it simply would not!—be pushed through the hole she had identified for it.

Do you really believe a husband does not know when his wife is a drunk?

There! The tip of the needle was through and now she was able to pull the gold thread through after it. Her task completed, she looked up at him.

'What a ridiculous thing to say!' she replied with a laugh. 'How can you say such a thing!'

But her reply seemed only to inflame him more.

'Your denial offends me. *You* offend me. The very sight of you offends me,' and making a disgusted noise he turned on his heels and left the room.

She remained quite still on the sofa and listened to these words and it was as though they had been spoken by someone very far away, in a distant room. She had made a mistake mentioning the maid, the locked cabinet. He had somehow decided this was proof she was a drunk.

She continued to sit quite still. No expression crossed her face. His words washed over her. They did not touch her. The end of her thumb was white and still she felt nothing. A tiny patch of blood appeared through the handkerchief and began to grow. How could it bleed so, from such a tiny scratch?

CHAPTER TWENTY-TWO

ON FRIDAY MORNING A LETTER arrived from Roger Brightside three weeks after the report of his death. It came with the first post and was all but lost amidst the letters of business, the tradesmen's accounts and the requests for charitable donations that were piled high on the silver letter tray that Mrs Logan handed to Mr Jarmyn at breakfast. When he thumbed through the pile he paused at the letter, not because it was clearly of a personal nature nor because it had colourful foreign stamps nor yet because the handwriting was unfamiliar to him. He paused because it was addressed to Dinah.

'Dinah, this one is for you,' he said, handing it over without thinking. Then he watched as his daughter took the letter and turned a deathly pale and withdrew from the room and he realised the letter had been postmarked Madeira on the eighteenth December and had been sent by her cousin a fortnight before his death.

—⫘—

THE REPORT OF THE COURT OF INQUIRY
HELD IN PURSUANCE OF AN ORDER
OF THE BOARD OF TRADE,
DATED THE 29TH DECEMBER 1877,
INTO THE CIRCUMSTANCES ATTENDING THE
ACCIDENT ON THE NORTH WEST MIDLANDS
RAILWAY WHICH OCCURRED NEAR
WOMBOURNE ON THE 27TH DECEMBER 1877.
PRESENTED TO BOTH HOUSES OF PARLIAMENT
BY COMMAND OF HER MAJESTY
APRIL 1878

In his study an hour later Lucas laid the three-year-old report on his desk and rubbed his temples. It would be another four weeks at least until the report from the Lea's Crossing accident was published. It hardly seemed to matter now, in light of yesterday's vote.

Yesterday's vote hardly seemed to matter now in light of last night's scene with his wife.

He stood up, walked two paces and returned to his desk and sat down. He would think about the report, the vote. These things were important. They required his immediate attention.

Had the board made the correct decision? Had *he* made the correct decision? How had it come down to his vote? Yet it had, and he had the whole weight of it on his shoulders. On his head. Well, the decision had been made. He hoped, he prayed, that it was the right one.

He picked up the Wombourne report once more. It was the worst accident in the company's history: the local branch line train travelling between Wolverhampton and Stourbridge had been delayed leaving Wolverhampton and had attempted to make up time as it entered the stretch of line a mile north of Wombourne. It had been travelling at top speed when it had ploughed straight into a track-maintenance gang who were replacing sleepers on the same stretch of line. The resulting accident had caused thirty-one fatalities and a hundred and twenty-one injuries. How the track-maintenance gang had come to be working on that stretch of line at that time and how the railway had failed to notify the driver of their presence was the main focus of the report.

He had attended the scene and the subsequent inquiry himself, had travelled up on the afternoon of the accident, hiring a man with a trap at Wolverhampton and arriving in time to see the chaos and the destruction that a train travelling at top speed could wreak on a gang of workers and eight carriages of passengers. He remembered stepping down from the trap in a daze, scrambling down the embankment, slipping but hardly noticing, righting himself and wandering the length of the train, taking in the twisted carriages, the people scurrying about, hearing the cries, the screams for help though the accident was already four or five hours old by then. The reek of burnt metal and smoke had filled the air. A pall of smoke hung over the front carriages so that the people from a nearby village who had come to help moved about like ghosts, appearing then disappearing.

Out of the smoke a figure had appeared, a woman in a full skirt, a shawl pulled tightly around her shoulders, a bonnet on her head but no reticule, no umbrella, no parasol. Nothing, in fact, in her hands at all. She had simply walked out of the smoke devoid of personal belongings like a soul arriving at the gates of Heaven.

He had assumed she had survived the accident. She had stopped when she saw him standing there watching her, and something had made him want to go to her, to rush over to her and—and—what? He had been confused, ashamed of his inability to assist her, a survivor of his railway, of the carnage that he was responsible for. In the end a man, a local from the village, had gone to her and led her away. Gone.

But he had not forgotten her.

The same woman had attended the inquest at Birmingham Assizes three days later and he had found out she was not a survivor at all. She had gone to the accident site, as he had, though she had gone to locate her husband. Her husband, it now came out, was not a survivor either. He had been in the front carriage of the train. His remains were in the mortuary at Wolverhampton.

So he had killed the woman's husband: Paul Logan, a wine merchant, employed by a large Birmingham-based wine wholesaler, a man who had set off from his lodgings in Wolverhampton one December morning to meet a customer in Stourbridge and another in Birmingham; a trip lasting two days, no more, in these days of fast, efficient rail travel. (Why did he remember these details? They formed no part of the Board's report and if Mrs Logan had told him she had certainly not referred to it since.) Paul Logan had set off one morning and he had never returned. He had left a widow. There were no children—he had pondered that at the time: three years of marriage but no child. Was that a Godsend or an even greater tragedy?

He had stayed just long enough to hear the inquest adjourned, the details for the forthcoming public inquiry arranged, and had returned to his hotel unable to get the details out of his head.

He had sought the woman out at a cramped and badly constructed tenement building in Wolverhampton to ascertain her situation. Was she destitute now her husband was gone? There were plenty who would be, after this day's work, plenty of breadwinners gone and wives dependent on the charity of the parish. But it was this woman whom he had sought out. She had come to the door, unsurprised, it had seemed to him, by his sudden and unexplained appearance at her home. She had asked him in, offered him refreshment, and he had offered her the position of housekeeper in his house in London.

She could read and write. Her father had been a clerk. Her mother's people had been clergy a generation back, in some Northern place. She had been in service herself before her marriage. They had a position vacant and would she take it?

She had asked a number of pertinent questions and ended by saying she would consider his offer. He had returned to his hotel and a telegram had awaited him. She would be honoured to accept his offer and would start at once.

The strangeness, perhaps even the impropriety, of this woman, whose husband had been killed by his company, coming to work for him had not even occurred to him. He had offered her the job and she had accepted. Now, three years later, it was impossible to imagine the house without her.

'Mr Jarmyn?'

He spun around and stared at Mrs Logan, aghast, as though his thoughts had conjured her up. She was looking at the Wombourne crash report that lay on the desk where he had dropped it, its frontispiece printed in a large bolded typeface. He wanted to snatch up the report, to remove it from her sight, but to do so would only draw attention to it. He faced her over the table with a level gaze.

'Mrs Logan?'

There was a slight frown on her face as she looked at the report.

'A package was hand-delivered whilst you were at breakfast,' she said, holding out a large, flat envelope. He knew what it was and he stared for a moment at it in her hands. He reached out to take it from her, looking up and seeing her studying him.

'Thank you,' he said, turning away. But she did not leave.

'Mr Jarmyn, I—it may not be my place to say so, but I overheard Miss Jarmyn tell your wife that she intends this morning to go out to her committee,' she said, and he turned and looked at her in surprise.

'Dinah said nothing at breakfast.'

'It was mentioned in my hearing last night.' She hesitated. 'Mrs Jarmyn was not concerned but then she is not, of course, aware of the threat that occurred on the night of the dinner party. I think she might not be so agreeable to the excursion were she in possession of all the facts.'

'But surely Dinah has resigned from her committee? She told me so herself.'

Mrs Logan offered no explanation for this.

'Did Mrs Jarmyn not question this?'

'Not in my hearing, Mr Jarmyn. She was engaged in some private business of her own. And we are to conduct an inventory of the cellar this morning—no doubt her thoughts were taken up with this.' Mrs Logan hesitated a second time. 'I would not have mentioned this were I not concerned for Miss Jarmyn's safety.'

He nodded. 'You were right to tell me, Mrs Logan. I shall speak to her.'

And Mrs Logan nodded and withdrew.

When she had gone Lucas picked up the large envelope that she had handed him. He dreaded to open the package and take out the papers that he knew were contained within. They were copies of the sworn depositions from the witnesses of the Lea's Crossing accident, which he had requested from the secretary of the Board of Trade. Urgent business here in London had meant that he and Kemp had attended only the first two sessions of the public inquiry and had missed many of the witnesses' accounts. He wished to read for himself what had happened. It would change nothing, but he owed it to the dead and maimed to at least know what had occurred.

He laid the envelope on his desk and slit it open with the letter knife, then he stopped and put the knife down with a sigh. It was not true: there had been no urgent business in London. They had fled—there was no other word for it—he and Kemp. The hostile mood of the inquiry had rendered their continued presence . . . what was the word Kemp had used? Ah yes: 'unproductive'; and they had fled back to London.

He put the envelope into a leather portfolio. He would take the reports to the office and open them there rather than read them here in his own house. He put the report from the Wombourne crash into his desk drawer and locked it. Then he went in search of Dinah, pausing outside her door and only now remembering the letter that had arrived at breakfast. Dinah had been distressed by it, as well she might be, though it was odd Roger having written to her, singling her out like that. But perhaps if Dinah were indeed planning to go out this morning the unfortunate arrival of the letter would be enough to dissuade her.

He knocked on her door and after a longish wait it opened. Dinah stood in the doorway and she said nothing, her face bore no expression but he felt suddenly—though quite illogically—unnerved. She was not dressed to go out, at any rate, and that was all to the good.

'Dinah.'

'Yes, Father?'

'I understand you were planning an outing this morning—to your committee? I know this will sound strange but I ask you not to do so today but to remain indoors. Please do not question me on this, Dinah. It is enough that I ask you not to go out. I would be obliged if you were to accede to my request.'

If she thought this an odd request she showed no sign of it. 'Of course, Father, but—as you see, I am not planning on going out,' and she indicated her indoor attire.

'Ah, good. Well then,' and he left her and returned to his study. But it was odd, he thought, that interview with Dinah, though he could not say why. Still, it was distinctly odd.

'Ah, Mrs Logan,' he said, seeing her passing before the door, and he waved her into the room. 'I have this minute spoken to

Dinah and advised her not to go out. I did not offer a reason and she knows better than to ask for one.' He paused, looking down at the portfolio that now contained the depositions. 'Thank you, Mrs Logan, for your intervention. I—'

He stopped then, not quite certain what he had been about to say.

She came further into the room. 'Are you unwell, Mr Jarmyn?'

'No . . . but I find myself suddenly . . . struck by the enormity of what it would mean to lose Dinah. To lose my other daughter.'

He could not believe he had said those words to her. He could not raise his face to hers for the shame he now felt. What must she think of him? But she put out her hand and rested it on his arm and after a moment he pressed his own hand over hers.

—⁂—

A letter had arrived from Roger. It lay now at the bottom of the trunk in Dinah's room where it would remain and Dinah sat at her dressing table brushing her hair. The letter had not been opened and it never would be. Its contents, whatever they might be, meant nothing, they could change nothing. Dinah laid down the brush and turned to her tray of ribbons and trimmings and began to pin up her hair.

The letter had arrived on the very morning of her outing with Rhoda to see the spiritualist who was bound to be a charlatan, and the absurdity of their outing and the inevitable disappointment it would bring was now clear to Dinah. She would cancel the appointment.

She had no sooner resolved on this course of action than her father had knocked on her door and asked her not to go out.

It was an odd request, she thought now, pausing and staring at her reflection in the mirror. Father had known she was intending to go out yet the only person she had told was her mother the previous evening. The feeling in the drawing room after dinner had been so disagreeable that she had fled rather than endure it and a short time later the door had slammed and her father had come upstairs. She could not imagine her mother mentioning the outing at such a time.

She must let Rhoda know the outing was cancelled but the effort involved seemed, for a while, too great. And she did not know what reason to give. After a time, when nothing further was resolved and it did not seem like anything would get resolved, she reached for her notepaper and wrote a note to her cousin. She left her room to take the letter directly to the post-box so that it should reach Rhoda, if not exactly in time to prevent her dressing to go out and waiting on the corner, then at least as an explanation as to why Dinah had failed to turn up. Her father's request that she stay inside did not, she presumed, include a trip to the post-box on the corner. Even so, she moved softly as she passed his study door, where she looked in and saw her father and Mrs Logan, and Mrs Logan's hand lay on her father's arm, his hand on hers.

Dinah fled. When she came to herself she found she was back upstairs in her own room, where she stood quite still in the middle of the floor. Her eyes settled on her dressing table—a chaos of hair pins and ribbons; her looking glass; the purple-bordered notepaper on her writing desk, a half-written letter to a dressmaker. These things made sense. They calmed her.

Mrs Logan's hand on her father's arm, his hand on hers.

She rubbed the palms of her hands into her eye sockets to erase the scene. What could it *mean*? Her mind baulked at the possibilities. She found herself staring at a map that had no compass points and no roads marked on it. One heard of such things—husbands having a mistress—though one could not imagine anybody one actually knew doing such a thing. And Mrs Logan resided *in the house with them*. Those sorts of women were housed in discreet little flats in St John's Wood, out of sight, away from prying eyes (or so Bill had once remarked, though how he knew this he had not said). She could not imagine her father visiting a woman in a small flat in St John's Wood.

She reached blindly behind for her chair, sitting heavily down on it.

Mrs Logan. But we trusted her, she thought. *We. Trusted. Her.*

'Dinah, where is Mrs Logan? I shall require her soon so if you see her, please send her to me.'

Dinah stared mutely at her mother, who had appeared somehow in the doorway of her room.

Did she know? If a man had a mistress surely his wife would know? But she must not know, otherwise how could she arrange to do an inventory of the cellar with her?

'But are you not going out this morning, Dinah?' her mother added, noticing Dinah still in her indoor attire at the hour she had said she was leaving.

'Father does not wish me to go out. And I have not seen Mrs Logan,' Dinah replied and her face flushed scarlet so that, in her dismay, she sprang up and fled to the window. She had wondered how her father had known that she was intending to go out this morning when the only person she had told was her mother, last night after dinner. But Mrs Logan had been there. Mrs Logan, she realised, was always there. Dinah could feel her face burning. She wanted her mother to leave now, at once; it was intolerable that she stood in the doorway asking about Mrs Logan.

'That is an odd thing for your father to request. And as for the elusive Mrs Logan, one would almost think she had reason to wish to avoid the inventory,' her mother remarked. 'If you should see her please remind her.' And she left.

The inventory of the cellar. Her mother's proposal, which had struck her as odd last night, now had an almost cataclysmic feel about it.

And Dinah, who had resolved to abandon her appointment with Rhoda and the spiritualist who was bound to be a charlatan not ten minutes earlier, now threw away her hastily written note to her cousin and pulled on her boots and her gloves and scooped up her cloak and threw it over her shoulders. She had an appointment and she intended to keep it. Besides which, it was insufferable to remain in the house another minute.

Downstairs the front door opened then closed and from her window she saw her father setting off, his head bent against the wind, in the direction of Cadogan Square, a small leather case under his arm, his cane clicking on the pavement.

This was just as well for she had no wish to run into him. Dinah left her room, closing the door. If anyone came looking for her, well it was too bad for them. She went silently down the stairs. There was no sound from Uncle Austin's room, her brothers were on an excursion with Mr Todd and she reached the front door unobserved, pausing only to tie the cloak beneath her chin. Ought she to carry an umbrella? It didn't look like rain. She would risk it—it was a day when nothing more could touch her.

'Miss Jarmyn. You're going out?'

She turned slowly and there was Mrs Logan standing in her way. For a moment Dinah could not even look at her. 'That is so, yes,' she replied, lifting her chin very high. 'I am paying a visit to the National Gallery,' she added, though she had no intention of going to the National Gallery and was not sure why she had said it nor why she felt the need to explain herself.

Mrs Logan replied in her usual calm, serene manner just as though everything was quite normal. 'I understood from Mr Jarmyn that you would not be going out today.'

'Did you? I wonder why he told you that?'

Mrs Logan did not hesitate. 'He seemed to think there was a good reason why you would not be going outside.'

'Did he? And what was that reason?' Dinah stood square-on, her eyes level with Mrs Logan's.

'I am afraid I am not at liberty to say.'

'But you know? Do you not think it odd that my father saw fit to tell *you* but not me? And not my mother, his own wife?'

'I could not comment—'

'Or, for that matter, that my father appeared to know I was intending to go out this morning in the first place, even though I said nothing and I am certain my mother made no mention of it to him?'

'I told Mr Jarmyn myself. I believed it was the right—'

'How *dare* you! How *dare* you spy on me and report my actions to my father!' The words came out in a rush as though a dam had broken and Dinah felt them as a heady release.

As for Mrs Logan, a fissure had appeared in her calm serenity and there was something, now, in her eyes that revealed the woman behind the housekeeper. The muscles on either side of her jaw tensed and colour appeared in her face where a moment earlier there had been no colour. Some line had been crossed, a line on the map that had no compass points and no roads marked on it.

Dinah pressed on, lightheaded and determined to crush her. 'You have *no* right! Do you think we allow servants to interfere in our private family matters? You have overstepped the mark and I shall ensure my mother is made fully aware,' and she threw herself at the front door, fumbling with the catch, then fleeing down the steps.

'Miss Jarmyn, *wait!*'

But Dinah would not wait! She set off along the mews, her head high, her stride purposeful, her gaze unflinching, displaying a dignity that was entirely at odds with what she felt inside, not pausing until she had reached the corner of Cadogan Square. Here she walked straight into a man standing on the corner who, startled by her purposeful stride and her unflinching gaze, shied away from her, and in another moment she had hailed a passing hansom.

'Miss Jarmyn, *wait!*'

But Dinah had not waited.

Hermione, who was standing at an upstairs window engaged in a bitter struggle with the drawing room curtains and a rug beater, paused in her struggle and looked down to see Miss Jarmyn sweep majestically around the corner and disappear from sight. She was astonished a moment later to see in the street below the deranged man who had attempted to storm the house on the night of the big dinner party.

Dropping the implements of her labour she ran down the stairs to find Mrs Logan standing on the front steps.

'It's 'im!' Hermione gasped, pointing.

'It *is* him,' Mrs Logan grimly confirmed, coming back inside and knocking the mud from her boots. 'I fear his intention is to follow Miss Jarmyn. He observed her getting into a cab and has this minute set off on foot in the direction taken by the cab. I confess myself somewhat concerned for her safety.' She reached for her shawl and began tying on her bonnet.

Hermione gaped at her. 'What will you do?'

Mrs Logan took a deep breath and lifted her chin. 'My duty is clear: I will follow him. I shall find Miss Jarmyn and assure myself of her safety and if that means I shall be obliged to inform her there is a madman on the loose, so be it. The fact of it can no longer be kept hidden. Then I shall go to Mr Jarmyn's office and inform him of what has happened.'

'Go to Mr Jarmyn's office!' gasped the horrified Hermione. 'Whatever will folk say?'

'It is of no interest to me what folk say. I see no other possible course of action. However, it is no concern of yours, Hermione. Please return to your duties—'

Mrs Logan stopped mid-sentence. Turning around, Hermione saw Mrs Jarmyn walking towards them. She curtsied but Mrs Jarmyn appeared not to notice her presence.

'Ah, Mrs Logan. There you are. We shall commence the inventory of the cellar at once, if you please.'

Hermione, who had no wish to become embroiled in the inventory or the discussion preceding it, threw in a second curtsey and scurried up the stairs.

'I am sorry, Mrs Jarmyn,' she heard Mrs Logan reply, 'I have to request that we postpone the inventory. Something—'

'I beg your pardon? Mrs Logan, is there some reason why you do not wish to undertake this inventory?'

'I believe something bad may happen unless we act at once. Miss Jarmyn has gone out—'

'Surely you are mistaken. I understood from Dinah herself that Mr Jarmyn did not wish her to go out?'

'Yes, that is correct and that is the reason for my concern. There is—'

'Well but surely this is a private family matter, Mrs Logan, is it not? I do not think you need to concern yourself.'

'No, you are wrong, Mrs Jarmyn—'

'I *beg* your pardon?'

For a moment no one spoke. Upstairs, though she was certainly not eavesdropping, Hermione held her breath. She had a dizzying sense of things moving beyond anyone's control, beyond, at any rate, her own sphere of experience. She gripped the top of the banisters and peered through them.

'I apologise if I appear impertinent, Mrs Jarmyn, but I believe Miss Jarmyn may be in danger—'

'What *can* you mean?'

'A man came to the house on the night of the dinner party. He was deranged. A madman. He attempted to enter the house by force. We managed to prevent his entry—'

'But this is nonsense! You forget that I was in attendance at the dinner party and I can assure you that this fantastical tale is nothing more than that: fantastical, and I am at a loss to know why you would invent—'

'Mr Jarmyn knows. He was there. The man wished to speak with him.'

'Mrs Logan, do you really think my husband would keep such a thing from me? From his *wife*?'

'Nevertheless it is true. He wished, for your own peace of mind, to keep it from you. '

'And now you suggest my husband colluded with you to lie to me, to lie to the members of his family? You have gone too far, Mrs Logan.'

No one moved. Mrs Logan's bonnet hid her face so that, upstairs, peering through the banisters, Hermione could see only that her hands tying up her bonnet had become still. Mrs Jarmyn she could see quite clearly but she had been in service long enough to avert her gaze at once rather than look on her mistress's face. What could she *do*? She looked about her for a large, ugly vase that she might drop but there was none and she realised that, even had there been one, she did not have the courage to drop it.

Mrs Logan's hands, still holding the ends of her bonnet ribbon, fell to her sides. A second passed, then another before she reached up and took the bonnet off. Beneath, her face was quite pale but composed.

'I am sure that was not my intention, Mrs Jarmyn,' she said, her voice steady though very quiet and contained as though she were in church. 'I am merely concerned for the well-being of the family. I realise now that this should be a private conversation between yourself and Mr Jarmyn. If you allow me a few moments to change into suitable clothing I shall be ready to undertake the inventory.'

Hermione, though not a little astonished at this sudden and total capitulation, breathed a sigh of relief and fanned herself, liberally, with the feather duster. She had only just got over her shock when Mrs Logan herself appeared before her on the first-floor landing, grabbed her firmly by the arm and marched her downstairs to the front door.

'You must go, Hermione,' she commanded, her face no longer composed, her voice no longer quiet or contained, and though Hermione was only dimly aware of what was being asked of her, she shook her head instinctively.

'No, Mrs Logan—'

'You must take a hansom to Mr Jarmyn's office in the city and tell him to return home at once.' And Mrs Logan slapped her own cloak around the girl's shoulders and her own bonnet on her head, thrust two half-crowns into her hand and pushed her out the door. 'Go! *Hurry!*' she urged as Hermione stood on the doorstep gaping at her.

CHAPTER TWENTY-THREE

THOMAS BRINKLOW HAD RETURNED TO Cadogan Mews the evening before minus his jacket, and this alone would have been cause for anyone who saw him to stare, for the air had been bitter and many poor souls would perish that night who wore more on their backs than he did. The train accident, he had noted, which had been reported that day and had happened many miles from here, had very little impact on this street. The white-fronted houses had been shuttered and silent. No one had arrived or departed. At Mr Jarmyn's house lamps had been lit and then extinguished by unseen hands. A solitary caped police constable had appeared as the clocks struck midnight, slapping his hands together and whistling tunelessly, causing Thomas to slip down into the basement area of one of the houses until the man had passed. Otherwise he had been alone all night and into the morning, until it had seemed no one was ever going to leave the house again. And then the door had opened and Thomas had felt a pulse beating in his head.

It was Jarmyn himself who came out, striding right past him, and not even noticing him. Thomas watched the man whose father had built the railway and he saw a cool contempt for the world in this man's face, a belief in his own righteousness that was unshakable.

A stiff breeze had got up but the cold did not touch Thomas, which was as well since he was in his shirtsleeves, having traded his jacket to an old soldier on the Euston Road in exchange for the man's knife. It was a military knife, scarred and chipped from use but still sharp. It nestled now in Thomas's arms, wrapped in a piece of oilcloth, and his thumb traced the shape of the handle.

He made to set off after his quarry but the Jarmyns' front door opened a second time and this time it was the young lady whose face he had seen in the window one evening a week or more ago. She was clothed in a many-layered emerald-green cloak with a fur-lined hood that all but covered her face and delicate fur-lined boots so intricate and beautiful it broke your heart to see them in the dirt and grime of the street. She carried an embroidered bag fastened with a gold clasp, a bag so tiny it must surely contain nothing more than a single gold sovereign, and she seemed to float along the pavement somehow with a sense of great purpose yet with an effortless glide. He thought how very young she was and yet she held herself like a princess, though he had never in his life seen a princess.

She was already some distance ahead of him and it seemed that she must glance behind her at any moment and see she was being watched. He looked about but there was no shadow to merge into, no place in which to take refuge. If she chose to look back she would see him. But she did not.

A cab had entered the square from the north and she hailed it and as she climbed in he saw her face, briefly, in the second that she waited to step inside. It was a perfect, angelic, untainted face. A face that registered no pain or misery and no joy. It was smooth and composed and then it was gone and somehow, in the moment after she turned away, he could no longer remember her features, the detail of them was gone. All he had was a sense of her, vivid but swiftly fading, like a dream in the moment after waking.

A pressure was rapidly building inside his head and he rubbed his temples to relieve it. His plan had changed in the moment that she had appeared. An eye for an eye. It was simple. So simple that the pressure cleared and was gone. An eye for an eye, a daughter for a daughter. And then they would have to listen, wouldn't they? The lawmakers and the Board of Trade inspectors and the directors of all the other railways. When they saw what they had caused, they would have to listen. He would make that sacrifice, and so would she.

He set off quickly on foot heading south after the cab.

A moment later Constable Matlock emerged from the basement of number 13 Cadogan Mews, where he was on friendly terms with the domestic staff, and, dabbing a handkerchief to his mouth to remove any traces of the muffin he had just consumed, resumed his rounds. He passed numbers 15 and 17 and then number 19, where he thought he could see a maid standing at an upstairs window. Giving the girl an acknowledging salute, he continued on his way.

—∞—

Folk were hurt, I could see, and I was very afraid. I found her,
my little Alice, lying at some distance from me, and she had
been thrown across the carriage and had hit something. I learnt
later that a metal rod had pierced her straight through though
at first I did not know this. I called her but she did not answer.
I went to her and thought at first she must be dead but she
was breathing though she stopped soon after and she was dead.

Lucas put the deposition down on his lap and closed his eyes
for a moment. The Metropolitan Railway's train jolted as it
pulled out of Gower Street Station and the pile of statements
on his lap almost slid to the floor. He reached out and grabbed
them just in time.

The first-class carriage was crowded, so much so that a
number of gentlemen were standing, their tall hats almost
brushing the curved ceiling of the carriage. He had been
fortunate to get a seat. Usually he enjoyed travelling on the new
subterranean railways. It seemed to him that they represented
some splendid monument to man's achievement, in the same
way that the first above-ground railways must have done to his
father's generation. Trains, travelling at unimaginable speeds
in subterranean tunnels! Surely it was a marvel. He never tired
of it, when others complained bitterly of sulphuric fumes and
smoke and the possibility of a breakdown. But these trains
were perfectly secure: they had a system of interlocking points
and signals that was fail-safe. There had been no fatalities, no
major accident, in seventeen, eighteen years of operation. They

were safer, at any rate, than taking a train on the North West Midlands Railway.

The underground train picked up speed and careered around a corner. The standing passengers swayed and staggered and reached up to grasp the leather straps that hung from the ceiling. Lucas looked up, observing his fellow passengers, his ear cocked to the sounds of the engine, avoiding the pile of depositions that rested on his knee. Usually he enjoyed travelling on these trains. But not today.

The girl who had died, Alice, had been nine years old. The same age as Sofia. Did that make it better or worse? He could not decide. The child had been impaled. A brass rod had gone straight through her. It was an appalling way to die. Better or worse than to be burnt alive, to lie in a state of near-death for ten terrible days? He could not decide. If she had been thrown a yard to the left, half a yard to the right, she would have dodged it. She was the only one in the carriage to die.

They had sat at the inquiry that first day, he and Kemp, and watched this man, Brinklow, give his account of the incident, and his simple, unemotional words had been worse than any of the hysteria and fury of the other witnesses. The man had gone to his child after the accident, unaware of her terrible injury. And the child had been alive. Then she had died.

Lucas rubbed his chin, frowning, but the image would not be dislodged. It was surely enough to turn a man mad, in a single instant. He remembered Sofia, a column of flames, then Sofia a blackened, destroyed thing that was not Sofia at all.

Did I go mad? he wondered. Did I go insane in that instant?

He could not decide. Who did this man, Brinklow, blame for his child's death? Fate, the train driver, the railway company? God?

The underground train had slowed, but now it picked up speed once more and the standing passengers braced themselves and tightened their grips on whatever came to hand.

He knew who he blamed for his own child's death and it was not God.

—⁓—

She does not want me here, Aurora realised. She wishes me away, gone—or dead—then she would be free to take over the household. To take over Lucas.

She stood at her window as down below Mr Todd and the boys returned home from an excursion and a heated discussion broke out in the street between Jack and Gus.

Could Mrs Logan—a housekeeper!—really picture herself the wife of Mr Lucas Jarmyn, director of the North West Midlands Railway Company, son of the celebrated industrialist Samuel Jarmyn? It was hard to credit. And yet the idea, once formed, would not be dislodged.

But the inventory was to go ahead. Aurora was still mistress of this house. She wrapped a shawl around her shoulders for it was sure to be cool in the cellar. Downstairs she could hear the boys moving about, bickering, then the querulous tones of someone older, and she thought for a moment that it was Lucas before realising it was Mr Todd, the tutor.

She had not seen Lucas since last night in the drawing room.

Do you really believe a husband does not know when his wife is a drunk?

She moved restlessly about the room. Mrs Logan had done this. Lucas had said nothing prior to Mrs Logan's arrival; now suddenly he was accusing her. It was Mrs Logan who had planted this idea of her drinking in his head, it had to be, and she had had six months in which to water and nurture the idea.

She pulled the shawl closer about her shoulders and made her way down to the kitchen, pausing to wish Cook, who gave her an astonished look, a brief good morning then making her way along the passage to the door of the cellar.

Since the events of last May Mrs Logan had been the custodian of the key to the cellar. If stock was missing, would it not cast Mrs Logan in a very different light? She thought of the maid—Clarice? Clara?—in the first years of their marriage. Some bottles of sherry had gone missing and one had been found in the maid's room. The girl had been dismissed at once though she had protested her innocence in an impassioned, rather pitiful way, to the end.

Mrs Logan was already there at the cellar door, awaiting her, her face composed and blank. The perfect housekeeper.

'Do you have the key, Mrs Logan?'

'Of course.' She produced it from a chain that hung around her neck and fitted it into the lock, turned it and opened the door. It creaked open and from beyond a cold, slightly musty smell seeped out. The cellar was really little more than a stone-flagged scullery that Mr Jarmyn Senior had had converted for wine storage sometime in the fifties. Four narrow rows of shelves ran parallel to one another leading away from the door; a single tiny window, barred and little more than a ventilation hole, had been placed high up near the ceiling. The temperature was distinctly chilled and Aurora again pulled her shawl closer about her.

She led the way in, raising the paraffin lamp to head height to light her footsteps. Mrs Logan had brought with her the ancient ledger that some previous mistress of the house in her father-in-law's day had started and in which had been listed, in minute, florid script, the details and dates of each consignment. The newer entries denoting the wine merchant's more recent deliveries were recorded in Mrs Logan's own handwriting towards the back. There had been a recent delivery, it appeared, for a number of crates were stacked on the floor near the door and some had been placed on an upper shelf, still unpacked, and Aurora silently noted this surprising oversight by her housekeeper.

She took the ledger and opened it, leading the way to the nearest shelf. Some of the Cognacs and Armagnacs dated back to the fifties and were stored high up on a handful of dusty shelves in the furthest corner of the cellar. The newer items—endless rows of Champagnes and Sauternes and the hocks and clarets that Lucas preferred—were on the shelves nearest the door. The bottles lay on their sides, the labels facing upwards, and in her former role as mistress of the house she had come down here regularly checking the bottles for cork seepage. No doubt Mrs Logan performed this vital task now though Aurora could not recall ever instructing her to do so. She studied the neatly written lists in the ledger.

'There should be two dozen Veuve Pommery, one crate of Jacquesson containing twelve bottles, then six Giesler and ten Bourlon.'

Why do we have so much Champagne? she wondered. We almost never drink it.

Mrs Logan counted. 'Two dozen of the Veuve Pommery . . . twelve Jacquesson . . . six Giesler and . . . ten Bourlon.'

Aurora recorded this in the ledger and moved to the next shelf. They continued in this fashion to the end of that side of the first row, then began to work their way back up the other side to the first of the Cognacs and Armagnacs.

'There should be two dozen of the Larressingle, an unopened crate of Janneau and one of Delamain,' read Aurora. She waited. Was there a longer pause than usual?

'The Janneau is opened and there are . . . four bottles used,' corrected Mrs Logan. 'The Delamain also is opened and . . . five . . . six bottles have been used.'

'No, it distinctly says both crates delivered last month and both unopened.'

There was a silence. From the kitchen they heard a roar of hissing steam and a curse from Cook. The cat yowled some way off.

'Could you have forgotten to record in the ledger that these had been consumed, Mrs Logan?'

Mrs Logan shook her head. 'Quite impossible. Every last bottle is recorded.'

'And yet here we have a distinct discrepancy. And oddly, I do not recall us consuming either of these recently. How do you account for this?'

Mrs Logan looked down at the stone-flagged floor and appeared to be considering the question. 'I cannot account for it, Mrs Jarmyn. It is inexplicable to me.'

'Could they have been taken without your knowledge?'

'I do not believe it likely that Mrs Varley or Hermione could have got in here without my knowledge. And Annie, the same. It is simply not possible. I never lend this key to a single person. It does not leave my sight other than at night when it, along with the other household keys, is locked in a drawer in my room. The lock on the cellar door has not been jimmied, the window is secure. When I come in here, I let no one in bar myself.'

'Then,' said Aurora, speaking in a low, steady voice, 'as it is not they who have taken the lost items, who can it be? Who else has a key? As far as I am aware there is only one key and you have it.'

For everyone knew there was only one key to the cellar.

'I believe you have a key, Mrs Jarmyn.'

Except of course only a foolish mistress had but a single copy of a key lest the original was mislaid.

'I? Is it likely I have taken items from our own cellar and not remembered it?'

She studied her housekeeper's face in the dim light cast by the lamp. Mrs Logan gazed at a spot over her mistress's left shoulder, her face composed. But was it composed? Was there not a small patch of colour on both cheeks? It was hard to tell in this light. Aurora felt her grip on the lamp, on the ledger, tighten.

'That is not for me to say,' said Mrs Logan in her quiet, dignified way.

The shadows jumped around them as though a sudden breeze had knocked the lamp though, aside from the tiny ventilation window high above their heads, the room was sealed from intrusions and no breeze had entered the room. Aurora stilled her hand and the shadows too became still.

'Then I ask again, how do you account for this?'

Mrs Logan drew herself to her full height, which meant she was eye to eye with her mistress.

'Are you accusing me, Mrs Jarmyn?'

—⁓—

The underground train had broken down and they were stuck in the tunnel between Farringdon and Aldersgate Street. The carriage had immediately filled with smoke and steam, generating much alarm amongst the passengers and making everyone cough and hold handkerchiefs to their mouths.

'This is intolerable,' someone said for the third or fourth time, and a young lady in an Empire-blue cloak fainted and had to be helped to a seat. Lucas gave up his seat to an elderly gentleman whose face was turning an alarming puce colour and who held a hand to his chest.

'Actually a breakdown is not an uncommon occurrence,' another man further down the carriage said.

'They ought to be able to guarantee by now that the trains do not break down in the tunnels!' the old man with the puce face retorted. 'And what about the smoke and fumes? It's poisonous, you know. It's a well-known fact the drivers die of it eventually.'

'Good Heavens!' said one of the ladies, though not the one who had fainted.

'I believe the company would dispute that,' Lucas observed, and they all turned to him. 'They use coke from the highest quality coal and pre-burn it. If you pre-burn it for long enough, that removes any traces of sulphur. In fact, it's probably better than the coke used on any of the main-line railways.' He smiled. And it was certainly better than the fuel used on the NWMR, he added privately.

'Naturally the company would say that,' said the man further down the carriage.

'There's really no need to be concerned. There have never been any major accidents.'

'What if another train comes up behind us!' said one of the ladies, fanning herself at a great rate, and a flutter of concern rippled the length of the carriage.

'I can assure you, that cannot happen,' Lucas replied. 'There is a signalman positioned at each station who indicates with the man at the next station if the line ahead is clear or if there is a train on the line. It's simple, but remarkably effective. And they have a fail-safe system of interlocking points and signals.' He smiled to back up his words because he could see they had no idea what he was talking about.

'You appear very well informed, sir?' said the elderly gentleman suspiciously.

'Just an interested amateur.'

(He did not add—at least not out loud—that they could also take comfort in the fact that, at this depth, it was safe to assume that the signals would not freeze.)

His fellow passengers were not reassured by his words, he could see that; indeed one or two of the gentlemen were looking distinctly uneasy and a loud clang followed by an echoing thump from further up the line did nothing to alleviate their anxiety.

But there really was no need to be concerned.

'This really is intolerable!' said the man in the tall hat for the umpteenth time, and the man further down the carriage told him, somewhat tersely, to be quiet.

It *was* intolerable. Lucas moved from one foot to the other. He had long ago stopped reading the depositions from the accident survivors. It seemed bad form to read them when stuck in an invidious position in a railway tunnel. And he had no wish to be quizzed further. It did not seem prudent to inform his fellow travellers that he was a director of a railway company.

He was feeling a growing sense of unease and the stationary underground train, stuck in such a vulnerable position in a tunnel hundreds of feet beneath the Earth's surface, was surely the cause of his unease. Yet there was something more. Something nagged at him: the decision at the board meeting; the deranged man at the front door, a man whose life he had helped to destroy; the lie to his family—though, surely, that was for their own good, their own protection? The collusion, then, between himself and the servants against his own family—how had he got himself into that situation? But again, it was surely for the best of reasons. He and Mrs Logan, side by side, moving the furniture in the dark as the deranged man attempted to break down the door; Mrs Logan barring his way and refusing to leave as he had opened his front door to the man; Mrs Logan coming to him in his study and laying a hand on his arm.

He shook his head, realising that he had reached the core of his unease. She had seen him break down and, for one blinding, dazzling moment, her face had not been the blank, neutral, composed face she had always shown to him.

The train shuddered and let out a blast from its whistle. A moment later it jerked forward and they were moving. The relief inside the carriage was palpable. A number of people cheered, some laughed; at once everyone was buoyant and brave except for the man in the tall hat, who said, 'I should jolly well think so too!' but no one cared what he said.

They pulled in to Aldersgate Street station and, though it was not his stop, Lucas jumped off the train and made his way up to the surface, where he stood for a moment in the rain, enjoying the cool drops on his face and the air filled with the smell of smoke and horses and the sounds of men and carriages. He was but a shortish walk from Half Mitre Street but the revelation of a few minutes ago had turned the world on its head and he stood on the corner of Beech Street unable to go one way or another.

A hansom passed and he was astonished to see the maid, Hermione, seated in the cab, leaning out of the window and waving at him like a lunatic.

—⁂—

The temperature in the cellar had fallen a degree or two. Aurora and Mrs Logan faced one another at the end of the first row, furthest from the cellar door, in a corridor perhaps two yards wide formed by the row of shelves on either side. The shelves had been solidly constructed; good British oak had been used. Yet these same shelves had been here getting on for thirty years, straining beneath the constant weight of hundreds of pounds of bottled wine. Every now and then the wood settled with a creak.

No one had spoken for a minute, two minutes.

Mrs Logan leant back against the nearest shelf, as though to give herself space between herself and her employer, and the shelf gave slightly. Above their heads, the crates that had been placed on the top-most shelf wobbled.

Aurora put out a hand to the shelf, touching the wood, pondering its construction. It became apparent to her that the shelving was free-standing and not affixed to the floor or the wall—an oversight, surely, by the joiner who had constructed it.

'I can assure you I am not in the habit of stealing from my employer,' said Mrs Logan.

'And, yet, the ledger clearly shows someone has taken those bottles. And once Mr Jarmyn is presented with this proof, there can be only one outcome.'

'I cannot believe Mr Jarmyn would think such a thing.'

'Really? You must feel very secure in your place here, Mrs Logan. You must have a very strong desire to remain. Why is that, I wonder?'

Even in the dim light she could see Mrs Logan turn quite pale and she seemed unable to reply.

Faintly, Aurora heard a door slam in the distance followed by footsteps above them. The force of the door slamming directly above their heads caused the ceiling to vibrate, and the crates above their heads creaked. Again, Aurora reached out to steady the timber shelves. Really, now that she studied them closely, it was quite shoddy workmanship. Old Mr Jarmyn Senior cutting corners as usual.

'Careful, Mrs Logan. That crate above your head appears quite unsteady.'

'*Watch out!*'

It seemed to Aurora that the shout came from a great distance, that one moment she and Mrs Logan were alone in the cellar, the next Lucas had appeared from behind her in the doorway and was running at them, just as the crate on the topmost shelf became dislodged. Both she and Mrs Logan put out steadying hands to the shelves on either side of them, both gaped upwards in wide-eyed horror as the crate teetered for an agonising moment. But it would not fall, it was secure. And then, somehow, it was not secure, it was plunging downwards towards them—towards Mrs Logan, who was directly beneath it. And Aurora saw that Lucas had not, in fact, run at them. He had run at Mrs Logan; his warning had been aimed at her alone.

He reached her and pushed her aside the second before the crate landed, with a terrific crash of glass and splintering wood, onto the very spot where Mrs Logan had been standing. Instantly the floor was awash with wine and broken glass. Aurora found herself standing amidst a pile of it, and she sidestepped to avoid the worst of it.

'Dear *God,* you might have been *killed,*' Lucas gasped.

Aurora looked down to see Mrs Logan sitting on the floor, a hand raised to her face, which was shocked and deathly pale, and Lucas kneeling beside her in the spilt wine and the broken glass just as though it were not there. He reached up and his fingers brushed against her cheek and he peered into her face and Aurora reeled.

She left the cellar, though afterwards she had no memory of walking outside. In the kitchen Cook was standing in the middle of the stone-flagged floor grasping a dead pheasant by its legs, its head hanging limp, its neck broken. 'Somebody have an accident, did they?' she inquired, and a trickle of blood dripped steadily from the pheasant's mouth onto the floor.

CHAPTER TWENTY-FOUR

DINAH HAD GIVEN THE DRIVER of the hansom an address in Seven Dials though she instructed him to go via Great Portland Street, which was in completely the other direction but it could not be helped for this was where she was to pick up her cousin, who was even now standing on the corner.

'I thought you were never coming!' exclaimed Rhoda indignantly as she climbed into the cab. 'Your note distinctly said ten o'clock. It is now half past!'

'I know and I'm sorry. It has been a horrid morning. Horrid.' For a moment Dinah saw the letter postmarked Madeira on the eighteenth December and she could not go on. But she would not tell Rhoda about the letter, no, she would not do that to her cousin. Instead she said, 'There was a development in our house.'

'What kind of a development?'

'Father forbade me to go out (though he would not say why!) and Mama did not know why either. But our housekeeper—'

Dinah paused and found she could not speak the woman's name.

'Mrs Logan?' suggested Rhoda, clearly mystified.

'Yes. That . . . person. She informed Father of my going out (even though I had said it in private and only to Mama) and then she attempted to prevent me from leaving—though she too refused to say why! It is . . .' she cast about for the correct word, '. . . an *outrage!*'

'Yes, indeed!' agreed Rhoda, readily enough. 'Though it does seem odd that Mrs Logan—'

'I hold her entirely to blame for my tardiness, for my being forced to go against my father's wishes and for—'

Dinah could not go on. She made herself look out of the window so that Rhoda would not see the flush that had risen to her face at the memory of what had passed in her father's study.

'This is all very odd,' was Rhoda's analysis as the cab turned into Oxford Street and became instantly entangled in a log-jam of cabs and carriages all trying to feed into Regent Street.

'What did you tell Aunt Meredith about our going out?' said Dinah, having got her emotions under control. She somehow found it difficult to imagine her cousin lying to Aunt Meredith.

'That I would be writing letters in my room all morning and should not like to be disturbed,' was the reply.

'Oh.' Dinah regarded her cousin in some surprise. 'What if she does disturb you?'

'Then she will find I am not there.'

The cab jerked forward and squeezed into the stream of traffic heading east.

'But she won't disturb me,' added Rhoda quietly. 'And if she did and if she found me not there, she would say nothing.' Rhoda looked down at her gloved hands in her lap with a frown and Dinah understood this to mean that, since Roger's death, her aunt was not the same. She understood this and did not question it.

And so she had liberated her cousin from deepest mourning and somehow she had assumed it would prove a bigger challenge than it had turned out. She felt a little deflated.

How would her aunt react, Dinah wondered, if she found out the reason for this excursion. She might be very angry. On the other hand, she might wish to have accompanied them. Rhoda, however, had been adamant her mother was not to find out. They sat in silence as the cab made its way slowly towards St Giles.

The spiritualist woman had replied to Dinah's letter by return-post, giving an address in Seven Dials to which they were to go at eleven o'clock. Dinah had brought money—the woman would want money, there was no question of it—but how much?

Of course, she would be a fraud.

The cab darted forward as a gap appeared in the traffic, then lurched to a juddering halt again almost at once and Dinah stared out of the window. The woman would be a fraud, of course she would, but if she was not? If she had really been contacted by Roger, would she not also be able to contact Sofia? And what would either of them have to say?

'But that was the man!' declared Jack, almost jumping up and down in his frustration at not being believed. '*It was him*, I tell you! The man I saw on the night of the dinner party trying to break down the door! It was him!'

They had returned from an excursion to the British Museum. Mr Todd believed strongly in excursions to broaden the inquiring mind. Today they had pondered the ancient treasures of Rome and Greece, returning on foot via Montague Place and thence into Cadogan Square, and passing them in something of a hurry, on the far side of the square, had been a wretched-looking fellow in a cap, ill-fitting breeches, workmen's boots and no jacket at all, though the air was bitingly cold.

Jack had at once started up and pointed after him excitedly.

Gus and Mr Todd had been less than impressed.

'I thought we had finished with all this nonsense about a man at the door,' observed Gus in a bored voice. He was consumed with the problem of how many antiquities (some unearthed and already crumbling in some poorly maintained foreign place, and so many others yet to be discovered) could be rescued and brought to London before they were destroyed forever. It seemed an immense, an insurmountable problem. He could not believe Jack could still be talking about an imaginary man at the door.

'I am afraid I do not follow you, Jack,' said Mr Todd with a confused smile. 'What man is this?'

'He believes he saw a man trying to enter our house by force,' explained Gus. 'Yet strangely enough no one else seemed to see it.'

'Mrs Logan saw it!' Jack retorted triumphantly.

Gus raised a quizzical eyebrow. 'Strange that she has neither said nor done anything about it.'

'She admitted it to me. She said it was our secret.' Even as he said this, Jack appeared to realise it seemed improbable.

Gus laughed. 'A secret? Oh well then, you had better keep the secret.'

'But she saw it!'

'Saw what, exactly?'

'Scuffs on the carpet!'

Gus scoffed. Even Mr Todd appeared unconvinced by this overwhelming and undeniable evidence of a struggle.

'Perhaps you had a bad dream,' he suggested, and Jack almost burst with indignant rage.

'Look—there is a constable! I shall tell him!' And with that he scooted off and flagged down Constable Matlock, who had reached the end of his beat and was preparing to turn around. By the time Gus and Mr Todd caught up to him Jack had relayed his sighting of the man and was defiantly awaiting the policeman's proposed course of action.

'I hardly think so, young sir,' the constable replied with an indulgent smile. 'I've been patrolling this stretch all morning and I think I'd have noticed if the man you describe had come anywhere near it.'

Dismayed and crestfallen, Jack had stormed up to the house and demanded to be let in. Gus, who was feeling much better now about all the lost antiquities, had followed at a more sedate pace, whistling to himself.

—⟋⟋⟋—

The address in Seven Dials was number 1 Brown's Passage Buildings, an inauspicious sort of an address that had caused their cab driver no end of problems and in the end he had had to ask directions. He had deposited Dinah and Rhoda on a corner, not wishing, it had seemed to Dinah, to venture further into the murky warren of passages and alleyways that made up the Dials. Then he had swiftly moved off, not waiting to pick up another fare.

When the cab had gone, Dinah stood perfectly still and Rhoda stood beside her, very close, her hand on Dinah's arm.

It had been a cloudy though still bright mid-morning when she had boarded the cab in Cadogan Square but here the daylight was little more than a feeble, smoky glow that allowed for only a glimpse of buildings and alleyways and doorways and the restless, moving mass of wretched people who resided within them. Instinctively they both moved backwards against the wall of the nearest building, clutching onto each other as a sea of gaunt and hollow-eyed faces reared out of the mist, stared at them and vanished, one after another. Something crunched beneath their feet and they both looked down at the detritus of fish remains, animal faeces and oyster shells that littered the ground and as one they held handkerchiefs up to their noses.

'I have been to Whitechapel,' Dinah declared, 'which is *much worse*! Do not lose heart, cousin. We are quite safe.'

But in Whitechapel they had had Mr Briers who had swept a clearway through which she and Miss Parson could safely pass. Here, it was just her and Rhoda.

'Come,' she said firmly, 'this must be the building.'

She had no idea if this was the building, but the cab driver's directions had brought them to Brown's Passage and Brown's Passage Buildings must be somewhere along this alleyway. They walked the length of it, stepping over rotting food matter and disturbing a feasting rat, and there was only one doorway to be seen so at this doorway they presented themselves. The door stood ajar. Dinah knocked.

'Hello? We are looking for . . .' she consulted the letter, 'Mrs Moore.'

There was no reply and they looked at each other.

'Perhaps this is not the place?' suggested Rhoda. If it was not, Dinah had no idea where else they would go. She knocked a second time, then, on hearing no reply, pushed the door open.

Inside was a passageway with a number of doors leading off it and a smell of boiling cabbage or rank meat or unwashed bodies or all three.

'Are you sure?' whispered Rhoda, clutching her arm, and Dinah was not sure but they had made an appointment and they would keep it.

'Hello? Mrs Moore?'

A man appeared at the far end of the passage, a short man in a patched waistcoat and a derelict hat. He stood and regarded the two ladies and pushed back his hat to scratch his head. He looked like he'd just woken up.

'What d'you want?' he demanded.

'We are looking for Mrs Moore. This is number 1 Brown's Passage Buildings, is it not?'

The man scowled at them. 'Who wants to know?'

'Obviously, we do,' Dinah replied.

The man growled at them and advanced down the passageway and, beside her, Rhoda said in a quavering voice, 'Oh dear.'

'She's not here,' he said, stopping directly in front of them.

'Then do you know of her whereabouts? Or when she might return?'

The man seemed on the verge of laughing but stopped himself as though he knew such an action might cause himself some physical damage.

'Nope,' he said instead. 'Might be gone a while. A long while,' he added mysteriously.

'I see. Well.' Dinah tried to think. 'In that case we shall reassess our situation,' she concluded.

They turned and beat a retreat.

'What do you think he meant, she might be gone a long while?' said Rhoda, clearly relieved to have come out of the building unscathed.

'I do not know,' Dinah admitted. She had not reckoned on the woman not keeping the appointment. The man's words had the unfortunate effect of suggesting that Mrs Moore had undertaken a dead-of-night flit from her wretched lodgings, an angry landlord or a constable or both in hot pursuit. She may already be languishing in a police cell. She would not, Dinah decided, voice these unsettling thoughts out loud. 'Let us wait for a short while,' she said, 'here on this corner to see if she comes.'

They waited but the woman did not come. Instead a horrible misshapen figure appeared out of the gloom and they stared at it, clutching at one another in terror. As it approached them they saw that the figure was a man with a long wooden pole across his shoulders, and hanging from the pole were a dozen dead blackbirds, tied by their feet with string and swinging in unison as the man staggered towards them beneath his load.

'Two for a farvin', lovely ladies,' he offered in a rasping voice through toothless gums, pausing before them and turning this way and that so that his dreadful load swung in a crazy dance and one of the dead birds brushed against Rhoda's arm so that she shrieked.

'No, thank you,' said Dinah firmly, reaching blindly for her handkerchief to cover her nose.

'Make you a lovely pic, they would.'

'Come, Rhoda. I think it is time we left,' and they grabbed each other's hands and hurried away, Dinah not at all sure which was the correct direction but aware that the horrid man was shuffling after them. Beside her, Rhoda stifled a cry. There were no cabs so they hastened in a crazy zigzag south and west, popping out into St Martin's Lane, gasping and reeling, and catching their breath. At a more ladylike pace they made for Trafalgar Square, reaching it just as the black clouds that had been gathering all morning began to squeeze out the first heavy, fat raindrops and they picked up their skirts and, along with everyone else, ran up the steps of the National Gallery to shelter.

She had told Mrs Logan she was going to the National Gallery, thought Dinah, and now, here she was.

'Oh, he was horrid!' gasped Rhoda, pausing on the top step to catch her breath.

'He was just trying to sell us his wares. I feel certain he meant us no harm,' Dinah admonished, though her heart was racing. 'And we are quite safe now—see, we are at the National Gallery! What safer place could there be in all of London?'

During their headlong flight they had not spoken of their abortive enterprise but now Rhoda exclaimed, and there was a heartbreaking catch in her voice, 'Oh I *knew* it would all be for nothing!' and she was evidently close to tears but as the rain was falling onto every face, no one noticed.

'But it was worth trying,' Dinah insisted, putting an arm around her cousin and leading her through the entranceway. They paused to shake the raindrops off their cloaks then drifted into the first gallery, making for the bench in the centre of the room before someone else claimed it.

'But if the woman was waylaid? Delayed somewhere? If she is awaiting us even now? Perhaps we should have waited a while longer.'

'It is gone twelve, Rhoda. She cannot expect us to have waited any longer. I am afraid this does rather suggest the woman was a fraud.'

Rhoda nodded slowly but said nothing and Dinah squeezed her cousin's hand. They sat quietly on the bench whilst around them the room filled up with fellow refugees from the storm and Dinah noticed how the raindrops that slid down her own face and onto her lips were warm and salty and not like raindrops at all.

—◊—

The rain was now so heavy that people were running in all directions in order to escape it. Horses ploughed through the rapidly growing puddles sending sheets of water over hapless pedestrians, the coach drivers hunched on their seats with their collars turned up and hats pulled low, the water cascading from the brims. In Trafalgar Square those who did not live nearby or could not hail a cab made for the shelter of the gallery, congregating in a sodden mass and clogging up the entranceway: young ladies and gentlemen in couples and singly, flower sellers and piemen, visiting American tourists holding their sodden Baedekers over their heads as they ran, the sick and the homeless, an old soldier minus a leg who had somehow made it up the steps and was now setting up his begging tin in the doorway.

Into this morass Thomas Brinklow easily slipped, weaving his way between the soaked people of London, a hand held to his chest, a knife clasped in his hand.

He had followed the young lady's cab which had made its way slowly, ensnared in the never-ending traffic. She had stopped once, to pick up another young lady, then seemed to double back, heading east. Here the cab had turned into a maze of tiny passages and he had finally lost her, and had for a time wandered aimlessly, buffeted by the swarming, hurrying, angry people who dwelt there. Finally, when it seemed that the endless maze of passageways must cover the whole of London and there was nothing else to the city but this horror, he had found his way out of the warren and onto a wide shopping street.

Standing and squinting in the sudden daylight he had not known which way to strike but there she was before him, Mr Jarmyn's daughter, and the other lady, her friend, walking straight towards him. Two angels. Or one angel and her attendant. A vision. Had he created this vision or had God?

Or had the Devil?

For a moment he had frozen. If he had moved they would have noticed him. He had stood quite still, almost leaning his shoulders on the window of the shop behind him, and they had passed right by, less than two yards from him. He had heard the swish of their gowns, the clip of their heels on the pavement, a faint scent of roses, lavender, camphor—he had not known what it was—in their wake.

Ahead of him the two young ladies had suddenly veered to the right as though the rain had caused them to change direction and for an instant it had seemed they had seen him, but they had continued on down the street in the direction of the great column on which Admiral Lord Nelson was perched and above which the storm clouds had gathered. The rain came steadily down and they had run up the steps of the gallery and a moment later Thomas had followed them.

The gallery attendant saw him and would have stopped him but Thomas dodged him, pausing only once he reached the hallway, where a second attendant hurried forward with mop and bucket. Looking down Thomas saw that a puddle had formed at his feet. But similar puddles had formed at the feet of each person taking refuge from the rain and the attendant was not singling him out. He turned left and found himself in a gallery. The room was vast and as high-ceiled as a church. Paintings, many of them religious, hung at intervals along the walls: Christ on the cross, the Last Supper, Lazarus arising from the dead, the tax collectors in the temple. How did he know all this? It had been years since he had attended the Sunday school but it had stuck in his head.

An eye for an eye.

He did not want it in his head. He did not want anything inside his head.

The two young ladies were not here. He turned and returned to the hallway, crossing it and going into the first room on that side.

And here they were, as though awaiting him. As though he had made an appointment with them, here in this very room.

—⁂—

And so the enterprise had come to an inglorious conclusion, thought Dinah, and what had been achieved? Here they were, she and Rhoda, sheltering from a rainstorm in the National Gallery. It was hardly a scheme to rival Miss Nightingale journeying to the Crimea with her team of plucky nurses. Yet they had attempted something and that was the important thing, though it was becoming disappointingly apparent that she, as the eldest—the only—daughter and granddaughter of men who had built railways and made fortunes and changed destinies could no more alter the course of events in her own life than could a tiny ant scaling a blade of grass in the garden. How small we all are, she thought, how utterly insignificant; a hundred years from now there will be nothing left of us; it will be as though we never existed.

If she had married Roger that too would have made no difference. He would still have gone off to war. He would still have died.

Rhoda seemed to have got over both her alarm at the advances of the horrid bird seller and her disappointment at the spiritualist woman's non-appearance and was now focussing her attention on the growing mass of people, mostly of the lower classes, who were pouring into their hall of the gallery.

'Such a very large number of people,' Rhoda observed, 'and of all types, Dinah. You can take my word for it they would none of them be here were it not for the rain!'

'We would not be here were it not for the rain,' Dinah pointed out.

'Ah, but there is every chance we would visit the gallery at some point, would we not, regardless of the rain?'

'Yes, every chance.'

'Whereas these people,' Rhoda made a movement of her hand to indicate the rabble pouring in through the door, 'would never come here otherwise. It is an unfortunate consequence of the gallery's free-entry policy.'

'No doubt,' agreed her cousin. 'Though perhaps a fortunate consequence of the free-entry policy is the potential for the lower classes to educate themselves.'

'Oh that,' replied Rhoda, dismissively. 'Yes, that is of course a possibility. Though a slim one.'

'An unlikely one.'

'An almost inconceivable one.'

'Though a possibility, none the less.'

Dinah smiled and took her cousin's arm, uncertain whether Rhoda was in earnest or in jest, but preferring to think the latter. At least she had got over her disappointment. And at least I have broken her out of the house, Dinah thought. How stupid mourning was! She was glad she had helped her cousin.

Perhaps I shall tell her, she decided, about Roger. One day.

A young man had come into the hall, or rather he had stopped in the doorway and was regarding them. He was a wretched-looking fellow, in a thin collarless shirt and no jacket though it was freezing outside, working-men's trousers soaked to the knee, and a cap and boots to match. His face was bruised and cut, adding to his disreputable appearance. He carried something in a bundle, wrapped in a cloth and held close to this chest, or perhaps he had hurt his hand for it was wrapped up and out of sight covered by the cloth.

'That man is hurt,' she said to Rhoda. 'Look how he holds his hand, like it is injured.'

'Do not look,' Rhoda hissed, staring fiercely at the opposite wall rather than at the man.

But Dinah, to her cousin's evident dismay, immediately got up and went over to the man.

'Are you hurt?' she asked, pointing to his arm, and his eyes widened and they were black, an unfathomable black, and Dinah took a step back.

—⁓—

Thomas could not move. His body, his arm had frozen. His heart was thudding painfully in his chest so that he struggled to breathe. He could no longer feel the handle of the knife that was clasped in his right hand. Perhaps he had dropped it? He could not look down to see if he had dropped the knife.

The young lady was standing before him, looking into his face quizzically, confused by his expression, perhaps also a little frightened. He wanted to reassure her, he wanted her to know that he would do her no harm.

But he was here to do her harm! That was his purpose! An eye for an eye. One girl for another girl. Justice served. And it did not matter that this was a public place, a gallery full of important people and important paintings. It did not matter if a dozen, a hundred people witnessed his actions for there was nothing beyond that point, he had no thought for what might happen to himself. The Thomas Brinklow who had boarded a train in Dawley to attend a fair with his daughter no longer existed. He had died that day.

'Your hand, I wondered if you had hurt your hand?' said the young lady again, offering a tentative smile, and Thomas Brinklow, the man who thought he had died along with his little girl in the train crash, found that he had turned and fled from the room, from the young lady, from justice and, as he ran, the knife dropped from his hand.

CHAPTER TWENTY-FIVE

MRS LOGAN REALISED IT WAS time for her to go.

She had not slept at all that night and now she sat by the window in the little armchair in her room, the curtains opened before her, and watched the moon sink lower in the western sky. It would be dawn in an hour. She would be long gone by then. She would leave, but not because Mrs Jarmyn had accused her of stealing or because Dinah had threatened to report her. She would leave because she could not be in the same house with Mr Jarmyn when he was married to another woman. He would see that, he would understand her actions. He would know what her departure meant.

She remembered another pre-dawn morning three years ago, herself seated on the bed, Paul, her husband, standing beside the shuttered window in their two-room tenement, holding aloft a tiny tumbler of some liquor—port, most likely, he had a taste for port. (Even now she shuddered at the smell when decanting a bottle.) The room was in shadows, lit only by the guttering candle, its meagre light catching the dark liquid in his tumbler and creating a myriad of crimson, flickering points. She had concentrated on those flickering points as they had seemed, almost, to transcend the mundane scene of his departure that far-off morning, of that horrid room, of their life together. If she concentrated on them she did not have to see him. They had not been blessed with children and this failure had been merely the most tangible manifestation of their brief and unproductive marriage. It was a failure neither had spoken of—she out of a growing realisation that she did not want a child with this man, he out of an inability to remain sober. She had rarely seen him during those three years without a glass in his hand.

When the railway accident happened she had received news of it within the hour. She had not believed, at first, that he had been killed in the crash. Had not dared to hope. Then her guilt had made her rush to the accident site to find him. She had convinced herself she was no different to the other frantic wives searching desperately for their menfolk. She had almost believed it. When she had seen his corpse laid out in a line with so many others, white and still, hardly marked at all, she had wept but her tears had been of relief.

And then Mr Jarmyn had appeared out of the smoke.

Why had he been reading the Wombourne report yesterday? Did he feel responsible for her husband's death? She had never thought of it that way before, but perhaps he did. Was that why he had come and sought her out after the inquest? It was an act of charity, she had always known that, yet she had thought at the time there was something more, some other reason that could not be voiced, and now would never be voiced. But now she wondered if she was mistaken, if it was simply that he felt responsible for Paul's death?

She stood up and walked restlessly about her room. She did not wish guilt to be the reason for Lucas's arrival at her door, for his extraordinary offer of employment. Yet, if it was guilt, why had he not sought out all the widows and offered them all positions in his household?

She stopped dead. Perhaps he had. Perhaps he had gone to half a dozen other houses and spoken to half a dozen other women, offering them all the position of housekeeper, and all had turned him down. Perhaps she had been last on the list. The only one desperate enough, foolish enough, to accept his offer.

For a moment she forgot to breathe. How could she not have realised this before now?

Well, then it was equally important that she pack her things and move on. She had outstayed her welcome.

Outside her window the moon was obscured by a bank of clouds. She steadied herself and in the dark began to pack her clothes into a portmanteau and a small trunk. By the time the clouds had drifted on and the moon had reappeared she had packed everything. She made the bed. Hermione would have to strip it next laundry day. Poor Hermione. She would have her work cut out for her. How quickly would they find a replacement? Would they get another housekeeper, or would Mrs Jarmyn insist on a second maid instead?

She realised it did not matter. It no longer concerned her.

She opened her door and listened. The house was silent. She waited. Somehow if she stood here, in the doorway, she was still a part of the household. Once she picked up her trunk and her portmanteau it was over.

A cat whined loudly in the street outside. She wondered if it was Mr Gladstone. He was loud enough to wake the dead and that she did not want. She picked up the two items of luggage, awkwardly managing both at once, not wanting to risk two trips. She made her way down the first flight of stairs to where the family's rooms were, then down again, finally reaching the ground floor. She had written a brief letter of resignation and she placed this now on the silver tray in the hallway.

She paused again but a sound from upstairs set her heart racing and she reached quickly for the front door and slipped out, closing it behind her. Once outside she made her way rapidly down the front steps and set off the short distance along Cadogan Mews half expecting to hear the front door open, an upstairs window slide up, and a voice calling to her. But no door opened and no window slid up and soon she had turned into the square.

Mrs Logan had left Cadogan Mews.

—◊—

Dawn broke over number 19 and, aside from Mr Gladstone, who had been out all night and was looking very pleased with himself having stalked and consumed a whole Prussian fowl, it was Cook who was first to stir.

She swung her legs over the side of her truckle bed and reached for her pipe. Once she had got it lit she shuffled off the bed and made her way from the antechamber off the scullery that served as her bedroom over to the boiler. Bending a stiff back, she poked about inside until she had got the coke alight and, filling the kettle, she placed it on the hob and heaved herself down into her rocking chair to recover from the effort.

The cat was yowling to be let in. Let it yowl, mangy fleabag, thought Cook, puffing on her pipe.

It was a Saturday, which was the day for scrubbing the front steps and the kitchen and passage floors, but traditionally the family had breakfast a little later on Saturdays so there was time for a cup of tea and a bit of something to eat first. She was feeling in a buoyant mood this morning. No guests were expected for dinner this evening, it would just be the family, and she had already plucked the duck she was intending to roast. The carcass of the chicken she had prepared for last night's dinner was on a shelf in the scullery and there was so much left she could make a pie out of it for lunch and a soup for tonight's dinner and there would still be a fair bit of waste left to go in the wash bucket. Being Saturday, the washman would be coming soon to buy whatever waste she had salvaged during the week. With all the food the family had not eaten these last few days, she had been able to fill two buckets, which would bring a pretty penny. They had begun to smell a bit, now, and Hermione had complained and said it made her feel sick so she had covered the buckets with a muslin cloth and moved them into the scullery last night. But it was no use being squeamish about smells and waste if you were in service, she muttered to herself. The sooner the girl got over that, the better it would be for her. Plenty more like her in the workhouse.

Cook shifted and stretched out her legs. She had an idea her knees were bad again today, which was a pity, it being floor-scrubbing day, as it meant she would need Hermione to assist. Nothing to be done about it, if your knees were bad, they were bad. You couldn't be on them scrubbing.

The water was boiling and she heaved herself to her feet and poured it into the teapot, swirling the hot water around to catch the tea leaves. As she waited for the tea to brew she shuffled over to the scullery and retrieved yesterday's roast chicken, bringing it into the kitchen and placing it on the table where it would be within arm's reach when she resumed her seat in the big rocking chair. Her pipe had gone out and she took a moment to relight it, then she poured the tea and settled back with a contented sigh. She reached out and pulled the wishbone off the carcass and stuck it in her mouth, tearing off the flesh then chewing the piece of bone.

She paused mid-suck and began to chuckle to herself as she remembered the big to-do yesterday. The mistress and Mrs Logan had been up to Lord knew what fun and games in the cellar—an inventory, according to Mrs L—when all of a sudden there had been the most almighty crash as though the Heavens themselves had fallen in, then a scream and the master had appeared from nowhere, shouting and carrying on, and Hermione right on his heels just as though the two of them had arrived together. She herself had made her way at a pace more befitting an elderly woman and there was Mrs Logan sitting in a pool of wine and broken glass, a crate and a dozen bottles shattered across the floor! Oh, what a lark it had been! And they had still been at sixes and sevens when Miss Jarmyn had arrived home, wet through from the downpour and in need of dry clothes, whereupon the master had set about kissing and hugging her as though she had escaped some mortal danger instead of just returning from some jaunt or other. What a lark!

Cook shook with laughter. She didn't remember laughing so much since that maid in her previous house had fallen headfirst down the main staircase and landed on the family dog. Killed it outright, the girl had. And suffered a concussion too, it came out later, though at the time the family were more concerned about the dog. Lord, how she had laughed!

The piece of wishbone splintered into two and one piece slipped down her throat.

Cook reached up to her neck and coughed, attempting to dislodge the piece of bone, but it had stuck fast. She coughed again, harder, and sat up in her chair. It would not be dislodged! She coughed some more and her face turned red. She coughed even harder, getting up out of the rocking chair. Her fingers clutched at her throat and her face began to turn purple. It would not come out, it would not budge! She coughed some more, causing tears to spring to her eyes, blurring her vision. She could not get her breath! The bone could not be moved, and panic seized her as she realised there was no one to come to her assistance, that she was choking, that she might, in fact, die. Tears streamed down her face and she let out a choking gasp, clutching at her throat, and into her mind, unbidden, came the faces of the four children whom she had lost all those years before, and had made no mention of to anyone: two dead in their cradles, buried before their first birthdays; one drowned in the river on New Year's Eve; the last dashed beneath the hooves of a horse crossing Whitehall. All dead. All so many years ago but she could see each of their faces clearly, could recall each of their names, and with one final gasp, she realised what she had lost and that she did not wish to die.

—⁓—

Hermione would, in fact, have arrived in time to come to Cook's aid had she not heard Mr Gladstone yowling piteously outside the front door and paused to let him in. The cat slid inside, instantly purring and rubbing himself ingratiatingly against Hermione's legs. Hermione, who had been born in a workhouse and did not remember her mother or her father and who had no siblings so far as she was aware, often felt lonely and was vaguely aware that there was some great lack in her life, so she reached down and tickled the cat beneath his chin, which only made him purr more and rub himself even more frantically against her legs.

'Stupid, daft cat,' she observed, because it is often easier to insult the things we treasure than to acknowledge how much we need them. 'You stink!' she added, which was perfectly true—Mr Gladstone did indeed stink, his nocturnal activities being mainly to blame, a general deficiency in the area of basic hygiene also contributing. He had dried blood down his front and a feather stuck to his ear. 'Ugh!' said Hermione, noticing this, and she pushed him away.

Consequently, by the time she made her way down the back stairs to the kitchen, tying her apron and taking the steps two at a time because she had delayed too long, Cook was slumped face-first on the kitchen table, stone dead.

And to be fair, even had she arrived in time to come to Cook's aid, it is doubtful Hermione would have known what to do. She may very well have done exactly what she now did, which was to scream, loudly and terrifyingly, and in a voice that raised the household and immediately threw it into chaos.

The master responded first, coming crashing down the stairs, a poker in his hand ready to repel any invaders. The boys were close behind, tumbling out of bed and clattering down four flights of stairs in a mixture of excitement and terror. Uncle Austin, in his room at the front of the house, awoke and was instantly alert, reaching for his sabre and being slightly confused when he couldn't find it. Dinah and her mother emerged from their rooms at a more sedate pace, glancing apprehensively at one another and, coming instinctively together, they waited at the top of the stairs, exactly as an etiquette manual on how to prepare for a home invasion—had such a manual existed—might have prescribed.

(Indeed the only member of the household who was not thrown into chaos was Mrs Logan who, at that moment, was disembarking from a cab before the great entranceway to Euston Station terminus and who no longer considered herself a member of the household anyway.)

Hermione's screams continued and, using them as his guide, Mr Jarmyn made his way down to the kitchen and discovered the cause of them.

'Good God!' he exclaimed, pushing the screaming housemaid aside and grabbing Cook by the shoulders. Her face was purple, her hands still clasped to her throat, her mouth was open, her eyes glassy and staring wide and unseeing. She was dead.

'Dear God,' he now said, though in a quieter voice. Hermione, her task fulfilled, had fallen silent and together they regarded Cook. 'She's dead,' Mr Jarmyn said, perhaps a little unnecessarily. 'What happened? Hermione, do you know what happened? Boys, stay out. Go upstairs, now! And call Mrs Logan, at once!' he added, hearing footsteps approaching. 'Hermione?'

'Don't know,' the girl replied, shaking her head. 'I just come down and found 'er like this.'

They both observed the shredded chicken carcass on the table, two small bones, picked clean, lying beside it.

'I think she choked,' Mr Jarmyn concluded. 'Or it may have been her heart. Better call Dr Frobisher. Hermione, go out and fetch the doctor. And get Mrs Logan!'

And Hermione fled.

—⁂—

'What is it? What's going on?' demanded Jack, waiting impatiently in the hallway, furious that his father had sent him and Gus away. If there was danger, they should be told! The ladies needed to be protected.

Hermione now flew up the stairs and almost bowled him over and he started to exclaim 'Hey!' in an appropriately indignant voice but one look at her pale, horror-stricken face forestalled him. So instead he said, 'Hermione, what is it?' but the maid, having a moment earlier almost knocked him over, now completely ignored him and shot out of the front door and threw herself down the front steps and could be seen, a moment later, tearing off down the mews.

Jack and Gus stared after her and Mr Gladstone, who had decided to conduct a rudimentary toilet, paused, his tongue poking out of the side of his mouth, to regard the fleeing maid, before resuming his washing.

In another moment Mr Jarmyn came slowly up the stairs, his head bowed, and Jack felt his stomach muscles tighten and his bowels loosen. The danger, whatever it had been, had evidently passed but something very dreadful had occurred.

'What is it, Father?' said Gus, getting in first.

'Boys,' said Mr Jarmyn, placing an arm around the shoulder of each child and drawing them away, then turning to face the female members of his family as they stood gravely at the top of the stairs. 'Aurora. Dinah. I am afraid I have some sad news. Cook has passed away.'

'Oh!' said Gus, clearly not anticipating this.

'Good Heavens!' said Mrs Jarmyn from upstairs.

'Oh dear!' said Dinah.

'Yes. It is not immediately clear what the cause of her passing was, though we may rest assured that it appears to be natural causes. At a guess I would say she either choked or her heart gave way. I have sent Hermione for Dr Frobisher.'

'But why, if she is already dead?' said Jack, getting in before Gus could.

'Because there will need to be a death certificate, of course,' said Gus. 'And only a doctor can sign one. And he needs to see the body to ascertain the cause of death. It is common sense.'

Jack was furious.

Mrs Logan was nowhere to be found. Hermione returned with Dr Frobisher half an hour later and the family waited solemnly in the drawing room whilst he conducted his examination.

What did she look like? Jack wondered. Could he ask? It seemed tasteless to do so. Certainly one would not ask if someone in the family had died but when it was Cook, perhaps one could ask? He glanced at his father, who was sitting in an armchair, his hands motionless on his lap, and decided against it.

With a discreet knock on the door, Hermione announced that Dr Frobisher had concluded his examination and was ready to see Mr Jarmyn. Once his father had left the room, Jack jumped up.

'I don't see why Dr Frobisher can't give his report here, to us all,' he said, and his mother gave him a disappointed look.

'Don't be tasteless, Jack,' she said.

Jack sat down. They had not had breakfast. Who was to get their breakfast? And lunch and dinner? He forced the questions back down, knowing how they would be received.

After an intolerable delay they heard the front door open and footsteps in the street outside and a moment later Mr Jarmyn returned.

'As we feared,' he announced, resuming his seat. 'It would appear she choked on a chicken bone.'

'Oh dear,' said Mrs Jarmyn. She glanced at the clock on the mantel.

'How could he tell?' asked Gus. 'Did he find the bone?'

'Really, Gus.'

'I believe so, yes. Indeed he did offer to show it to me but I declined.'

'I should like to see it!' gasped Jack, thrilled.

'Really, Jack!'

'Too late, I am afraid. He took it away with him.'

'Oh!'

'Someone will be coming to take her away soon so I suggest we remain here until that task is completed.'

So they sat quietly in the drawing room, reflecting on the life and death of Cook, and Jack's stomach rumbled loudly.

It was an age before the men came for her and by then Jack was so famished he felt faint. Hermione had been commanded to produce toast and coffee, which she did, though her hands shook as she served it.

Consequently, it was mid-morning before anyone began to wonder at Mrs Logan's absence.

—∞—

It was Dinah who found the letter. It was lying, by itself, in the silver letter tray in the hallway and at first Dinah thought it had arrived in the first post but, when she picked it up, she saw it had no stamp. It was addressed simply: *Mr Jarmyn*.

That was odd. It must have been hand-delivered. She had heard no one come to the door—though in all the chaos it was likely she would have missed it had someone come. And then a bizarre, a terrifying thought crossed her mind: the letter was from Cook and she had taken her own life! Or she had had a premonition of her coming death. Dinah stood very still, the letter clasped to her chest. A letter from a dead woman! Then she inspected the envelope again and decided that, on the whole, the handwriting could not possibly be Cook's. Indeed it was debatable whether Cook could even write.

She took the letter to her father.

'It was in the silver letter tray in the hallway,' she explained, and it was a measure of the topsy-turvy nature of the morning that her father took the letter and opened it at once without retiring to his study to do so.

She watched his face as he pulled out a single sheet and unfolded it, reading what appeared to be a few lines at most, and as he did so his expression did not change. Then he slowly refolded the letter and met her inquiring gaze.

'What is it, Father?'

'Mrs Logan has decided to leave us,' he said simply.

Dinah's hand flew to her mouth. 'Oh but—oh!' she said.

'Here, read it for yourself,' and he handed the letter to her. It said simply:

Dear Mr Jarmyn,

I am hereby tendering my resignation from the position of house-keeper in your household. I very much regret the lack of notice and the upset my actions will inevitably cause. I am unable to provide you with a suitable reason for my sudden departure and understand that it will seem strange, however I beg that you respect that my reasons are both just and compelling. Please accept my warmest wishes for the future.

Yours faithfully,

Christabel Logan.

Dinah turned away, holding out the letter to her father and walking quickly from the room. She recognised that a crisis had been reached but her own part in it—*had* she played a part?—was worryingly unclear to her.

—∞—

When Dinah had gone, Lucas closed the drawing room door and sat down on the nearest chair. For a moment he could not conceive that she had gone. That she could pack her belongings, write a letter and leave and he not know. *When* had she gone? Sometime between them all retiring to bed last night and Hermione's scream this morning. A long time, certainly time enough to get far away from Cadogan Mews. She could be on the other side of London by now. She could be on a train heading anywhere.

Why would she leave? Her reasons were both just and compelling. What the *Devil* did that mean?

He stood up, furious. It was an outrage that she just leave after all he had done in bringing her here, after all they had done to make a place for her here, in their house.

He sat down. What had he done, really? Offer her a position out of pity, guilt? And what had the family done? Devolved the entire running of the house over to her so that the idea that the house could function, that the family could function, without her seemed . . . inconceivable.

He unfolded the letter again and reviewed its contents. *It will seem strange . . . !* Yes, it damn well did seem strange! What was the woman thinking of? What had happened? Something must have happened to precipitate this.

He refolded the letter. He saw his hand covering hers and, later, the horrifying moment when the crate in the cellar had tipped over and he had thrown himself at her to save her.

And afterwards, as he had knelt on the floor at her side and touched her cheek.

He stood up. What should be done? What ought he to do? He would seek out the maid. He rang the bell urgently.

'Hermione, Mrs Logan has resigned and departed. I wonder did she give any indication of where she might go?'

And Hermione, receiving news of a second calamity fast on the heels of the first one, groaned with dismay and clapped a hand to each side of her face, which was enough for Lucas to conclude that the girl had not been privy to Mrs Logan's plans. He dismissed her and went out into the hallway. Then he stopped dead. He had been about to summon Mrs Logan. A crisis had occurred and she would fix it.

But she *was* the crisis. And the Jarmyns were on their own. For a moment he couldn't quite catch his thoughts. He was almost relieved when various members of his family began to appear.

'Is it true, Father, that Mrs Logan has left?' asked Gus, bug-eyed.

'It is looking very much as though she has.'

Behind the boys Aurora had come halfway down the stairs. She paused now, her hand resting on the banister and her face quite still and composed. He tried to read her face but could not.

'I bet Mrs Logan murdered Cook and that is why she has fled!' said Jack, fairly bouncing up and down in his excitement.

Lucas rounded on his son, furiously. 'Mrs Logan did *not* murder Cook! Do not be so *absurd*, Jack!'

And Jack cowered and crept up to his room and did not reappear until teatime.

'Well. This is very awkward,' observed Aurora, still not moving from her place on the stairs.

'*Awkward?* Yes. Yes, it is indeed awkward,' he agreed and he began to experience a dizzying sense of things moving outside of his control. He needed to say something, there was no doubt something definitely needed to be said, but he did not know what it was. He turned abruptly and went downstairs to the hallway. His coat and umbrella and gloves and hat were all there, where she had placed them last night. He put them on and grabbed the umbrella and made for the door.

'Where are you going?'

'Out,' he replied, not turning around. He pulled the door shut behind him and plunged down the steps and away, putting as much distance between himself and the house as he could. It was only as he turned into Cadogan Square that his pace slowed.

Where *was* he going? He would find her, of course he would.

He hailed a cab but when the driver asked where he wished to go, he realised he did not even know where to begin.

CHAPTER TWENTY-SIX

THE DAY WENT ON AND a lunch of sorts was served, consisting of last evening's soup, heated up on the hob by Hermione, who spilt some of it on Gus's lap, and a chicken salad. True, it was not traditional salad weather (last night's frost still lay on the ground outside) but no one commented. Jack did inquire whether or not this was the self-same chicken on which Cook had choked to death, but he was silenced by a look from his sister that was almost as frosty as the pavements outside. There was a tart to follow though, wisely, no one inquired as to its provenance, and when no custard arrived to accompany it, the family dealt with that too.

Mr Jarmyn did not join them for lunch and no one seemed to know where he was but, as there wasn't very much soup or salad, it was perhaps just as well. After lunch Mrs Jarmyn retired to her room and asked not to be disturbed. It was assumed that she had a headache.

Aurora closed her door but she did not at once sit down. Instead she leant against it, her forehead pressed to the wood panelling. She closed her eyes.

Mrs Logan had gone. And in the end she had simply packed her things and, with the minimum of fuss, had left them. Unquestionably it was right that she go. It was for the best. It was, on the whole, a relief. That horrid little scene yesterday, and the ghastly incident in the cellar. It had been awkward. Untenable, it had seemed at the time. But now, miraculously, it was all resolved. Mrs Logan had gone. She was no longer a presence in their lives.

She wondered when Lucas would return. It was Saturday, he would not have gone to the office. He rarely went to his club any more, though perhaps today he had. Yes, that was it: two of the staff had gone—one had died, one had fled—what self-respecting gentleman would wish to remain a moment longer in the house? The home was her responsibility, her domain, and it was her duty to ensure it was a haven of peace and calm, a place where a husband felt secure and contented, a place to which he would wish to return each evening.

She would make this a haven of peace and calm.

The dinner gong did not sound. Realising it was past the usual hour, Aurora made her own way down to the dining room and found Dinah already seated. Of Lucas there was still no sign.

'I don't know where Father is,' said Dinah.

Aurora put her hands on the back of her chair to steady herself, aware that Dinah studied her. After a moment she sat down. Then she gave her daughter a bright, encouraging smile.

'I do believe it is a little warmer this evening,' she observed.

'Yes, perhaps it is,' Dinah replied, sounding unconvinced.

They lapsed into silence and Lucas's unexplained absence and the inexplicable and sudden departure of Mrs Logan hung over them.

'I wonder what we shall be having for dinner,' Aurora remarked. She had intended to go downstairs this afternoon and address Hermione. It was important that the girl receive some instruction in order to carry out all the duties that now fell to her. But somehow she had not. She had stayed in her room. She had had a headache.

'Are you all right, Mama?'

But before Aurora could reply the dining room door opened. She looked up, a welcoming smile ready on her face. But it was Uncle Austin who shuffled through the door and now regarded them. Aurora looked down as the old man shuffled towards a chair and fussily arranged himself in it.

'Good evening, Uncle,' she said, more for Dinah's benefit than his. 'How lovely of you to join us.' His attendance at dinner—at any meal—was sporadic. Often the maid took a tray up to his room and they did not see him from one day to the next. But tonight he had appeared.

'Good evening, Uncle,' said Dinah. 'I am very much afraid dinner may not be quite what you are expecting. Indeed, there is every chance it may not happen at all.'

The major sat and smiled politely at her. He mumbled something they could not catch and began to rock gently back and forth.

No one spoke.

'I wonder what has happened to dinner?' said Aurora eventually and Dinah pushed back her chair and stood up.

'I shall go and see what is happening in the kitchen.'

'Perhaps that would be for the best.'

They were alone, she and Austin. Aurora looked down at the tablecloth and Austin sat and rocked and mumbled. She had a vivid memory as a child of him in his dark blue and gold cavalry officer's uniform visiting her father's house in Cheyne Walk. He had sported a great, bushy moustache in those days—the mark of the cavalry officer—riding boots, a tall hat with a crest on top and a sword at his side. The next time she had seen him had been during the second year of the war. The dark blue and gold had gone, the boots replaced with soft house slippers, the great bushy moustache replaced by a gaping, vivid gash from mouth to temple. She had been frightened of that terrifying gash, of the empty and unseeing eyes that sometimes frightened you even more by becoming unexpectedly focussed and intelligent. But gradually she had grown used to him. She had brought him into her husband's house—he was her final link to her father, after all.

She poured herself a glass of water and drank it.

And now she was preparing to send him to an asylum.

'I'm afraid dinner may be some little time yet,' said Dinah, returning and resuming her seat.

'Oh?'

'Yes. There is duck, apparently, but it is some way from being roasted. I suggested we have our soup and some hot bread rolls and await developments. It may be that we have the duck for breakfast instead.'

'What happened to the child?' said Uncle Austin suddenly, looking up with an inquiring but perplexed expression.

A chill seemed to settle over the room and Aurora's throat constricted. 'Now, Uncle,' she murmured in a soothing voice, keeping her eyes on him and willing him to say no more.

'But she was here,' Austin insisted. 'A girl. Sweet little thing,' and he gave a wistful smile.

'Mama, shall I go to the cellar and get a bottle of claret to have with the duck—if we get the duck—in case Father returns?' Dinah suggested.

'Yes, if you wish, dear, though I shall not join you. I shall just drink water, I think, this evening. Oh, Dinah be careful. The accident yesterday—the floor may still be slippery or there may be broken glass. And you'll need the key.' For Aurora was once more custodian of all the household keys—and everyone knew there was only one key to the cellar.

'Thank you, Mama. I will be careful,' and Dinah got up and left.

They were alone again.

'Uncle, why don't you have your dinner in your room? I can bring you up a nice bowl of soup and a hot bread roll. I am sure you would prefer to eat in your room, wouldn't you?'

He ignored this, a look of distress appearing on his face. 'Something happened.'

Aurora put her hands flat on the table before her and took a slow, calming breath. 'Uncle, please—'

'To the child. Something bad.'

She didn't want Dinah to return. She should get Austin up to his room. Mrs Logan would be able to manage him.

But Mrs Logan had gone.

Dinah returned at last, carrying a bottle which she had already uncorked, and resumed her seat. Mother and daughter faced each other across the table and Aurora thought, things have come to a pretty pass when we have to fetch our own wine and pour our own glasses. But everything appeared to be different this evening, the dinner and the wine was the least of it.

Dinah poured herself a small quantity of the claret and Aurora watched her over the top of her glass of water. She could smell the pungent fumes of the claret but she would not drink. Mrs Logan had gone. She was going to make this a haven of peace and calm.

Austin moaned, rubbing a hand agitatedly against his cheek over and over. 'The child caught on fire and no one could save her.' He clutched his hands to his head and groaned. 'No one could save her.'

At this Aurora pushed back her chair so violently it fell backwards onto the floor. No one spoke. Dinah's face had a ghostlike appearance in the lamplight. Her uncle's eyes showed black with tiny pricks of reflected light and she shivered because she could not tell if beyond that light was absolute clarity or an unimaginable void.

She pleaded a headache and fled to her room, leaving him in Dinah's care to say or not say whatever he might. Once alone, she sat motionless to calm herself. Mrs Logan had gone. All would be normal once more. But she saw again—she kept on seeing—Lucas's expression as he came to Mrs Logan's assistance in the cellar the day before, and his hand reaching up to touch her; and she saw him again this morning as he had announced Mrs Logan had left, and his face as he had curtly informed her he was going out.

She stood up as a terrible fear gripped her and her fingers curled themselves into tight fists. In a moment it passed but she found herself at her desk drawer, the key already in the lock, the drawer sliding open where an Armagnac, one of the Janneau that had been unaccounted for in yesterday's inventory, lay. She had had no intention of drinking them, they were an insurance, that was all; an insurance that had not, in the end, been required, for Mrs Logan was gone of her own volition. But she had earned one drink and she poured herself a quantity, taking a sip and letting the brandy roll over her tongue. She was not a drunk, though in the early years of their marriage, in the dark months following her mother's death, she had almost gone down that path, had come perilously close, and Lucas had almost discovered it but in the end a maid had been dismissed instead and this sacrifice—it was Clara surely, not Clarice—had saved her marriage. She had not let herself fall like that again. She was not a drunk like her poor dear Mama, but she had earned one drink on this night of all nights.

She sat up with a start, breathing quickly, awake.

'Who's there?' She got unsteadily to her feet but she was alone. The room was almost in total darkness; only a thin shaft of moonlight lay across the bed and the spluttering remains of her candle made dancing shadows against the wall. What time was it? It was impossible to know. She could not remember hearing any clocks chiming for a while. She reached for a shawl and put out a hand to the door handle, listening.

Someone was there, just outside her door. She thrust open her door and all but walked right into him.

'Well, you have driven her away. Are you satisfied?'

She stifled a gasp. Lucas was standing at the top of the stairs, a smell of chimney smoke and horses and night air clinging to him as though he had just this minute returned home. It was a moment before she realised he was referring to Mrs Logan. The hatred in his words nailed her to the floor but when she replied her voice was quite calm.

'I? I hardly see how I am responsible.'

'Do you not?' he said, and his tone chilled her. 'No doubt you absolve yourself of that too.'

'I am afraid I do not follow you, my dear.'

'Then let me enlighten you: our daughter whose death you caused. Our daughter who was burnt alive due to *your negligence . . .* your *drunkenness*—'

She heard herself gasp.

'—and now you attempt to lay the blame at your uncle's door, and do not think for one minute that I do not see what you are doing! Let the old man take the blame. He is an imbecile—who is to know? And once he is removed, then who is to know the truth?'

Aurora put a hand to her mouth. The flesh on her face felt cold, clammy, as though there was no blood left in it.

Lucas took a step towards her and peered into her face: 'My God. You are drunk,' and he turned and went into his room.

She stood for a time in the darkness, listening to the sounds of the house around her: the floorboards settling, a window rattling in an upstairs room. Each sound was amplified and thick with portent. There was no sound from Lucas's room and no light from beneath his door.

He believed she had killed their daughter.

Their daughter. Their beautiful, innocent daughter.

'I wish to look as beautiful as you, Mama.'

She had asked her child, *'Have you thought about what type of dress you are going to choose?'* and Sofia had answered at once: *'A princess line with a cuirasse bodice in sapphire or perhaps crimson silk, but certainly not in green and not in taffeta though I do like taffeta but I think it will be a little stiff and bothersome to wear,'* and she had smiled at this for it sounded like something she herself might say. *'I am not sure that sounds entirely suitable for a little girl,'* she had observed, and Mrs Logan had gone outside to whistle for a cab. But in the end the outing to the dressmaker had been abandoned. *'We will go to the dressmaker another day,'* she had said, but they had not gone to the dressmaker on another day for there had been no other days.

A sound from the street below startled Aurora and she listened—a man calling drunkenly, a carriage passing the end of the square, a dog barking in the mews, the clock at St George's striking the hour. She found she was lying on the floor, curled up, and she had no idea how long she had lain here. She did not move, could not imagine how she would ever move again.

I have tried, she thought, Lord knows I have tried so very hard.

But it would not be dislodged, the coldness, the void, all she had done was to push it down, to pretend it did not exist. She had thought Lucas would help her. But he had not. Instead he blamed her.

A second clock struck, though whether it was for the same hour or if another hour had passed she didn't know. She lifted her head and the room swam horribly, her eyes refused to focus. She had drunk, and she had drunk a great deal, and the irony, the wonderful, funny, stupid irony was that she had drunk because he had accused her of being a drunk! It was funny, wasn't it? It was ironic!

She pulled herself to her feet, filled with a purpose now that had been entirely absent a minute earlier. She reached for her cloak and her shoes and went down the stairs in the dark, opened the front door and, like Mrs Logan a few hours before her, she went out of the house and down the front steps. Outside she paused, breathing slowly. It was bitterly cold—wasn't it? She couldn't feel the cold.

She walked out of the mews and into Cadogan Square. It was deserted, no lights showed from any of the houses. To the south, she could hear the never-ending clatter of carriages on Oxford Street. It was a comforting sound when the silence of the square was unsettling. She walked towards the clatter, down Southampton Row and crossing Oxford Street, and at once she was surrounded by people and horses and cabs. One cab appeared out of nowhere, its horse rearing up, and for a moment all she could see was hooves and the froth on the animal's nostrils and the terror in its yellow eyes. The driver shouted at her and a whip cracked frighteningly near her head.

She plunged onwards through the maze of streets between Lincoln's Inn Fields and Drury Lane, crossing the Strand, and reaching the Embankment where the river finally halted her.

The river flowed swiftly, swollen with a high tide, and looked impenetrable, its black depths so wide one could not make out the opposite bank. The clatter of hooves on Waterloo Bridge echoed across the silent expanse of water and a barge laden with coal slid past heading eastwards towards the Estuary, a lamp burning at bow and stern. The clouds parted and a three-quarter moon appeared, transforming the scene and bathing the river in a pale ghostly light, and Aurora saw the figure of a child on the far bank. A little girl, a beautiful, perfect nine-year-old child, miraculously saved from the fire! She started forward with a cry but the figure transformed itself into a stranger. The clouds closed in again, the river became black and the figure was gone. It was not her child. It would never be her dead child.

—⁓—

A mile or two north of the river, Dinah could not sleep. Giving up, she pulled back the curtains. Ice had created delicate patterns on her window and in the moonlight the frost on the branches of the plane trees glistened so prettily she felt a moment of light-heartedness. Then a shadow fell as she remembered that Cook had died in the kitchen and Mrs Logan had gone.

How instantly everything could change.

She let the curtains drop and turned away, pulling a shawl over her shoulders. Mrs Logan had gone and it was right that she go, indeed it was the only possible outcome. Father had gone out all day, searching for her. He had returned very late and one presumed—one prayed—he returned alone. *Had* she played a part in Mrs Logan's departure? At any rate, things would return to normal now. A sort of normal. They would find a new housekeeper. And a new cook.

In the meantime she could not sleep.

The clock struck five and dawn was many hours off yet, not even a suggestion of it showed in the mid-winter eastern sky.

A rapid but soft rap on her door flew her into a terrified panic. She got swiftly out of bed and opened her door, just a crack to see her father and he was not in his dressing gown but was fully dressed, so that she was confused and a little frightened.

'Dinah, your mother—is she here with you?'

Dinah gaped at him and silently shook her head, the confusion becoming now a cold knot of fear.

'All right.' He nodded, a slow, reassuring nod, but she could tell he was not calm at all and the cold knot hardened inside her. 'Then I do not know where she is,' he said. 'She is not in her room or any of the other rooms so far as I can tell. I have gone down into the basement and into the garden and into the street as far as the square but I cannot find her.'

'But I don't understand,' said Dinah.

He nodded again, taking both her hands in his. 'I thought I heard her go out—hours ago—but I wasn't sure. When I went to check she was not in her room but I will find her,' and he went out again to search.

When he had gone Dinah ran silently from room to room, convincing herself with each room she entered that he was mistaken, and in each room her hopes were confounded. She went lastly to the drawing room and awaited her father there. His words '*I thought I heard her go out—hours ago*' frightened her. *Why* had her mother gone out late at night, and alone? And why had Father let her? It was inconceivable, inexplicable. She began to pace the room.

Eventually her father returned alone, silent and thoughtful and in need of a brandy to warm his frozen limbs, but he was prevented from having one because the liquor cabinet was locked and Mrs Logan had not seen fit to reveal the whereabouts of the key before her departure.

'Damn and *blast!*' he exploded, pulling at the handle and too angry to see the irony of it. Dinah found the keys in her mother's room and hurried down to the cellar, snatching up the first bottle that came to hand, which turned out to be the last of the Quinta dos Calvedos cellared by old Mr Jarmyn in the fifties. But what did it matter, and she brought it upstairs anyway and watched her father open it and pour a quantity into a tumbler.

Could this be my fault? Dinah wondered again. Have I caused this?

'Mama must have gone to Aunt Meredith,' she said for the third or fourth time, though her father had been to the house in Great Portland Street already and received no word of her. She thought of her mother in the weeks following Sofia's accident, how she had seemed to lose something of herself. Dinah had lain awake night after night, thinking, What if Mama, too, should die, of a broken heart? Seeing her mother so altered had made the idea of it—of dying of a broken heart—no longer fanciful but something real and present.

The Quinta dos Calvedos was clearly not to her father's taste for he threw down the glass half drunk and returned to the liquor cabinet to tug vainly at the door. 'Damn and *blast*! I know there's some decent Scotch in there.'

'I'm afraid Mama or Mrs Logan must have locked it and forgotten to unlock it,' said Dinah. 'It must date back to that time we saw Sofia in there about to help herself to the sherry—do you remember? I think one of the boys put her up to it—a silly dare or something. Uncle Austin got in a terrible state about it. You know, I don't think he ever really knew who Sofia was. I think he always had some crazed notion that she was the child of one of the neighbours—or one of his neighbours from his father's house in the 1840s. He always thinks Mama is the child of the house. He always calls Mama the pretty little girl, haven't you noticed? It's as though he still sees her as the little girl at his brother's house all those years ago—'

Dinah made herself stop. She did not know why she was babbling on about such nonsense except that it was better than just sitting here with her father who was getting more and more angry.

But a strange thing had happened.

At her words, which had seemed to Dinah innocuous enough, her father groaned and violently shook his head, pounding the side of his temple with the flat of his hand with a force that alarmed her.

'*She oughtn't to have been drinking. She got too close to the fire and the pretty little girl tried to save her,*' he said as though reciting something he had learnt or had been told, and Dinah was lost. '*She tried to save her but her dress caught alight.*' Dear

God,' he whispered, 'it was the other way around. She tried to *save* Sofia.' He got slowly to his feet, and his face frightened her. '*We must find your mother.*'

—⁓—

Aurora had thought she had seen a little girl on the far bank but she had been mistaken. Had she looked up, instead, at the great iron edifice of Waterloo Bridge she might have noticed a solitary figure standing at the apex of the bridge leaning out and silently watching the flow of the great river beneath him.

At first this solitary figure did not see her either: he saw Alice and, other than her, everything was black: the river, the night sky, his heart.

Thomas had wanted to kill the young lady. He had purchased a knife and followed her with the intention of killing her. It was to be retribution. Justice. The horror of it surpassed even the horror of the train accident. He could not shake the image of it out of his head and he wondered if he might possibly go mad with it.

He could not go home and he dared not return to his lodgings—which was a pity for a letter from his wife awaited him there, informing him of her intention to return home to him, and that she was carrying his second child.

He had made things worse, a hundred, a thousand times worse, when it had seemed that the very worst thing had already happened.

He looked down into the fast-flowing river and he understood what it was that made people jump. They said the Thames overflowed with the corpses of folk who had drowned themselves. He could well believe it. The miracle was that so many millions chose *not* to throw themselves in.

He heard the muffled cry of a woman and saw on the river bank below the bridge a cloaked figure walk down the little steps at the water's edge and rather than stop at the water that lapped over the lowest step, the figure simply continued onwards, walking very steadily into the water. For a moment he stared transfixed because the figure was ghostlike, a vision he must surely have conjured up from his own deranged mind, but the woman gave an involuntary gasp as the cold waters sucked against her cloak and pulled her under and he knew she was real.

He cried out and ran down the steps at the side of the bridge then down the little steps at the water's edge and he plunged in, wading, and the shock of the icy water numbed his brain. He could not swim and he could no longer see her but he plunged under the water and thrashed about like a madman, finding something that was soft and material-like and grabbing at it with both hands and pulling and pulling, and she came at last, a dead weight, and he slipped and they both sank beneath the surface and he felt a moment of sheer panic but he found his footing and, slipping and scrambling, he burst out of the water gasping for air and dragging her with him to blessed dry land.

He lay there for a time on his back, and directly overhead was a single star burning very brightly. He did not believe it was a sign, he knew it was just a single star burning very brightly, but he wept and could not stop.

CHAPTER TWENTY-SEVEN

London and the Midlands

ON A SUNDAY MORNING IN late January the city was slow to come to life but the river had been awake since dawn, since long before dawn. The first barges taking coal upstream and bringing goods downstream were already chugging beneath the capital's great bridges. Wherries dodged in between, taking passengers and cargo from one bank to the other. A naval frigate, here for a ceremonial duty, was being led by a tug to moorings on the south bank. Only the pleasure craft were tethered and silent, and would remain so until the spring.

Those who had business to attend to were already working. Those who did not put on their Sunday best and prepared to attend church. And those who had neither business nor church to attend sheltered in doorways and beneath the arches of the same great bridges, shivering and praying they would make it through another day.

Not all did.

Thomas Brinklow, a lone figure on the river bank not far from the bridge where he had intended, the night before, to contemplate his future and had instead found himself saving a woman's life, watched as a group of constables in a police launch pulled a body from the river.

You could not save everyone, it seemed, and the profound elation he had experienced last night at the life he had saved was quelled a little. This person no longer needed his help, or that of any mortal man. The constables heaved the corpse onto their craft and turned towards the shore and Thomas removed his cap, though it felt like a futile enough gesture. There was little point in wondering who it was—there were too many things that could happen to a person in this city to make it worthwhile speculating on which of them had finished this poor soul off.

The police launch reached the shore not ten yards from where he stood, and if they wondered at this strange-looking figure on the river bank in sodden clothes that smelt like the river they made no remark. Instead a constable leapt out and secured the moorings with an expert hand and they manhandled the corpse out of the boat and onto the jetty where they laid it whilst they paused to light their pipes and stand and smoke in the misty dawn.

Thomas looked and saw this one, too, was a girl, her long skirts tangled and sodden and wrapped around her slim torso, her long, dark hair matted and stiff with the river's detritus, her face bleached and empty of expression. After a time the constables roused themselves to lift her onto a stretcher. One of them tossed an oilcloth over her and they heaved the bundle onto their shoulders to carry her off, at which point Thomas turned away.

The corpse was that of a starving, homeless girl called Annie who had once worked as a maid in a big house in Bloomsbury. She was taken to a mortuary and as no one came to claim her she was eventually buried in an unmarked pauper's grave at Houndsditch.

After many hours, his clothes still damp and reeking of the river, Thomas Brinklow returned to his lodgings and found the letter from his wife.

And though he did not know it, a short distance away the woman whom Thomas had pulled from the river lay insensible in the house of a retired clergyman who resided in a modest house on the river's edge and who had witnessed—as he witnessed on many winter nights—a poor soul attempt to end their life. But this soul was saved and the fact of it surprised him so much he was roused to leave his house and, rather than see the poor wretch arrested for her unlawful act, he had brought her to his house. Here, and to his great surprise, he found her to be, not a poor wretch at all, but instead a lady. It was many hours before the lady regained her senses enough to allow him to contact her people. For she had a family, and a husband, a pleasant-looking fellow but with a face ravaged by worry, who was even now at her bedside, pacing the floor in a way that caused the retired clergyman to question why it was the lady had attempted what she had the night before. But no doubt it was all part of God's plan.

The sky continued to be clear for the next two days but the temperature dropped and snow fell on Monday night and again on Tuesday night, blanketing the city and causing havoc on the roads. Horses slipped on the ice and had to be destroyed where they fell, carriages overturned in Regent Street, breaking bones and blocking the main thoroughfares. A hundred souls perished in the night, frozen solid in the doorways and beneath the arches in which they huddled, and a number of performances had to be cancelled at some of the more important West End theatres, generating a flurry of angry letters to the editor of *The Times*.

Outside the city, the snowfalls were even heavier, and by Wednesday morning transportation in the provinces had all but ceased.

In Birmingham, Christabel Logan looked out of her window and wondered if she would be able to catch her train. She had been staying at the Railway Hotel for the past four nights, awaiting a reply from a sister near Wolverhampton with whom she was hopeful of staying, but the sister had failed to reply until late last night. Now, dependent on the snow, Mrs Logan was in a position to leave the hotel and travel north. Would the trains be running? she wondered. They had been sporadic yesterday and she had sat by the window watching the comings and goings on the platforms below. She had stayed away from the hotel's public bar downstairs, taking her meals in her room, feeling it was not quite proper, her a widow travelling alone.

The letter, received at long last from the sister, had been brief and surprised, but she had offered her older sibling a place to stay, at least for the time being.

Mrs Logan reflected that she had not seen her sister since her own marriage to Paul Logan, six years earlier. This particular sister, her youngest, had herself married a blacksmith and now resided in a small village to the north of Wolverhampton. They had a number of small children and, reading between the lines of the brief note, not much free space for a guest. But she could help with the children, could she not?

At least for the time being.

Mrs Logan put her things in her trunk and called the porter to take her luggage downstairs. She settled her bill and the porter, a kindly man who seemed to have some inkling of her dilemma, carried the trunk and her portmanteau across to the station and waited whilst she purchased her ticket.

The platform was busy. A number of cancellations earlier that morning and the previous day had stranded people who otherwise would have travelled earlier. A farmer, perched on a crate of week-old chicks, waited wearily, sucking on a clay pipe, clearly not expecting the train to turn up. It did, twenty-five minutes late: the 11.50, a local stopping train scheduled to reach Wolverhampton a little before one o'clock. The train pulled into the platform and there was a flurry of doors opening and a bustle of trunks and crates and parcels loaded on board. The farmer with the chicks helped her to get her trunk on board and saw her settled on a seat in the second-class carriage before tossing his crate into the neighbouring third-class carriage.

As she settled herself for the journey Mrs Logan hoped her sister or her sister's husband would be waiting at the other end to meet her. She had replied to her sister's letter by telegram to say which train she would be on but had received no reply.

Well, no matter if they were at the station to meet her or not, she had the address and, if need be, she could hire a man and a cart and get herself there.

All would be well.

The train let out a great whoosh of steam and sounded its whistle. As it heaved its load out of the station and started on the journey northwest towards Wolverhampton, the train passed beneath the first of thirty-two sets of signals on the stretch of line between the two cities. A defective goods train, some distance away and travelling on the main Birmingham to Liverpool route, had been shunted onto the local line in order to make way for the oncoming Liverpool express. It was now blocking the Wolverhampton branch line, just north of Moxley. But both the stationmaster and the signalman at Moxley had been notified and the signals on the branch line would be set to 'danger' which would be enough to alert the driver of the oncoming local stopping train of the hazard up ahead.

All would be well.

She looked out of the carriage window, separated from her fellow travellers by her loss. And yet, despite her situation, Mrs Logan could not help but marvel at the wintery wonderland of snow-covered fields and white-roofed cottages and the frozen canal, the barges set solid in its midst. The snowfall of the previous two nights—surely the last snowfall of the winter—had even caused ice to form on the signals in pretty icicles that glistened in the late morning sunshine.

CHAPTER TWENTY-EIGHT

London and Oxford: February

IT WAS A MONDAY MORNING, the last day of February. In Oxford, Hilary term was in full swing and Bill Jarmyn, standing at the window of his rooms, smiled as some unfortunate fellow was carried, wriggling and protesting, into the Quad and was ceremoniously tipped into the pond to a chorus of cheers. After some splashing about, the chap stood up, the water cascading off him, and made a sweeping bow which was greeted with a chorus of boisterous 'hurrahs!' from the crowd of onlookers. That same chap had been tipped into the pond before Christmas, Bill noted, and looking at the other chaps in the crowd, he saw that every single one of them had, at some time or another, ended up in the pond. Now the fellow was being hoisted onto someone's shoulders and paraded around the Quad, dripping water, to a spontaneous rendition of 'Rock of Ages'. The procession made its way through the gate and out of the Quad and all was quiet. And Bill stopped smiling and wondered why it was that no one had ever tipped him into the pond.

—⚔—

Sixty miles away at number 19 Cadogan Mews the schoolroom was silent and deserted. The boys had started at a small prep school and, in the autumn term, Gus would be starting at Eton. Mr Todd had been forced to find himself a new position with a doctor's family in Chiswick but, as that family had just commenced a one-year Grand Tour and had taken him with them, he was not complaining.

—⚔—

Uncle Austin was not in his room either. He was in the third hour of the battle, his troops had just charged the Russian lines and Austin found himself temporarily cut off from his men. The smoke from the battery of guns up on the hillside and from the shot of the percussion muskets created a fog that smothered everyone and everything, a fog that caught at your lungs and made you choke and that reduced visibility down to an arm's length. It was disorienting, even for the most hardened soldier. It made you lose your way. He realised he had become cut off from his men.

—⚔—

It was a Monday morning, the last day of February. There was a definite hint of spring in the air and in a downstairs front room of number 19 Cadogan Mews someone had placed a sign in the window that read *Cook wanted. Apply within.*

In the kitchen Hermione, surrounded by a mass of unwashed pots, pans and dishes and an unscrubbed kitchen table, regarded

Cook's book of recipes which lay open on the table before her, a look of controlled panic on her face. Who had written out Cook's recipes was not immediately clear to her as Cook had boasted on more than one occasion that she could neither read nor write. And, what was more concerning, none of it seemed to bear the slightest resemblance to the dishes Cook had prepared. This morning Hermione had made a beef and onion pie. The pastry had been too crumbly and then it had been too soggy. But she had pressed on and made the filling and placed the pie inside the range. Now she pulled open the range door, glancing over at Mr Gladstone, who stopped washing himself and seemed to hold his breath, and she pulled out the pie. It was burnt to a crisp on the top and, as she gazed at it, the centre of the pie collapsed and Hermione burst into tears.

Mr Gladstone tactfully resumed his washing and made no comment.

—∽∿∽—

It was a Monday morning, there was a hint of spring in the air and Mr Jarmyn had gone, not to his office, but to Regent's Park. He purchased a newspaper and sat down on a bench where he read on page five the headline *'Defeat of the British Troops. Reported Death of General Colley.'* There had been a great battle, it appeared, which the British forces had resoundingly lost and during which their commander had been killed. There was a list of casualties. One of those listed as killed was Lieutenant Francis Graves of the 58th Regiment. Roger's old regiment, and the boy Meredith had hoped to speak to upon his return in order to find out more about her son's death. Well, she would not be speaking to him now. There would be no more information and the campaign, it appeared, had been a failure.

Lucas put down the newspaper and watched for a while the carriages and riders going past. Two young ladies in green riding habits rode past, their groom on another horse a few lengths behind them.

'*Board of Trade Report on Near-Fatal Collision: Signals to Blame!*' reported *The Times* on page six:

A Board of Trade report released today, following the near-fatal train accident at Moxley near Wolverhampton earlier this month, commended the owners of the North West Midlands Railway Company whose safety measures undoubtedly prevented what would surely have been a catastrophe resulting in numerous lives lost. On Wednesday, 2 February, a defective goods train had been shunted onto the branch line of the aforementioned railway and into the path of the oncoming 11.50 Birmingham to Wolverhampton passenger train. It being an uncommonly cold day with snowfalls reported the previous two nights, the signals on that stretch of line had frozen into the 'clear' position, meaning the driver of the oncoming passenger train was unaware of the mortal danger ahead. Less than two hundred yards from the goods train the passenger train came in sight of a third signal. This signal had, however, the previous day been replaced with the new safety signal. This signal too had frozen, but the design of the new signal was such that it had frozen in the 'danger' position. Consequently, the train braked, stopping a mere twenty yards from the last carriage of the stranded goods train. No injuries were reported. The company had initiated the installation of the new safety signals following the Lea's Crossing accident last December which resulted in three fatalities and 29 injured. The Board of Trade report ended by commending the company for its timely response to the earlier incident, which has undoubtedly saved many lives.

Lucas looked up. The riders on the bridle path had gone and for the moment he was alone with the neatly trimmed floral beds and the row of elegant black railings that bordered the boating lake. The company had received a letter from the widow of the fireman, Evans, who had died in the Lea's Crossing accident. The funeral costs, she had explained, had not been paid. They had not been paid either, it had transpired, for the dead driver, Proctor, or for the little girl, Alice Brinklow. Somehow it had been forgotten. A clerk had been threatened with termination but in the end had been served with a reprimand, and it seemed entirely possible the wretched man had never been charged with this task in the first place. Which of them, he wondered, had failed in this duty? Had they all failed? But the three funerals were now, finally, paid for and next time they would do better.

Mr Jarmyn closed the paper and folded it up. Today was not a day to be thinking about railways, to be thinking about anything more exacting than the two pigeons squabbling over a breadcrumb at his feet or the small boy who now appeared chasing a kite in the distance. The insanity of a few weeks back—it *was* surely an insanity—had vanished so utterly that it was hard now to remember what he had felt or how it was even possible to have such thoughts about one's own housekeeper.

He decided to leave his newspaper on the bench for the next visitor. He no longer had need of it.

As he prepared to depart a closed carriage passed by led by a team of horses and liveried grooms at front and back with more riding behind. The door of the carriage had a familiar crest on it and when Lucas strained to see inside he saw the Queen, though she did not see him.

A battle had been lost but Her Majesty still took her ride in the park. The Empire, it appeared, would survive.

He stood up. He would not go to the office today. He would go home.

—⁂—

Dinah, coming in from the garden, looked up at the shock of blue sky above and removed her shawl.

'I heard the first cuckoo,' she exclaimed. 'I've never heard one so early in the year.'

'Yes, I heard it too,' said her mother. Neither of them said: perhaps it is an omen, for neither of them believed in such things. It was pleasing though, the first cuckoo of spring so early in the year.

The second post had come and letters lay in the silver letter tray in the hallway but Dinah ignored them. She saw a button, a tunic button, brass and round, and shiny as though someone—the maid presumably—had polished it but, perhaps not knowing its proper place, had left it where it had lain on the hallway table since December. Dinah slid the button into her hand and her fingers closed around it. She would find a proper place for it.

Roger's letter had lain for a month unopened in the trunk beneath her bed and perhaps, finally, it was time to open it.

She returned to the morning room where a roaring fire was burning in the grate though they hardly required such a blaze on this fine spring day but her father had said there were to be fires in every room. Her mother's shawl was on the floor where it had fallen and Dinah stooped to retrieve it and placed it over her shoulders. Mama was still weakened by her illness but today there was definitely a patch of colour in her cheeks and a lightness in her eyes, and Dinah was glad. 'I think I hear Father in the hallway,' she said. 'Perhaps he has forgotten something. Or perhaps he has decided not to go to his office today.'

Beside her Aurora smiled. There had been many occasions recently when Lucas had decided not to go to the office. For reasons she could not fathom but she did not question, her husband had been returned to her. And a fire burned in the grate. She held her hands out to the flames and felt its warmth.

'Come, Dinah,' she said, getting to her feet and casting off the shawl Dinah had placed over her, 'I do believe there is a hint of spring in the air. Let us go into the garden and see if we cannot locate the first crocuses.'

As Dinah and her mother stepped out on the lawn and began to take their turn about the garden, Mr Jarmyn was returning from his walk, making his way at an energetic pace along the Marylebone Road, his cane clipping the pavement with each stride just as though he was in a hurry to get home, so that for the time being, 19 Cadogan Mews was empty.

Or not quite empty.

In the basement kitchen Hermione, who had been born in a workhouse and who had been scalded by spilt bisque, who spent her loneliest moments with a large orange cat and who had once dropped a very ugly vase in front of a house full of dinner guests, took a deep breath and opened the range door. She pulled out a tray of six perfect cottage loaves. Gasping, she clapped her hands together with delight, carefully placed the tray on the table and ran upstairs and, when she was sure no one was looking, she removed the *'Cook wanted'* sign from the window and hid it.

EPILOGUE

June 1880

'SHE WILL NOT LAST THE night,' Dr Frobisher said, but Sofia did last the night and there followed a terrible time with the child alive, though barely; unable to speak, to eat, to drink even; in such silent and terrible pain it was more than anyone could bear. In another room, Mrs Jarmyn, her arm bandaged, and heavily sedated on the draughts Dr Frobisher had left for her, lay silently in her bed, unable to speak, tormented by the horror of what was in the next room.

On the tenth night, as the clock in the hallway struck three, she fought off the sedatives and rose from her bed. Outside in the corridor her husband slept on a hard chair and she thought: no one has slept and yet they do all sleep. They just forget. At first Lucas had stayed with her, stroked her hair and kissed her eyelids, willing her to remain asleep. But how could she sleep? She would never sleep again.

She needed him now to do what could not be spoken but he had failed her—and how could you command what was

unspeakable? Lucas had not heard her or had chosen not
to hear.

Aurora stumbled, steadied herself, holding her breath but
he did not stir. She made her way silently and without a candle
to the horror of the next room. Opening the door she slipped
inside and all of Dr Frobisher's little powders could not have
stilled her heart. She ignored the smells in the room, not
allowing her senses to begin dissecting the various odours
and sounds, the dark slow-breathing shape on the bed before
her. She did not pause because she knew her courage would
fail her but lifted, gently, a pillow from the bed and placed
it over her daughter's face, shutting out all the sounds and
movements that then followed.

When it was done she offered up no prayer because what
she had done she did not wish God to observe.

Acknowledgements

THANK YOU TO CLARE FORSTER and Annette Barlow for patience and understanding far beyond the call of duty; to my family Sheila Joel and Anne Benson for your love and support; to my dear friends Tricia Dearborn, Liz Brigden and Sharon Mathews for coming to the rescue at every emotional, domestic, technical and spider emergency; and to all the wonderful people at Curtis Brown and Allen & Unwin, in particular Christa Munns and Clare James, for your assistance, support, expertise and encouragement during the—at times torturous—writing and publication of this book.

Author Note and Sources

WHILST I AM REASONABLY CONFIDENT that no one who was alive at the time that this book is set is around now and in a position to read it, I have nevertheless taken every care to produce a work that is, as far as possible, historically correct. Some inaccuracies will inevitably have occurred, and for these I beg the reader's indulgence and trust that they do not detract from the reading experience.

The following publications, reports and articles proved invaluable during the writing of this book, in particular Judith Flanders' wonderful and extraordinary book *The Victorian House* and Liza Picard's *Victorian London: The Life of a City 1840-1870*, both of which provided me with the sort of rich and colourful detail no writer of historical fiction can exist without:

'Affairs at the Cape' article from *The Times*, Monday, 13 December 1880, issue 30062, p. 5.

'Comfortable Carriage' by Hamilton Ellis from *Steam Horse: Iron Road*, edited by Brenda Horsfield, published by The British Broadcasting Corporation, London, 1972.

Daily Life in Victorian England (second edition) by Sally Mitchell, published by The Greenwood Press, Westport and London, 2009.

'The Disaster in the Transvaal' article from *The Times*, Saturday, 25 December 1880, issue 30074, p. 5.

The Forsyte Saga by John Galsworthy, published by Wordsworth Editions Ltd, London, 1994.

Going Green: The Story of the District Line by Piers Connor, published by Capital Transport Publishing, UK, 1993.

'Historic Accidents' by O. S. Nock from *Steam Horse: Iron Road*, edited by Brenda Horsfield, published by The British Broadcasting Corporation, London, 1972.

London Buses: A Brief History by John Reed, published by Capital Transport Publishing, UK, 2000.

The London Underworld in the Victorian Period by Henry Mayhew and Others, Dover Publications, New York, 2005.

London's Shadows: The Dark Side of the Victorian City by Drew D. Gray, published by Continuum UK, London, 2010.

'News in Brief' article from *The Times*, Tuesday, 16 November 1880, issue 30040, p. 5.

News in Brief' article from *The Times*, Wednesday, 22 December 1880, issue 30071, p. 5.

Nobody's Angels: Middle-Class Women and Domestic Ideology in Victorian Culture by Elizabeth Langland, published by Cornell University Press, New York, 1995.

The Report of the Court of Inquiry into the Circumstance Attending the Accident on the Great Western Railway which Occurred Near Shipton-On-Cherwell on the 24th December 1874: Presented to both Houses of Parliament by Command of Her Majesty April 1875, printed by George Edward Eyre and William Spottiswoode for Her Majesty's Stationery Office, 1875.

Royal Gardeners: The History of Britain's Royal Gardens by Alan Titchmarsh, published by BBC Worldwide Ltd, London, 2003.

'The Rising in the Transvaal' article from *The Times*, Wednesday, 29 December 1880, p. 4.

'The Rising in the Transvaal' article from *The Times*, Saturday, 1 January 1881, issue 30080, p. 5.

'The Rising in the Transvaal' article from *The Times*, Wednesday, 12 January 1881, issue 30089, p. 5.

'The Shipton Railway Accident' article from *The Times*, Thursday, 31 December 1874, issue 28200, p. 7.

'The Shipton Railway Accident' article from *The Times*, Monday, 28 December 1874, issue 28197, p. 9.

'The Shipton Railway Accident' article from *The Times*, Wednesday, 6 January 1875, issue 28205, p. 10.

The Subterranean Railway: How the London Underground was Built and How it Changed the City Forever by Christian Wolmer, published by Atlantic Books, London, 2004.

'South Africa' article from *The Times*, Thursday, 11 November 1880, issue 30036, p. 5.

'South Africa' article from *The Times*, Tuesday, 30 November 1880, issue 30052, p. 5.

'South Africa' article from *The Times*, Tuesday, 14 December 1880, issue 30064, p. 5.

'South Africa' article from *The Times*, Tuesday, 21 December 1880, issue 30070, p. 5.

'South Africa' article from *The Times*, Thursday, 23 December 1880, issue 30072, p. 3.

'South Africa' article from *The Times*, Friday, 24 December 1880, issue 30073, p. 3.

'Terrible Railway Accident' article from *The Times*, Friday, 25 December 1874, issue 28195, p. 3.

'The Transvaal. Defeat of the British Troops. Reported Death of General Colley' article from *The Times*, Monday, 28 February 1881, issue 30129, p. 5.

The Victorian House: Domestic Life from Childbirth to Deathbed by Judith Flanders, published by Harper Perennial, London, 2004.

Victorian London: The Life of a City 1840–1870 by Liza Picard, published by Weidenfeld & Nicolson, London, 2005.

The Years by Virginia Woolf, published by Penguin Books, London, 1968.

The following websites provided historical detail about Majuba, Laing Nek and the 58th Regiment:

http://www.thehistorychannel.co.uk/site/encyclopedia/article_show/Majuba_ Battle_of_/m0046565.html?&searchtermold=&searchtermold=

http://www.britishbattles.com/first-boer-war/laings-nek.htm

http://www.britishbattles.com/first-boer-war/majuba-hill.htm

http://www.sahistory.org.za/pages/chronology/thisday/1881-02-27.htm

National Army Museum website: http://www.nam.ac.uk/research/ famous-units/58th-rutlandshire-regiment-foot